Daniel Owen is the foremost Welsh novelist of the nineteenth century. He was born in 1836 in Mold, Flintshire. The following spring, his father and two of his brothers were drowned in a mining accident that left the family 'in poverty if not in destitution'. Although he received a little education in the town's British School, he received his true early education in the Calvinistic Methodist chapel to which his widowed mother belonged. When he was twelve he was apprenticed to one of the chapel's deacons, a wise, cultured tailor called John Angell Jones. The camaraderie in that tailor shop, Angell Jones's prompting, and the encouragement of his minister, the Reverend Roger Edwards, turned the boy into a youth who loved literature. In his twenties, now a fully fledged tailor, he published character sketches of local characters, and translated an American novel. Also, like hundreds of his talented contemporaries, he started to preach.

In 1867, he enrolled at Bala College, an academy established by Dr Lewis Edwards mainly for the education of men who wished to enter the ministry. His fellow students thought highly of him as an observant, sagacious young man, as, no doubt, did the Principal. But after eighteen months Daniel Owen returned to Mold—ostensibly to look after his mother and sister. I think he left college because the vital part of him could not abide the pieties of Nonconformity or its ministerial demands. He returned also to Angell Jones's tailor shop. He continued to preach on Sundays, he read avidly, and he regularly wrote and published portraits and stories and some poems. In time he established his own tailor shop.

Then, when he was forty, he ruptured a blood vessel in one of his lungs, and from then on he was never in the best of health. But ill as he often was, the life of his imagination flourished brilliantly. Some of his sermons and stories about Methodist chapel affairs were published in *Offrymau Neillduaeth; Sef Cymeriadau Beiblaidd a Methodistaidd* (1879), after which Roger Edwards persuaded him to write a novel. *Y Dreflan* (1881) and *Rhys Lewis* (1885) were first published in monthly parts in Edwards's *Y Drysorfa*. *Rhys Lewis*, perhaps the best of his novels, an autobiographical account of the life of a minister, mirrors Daniel Owen's own life and times, and is a masterly analysis of the complexity of fervour, faith and faddishness that was Welsh religious society in the second half of the nineteenth century. Other novels followed, *Enoc Huws* (1891) and *Gwen Tomos* (1894). In 1888 he published a collection of essays, portraits and poems, *Y Siswrn*. And, in 1895, the year of his death, *Straeon y Pentan*.

Rhys Lewis, written as the autobiography of a Victorian Methodist minister, is a novel that richly portrays the contrast between the Christian belief of his mother Mari Lewis' generation and the secularisation of chapel life in industrial Flintshire in the middle years of the nineteenth century. It describes a godliness that had cooled to become 'a great degree of common sense'—not philosophically (though there is some philosophy) but through a host of memorable events and classic characters that reflect wonderfully the ever-changing complexity of modern society. It is, in my opinion, Daniel Owen's finest work, and probably the best of all Welsh-language novels.

DEREC LLWYD MORGAN

RHYS LEWIS
MINISTER OF BETHEL

By

DANIEL OWEN

A new translation by Stephen Morris

www.browncowpublishing.com

WELSH CLASSICS FOR ENGLISH-SPEAKING READERS
—
DANIEL OWEN SIGNATURE SERIES

First published by
Brown Cow Publishing, 2015

www.browncowpublishing.com

This paperback edition 2015
1

© Jaffa Design Limited, 2015

A catalogue record for this book
is available from the British Library

ISBN: 978-0-9567031-3-2

Nid i'r doeth a'r deallus yr ysgrifennais,
ond i'r dyn cyffredin.

Not for the wise and learnéd have I written,
but for the common people.

DANIEL OWEN

CONTENTS

ACKNOWLEDGEMENTS IX
I FOREWORD TO THE TRANSLATION XI
II PREFACE TO THE FIRST EDITION XVII
III DANIEL OWEN'S ORIGINAL PROLOGUE XIX
1 MEMOIRS 1
2 THE EARLIEST PERIOD OF MY LIFE 4
3 EARLIEST MEMORIES 7
4 EVAN JONES, THE HUSBANDMAN OF GWERN-Y-FFYNNON. . 11
5 THE CHILDREN'S MEETING 17
6 THE IRISHMAN 24
7 THE TWO SCHOOLS 30
8 UNDER INSTRUCTION. 39
9 MATTERS ECCLESIASTICAL 47
10 THE SUBJECT OF EDUCATION. 57
11 WIL BRYAN ON ECCLESIOLOGY 66
12 AROUND THE HEARTH 76
13 SETH 86
14 WIL BRYAN 99
15 THE BEGINNING OF SORROWS 108
16 THE DAY OF TROUBLE. 119
17 MORE TROUBLE 133
18 THOMAS AND BARBARA BARTLEY 143
19 ABEL HUGHES 152
20 THE PARISH PARSON 164
21 CONVERTS. 174
22 A VISIT BY MORE THAN ONE RELATIVE 187
23 BOB 200

24 MEMORIES OF SADNESS AND COMFORT 214

25 AN ELEGY IN PROSE. 227

26 VANITY AND VISION. 238

27 DAYS OF DARKNESS 251

28 MASTER AND SERVANT 264

29 THE CLOCK CLEANER'S ADVICE. 278

30 THE POACHER. 293

31 DAVID DAVIES. 310

32 A MULTITUDE OF COUNSELLORS 324

33 MORE ABOUT WIL BRYAN 339

34 THOMAS BARTLEY ON COLLEGE EDUCATION 354

35 TROUBLESOME 370

36 A FAMILIAR CHARACTER 384

37 THOMAS BARTLEY'S VISIT TO BALA 401

38 A FORTUNATE ENCOUNTER. 423

39 WIL BRYAN IN HIS CASTLE 436

40 THE AUTOBIOGRAPHY OF WIL BRYAN. 451

41 THE FIRST AND LAST TIME 464

42 THE MINISTER OF BETHEL 475

IV APPENDIX. XXI

V EPILOGUE. XXV

ACKNOWLEDGEMENTS

I would like to thank my wife, Tina, for the initial suggestion that this book should be translated into English so that she could read it for herself. I'd also like to thank her, and my daughter Anna, for tolerating the many hours I spent in the back bedroom, usually on Sunday afternoons and evenings when I'd otherwise be spending time with them, to get the job finished.

Mark Turner, whom I knew from the time I spent worshipping at Ebenezer Baptist Church in Mold when I lived in Ruthin in the Vale of Clwyd, made the suggestion that I should publish it alongside the English translations of some of Daniel Owen's other books that Brown Cow has published in recent years. He introduced me to John Mainwaring, the proprietor. John has been immensely supportive throughout, guiding me through the process of preparing the text for publication and sharing with me his own extensive knowledge of Daniel Owen's background and the local history of the Mold area, not to mention its flora and fauna. He in turn introduced me to Adam Pearce of Bangor University who was able to share with me some of his academic work on the previous English translation of this book, of which I'd been wholly unaware. I was also introduced to Les Barker, the translator of the Brown Cow edition of Enoc Huws, with whom I was able to compare notes on some of the characters who occur in both novels, and to Professor Derec Llwyd Morgan, formerly Vice Chancellor of the University of Wales, Aberystwyth. Professor Morgan is an acknowledged expert on Daniel Owen's literature and was good enough to examine the first draft to check its consistency with the text, and to help get some of the author's more obscure phrases translated accurately. He also kindly provided the biographical introduction to Owen's work that appears on the first page of this volume.

My thanks to Linda Moores and Rose Price for proofreading the manuscripts, and to John Mainwaring (again) for providing the typesetting and layout.

Special thanks go to Martin E. Leckebusch for writing a brand new hymn based on my literal translation of '*Y gwaed a redodd ar y groes*', which is quoted on page 61 and given in full in the Epilogue; also to Professor E. Wyn James of Cardiff University for revising the literal translation, and Mrs Gill Berry of the Praise Trust for bringing the parties together.

I would not have been able to research the background to the text in order to generate the many footnotes, even ten years ago, without spending many hours in university libraries looking up references. The fact that I can now access an immense corpus of information without leaving my own home is a miracle of the 21st century, so I would like to thank the many unnamed people who have put this information online, particularly at the National Library of Wales (which maintains the Dictionary of Welsh Biography) and Wikipedia.

Diolch i chi i gyd.

FOREWORD TO THE TRANSLATION

Rhys Lewis was Daniel Owen's first full-length novel, originally published in serialised form between 1882 and 1885 in *Y Drysorfa* (*The Treasury*), which was the monthly magazine of the Calvinistic Methodist church—at the time by far the largest of the Welsh Nonconformist churches. It was then published in book form in 1885, by Hughes & Son of Wrexham.

Translating this novel has been a labour of love, in two ways: firstly, I did it principally for my wife, and at her request, so that she (as a non-Welsh speaker) could enter in to the enjoyment of the book that I clearly had myself when I read it. The loud guffaws from the corner of the room where I was sitting needed some explanation, and translating the work as a whole rather than trying to explain each part in isolation seemed like the best way forward.

Secondly, the novel occupies a period of history to which I personally love to return and vicariously experience. Between about the middle of the eighteenth century and the third quarter of the nineteenth, Wales experienced one of the most comprehensive transformations of its culture that any nation has ever experienced, and this not as a result of any outside influence but as an entirely home-grown phenomenon. A country that had been largely bypassed by the intellectual movements of previous centuries, in particular by the Protestant Reformation, all-too-briefly became one of the most thoroughly evangelised, best-educated and generally civilised nations on earth—entirely as a result of the multiple religious awakenings that started with the conversions of Daniel Rowland and Howell Harris in 1735 and continued for nearly 200 years. The religious culture that arose, primarily but not exclusively within the various Nonconformist denominations, was (in the translator's personal opinion, naturally) one of the most godly, biblical and generally edifying that history has seen—sometimes referred to by scholars as 'Y Gwareiddiad Ymneilltuol', or 'the Nonconformist Civilisation'. The largest of the Nonconformist denominations by far were the Calvinistic Methodists, amongst whom the action in this novel takes place.

Of course, the period didn't last. Already by the third quarter of the nineteenth century, this civilisation was under attack from all sides. Intellectually, the desire to be seen by the outside world as 'respectable' had led to its colleges becoming open to the liberal theological ideas that had come over from Germany in the mid-nineteenth century[1] and already enthralled much of English academia. Culturally, the great flowering of poetry and music that had taken place within Nonconformity became an end in itself, so that hymn books became more important than Bibles and eisteddfods more important than preaching meetings. Politically, the essentially conservative (small 'c') values of Nonconformity— diligence, education, self-improvement, humility—became eclipsed by the new ideas of socialism and social activism, seen most clearly in the Temperance movement and the rapid rise of the Labour party to the position of dominance in Wales that it has enjoyed ever since. Already by the early 20th century, the life-force within Nonconformity had been virtually extinguished; but its corpse mouldered on for another hundred years or so and in the process alienated several generations of Welsh people against religion in all its forms.

The action in *Rhys Lewis* takes place in the middle years of the nineteenth century—roughly the 1850s, '60s and '70s. Though a novel, a great deal of its content is autobiographical, and a number of the events and characters it describes can be identified with real people and events, though the latter are not always in chronological order. All of the events in the novel take place in one of three distinct locations: the author's home town of Mold in Flintshire, the town of Bala in Meirionydd where the Calvinistic Methodists had their principal theological college, and a large English town which the author only ever refers to as 'B_____' but is almost certainly intended to be Birmingham, since other nearby places such as Warwick and Leamington Spa are referred to explicitly by name. It is clear from what the author writes that Calvinistic Methodism was already at a crossroads. On the one hand, its ascent to cultural dominance and general respectability was far from complete, with the imposing theological college at Bala yet to be built. On the other, the rot had clearly started to set in, with the elderly saints expressing their alarm at the younger generation's obsessions with hymn books and hairstyles.

The author navigates this period skilfully. It seems clear that the author has nothing but love and respect for the elderly saints, despite the distaste that he felt as a child towards their staidness and severity. One of them, the terrifying chapel elder Abel[2] Hughes, ultimately emerges as the true hero of the book. At the same time, he doesn't hesitate to point out the frequent hypocrisy and absurdity that was present even in that generation, and amongst its most revered leaders. He is just as sharp in his satire of the obsessions of the younger people, even though he is one of them himself.

Despite its subject matter which is superficially unappealing to modern eyes—a young boy from a broken home who nurtures a secret desire to be a Methodist preacher, while constantly haunted by his family's dark secret about which he longs to find out the truth for himself—*Rhys Lewis* is probably the most light-hearted of Owen's books. The comedy comes mainly from the cast of characters that the author succeeds in creating: Thomas Bartley,

---

[1] Those of the so called 'Tübingen school'—I've heard it said that Germany caused more damage to Europe in the 19th century through bad theology than it did through two world wars in the 20th.

[2] In Welsh 'Abel' is pronounced 'Abbel' with the emphasis firmly on the first syllable, almost but not quite rhyming with 'rabble'. It sounds nothing like the English word 'Able'.

Mr Jones the parson and, more than anyone, Wil Bryan, stand out and if ever portrayed on the stage or screen would require great comic talents to do justice to them. The author seems consciously to make his own character seem grey and sombre so that these others stand out all the more colourfully by comparison.

One of the challenges facing any translator is how to convey the various nuances of the language used in the original, and also how to present the language used by the author in a credible style. There is no escaping the fact that this is a Victorian novel, contemporary with the works of Dickens, Hardy and Trollope. When I was already halfway through the work of translating it, a Victorian translation of which I had previously been unaware—that of James Harris published in 1888—was brought to my attention. The Harris translation is of its time, and is what one would expect: a Victorian novel rendered in Victorian English. I decided to press on with my translation from the original Welsh, and have tried to strike the correct balance by avoiding both a literal rendering of the author's original rather flowery nineteenth-century style on the one hand, and an implausibly modern idiom on the other. The result is intended to be digestible to a modern English reader without too much effort getting used to the author's style, while at the same time staying in tune with the subject matter.

I have also tried to retain as close a correspondence to the author's original sentence-structure as possible, so that someone reading this translation side-by-side with the Welsh original should have no difficulty in synchronising the two. It is not my intent, by providing an English translation, to discourage anyone from reading the original in Welsh; on the contrary, I would be absolutely delighted if by unlocking another of the language's treasures I can encourage people to learn it for themselves. It is well worth the effort.

A peculiar challenge to a translator of a novel like this from Welsh into English is how to deal with the fact that the original contains a certain amount of English itself, often deployed by the author to great dramatic effect. With so many of the events described taking place within fifteen miles of Chester city centre, it is hardly surprising that English words were occasionally dropped into conversation by even the most cultured Welshmen, and where the author wants to quote a contemporary saying, song or poem in English, then he does so in the original language. By and large I have left this unremarked upon and melded the translated Welsh text and original English expressions seamlessly together, adding the occasional footnote where I consider it helpful for the reader to understand how the two languages were originally used. The one general exception to this is Wil Bryan, who uses English words in almost every sentence and always to great comic effect. In his case, I have followed a policy of always putting his English words into italics. If the reader, when following Wil's speech, were to speak the italicised words to himself in a broad Scouse accent, then that would probably capture the overall effect quite well. I must also say a word about Mr Brown the parson, obviously an Englishman who has made some effort to learn Welsh but speaks in a kind of halting pidgin which is very, very funny to read in the original but to which I've completely failed to do justice in the translation. If the contemporary reader can bring himself to imagine a respectable nineteenth-century parish parson speaking in gangsta hip-hop patois, then that would more or less capture the essence.

Any book about Calvinistic Methodist folk in mid-nineteenth century Wales is bound to have a lot of religion in it, and I make no apology for that. In fact, to nail my own colours to the mast, I am one of that tiny minority of contemporary Welshmen who hold to the ancient faith in its entirety, and regard the Calvinistic Methodist confession of faith as being not only fully true but one of the most comprehensive and accurate expositions of biblical Christianity that have ever been set out. The remnant of what was once Calvinistic Methodism lives on in the churches of the Evangelical Movement of Wales. I myself worshipped in such churches from my conversion as a teenager to the time when I moved to live in England, where I now attend a Baptist church. People of a similar background would find the world of Rhys Lewis familiar to them and probably be able to spot the numerous biblical allusions with ease. I have done my best to capture all of them and mark them with footnotes, along with the many other references to hymns, theological works and sacred poems which the author liberally scatters throughout the book. This isn't just an everyday story with some cultural religion thrown in, however: there's some deep stuff in here. As with anyone who lived at a time when the culture was permeated with religion and its language and idioms, there is room to ask whether the author himself was a believer or had simply absorbed the manners of his times and knew how to 'talk the talk'. All I can say is that, having read the author's account of Rhys Lewis' conversion in Chapters 22 to 28, it is hard to see how he could have written such things without knowing something of his character's experiences first-hand.

Stephen Morris
Shropshire, September 2015

PREFACE TO FIRST EDITION

If an obscure author ventures to publish a book in Welsh, priced at four shillings, chances are that he will find himself one day with his head in his hands, sitting in the seat of the penitent; especially if the greater part of his book's content has already appeared in a monthly magazine, as happens to be the case with *Rhys Lewis*. It is this unpleasant consideration that accounts for such an awkward thing, at least in some people's opinion, as a list of subscribers for a work such as this. I was not inclined to finish the work, far less publish it as a volume, had I no grounds to believe there would be a demand for it. I am therefore taking this opportunity to thank my compatriots for the support—almost unheard-of in Welsh literature—that I have received.

I could say something about the disadvantageous circumstances under which the book was composed, were I not thereby to appear as one seeking to blunt the edge of criticism. He who publishes a book must learn to be patient when the day of reckoning comes. I don't expect to be an exception; rather, just as Wil Bryan would, I'd say to any who feel that way inclined, '*fire away*', you won't find more defects in the work than the author is already conscious of. I have not written for the wise and learned, but for the common man. If the work has any virtue, it is the Welshness of its characters, and the fact that it is not indebted for its material to foreigners. If there is anything in it that does not tend to edify as well as entertain the reader, that will grieve no-one more than

The Author.
Mold, April 30th,
1885.

DANIEL OWEN'S ORIGINAL PROLOGUE

The minister of Bethel has, for some time now, been lying quietly in the folds of the valley. In his day, he was considered a wise and unassuming man; those who knew him well knew that there was more to him than met the eye. Although he was, as a minister of the Gospel, a 'public man', so to speak, he was never anxious to push himself to the fore. He was not popular as a preacher, mainly because he could not sing, which was his great misfortune. Even so, he always had something to say that was worth hearing; I have heard men of discernment say that if his sermons were put into print they would bear comparison with the best of the Welsh pulpit. Indeed, the few articles he wrote for the *Traethodydd*[1] were attributed to Dr _____;[2] and they were read with relish. This was in the period when it was not customary to name the authors within that august quarterly. Perhaps, had it been, nobody would have gone to the trouble of reading the works of Rhys Lewis. As a pastor, he was tolerably happy and successful; but this was mainly because the majority of the church under his care possessed a good dose of common sense, and little Christian sentiment.

Although Rhys Lewis was a genial and very sociable man with those he knew well, his favourite place was the solitude of his study. At times he would forget himself, and give way excessively to this tendency for contemplation; and on more than one occasion it was necessary for the deacons to call his attention back to his

---

[1] The *Traethodydd* (literally Essayist) was the leading Welsh literary periodical of its day.

[2] The author has a habit of using this style to hint at a real person or place that would have been well-known to his readers.

public duties. He was afflicted sometimes by melancholy; some thought that there was something pressing on his mind, which was not manifest even to his closest friends, while others surmised that a disorder of the nervous system was the cause. Perhaps the following account, from his own pen, will throw some light on which of the two opinions was correct. The minister of Bethel died in the midst of his usefulness, without a stain on his character, while he was still relatively young.

Lately, while under the instructions of his executor I was putting his books in order, in preparation for sale, I hit upon a substantial manuscript; and on browsing through it I realised that it was his autobiography. Thinking that there might be in the manuscript something of interest, and having obtained the permission of his executor, I took it home with me; and when I had leisure, I read it in detail. Besides the fact that the author himself said clearly (as will be seen), it was obvious from the style and content of the manuscript that it was not intended to be published. Even so, such was the pleasure I obtained from reading it that I sought permission to do so. At the same time, I feel that an apology for the story is in order. The early chapters are somewhat lightweight and childish, though innocent and, I believe, *true to nature*, and they reflect the experience of many. As the story goes on, it becomes more substantial, and contains descriptions of some remarkable and devout characters. I took the liberty, for various reasons, of changing the name of the author and of others that he mentions. I did not feel that I had the right to make further changes. If the reader finds some things disagreeable, or is offended by the casual style that occasionally touches on comedy, and the excessive detail that appears when describing inconsequential things, I would bid him remember that it was not the author's intention for the work to be published.

MEMOIRS

Throughout my lifetime I've read numerous memoirs, and I can't measure nor value the amusement and benefit I've had from them. It's possible that as much talent, and especially common sense, is displayed in biography as in any branch of literature, since an author must know something of his subject and this cannot be taken for granted in other branches; how often one finds men writing on subjects they know nothing about! At the same time, however capably and faithfully the biographer describes the public character of his subject, I often lament how little he knows, all told, about the feelings and inner workings of the one that he's writing about. I feel that the writer, as much as the reader, would like to ask many questions of the one who by now is lying in his quiet grave. In this, an autobiography has a great advantage over other biographies. On second thoughts, perhaps a memoir written by another, rather than by the subject himself, is the more accurate on the whole. It is true that there are materials at the disposal of the man writing his own story that another, no matter what his capability and faithfulness, could never guess. Even so, when one writes his own story, while conscious that the account is to be published, if he is a man of manners and refinement then he will be so afraid that others may think he overvalues himself, that he will not claim for himself the reputation that is attributed to him by others.

I have thought many times how glad I would be to have an accurate biography of an ordinary man such as myself. All of the biographies I have read have had as their subjects great men, remarkable for one thing or another, who have moved in circles wholly alien to me and been through circumstances of which

I know nothing. Even though this may have been what made them worth writing a biography about, I have thought at the same time how good it would be to read the story of an ordinary man—one who had moved in the same circles and been through the same circumstances as myself. Isn't there here a category of thoughts and feelings that have never been conveyed, and that because of their ordinariness, just as many of the beauties of nature pass unnoticed because they are to be seen everywhere? Is it because the daisy lacks beauty that it is overlooked by the botanist, and fails to attract the praise of poets, or is it because it is to be seen in every field and trodden upon by every cow? If the robin redbreast and the goldfinch struck up a discussion about beauty in nature, the wild primrose would draw much of their praise, even though it adorns the uncultivated ditches. I tend to the view that there is hardly any man whose story, honestly told, would not be interesting. Are there not in the life of every man events worth chronicling, and thoughts in his heart that neither he nor anyone else has conveyed? I've often thought that the difference between the ordinary man and the extraordinary man is that the latter is able to articulate that which he has thought and felt, whilst the former is unable to do so, or at least has not made the attempt. My reason for thinking so is this: when I have read famous authors, or listened to masterful orators, I have often felt that they have not said anything particularly novel, but have merely been able to give form to, or put into words, that which I myself have thought or felt but could not quite get across. Or, in other words, they have been able to read from my own heart things that I have not been able to spell out after years of trying. I have been conscious that the thoughts and feelings have been there already in my heart, but sleeping, or at least napping, and what these gifted men have been able to do is to knock on their bedroom door so effectively that the sleepers jump up and open their eyes!

I have the urge to write the story of my own life, not for others, but for myself; and certainly not to print, but rather as a sort of self-reflection. I know very well that there is no danger of anyone else writing a biography of me after I am dead. A hundred years from now, the world will know no more of me than if I had never been in it. With thousands and thousands of my contemporaries, I will by that time be lying quietly in obscurity and forgottenness. Yet I don't like to think of this. But what help is there for it, as this is the fate of all us common people? Why is it, do you think, that a man is so reluctant for his name to slip into obscurity when neither recollection nor forgetfulness can do him good nor harm? The dead, perhaps, have as much satisfaction from the stone that marks their grave as the close friends who put it there. The bones of the dead lie more quietly if there is a memorial upon their heads! Immortality! Have you anything to do with this?

I am writing my story, I repeat, not to be printed—thank goodness!—because if it were then I would not be able to tell the truth, and only the truth, because under those circumstances I would need to study the reader as well as myself. Rhys, what will you say about yourself? Remember to tell the truth. That I will do; and if a friend or relative encounters this manuscript, he may know that there is not a word I would retract.

THE EARLIEST PERIOD OF MY LIFE

When I was first struck by the concept of writing the story of my own life, I thought that I could do this without the help of any living soul. How foolish of me! I see at the very beginning that I must depend entirely on the testimony of others about the earliest part of my life; and as I am decidedly trying to keep to the facts, I must admit to myself that I have no recollection about the time I first came into the world.

In the face of this deficiency in my own memory, I feel I can rely wholly on the veracity of my mother. She told me more than once that it was between two and three in the morning, on the fifth day of October, in the year 18__, that I first saw the light of a halfpenny candle. Whether it was the fact I was offended that the preparations for my coming had been so poor, or some other reason, that caused me to be so bad-tempered, shouting and screaming as much as I was able, only the two neighbours who were there at the time can decide. In any case, the aforementioned two neighbours thought me wholly unfeeling and inconsiderate to make so much noise when I knew, or should have known, that my mother was in such a poor state that morning. I know this—I had not been consulted at all about the circumstances I refer to, and perhaps that is what made me so unruly. Of course, this is only a guess, and I can't put it down as a fact. If I were not perfectly certain that my mother would never tell me anything untrue, I'd hardly believe that I was at that time, and as I nearly am now, bald and toothless, and that my nose—often thought of as Roman in form—was, I say, at that time, not only flat but like a crescent moon with its two horns pointing upwards, and that I was so fleshy that there were dimples at my knees and elbows where now there are only bones to be seen. I cannot remember either a time when I could not, and was not quite keen to, walk; but my mother told me that I was at one time wholly against the idea, and would lie on my back and kick and scream unless someone carried me. I'm sorry that I am guilty of such behaviour, even though I have no memory of it. It's strange now for me to think that three years of my life went past about which I remember nothing; and if those who knew me best at that time, in whose veracity I could trust entirely, were to make the most heinous accusations against me, I would have no option but to believe them. Didn't I have at that time reason, mind and feeling? Was I just a lump of living clay? If so, where did reason, mind and such things come to me from?

One thing I did have, I know, from my mother's testimony—and I fear I still have too much of it today—was naughtiness. I broke, she said, a great deal of crockery; and I know that she was telling the truth. I destroyed the few ornaments she had, and scratched the faces and pulled the hair of numerous relatives and neighbours. I pulled the earring of one young girl clean through her flesh, until the blood poured over her shoulder. I killed three kittens by crushing the breath out of them; and performed various other deeds that I can scarcely confess to myself, though I feel no guilt over them. What surprises me most is that everyone put up with me, and behaved towards me as if I were very profitable for them, when in fact I was good for nothing. Not only was I profitable for no-one, but I was the cause of a great deal of misery and trouble. My mother lost many nights' sleep because of me; and scores of times she had to rise in the middle of the night to make cinder tea for me. At times I would yell for hours on end; and because I had it in my head not to talk for nearly two whole years, no-one knew what I was yelling about. In spite of everything, my mother said that she would not part with me for the world, even when I yelled most.

I was a big, heavy child, considering that I lived almost entirely on milk; and even though I was so heavy, my neighbours vied with each other to carry me. It seemed I liked being toothless; because when those members began to appear I was very displeased, so much so that my flesh wasted away. Apparently I gave way to my bad nature to the point that in the end I suffered convulsions. How foolish I was! If only I had the opportunity to grow teeth now! But I have one advantage from being as I am now: no-one can ever give me a kick in the teeth!

Well, that's enough about the time of which I have no memories; I'd much prefer to turn to the time about which I know something from my own experience and memory.

3

EARLIEST MEMORIES

I think, in fact I'm certain of this, that one of the first things I remember is going with my mother to chapel. I'm not at all sorry that my earliest memories concern the big chapel. Dear old chapel; you have left many a mark on my memory, and on my conscience also, I hope.

Whether it was the first, or the second, or the twentieth time that I had been there, or many times fused together that left such a deep impression on my mind, I cannot now make out. I am sure, though, that I went hand-in-hand with my mother, and that it seemed a very long way—and that I insisted on being carried for most of the journey. It must have been a Sabbath night; because the chapel was full of people, and it was lit up, not with gas at that time, but by candles. I was terrified to see so many people, and broke out in tears; and I remember my mother putting her hand over my mouth until she nearly smothered me, and it was only when someone nearby gave me a Nelson ball that I stopped yelling. What happened to those famous sweets? I don't see anything like them these days. Have I changed, or have the sweets? The chapel floor was very different then from how it is now. It was open, and there were rows of backless benches across it, with some deep pews around it set against the wall. In the middle of the floor there was a great stove, with many children clustered around it, their faces as red as a cockscomb. It must have been the winter time.

I remember the 'Great Seat',[1] and the 'Singing Seat' to its left, and Abel Hughes in his velvet cap sitting beneath the pulpit,

---

[1] The fenced-off area at the front of the chapel where the elders and deacons sit, a feature of traditional Welsh chapels.

who—Abel, that is—would go around now and then snuffing the candles. I'll have more to say about Abel Hughes. The pulpit was set against the wall, standing on two columns, and so high that it made me think of the swallows' nest that had been left under the eaves of our house the previous summer. I wondered how 'the man', as I called him, who was in the pulpit, had been able to climb to such a place, and what he intended to do on getting there. I wondered whether he ever fell down the stairs, as I had done more than once on coming down from my loft,[2] or whether someone carried him down as my brother Bob carried me down from the loft. I thought it very strange that no-one was saying anything apart from 'the man in the box', and stranger still that he had so much to say. I understood nothing of what he said except the name 'Jesus Christ', and thought at first that he was the 'Jesus Christ' whom my mother talked so much about. I waited for him to stop talking, but he wouldn't. After he had been talking for a very long time, so it seemed to me, 'the man' began to look angry, and his face turned red, and he shouted loudly; and I decided at once that he wasn't Jesus Christ. I thought that 'the man' was telling me off harshly—for what, I don't know; but because he had looked at me many times I knew for sure that he was referring to me, and I started crying again; and once again I was half smothered and given a Nelson ball before I quietened down.

I looked around, and up and down. I was surprised to see so many people in the loft of the chapel. Did they all sleep up there? Where did they find enough beds? I saw the chapel start to darken, and the man in the box was getting further and further away from me, even though he was still shouting louder and louder. I felt my mother cuddling me, and in a minute lost sight of everyone and

---

[2] The Welsh word 'lloft' used here and in the next paragraph refers literally to the type of elevated loft or gallery, not filling the whole area of the house or building and accessed by steep steps or a ladder, where people were accustomed to sleeping. Though the sleeping arrangements in modern Welsh homes are a great deal more comfortable, it is still common to use the word 'lloft' just to mean 'bedroom'.

everything—I was fast asleep. I don't know how long I slept for, but it was very hard for them to wake me even though the whole congregation was singing. I liked the singing much more than the sermon. I felt somehow that I understood the singing, though I can't now explain that understanding. By now, the man in the pulpit was sitting down, wiping the sweat off his forehead and tying a scarf loosely about his neck. I saw Abel Hughes climbing the pulpit steps, and concluded that he was going up there to carry the man down on his back, just as Bob carried me down from the loft. I was very disappointed to see him standing halfway up the stairs and saying something to the people. Some time afterwards I understood that he was announcing the meetings for the coming week. Most of the people went out; but my mother and a few others remained behind, and the chapel doors were closed. I thought we were never going to go home, and I started crying again; but my mother told me earnestly that we would be going home 'just now'. I saw the man who had been, I thought, telling me off, climbing down the pulpit steps; and I watched him closely in case he fell. He reached the bottom safely. After this I saw Abel Hughes lifting the cloth that covered something at the front of the great seat, folding it neatly, and setting it to one side. I was amazed to see what was under the cloth—such beautiful crockery! I saw the man who had been speaking for such a long time going to the crockery, and to some bread that had been cut up very small, and after he had said something else about Jesus Christ he began to eat. I thought he was having his supper. Even so, all he had was a small piece of bread and a small drink; and I thought that perhaps he didn't like it. I was greatly surprised when I saw him picking up the bread and going around, giving a little piece to everyone. I was hungry, and I thought that this was a kind man after all even though he had told me off so harshly. When he came to my mother, she took her piece and I reached out my hand for some, but I was refused. I was furious with him, and burst into tears for perhaps the sixth time that evening. It was obvious to me by now

9

that the man had something against me. My mother had a great deal of trouble calming me down; and when the man came back again with the cup, I hid my face in my mother's cloak so I didn't have to see him, and he didn't get the opportunity to refuse me again. Between the night being cold and me, so I thought, having been insulted by the preacher, I was in a very bad temper and my mother had to carry me all the way home that night.

How fortunate I am that this story is not intended for publication! Because if it were, I would not be able to relate what I have related, as it would be too simple and childish, even though it is true, and even though perhaps it would be new in literature, though not new in the experience of many readers.

4

EVAN JONES, THE HUSBANDMAN
OF GWERN-Y-FFYNNON

As I cast my mind back to my childhood, it is strange to think that I have been the same person all along despite the many changes that have taken place in my ideas and inclinations. Comparing the child and the man, how different and yet how similar they are! I wouldn't for all the world want to deny my selfhood, or exchange my consciousness for that of another. I have many times felt pity for the river Alyn at the point where it loses itself in the Dee. From Llanarmon-yn-Iâl down to Cilcain, through the Belan and all along the vale of Mold, how independent, bright and cheerful it looks! But as it approaches Holt, its face changes, and its obvious dismay at the prospect of losing itself in the Dee can be seen in the way it flows. I don't know how other men feel; but I'm glad to think that I am always the same, and I would not for anything want to lose my Self. Isn't this what madness is? 'He forgot himself' is the expression used, isn't it, about one who goes mad? Well, I'm glad to be able to cast my mind back, and follow the course of my life through various periods, circumstances and prospects through to now, and remember that I have always been the same person. And I'm more glad still to think that when, who knows how soon, I leap into the great world of eternity, I'll still be the same, and will not lose myself in anyone else in the same way as the poor Alyn. How wonderful! After thousands of ages, I will have the same consciousness as I had when I went hand-in-hand with my mother to chapel for the first time!

But to return to the time of my childhood. And to tell the truth—which I am determined to do—I must admit that I did not like going to chapel. The service was far too long for me. I couldn't always manage to sleep through it. When I was awake, nothing was to my taste except for the singing. When the preacher went on endlessly, as it felt to me, my legs would ache insufferably, and it was as much as my mother could do to keep me occupied. My mother was a Methodist of Methodists, and cleaved closely to the ideas and traditions of the fathers. Bless her! One of the things she held most sacred was keeping the Sabbath. It wasn't acceptable for me to mention playing or to look at my toys on the Lord's day. I had to sit quietly, and seriously, when I did not have the least idea about the difference between one day and another. If I was restless and playful, my mother would tell me that Jesus Christ would be angry with me, and I'd never be able to go to heaven, and that He would throw me into the 'hot fire'. This caused me great distress. At the same time, I failed to understand why, if Jesus Christ was so fond of little children as my mother said He was, He was so exact and so opposed to me playing on a Sunday. I hated to see the Sabbath approaching, as I knew I was bound to annoy Jesus Christ. One time I asked my mother what sort of place heaven was. She replied, no doubt trying to reply at the level of my understanding, that it was a land where all the inhabitants kept the Sabbath for ever. My face fell that very moment, and I told her that for certain I would never go there. What a blow I gave her! I can see now her dear face sadden, with tears in her eyes. I put my arm around her neck, and said that I would go to heaven for her sake, but I'd hope that Jesus Christ would let me play a little bit.

My poor mother! With the best intentions, she went about my religious education in the most inept way that can be imagined. Well, my dear mother, you were uneducated and ignorant, but in spite of that were the best mother in the world to my mind. I have no doubt that your prayers for me have been answered in large part. I am now of age as a man; but what I would give to see your face once more! What I would give for the chance to make up for every hateful word I said to you, and every unkind act towards you!

I wonder what you know about my trials and tribulations since I carried you to the cold cemetery? How wonderful it is to think now that all my disobedience and wickedness did not diminish your love for me by one jot! I have met many faithful friends but no-one who has loved me as you did—more than your own life. The world is cold and strange to me without you. I have no-one who understands me, nor who can empathise with my feelings, as you did. Before I write another sentence, I will take a walk to your 'bare stone with two letters',[1] whatever anyone else may think of me.

My memories of Sunday School are mixed up and indistinct. I'm sure of this—it wasn't in Sunday School that I learned my letters. I don't remember ever learning my A B C; either I knew them by nature or, more likely, my mother had taught them to me during the times of which I have no memory. I am sure that it was Evan Jones, the husbandman of Gwern-y-ffynnon, who was my first teacher; and I'm just as sure that it was out of a small book, similar to the *First Part* which is used in our schools today, that my lessons came. What makes me so certain is this: it was 'a b, ab' that I called Evan Jones when talking to my mother, because this was the lesson—a b, ab, e b, eb, o b, ob, etc. Evan Jones was a kindly old man, who dressed for the Sabbath in a blue coat with shiny buttons, and breeches with grey leggings. There were six or seven of us in his class; and Evan's teaching method was to take one of us at a time onto his lap and teach us the lesson, while the rest of us played. Once he had taught each of us, he felt that he had done his duty, and took a nap. As he did so, with his chin sunk deep into his waistcoat and the great collar of his coat almost level with the top of his head, it wasn't once or even ten times that I counted all the buttons on his clothes. I can remember their number to this day. If I were to take an oath on anything, I would take it on this,

---

[1] The author is quoting a poem 'Bedd y Dyn Tylawd' (The Poor Man's Grave) by Ioan Emlyn, a contemporary Baptist minister.

that there were seven buttons on each legging, five on each knee of his breeches, four on each side of his coat and two behind it, and seven on his waistcoat. I'm sure of their number, as I counted them hundreds of times while he was asleep. Evan had a large watch—as large as what would nowadays be called a *timepiece*,[2] and he kept it in the pocket of his breeches. One time I asked my mother why Evan did not wear his watch in his waistcoat pocket, like the Squire did? She answered that it was a great sin to wear a watch in one's waistcoat pocket, and no-one would do such a thing except those who hadn't 'felt the cord'. I did not understand at the time what 'felt the cord' meant,[3] but I knew it was something great and indispensable to make a good man; and I was so fond of Evan Jones that I can hardly describe my satisfaction that it was in his breeches pocket that he kept his watch and not in his waistcoat. Tied to Evan's watch there was a black ribbon and, to that, two white shells, an old coin and a red seal.

We, the boys in his class, felt a great urge to get Evan's watch into our hands. One hot Sunday afternoon, Evan had done his duty and had fallen into a deep sleep. We knew this because he was snoring loudly—something we had never heard in our class before. Behold, the long-awaited opportunity had arrived: Wil Bryan, the eldest in the class, volunteered and was not opposed by anyone. The watch was duly pulled out, and each one of us had our chance to handle it and to put it to our ears. The location of our classroom was in the chapel gallery, in the highest corner that was nicknamed at that time 'Gibraltar', and therefore quite private. Evan's watch had made its way around the class twice, and at the time was in my hands. We were in the process of putting

---

[2] The original uses the English word for '*timepiece*' and italicises it for emphasis.
[3] Translator's note: …and I still don't. The original Welsh expression 'teimlo'r cortyn' occurs nowhere in Welsh literature besides here, as far as I have been able to find. It may be a reference to Hosea 11:4, 'I led them with cords of kindness, with bonds of love', but the context suggests that it may be a reference to the experience of the condemned man feeling the rope tightening around his neck, and grateful for any means of escape.

our heads together to decide how to put it back in its original place without waking its owner, when a voice thundered above our heads, "What are you doing here?" In my fright, I dropped the watch so that its glass broke into smithereens, and at the same moment our respected teacher jumped up as though someone had stabbed him in the small of his back. The thunderer was Abel Hughes the superintendent, he who, wearing his velvet cap, would peer crossly at people from the Great Seat. Our teacher was so shaken that he did not notice his watch. "Sleeping, were you, Evan Jones?" asked Abel Hughes reproachfully.

"Meditating," said Evan, flustered.

"Meditating, indeed, while your class plays with your watch. I must take your case before the teachers' meeting," said Abel, and went away indignantly.

As Evan began to notice the situation around him, I began to cry—something at which I was very accomplished. No-one had touched the watch since it had fallen from my hand. Evan looked at it, then at me, one after the other for a while, then he picked it up, wrapping it in his handkerchief and putting it in the breast pocket of his blue coat. Seeing my grief, although I know he believed that I was the sole guilty party, he took me on his knee and said to me kindly, "Well, don't worry my boy; it's no big thing." I thought afterwards that it was some sort of *fellow feeling* of guilt that made Evan so kind towards me. Even so, his kindness made me weep all the more; and by the time I went home my eyes were so swollen that I couldn't hide the story from my mother. The only thing she said to me was, "Well, we'll see tomorrow." She was true to her word: she saw, and I felt.

I don't know for sure whether the case of Evan Jones, Gwern-y-ffynnon, was heard by the teachers' meeting; but I have every reason to believe that it was, because after that whenever he got ready to have a nap, he would charge us to be on the *look-out* and to wake him up if Abel Hughes came anywhere near—to which charge we were faithful. I remember well that we as a class saw

Abel Hughes' action in forbidding Evan Jones from having a nap, after he had given each of us our lesson, as unforgivable tyranny and oppression.

If this story were printed, it is possible that someone might say, 'How much better are our Sabbath School arrangements and our teachers today, than they were then'. Perhaps. Evan Jones was just one of many like him. But taking his virtues as well as his failings into account, Evan was as good a teacher as the majority of today's. I have double respect for him, as it was under his wing that I learned to read, though he died when I was still young. I remember various expressions of my mother's when she was talking about Evan Jones, such as the following: 'Evan Jones is a man who has the root of the matter'.[4] 'Evan Gwern-y-ffynnon is greater when kneeling than when standing'. 'Evan knows well what it is to feel the cord'. 'A man of the secret place is Evan Jones'. 'If Evan had as much learning and money as he has grace, he would have been a Justice of the Peace since many years, and the Squire would be just a beggar alongside him'. These sayings, and many like them, were like Latin at the time, but many years later I came to understand them. I'm glad to remember the time when I studied classics with my mother. As I have already suggested, I have every reason to believe that Evan Jones, despite his many failings, was a transparent character who had experienced the great things of religion. When we were in his class, we saw his act of taking a nap more as a virtue than anything, as it gave us children a time to play; and looking back to that time, and remembering that he was one who had to work hard and wake every morning at five o'clock, I can forgive him from the bottom of my heart. If I can get to heaven, I will make a search for him so that I will be able to thank him. How foolish I am! I see Evan, in heaven, in his breeches and leggings and blue coat. I can't think of him in any other way than that.

---

[4] Job 19:28.

5

THE CHILDREN'S MEETING

When I was a boy one of the most valuable religious institutions was the Children's Meeting or, to give it its usual name among young and old, the children's *seiat*.[1] It was held weekly without fail, summer and winter; and I think I can confirm there was not a single boy or girl, if their parents were church members, who would not always be present unless prevented by illness. If anyone absented themselves for more than one consecutive week, without adequate reason, then as sure as anything Abel Hughes would call their parents to account at the next general *seiat*; and unless a satisfactory reason was given, they would be publicly rebuked for their negligence. What degeneration has taken place in our own day! It's almost impossible now to get a Children's Meeting together for a couple of months in the winter. And what if parents were publicly rebuked for neglecting to send their children to the *seiat*? Imagine for a moment rebuking Mrs Dowell the shop, whose children are not seen in church for one meeting out of every four. Heaven help us—if anyone did such a thing, I don't think that she or her children would ever come to chapel again, let alone come to the *seiat*. But if Abel Hughes were alive he would have called Mrs Dowell to account, and a great deal of other Mrs's, no matter what the consequences. He would surely have told them that the right place for them was the Church of England, and the sooner

---

[1] The Welsh word *seiat* refers to a type of highly interactive church meeting in which people share their experiences and others seek to comment on these in the light of the Bible. Even so, all is done with a certain amount of order and formality. The word itself derives from the English word 'society', and the ground rules were formalised in the 1777 book by William Williams Pantycelyn (better known as the hymnwriter) "*Drws y Society Profiad*" ('The door to the Experience Society'). Hence *seiat* is sometimes seen translated as 'experience meeting' but this implies something a great deal more airy-fairy than a *seiat*, at its best, actually is.

they went there the better. Have all the honest old elders died? As I bring some of them to mind, I have to admit that they were somewhat severe; but with all their severity, they had an integrity, and an honesty, which compares favourably with this generation of velvet-tongued hypocritical churchgoers.

As soon as I could get my tongue around 'Remember Lot's wife',[2] I was sent to the children's *seiat* under the care of Wil Bryan, who was some years older than me. Throughout my story, I will have to refer frequently to Wil Bryan, sometimes with grief. Perhaps it would have been better for me if I had never met him, though I once believed that he had no equal in all the world. I was very reluctant to memorise Bible verses, and therefore 'Remember Lot's wife' had to serve me on scores of occasions, unbeknown to my mother. She would always take care to teach me a new verse for every *seiat*; but by the time I got to the meeting, the verse would have taken flight, and there was nothing for it under the circumstances but to fall back on 'Remember Lot's wife'. I remember on more than one occasion beginning a new verse, like, 'This is a faithful saying and worthy of all—';[3] but failing to follow it through to its conclusion, I would invariably end with 'Remember Lot's wife'. As I was so small, they put up with this from me for a long time; and only when the other children started calling me 'Lot's wife' did I shut up about her.

My practice of reciting this well-known verse so often gave frequent occasion to those leading the meeting to make some observations on it; and I believe that before I was five years old I knew everything there was to be known about Lot's wife. At least, I'm not conscious that my ideas about the men of Sodom, the angels, the fire and brimstone, Lot and his family, the pillar of salt, Soar, and so on have changed very much since I was five years old. Bible history dripped into our consciousnesses like this without us being aware of it, and I'm sure that Bible knowledge was much wider and fuller among the youth of that generation than in 'this enlightened age'. The other day I was asking the son of Mrs Frederick Dowell the shop, who is about fifteen years old, 'Who was Jeroboam?', and his answer was that he thought he was one of the apostles. I have cause to think that there are many children of churchgoers in these days who little excel Solomon Dowell in their knowledge.

What commitment and zeal John Joseph and Abel Hughes showed with us children, even though the latter was an old man; 'old' as I remember him, at least. Nothing pleased John Joseph more than teaching us to sing verses, such as,

> 'Oh! That will be joyful!'[4]

and

> 'Never will there be an end
> To the sound of the golden harp'.[5]

In contrast Abel Hughes would be as serious and sober in listening to our verses, and commenting on them, as if the day of judgement were to take place tomorrow. We children preferred John Joseph to Abel Hughes; because if Abel was not present, John Joseph would use his tuning fork, and we'd love to see him striking it on the stove, and putting it by his ear, and closing his eyes and inclining his head to listen to the sound, and then give out two or three notes before beginning to sing, though we didn't know what good in the world was achieved through this. It wasn't fitting for John Joseph to go through this ceremony when Abel Hughes was present. I remember him trying it once, but Abel Hughes told him bluntly

---

[2] Luke 17:32.

[3] The complete bible reference, 1 Tim 1:15, reads, '*This is a faithful saying, and worthy of all acceptance, that Christ Jesus came into the world to save sinners; of whom I am chief*'.

[4] 'O! hyn fydd yn hyfryd! Hyfryd! Hyfryd! Hyfryd!', a Welsh translation of a Sunday School song written by Thomas Bilby in 1832. I cannot find it printed in any contemporary hymn book, though I'm sure I remember Huw Llywelyn Davies quoting it while commentating on an international rugby match in the 1990s.

[5] 'Ni bydd diwedd byth ar sŵn y delyn aur', the last line of the verse 'Dechreu canu, dechreu canmol' ('Begin to sing, begin to praise') by William Williams Pantycelyn (1717–1791).

to keep such gimmicks at home—they were not appropriate in the house of God. What if Abel were alive today? What if he heard a man in the 'Great Seat' announcing that such and such a tune would be sung in the key of *La*, and then a couple of dozen men started singing across each other, 'Doh, soh, doh, soh'? I'm sure that poor Abel would think that religion had fallen to ruin; and I'm afraid it would have driven him mad. How things change in less than half a lifetime!

Abel Hughes was very particular about starting and ending the children's *seiat* on time. We knew to the minute what time he would arrive at the chapel. I remember that my mother would applaud Wil Bryan for calling for me so promptly to take me to the meeting; but little did she know that our aim in going so early was to be able to play hide-and-seek in the chapel gallery. Wil had found out somehow that Abel began the meeting according to the time on his watch, and ended it according to the chapel clock. One evening, while we were all in our seats waiting for Abel to arrive, Wil said he would go to the gallery to move the clock half an hour forward; and on his word, he did. We were all very worried that Abel would come in. Just as Wil had reached the pew below the clock, and was about to put his hand on it, the door opened and Abel appeared. Wil ducked down at that moment. Our hearts beat heavily, as Abel Hughes was not a man to joke around with. As Abel prayed to begin the meeting, with his eyes tightly shut, we all seized the opportunity to look up towards the clock. We were amazed at Wil's boldness, as we saw him moving the hands of the clock, and then leisurely kneeling down at the front of the gallery, winking at us. Then, we saw him searching in his pockets for crumbs and dropping them down on old Abel's head. As he was so absorbed in his prayer, or perhaps because he was wearing his velvet cap, he didn't appear to feel a thing.

John Joseph was not present that night, and there was no *hwyl* [6] on the meeting at all. We recited our verses very imperfectly, as our thoughts were in the gallery with Wil Bryan, whose head appeared above the parapet now and again. Every time we caught a glimpse of his face, he was smiling and appearing to enjoy himself greatly. I think he was the only one whose heart was not pounding with fear. We were scolded many times by Abel Hughes for reciting our verses so poorly, and because we were continually watching the clock as though we were in a rush to go home. He little knew that we were looking up, not at the clock, but at the top of Wil Bryan's head. Though our faces were serious, Abel tired of trying to get us to concentrate on the verses, and then he looked at the clock and showed surprise that the time had passed so quickly. At that moment the door opened and Marged[7] Ellis, the minister's wife, came in. She started to complain to Abel that we children had come early to the chapel to play before the meeting, and that we made a dreadful racket. Abel asked Marged who was guilty of this, and she replied, "Hugh Bryan's boy is the worst of them all; he was particularly bad tonight."

"Well, Marged dear," said Abel, "you and I are both getting old; William Bryan has not been here tonight at all, though that is strange because William is very faithful to the meeting."

"Do you think, Abel Hughes," said Marged, "that I don't know what I'm saying? I heard him and saw him with my own eyes tearing around the chapel!"

"Rhys," said Abel, looking me straight in the eye, "did William Bryan take you to chapel tonight?"

Despite my best effort, my eyes flitted to the pew below the clock, and I saw Wil shaking his fist at me lest I say a word.

---

[6] Hwyl, in this context, lacks an obvious English translation. The word itself has two literal meanings: 'fun', in the sense that 'cael hwyl' is to 'have fun', or 'sail' as in the sail of a boat. However, it also has a particular meaning when used by Welsh evangelicals, where to 'cael hwyl' in a church meeting is to sense the presence of God in a particular way and to experience a particular freshness and fluency in all that takes place: the breeze of God's Holy Spirit 'fills the sails' and carries all before Him. Here the author plays with both meanings of the word.

[7] The Welsh form of Margaret, pronounced 'Marr-ged' with the accent firmly upon the first syllable.

I didn't dare so much as open my mouth once I had seen Wil's fist; but there was no need for me to say anything. Marged caught a glimpse of the top of his head disappearing below the parapet. "Abel Hughes," she said, "he's in the pew by the clock; I saw him just now." We all trembled in our places as Abel took a step back and looked up, but for the life of him he couldn't see Wil. "Go and fetch the wicked boy down, Abel Hughes; he's there, you can be sure," shouted Marged.

Abel was shaking as he went up to the gallery. I felt my heart in my throat as I saw him approaching the pew by the clock. However, before Abel reached it, Wil leapt to the next pew, and then to the next; and he leapt like a cat from pew to pew until he reached the top of the stairs, and ran down them as if by a single leap. At the bottom Marged tried to catch him, but flying past her Wil nearly knocked her over. Wil was well on his way home before poor Abel could turn on his heels. While Marged stated unambiguously what she thought about Wil's conduct, the venerable old elder struggled to regain his composure; but he was so worked up that he had to dismiss us that night without praying, though he charged us to go home quietly, to be good, and not to follow the example of William Bryan. Abel went on to remark to Hugh Bryan about the unbecoming conduct of his son; and I heard the latter saying the next morning that he had never in his life received such a beating from his father as he had that night.

The above story is only simple and childish, and wouldn't be worth repeating except to myself; and yet I remember a time when I'd look back at the events of that night and attach to them the significance that Wellington attached to Waterloo. At that time it was the great night of my life. In my childish folly, I admired above everything Wil Bryan's bravery and fearlessness, and thought that he had no equal in all the world. Casting my mind back now to the events that took place in the children's *seiat*, I can't avoid seeing in Wil's character the seed that later grew into a great tree.

Shame, shame, Wil, that you did not listen to the sober advice of Abel Hughes and John Joseph in the Children's Meeting. If you had, then you would not be where you are today. You would have saved all the misery you later went through, and the guilt that today loads your conscience. Do you remember, Wil, from where you are now, how Abel Hughes would counsel us to avoid every kind of evil, showing us time and again the dangers of walking in the way of the ungodly? Do you remember, I wonder, how fervently he would pray for us, and commend us to the care of Him whom he himself had found to be a faithful leader and a mighty Saviour? If you do, and I have no doubt that you do, these recollections will be as fire in your conscience today!

6

THE IRISHMAN

I suppose that my experience is no different from that of others who have tried to go back to the beginnings of things. How hard it is for me to get a hold on the beginning of anything in my story! For example, when did I come to understand that I had a closer connection with my mother than with any other woman? When did the concept of God first form in my mind? When did I come to understand that I was distinct from everyone else? When did the ideas of responsibility, of sin, and of another world become part of my consciousness? And so on. When I try to work back, and settle on some point as the beginning of these ideas or their like, I see immediately that I am mistaken and that the actual point was much further back; and as I follow it, I lose it in amongst the things that had no beginning. I don't know how to account for this. Doesn't the memory record the beginnings of things in the mind? Does a thing need to be in the mind for a certain amount of time before the memory can receive an impression of it? Or, is the beginning of something, and the memory of it, simultaneous? Are all the ideas that a man comes to hold already in his soul since he was created, but in some sort of slumber until they are woken up by circumstances, or does the soul have some adaptability to receive impressions, which then become deeper each time they are reinforced until at last they form into ideas?

About the time I'm trying to go back to, I think I was about six years old and my brother Bob about eighteen years old. Bob was, as I saw it, a big strong man; and proof enough of this was the fact that he was able to carry me on his back with no difficulty. He worked in the coal mine, and no-one ever admired their brother more than I did Bob, when he came home in his clogs, with his lamp in his hand, and his face as black as a chimney. Before that time, I don't think I had ever wondered about where my mother and Bob and I received our sustenance. However, at that time, or soon after that, I came to understand that none of the good things of this world were to be had without money—a truth which, alas, I have experienced thousands of times since then. Perhaps the means of my understanding this was my habit of asking my mother every day for this and that, and her saying that she didn't have the money to get it. I remember the great fascination I had with the time that Bob would bring home his pay. The three of us would sit around the fire while Bob emptied his pocket into my mother's apron. My mother would count the money many times over. It seemed to me that it was an enormous sum of money, and I couldn't understand why my mother always said she didn't have money, when she received so much from Bob. I noticed that my mother, on counting the money, would sometimes look joyful, and sometimes very sad; but afterwards she always looked contemplative. I imagined that she was lost in wonder at having so much money. How foolish I was. What if I had known that she was planning and agonising over how to make ends meet, how to be able to pay everyone with the few shillings that lay in her apron! As I think back, and remember how much Bob was paid, what a *chancellor of the exchequer* my mother must have been! I remember well that my mother and Bob, after counting the money, would talk long and secretively, in words that I didn't understand apart from words like 'rent' and 'shop'. Around this time I came to look forward longingly to payday, as my mother, after receiving the money, would go to the shop to buy food; and for one day we would have plenty to eat! How few people have really known the great pleasure it is to have enough to eat! I think that no-one knows that except for those, like myself, who know what it is not to have enough. Not enough, did I say? Yes, nothing at all! But I will tell of that another time.

As I have already mentioned, Wil Bryan and I were great friends, and I cannot but connect the formation of my thoughts and ideas with him. I remember vividly how jealous I was of him. His father kept a big shop, so it seemed to me, where there was an abundance of everything. Wil had meat and potatoes for his dinner every day, while I had bread and water.[1] Wil had new clothes often, while I had Bob's old clothes repaired by my mother. Wil had a penny every Saturday, while I never even saw one except for when Bob emptied his pocket into my mother's apron. But the one thing that made me regard Wil as the happiest boy on the face of the earth was that he had his own real live mule! At that time I don't think there was anything in the whole wide world that I wished for more than to have a little mule just like Wil Bryan's. I was not the only one to admire Wil's happy state; it was a general feeling among my contemporaries. Neither was Wil ignorant of his ascendancy over all of us; because if any one of us committed an offence against him, the most severe punishment possible was to be forbidden to come close to the little mule, and this usually brought us quickly to repentance at his feet. In a word, Wil, with his mule, oppressed us harshly; so much so that on one occasion I remember well, in one of our gatherings, when one of us wandered off the point—he gave out a command that not one of us, without his permission, was allowed to say three words on any subject other than the little mule, and there was nothing for it but to submit meekly to the command. As I think about it, how many fully grown-up people there are, in every walk of life where I have encountered them, who make capital out of their little mules!

Well, I wouldn't be mentioning this were it not for the fact that Wil's little mule was the means for arousing, or creating, a question deep in my soul. I remember one time being amazed and jealous about Wil's happy situation and huge advantages relative to myself, and trying to account for the difference, and I came to the conclusion that the only reason was this—that Wil

[1] Actually 'browes', a sort of gruel made from bread, butter, water and salt.

had a father, whereas I had not. Why was I without a father? When I asked my mother this question, she looked distressed, and tears leapt up into her eyes; but she did not answer a word, and tried to change the subject. I pressed the question with her again, and asked if my father was dead.

"Yes," she said, "your father, my dear boy, is dead in trespasses and sins."

My mother would commonly talk in scriptural language. I didn't understand the expression; but I took it to mean that my father had been put in the 'black hole', as I called the grave at that time. This thought caused great sadness to me at the time; though it passed quickly.

Not long after this—I can't be more accurate than a few months—I remember that my mother had been in the shop; because it was pay day, and we had just finished a good supper. The three of us sat around the fire, and I felt very happy, no matter how my mother and Bob felt. My mother would let me stay up late for an hour or two on the days when Bob received his pay. I can hardly put into words the immense happiness that being able to stay up late gave me. As I think of how such small things gave me such great happiness when I was a boy, I grieve in my heart that it wasn't possible for me to stay a boy forever. The three of us sat around the fire, as I said; it was winter, and the night was cold and stormy. I sat on my little stool, listening to the wind howling down the chimney and whistling through the keyhole. I felt very sleepy, but I made a great effort not to close my eyes in case my mother sent me to bed, and I forfeited my chance to be able to stay up late the next payday. Just as I was about to be overcome by sleep, I heard someone knocking on the door, and that made me wide awake. Before anyone had time to open the door, an unbecoming man came in and closed the door behind him, and walked straight towards the fireplace without saying a word. As soon as I saw him, I made up my mind that he was a bad man. He was dirty and unkempt, and the house was filled with an unpleasant odour. Even when I heard him speak in Welsh, I was sure in my mind that he was an Irishman. As he came into the house, Bob leapt to his feet, his face as white as chalk, and his whole body shook. I knew from Bob's manner that he was all for grabbing the man's collar and turning him out; something he could easily have done, as the man was thin and weak-looking, while Bob was barrel-chested and strong. My mother understood his intention, and pleaded with him to refrain.

In my mind, I had never seen anyone so ugly, servile and filthy as this stranger, and I was amazed at his boldness in coming like this into our house. I had never seen my mother so agitated, and having such trouble to control herself, as she said something to the effect of, "James, I have told you many times that you are not to come here; I never want to see you." The stranger pretended not to hear, but instead tried to befriend me, speaking kindly to me and calling me by my name. I was amazed that he knew my name, and I recoiled from him as one would from a snake. Eventually he took hold of me and tried to put me on his knee, and I went wild; with my little fist I gave him my best shot right in his face, and at the same moment Bob yanked me from his grasp. My mother asked him again to go away; but he would not, and Bob rose to his feet again ready to throw him out; but he was prevented again by my mother. I felt very angry with her for not letting Bob throw him out. The 'Irishman', as I called him, asked for food; and I was astonished to see my mother put food before him. He ate unashamedly, and I thought at the time that he wasn't going to stop. I would have refused him so much as a morsel, and I knew that Bob was of the same mind; as I was sitting on his knee, and I could feel him shaking with rage the whole time.

Once the Irishman had finished eating, he strode sedately across to the fireplace, as if he were planning to stay all night. My mother pleaded with him again to go; but he would not go without money. To my amazement, I saw my mother give a sum of money to him. This caused Bob to fly into a temper, and I remember him saying angrily that my mother was out of her mind, and that he wouldn't go down the coal mine to sweat and toil if she was going to give his hard-earned wages to such a thieving drunken scamp. I was angry that my mother had given the Irishman more money than it would have taken to buy a little mule just like Wil Bryan's. At the same time, although I was so young, I felt a great sympathy with my mother; I had an impression that this stranger had some profound influence upon her, and that she couldn't help but do what she did. Bob's rage had no effect at all on the Irishman. Once he had the money, he appeared even more determined to stay. He lit his pipe, and began to undo his shoelaces.

Seeing this, Bob lost all patience; he leapt to his feet, opened the door wide, grabbed the Irishman by the throat and threw him out into the road like a corpse, then barricaded the door shut. All this took Bob about a quarter of a minute; and I clapped my hands joyfully, until I saw my mother faint. I thought she had died, and I was almost out of my mind with grief. However, after Bob had thrown cold water over her face, she came round and started to weep; and for a while she was joined in this by both Bob and myself. Once we had calmed down, my mother and Bob spoke secretively; but I understood perfectly well that the Irishman was their subject, the one they just called 'him'. Though I asked my mother and Bob over and over, I failed to find out who the stranger was. The only answer I got was that he was a bad man, and that I was not to talk about him to anyone.

Well, it would have been good for me had I not learned any more about him as time went on. But that was not how Providence saw fit. Hasn't it been the Irishman who has made my whole life bitter? Hasn't he mixed wormwood into my sweetest drinks? How different would my story have been were it not for him! When my friends have thought that I was happy and carefree, he has been like an evil spirit turning every pleasure sour, and like a nightmare whenever I should have been at rest.

7

THE TWO SCHOOLS

I expect that every man, everywhere, possesses an idea, however correct it may be, about himself: his personal appearance, his physical and mental powers, and his social status. In other words, every man has an idea of his greatness; but he will not always be prepared to reveal it to others. As a rule, he keeps it to himself. Perhaps there are compelling reasons for this. It stands to reason that it is the man himself who knows best about himself; and he is the best qualified to form a correct assessment. But, if he is a moderately able man, he would not dare to make this known for fear of diminishing himself in the opinion of others, and being lower in their estimation than in his own. Perhaps one in a million may dare, like the apostle Paul, to state, without shrinking, his superiority over others; but the proportion of those who believe they are superior is far higher. Humility has such lustre and beauty in the sight of men, that even honesty must cover its eyes in its presence. How great He[1] must have been who could make the sorts of statements and claims that he did, without detracting in any way from his humility and meekness.

It is often thought that greatness and humility should go together; yet there is cause to think that what is called humility amongst men is, very often, nothing but another form of wisdom, or perhaps even craft. Suppose that Dr _____,[2] in the midst of his brothers at the association meeting,[3] were to address them thus: 'Well, my dear brothers, you know that I am more capable than any of you—I can write an essay or compose a sermon, when I choose to, far better than any of you. In a word, you know that as far as natural abilities and refinement go I am worth more than a dozen of some of you, and more than two of the best of you'.

What would his brothers say? Would they not look at one another? And would there not be, in their expressions, a suggestion that the speaker had taken leave of his senses? And yet the speaker knows as well as anyone that every one of the words I have put into his mouth are true, even though he wouldn't say so for the world. A truly great man knows that he can trust others to form their opinions of him without his directing them, and the chances are that they will think too highly of him; and he'd rather their error be in this direction than the other way. Neither the great nor the small are anxious to correct others, if their tendency is to think too highly of them.

I can say from experience that it is an uncomfortable thing to feel small; and perhaps this is the reason why the small always make an effort to show all of themselves off to best advantage. This can be seen among other creatures, besides men. The other day I was watching two cocks on a dung heap—the long-legged and high-headed Cochin China, and the little dandy. The former looked surly and disinterested, entirely satisfied with its position. But as for the dandy, oh how he pushed his breast out, standing on the tip of his toes, and holding his head and tail so upright that they almost touched each other! He crowed and crowed again in a clear voice, and he tried, or so it appeared to me, to pick a fight with the Cochin China. He turned around and around, and seemed to say, 'Don't you see my breast and tail? You don't have a tail like this'. The Cochin China seemed not to notice. In the end, he crowed, but it sounded more like a groan than anything else, as though in pity at the smallness of the dandy. I'm not sure whether the Cochin China and the dandy were imitating men, or whether men

---

[1] The use of the capital 'H' implies that the author is here referring to Christ, even though his awkward sentence construction makes it look like he is referring to the apostle Paul!
[2] In many places the author resorts to the irritating Victorian habit of giving a blank line instead of the name of some real person who his readers would be expected to know about. In some cases it is possible to guess whom he meant, but in this case it really could be anyone in the Calvinistic Methodist firmament.
[3] In the original, 'cymanfa', implying a particular sort of gathering of senior Methodists.

imitate them, but the similarity between them is obvious. But this is what I was going to ask: 'Rhys, what opinion have you formed about yourself? No-one else here is listening, so you can answer honestly, with no great danger of anyone thinking that you are being self-centred nor falsely modest. You are a preacher, a pastor, a poet sometimes, and occasionally you write for the periodicals. What position do you hold in your own mind?' Well, I will try to put my foot on the throat of pride and answer honestly without deceiving myself, as there is no-one else here to listen.

He who knows all things knows that in the thing I ought and wish to be greatest in, namely religion and the experience of spiritual things, I am woefully small. The more I strive to engage in things divine and eternal, the more I feel the grip of the world upon me, and the heavier are the weights that hold me down. If the declarations of the inspired word about the power and grace of the Saviour were not so emphatic and strong, I would have sunk into despair beneath the load of a defiled heart and a guilty conscience. My prayer from the depth of my heart is for Him to strengthen me in the faith.

With respect to my personal appearance, I know that there is nothing charming in me, and I find it remarkable to think that there was one, one time, who loved me, as I shall, perhaps, be able to touch on another time. I have often been jealous of the conversational abilities of Glan Alun,[4] which make everyone overlook his appearance. You dear man! I prefer you to a hundred of these handsome, tidy but soulless men. At the same time,

---

[4] It was common at this time for people who wrote poetry to use a pseudonym, often geographical in nature; 'Glan Alun' just means 'the banks of the river Alyn', which flows past Mold. In the case of well-known poets their pseudonyms replaced their actual names in day-to-day usage. Glan Alun was actually Thomas John, or Jones (1811–1866), a colourful character who ranged through various occupations including being a pharmacist and publisher in Wrexham, a Methodist preacher (though he was for a time disqualified due to intemperance), a candle-maker and a commercial traveller. He authored the Welsh edition of Aesop's fables, and his son-in-law John Roberts became a pioneer missionary in Assam, India.

I'd like to think that there is nothing actually repellent about my appearance. Perhaps I am wrong? In any case, I'd be more than happy to be Thomas John if it were possible to have his remarkable soul. Even so, a handsome and princely appearance is a huge asset for a preacher; and he who climbs into the pulpit without it is at a discount.

As for natural abilities—well, all right, no-one is listening—I believe that mine excel some of my brethren. They know this, or at least they ought to know. I would not say as much to anyone, and if anyone were to say so to me then I would protest to the contrary; and that, perhaps, would be counted as modesty on my part.

Regarding my knowledge, I am neither here nor there. Indeed, in this church there are lads who know much more than me about some things; and I often have to do my best to prevent them coming to realise this. Take geography, for example: I know next to nothing about that valuable subject; when one of the lads in the meeting asks me a question in that area I must exercise great cunning to hide my ignorance, as it wouldn't do for them to realise that I am ignorant, and me the minister of the church; the poor boys think that I know everything. I have various ways to get out of this awkward situation. If I am asked a question that I don't know how to answer, I will refer the question to a boy in the class who I think may be able to answer it; and if I have a rough idea that he has answered correctly then I give a reinforcing nod. But if I am asked a question that neither I nor anyone else in the class can answer, then I try to impress on the minds of my pupils the importance of everyone reading and learning for themselves, and that knowledge gained in that way is far more valuable than any answer I could have given them at that time. I may add that I will keep the question in mind until the next meeting, by which time I expect everyone to be able to answer it. In the meantime, I look up the answer for myself. Of course, no-one knows this, and wise men would not blame me if they did know; because if I were to confess my ignorance before the boys, this would detract greatly from my usefulness.

The thing that gave cause to me writing such a lengthy introduction to this chapter was the thought of what a misfortune it is for a preacher, of all people, to miss out on the advantages of education in early life. He daily stumbles across something that he should have learned in school when he was a boy; and he can never rise to the position of usefulness of those who received a thorough elementary education while they were children. When I was a lad, my native town had just two day-schools. One was kept by a gentleman of the name of Mr Smith, of whom I have fond recollections. Mr Smith was the great wizard of the town. He was looked on by some with the sort of admiration that almost touched on worship. It was believed that he was fluent in seven languages, and that he could speak words that no-one could understand. I heard my mother insist that Mr Smith and Dic Aberdaron [5] were the two greatest scholars that the world had ever seen. Whatever I think now about the accuracy of my mother's statement, I know that I believed it without question at that time. This would cause me to stand on the roadside whenever I saw Mr Smith, watching him in indescribable amazement as he passed. He was a tall, frail, long-haired man who wore black clothes and spectacles. I think he was the only man in our town at that time who allowed his beard to spread to his upper lip. Mr Smith's school was considered an eminent and very honourable institution, and no-one would imagine sending their children there apart from the gentry and the well-to-do. I remember thinking there must be a great mystery connected with the green bags in which the boys from Mr Smith's school carried their books.

I have strong cause to believe that my mother would not have dreamed of sending me to Mr Smith's school, even if her circumstances had allowed it, as she believed that he was a man without grace. She had various reasons for forming this idea about

---

[5] Richard Robert Jones (1780–1843), compiler of a Welsh-Hebrew-Greek lexicon and reputed to have spoken a total of 14 or 15 languages.

him; for one thing, because he frequented the parish church on the Sabbath rather than being 'with religion'; or, in other words, he went to the Church of England instead of to Chapel. The words 'Church of England' and 'religion' were very far away from one another in my mother's dictionary. Another thing that caused her to believe that Mr Smith was a man without grace was his custom of taking a walk on Sunday afternoon rather than meditating in the Word and doctrine. Also my mother had heard from an old maid of Mr Smith's that he had in his house a 'book for raising demons', which he read every day 'at nightfall'. There was no doubt about the veracity of this story, because one night Mr Smith had left the book open on the table. The maid saw it the following morning and carelessly moved over to it and tried to read it, but the only word she could make out on the page was 'Satan'; and the next time she went into the room, the book had disappeared. It is true that the maid did not understand a word of English. As additional proof of this, my mother recalls clearly that Mr Smith accompanied Mr Brown the parson when the latter went to Tynllidiart to exorcise a spirit, and shut it up in his tobacco box. My mother's conclusion was this: if Mr Smith, and he not being a parson, could help Mr Brown to exorcise spirits, then he would be no stranger to the work of raising them as well. But the main reason my mother had for believing that Mr Smith was a man without grace was the fact that he had a moustache. No-one would be able to persuade her, she maintained, that anyone who had experienced the great things of religion could leave his beard to grow on his upper lip. She had never seen anyone worthy of the name of Christian who would do such a thing. Would Mr Elias or Mr Rees wear a moustache? A bit of hair straying around the ear is something quite different. As I said, these things, even if my mother had been able to afford it, were an insurmountable obstacle to my going to school with Mr Smith. Apart from that, my mother didn't hold with higher education. I heard her say many times that she had never seen any good come from giving higher education to children, and that too much education had led some to the gallows. 'For poor children', she said, 'if they can read their Bible, and know the way to Life, that is plenty for them'.

The other school was kept by one Robert Davies, or as he was generally known, 'Robin the Soldier'. He was a solidly built and portly man, and very elderly. He had spent the flower of his youth in the army of Great Britain, where he had distinguished himself as a brave and honest soldier. When the old Soldier returned to his home town he was missing his right leg, which he had left behind in Belgium as a sign of his zeal and faithfulness to his country when he was fighting against Boney. Robert made up the lack with a wooden leg of imported material, but fashioned by himself, with an iron ferrule on the tip. On leaving the army, the government of the day felt the obligation to award him a pension of sixpence a day for the rest of his life, in recognition of his valuable service as a soldier, and as a substantial attempt to compensate him for losing his leg; and for this reason Robert often called the wooden leg 'this old sixpence leg'. For some weeks after Robert returned from the army, he was frequently called upon to dine with his old friends, for them to hear him tell the stories of his battles and all that he saw and heard. However, Robert soon came to the end of his repertoire, and his stories became dull before his stomach lost its appetite; and by this time the only place where his stories were listened to with a degree of interest was the Cross Foxes, where Robert was a frequent visitor.

As the income from the wooden leg scarcely covered his weekly bills from the Cross Foxes, the old Soldier quickly fell into straitened circumstances. But there soon came help for the old brother; Providence opened the way for him to keep a toll booth. In this state the old Soldier had, for a while, a life of daily plenty. There was a polished and comfortable look about him at that time; and no doubt things would have continued that way had the highway inspectors not discovered that, rather than Robert keeping the gate, the gate was keeping him. After deliberation, they concluded that this had not been the original intention of the toll booth; and as some of the inspectors were somewhat selfish, and hard-hearted, they wished to restore the toll booth to its original purpose; so Robert had to leave.

Mr Brown the parson was a philanthropic man and extremely kind to his parishioners, especially the ones who weren't heretics. In so far as the old warrior was one of his 'dearly beloved brethren' and a pious man—that is, he went to church every Sunday morning, went to bed every Sunday afternoon, and went to the Cross Foxes every Sunday evening—Mr Brown took a particular interest in his circumstances, and he was the first to suggest to him the appropriateness of his starting to keep a school. 'Robyt,' said Mr Brown—or so I heard my mother report it—'you're a scholar [6] —you can read and write and say the catechism—you could start a school in the old empty office—I'll help you. Lots of children are uneducated, Bobyt, you can charge them a penny a week—and make a *lot* of money—and live comfortably—I'll do my best for you. You, Robyt, have been fighting for your country, and I'll fight for you now'. Fair play to Mr Brown; he had a warm heart, and didn't rest until he had put Robert on his feet, or rather on his foot, in the matter of the day-school.

Robin the Soldier's school was an established institution by the time I was old enough to go to it. As for how it came about that my mother sent me there, my memory isn't fresh enough to supply the details. Certainly, it was not motivated by any over-eagerness to learn on my part. I'm fairly certain, also, that it wasn't because my mother was convinced of Robert Davies' piety. The most likely reason I can think of now was that Mr Brown had exercised his influence over my mother in the matter. Although she believed that Mr Brown had no experience of the 'great things', I know that she had a high opinion of him as a philanthropist and neighbour.

---

[6] In the original, Mr Brown speaks in a sort of deliberately mis-spelled pidgin Welsh, which is very entertaining to read. A very rough English equivalent would be along the lines of 'u skolur—u kan rid and rite und say katekism—u start skool…' and so on.

The only thing that reconciled me to the idea of going to the school was that Wil Bryan was a member of the august institution. Even so, I remember well that I felt I was doing an act of heroism in going to school, and that I deserved some sort of tribute for my self-sacrifice. I have noticed from reading other autobiographies that their authors regard their first day at school as no insignificant thing. That day is clear in my mind and I remember the day and its events, not as they do, for the entertainment of others, but for my own entertainment, the only one perhaps who can find amusement in it. Perhaps it would be better for me to take another chapter to tell of the day's events.

8

UNDER INSTRUCTION

If this story happens to fall into the hands of any of my friends after I have laid my head down, and if they go to the trouble of reading it, I know that they will be surprised that I have spent so much time recording such small and inconsequential things. I have just written seven chapters about the short period between my birth and my first day at school. If I were writing this for one of the periodicals,[1] no doubt the editor would have lost all patience some time ago, and urged me to speed up a bit, or knock the whole enterprise on the head. But, I have the advantage of writing to please myself, and not the public. The man who is delivering a message goes straight ahead, on the most direct route, and may manage to walk at four miles an hour according to his watch. But the man who goes to ramble in his native land is blind to all milestones; he climbs over ditches, wanders around the groves, hunts birds' nests, collects nuts and blackberries, sits on mossy hills, loafs around by the river, and all this without remembering that he has a watch in his pocket. Give me the latter. What freedom I have! No-one calls me to account for writing a preface to every chapter, if I choose; there's no need to rephrase sentences, if they read a bit awkwardly or don't flow well, and there is no need for me to ask myself what the reader will say about this or that.

I was remembering last night about Dafydd Dafis, the old chapel elder here. A remarkably good and godly old man—one of the faithful ones of the old school, who has not moved from the rules of the founding fathers so much as to part his fringe from his forehead. I have great respect for his good sense and his prejudices. I know

---

[1] ...which, don't forget, he was.

that Dafydd Dafis thinks highly of me, and perhaps that's why I think so highly of him. Indeed, now I come to think about it, I find that this is the rule according to which I form my ideas about my brethren. If I come to understand that so-and-so thinks well of me, then somehow, even against my better judgement, I come to the conclusion that there must be something in the fellow. And vice versa. I remember one time, I had a high opinion of the fellow in the post office; but when I came to understand that he did not have the same opinion of me, then my appraisal of him fell immediately. Ever since then I have regarded him as someone deeply flawed, though I have not been able to put my finger on the nature of the flaw. But what if Dafydd Dafis were to know that tonight I was writing something so childish as the story of my first day at school? I fear that his opinion of me would fall. Fortunately, he knows nothing of this work. I often find myself doing certain things, and refraining from certain other things, entirely because of the influence of Dafydd Dafis. When talking to him I have often been tempted to crack jokes, but have held back out of respect for the old man. Some time ago I was seized by a strong urge to grow a moustache, as many young preachers do so these days; but I remembered that minute about Dafydd Dafis; I could not do such a thing without offending him, and so I continue to shave. As Dafydd Dafis knows nothing about what I'm doing, I am going for my own entertainment to write a detailed account, without holding anything back, about the first day that I went to school.

It was a Monday, and it was winter. Wil Bryan called for me early, and was charged emphatically by my mother to take good care of me. Wil suggested to me on the way that it was fairly likely I'd have to fight with one or two of my fellow scholars—it wouldn't be pleasant, but this was always the custom with new pupils, and he would make sure he was behind me to see that I got fair play. This suggestion was anything but reassuring to me—mainly because I was convinced that my talents did not lie at all in that direction, and also because I could see the possibility of the event, if it happened, being reported back to my mother at home and to Abel Hughes in the Children's Meeting. I was ashamed to admit this to Wil Bryan; and I told him I would follow his lead; and indeed, I didn't want to do anything to annoy him, so high was my opinion of him.

The office where the old Soldier held his school was a long and narrow building. Around it there was a rough and crooked bench, and connected to it there was a desk resting against the wall. One of the first things I noticed was that there was not so much as a square inch on the desk that had not had cut into it, with a knife, a picture or a figure or a name. At the far end of the schoolhouse, by the fire, was the schoolmaster's desk, at the bottom of which was a large hole, whose purpose, as I saw later, was for the master's wooden leg to fit through while he was sitting down. On my first entering the school, I saw a sight which was very strange and new to me at that time. The boys were all present, some sitting on top of the desk, others sitting on one another playing horses and galloping around, others in a pile on the floor rowing through one another like eels in mud. One—a lame boy who had a crutch—was pretending to be the master, sitting at his desk and poking his crutch through the hole, and shouting for quiet, but to no effect. The scene changed every minute, and everyone was shouting at the tops of their voices the whole time except for one boy, who stood on top of the desk by the window, dividing his attention between the play and the direction from which the master would come. I felt strange at the time, and thought I had come into the midst of some very naughty children; and that if my mother knew what sort they were, I'd never be allowed to go there again. Conversely, I was thinking that this was the best place I had ever seen for having fun. Nevertheless, my overwhelming feeling at the time was one of isolation and painful shyness, as Wil Bryan had left me on my own and joined in the playing with gusto. As I was possessed by these feelings, I saw the boy standing on the table putting his two fingers into his mouth and whistling clearly; and in a blink of an eye every boy was sitting in his place, panting for breath. I knew very well that I looked silly

41

standing on my own by the door like a monument when the Soldier came in. He walked past me as though he didn't see me. He looked agitated and angry, and I soon understood that the watchman had not given the sign soon enough, and that the master had heard the whole deafening din. He went forward to his desk, and pulled out a long, strong cane. I saw each of the boys getting their necks ready as the old Soldier paced around the room, beating each one cruelly and indiscriminately. I was the only one who had no taste of the cane, and the only one who burst into tears, because I was so frightened. As for the other boys, it seemed they were well familiar with the regime. After the last boy had had his beating, the master went back to his desk; he raised his hands and said, "Let us pray," and repeated the Lord's prayer thoughtfully, with the boys following him. I came to understand later that some of the naughty boys were reciting under their breath something rather different from the Lord's prayer, which caused quiet giggling among those sitting close to them.

After the prayer had been recited, the old Soldier shouted authoritatively, "Rivets, my boys," the sign every Monday morning for the boys to come forward with their pennies. If a boy had failed to bring his penny with him, he would need to hold his hand out for the purpose of receiving the hot impress of the cane, which as a rule would send him back to his seat squeezing his hand between his knees, or under his arm, or into his mouth, or otherwise shaking it as though it had newly been pulled out of the fire. This was the effect that a slap with the cane generally had, especially if the boy had not had time to spit on his hand and place two crossed hairs upon it. In passing, I remember that the boys had an unshakeable belief in the magic of the spit and two hairs to allay the burning effect of the cane. My own belief is, despite much experimentation, that I never saw much effect from the practice. It was an infrequent sight for a boy to cry after one slap on his hand; but if he had two or three, then he was regarded as having the right to weep without being considered a sissy. I would cry every time after one slap; I was famous for being a crybaby, but I couldn't help it.

But to return; after Wil Bryan had presented me to the master, and he had put my name in the book, and received my penny—which was, as I recall well, hot because of how tightly I had been holding on to it for fear of losing it—he said I was to go to my seat, and I would know soon what my first task would be. I had the privilege of sitting between Wil Bryan and one John Beck. The latter immediately asked me if I had a ha'penny. I answered no. He asked me again if I knew when I would have one—he knew of a shop where a great deal of toffee could be obtained for a ha'penny—and that he knew the shopkeeper, and that I would have nearly twice the usual amount if I were with him. Wil Bryan told him to be quiet, and that if he did not then he would have cause to regret it; and more or less implied that I would beat him up. I knew little at that time how mischievous a boy Wil Bryan was. Beck said that it would be beyond me to give him a beating. Wil asked me if I was afraid of Beck. I bravely answered that I wasn't, even though I felt the opposite. "All right," said Wil, and within five minutes the news had been whispered in the ear of every boy in the school that there was going to be a fight between Rhys Lewis and John Beck. My conscience was tender, and I was very disturbed as I thought of such a thing; but I couldn't bring myself to tell of this to Wil Bryan, who was whispering into my ear various directions in preparation for the coming event. I had been taught by my mother at home, and by Abel Hughes in the Children's Meeting, that fighting was a great sin; and my conscience was burning with the thought that I was about to fight a boy who had never said an unkind word to me, and towards whom I bore no enmity. I remember comforting myself with the thought that, if the event happened to reach the ears of my mother, she might be more ready to forgive because my opponent was a Church boy, as I knew that she did not have a high opinion of Church people. I was confident, therefore, that she might look on the thing as an accidental collision between Church and Chapel.

For about an hour, it didn't look to me as though any work was going on in the school. The old Soldier spent most of the time with his head down—either reading or writing—and the boys, even though their books were open in front of them, were whispering the whole time. I knew full well that John Beck and I were the subject of their discourse. If the chattering happened to get a bit loud, the master would shout "Silence!" at the top of his voice, and for a few minutes there would be silence. At quarter to eleven, the command was given for us to go to play, and everyone jumped up and rushed out like sheep going through a gap in the hedge. My heart beat quickly as I thought of what was about to happen. Almost before I knew it, I found myself in the yard fighting with John Beck. I did my best under the circumstances, though I wasn't conscious of how I was getting on because my eyes were closed most of the time, not because of the blows of my opponent but because I was afraid. The contest did not last for long, and my heart was glad when I learned that everything was over, and I had won. I believe to this day that I must have had help from Wil Bryan. I don't know what I was most pleased about, whether it was because the fight was over or because I had come out of it victorious, and in one piece, but my heart was immediately shot with fear as I heard the commanding voice of the Soldier calling us into the school. It was obvious that he had seen the whole thing; and I heard some of the boys whispering straight away that the son of the woman who cleaned the church, who was nicknamed 'Slate', had carried the news to the master; and many were the threats which were piled upon his head.

After we had gone into the school, Rhys Lewis and John Beck were called to the desk to give an account of their stewardship. These were awful minutes, but Wil Bryan proved as good as his word. He came to the desk unbidden to give his testimony. He said to the master without shaking that Beck had challenged me, and hit me first. This was denied absolutely by Beck. Another witness was called, and he happened to be an enemy of Beck, so he confirmed the testimony of Wil Bryan. The old Soldier said that, inasmuch as this was my first day at the school, he would let me go unrebuked for this time, but as for Beck he would have three strokes of the cane; one for fighting without cause, one for being beaten by his opponent, and one for denying the charge brought against him. I felt great sympathy for Beck. He was held by the strongest boy in the school, a certain part of his body was made bare, which at the time I did not care to see and now I do not care to name, and the aforesaid punishment was administered to him. Before each stroke, the old Soldier gave a preface (in English) as follows: "*This is for fighting without reasonable cause*" (stroke); "*this is for coming out of the fight the vanquished*" (stroke); "*and this is for denying the true accusation brought against him*" (stroke). In the time after that, I heard this palaver scores of times—which is how I remember it so well. The old Soldier's sermon was particularly well-directed and influential, and for that reason he preached it often. In turn I saw every boy in the school except one jumping and shouting under its effects, though not with joy. The 'except one' was Wil Bryan. Whatever *hwyl*[2] the old Soldier had, he could not make Wil shout, and this made him a hero amongst the children and the epitome of courage. It seemed to me that the boys, in general, took great enjoyment from seeing Beck's punishment; and I took this to be great cruelty on their part, especially as they did not know which of them would be next to receive the same treatment.

Great guilt lay upon my conscience because of what happened; and I was in a hurry for my bedtime, so that I could ask forgiveness for the sins of the day, as I had been taught. Fortunately, the incident did not reach my mother's ears; and as far as I know, Abel Hughes did not hear of it. Nothing in particular happened that afternoon. I'm sure that I had just one lesson, and that in spelling, on my first day at school; and I don't think that any of the boys had more than one. In general, I am certain that each boy had more strokes of the cane than lessons. One thing happened that day that greatly quietened my conscience, and which gives me comfort to this day.

---

[2] cf. note 2 in chapter 5; the allusion is to a preacher who, experiencing *hwyl* as he preaches his sermon, moves his congregation to shouts of joy.

When I went home for my lunch, I was given a ha'penny by a relative as a reward for going to school. I lost no time before sharing the news of this with John Beck, and making peace terms with him. He took me to the shop where the ha'penny had great value, and Beck had the best part of the toffee, and the sun did not set on our anger.[3] In my innocence I remember believing that, because things had turned out so well in the end, there was no need for me to pray for forgiveness as I went to rest, and I did not. As far as I remember, the events of my first day in Robin the Soldier's school were as I have related.

---

[3] Eph. 4:26.

9

MATTERS ECCLESIASTICAL

The other day I had the pleasure of visiting the British School [1] in this town; and as I observed its wonderful orderliness, the good and wholesome education that was provided in it, the careful and gentle discipline that was administered, and the clean, happy appearance of the children, I couldn't help recalling the great disadvantages under which I had laboured in the school of Robin the Soldier. My blood boils even now when I think of his hypocrisy, his stupidity, his idleness and his incomparable cruelty. To do justice to my story, I must say some more about him in the chapter, before turning to more substantial things; and then I will say farewell to him forever, unless I have to bear witness against him in a day which is to come. However, I trust he will receive mercy, just as I hope for the same.

The most important thing for the old Soldier was getting his money, and the next thing, for his entertainment, was to be able to break his strong cane into shards on our backs and hands every week or, at most, every nine days. The harsh treatment that we received at his hands was not a secret from our parents; but in their ignorance, they considered it necessary for our well-being; and we, the boys, looked forward to this sharp discipline with the same consistency, though not with the same appetite, as we did to our dinner. As far as I can remember, not one of the boys cared any more than I did about learning anything; and the one to whom our education had been trusted cared even less. It appeared to me that he had more pleasure in our work when we failed a task than

---

[1] The 'British Schools' were a network of non-denominational charity schools across Wales and England; they stood in contrast to the 'National Schools', which were run by the Church of England.

when we succeeded, as that gave him an excuse to chastise us. He expected—if that is the word—that we would learn without being taught. We often thought that he felt disappointed if we happened to learn something in spite of his efforts. He never attempted to create within us a love for knowledge, or an ambition to succeed; instead he created a hatred for every sort of education, and an unnatural desire in every boy to be strong enough to give him a hiding in return, which I am sure every one had promised himself the pleasure of doing once he had become 'a man'. I remember well how I would, after having a severe hiding from him, when my back stung and my heart was heavy, gaze at his wooden leg and try to guess how many Frenchmen he had killed, when he was fighting against Boney. John Beck said he had heard that the old Soldier had killed three hundred. Wil Bryan gave a much higher number; and added that nothing would give more pleasure to the Soldier than killing all of us, except that he was afraid of being hanged; and with this sentiment we all agreed. No great effort of mind was needed to believe this; because whenever he was punishing a boy, such fury could be seen in his face—the sharp bones of his chin sticking out, the veins of his forehead swelling and turning black, and his appearance terrifying to behold.

At the same time he had a remarkable ability to change his facial expression. I remember seeing him more than once in this frenzy, when Mr Brown would suddenly come into the school. Mr Brown was a fat, generous and kind man, devoid of suspicion towards his neighbours, especially if they went to church. I saw, as I said, Mr Brown coming suddenly into the school while the old Soldier was in a frenzy; and in the blink of an eye the old hypocrite would change his face, and wear an almost heavenly expression. He would call one of us forward to say the catechism or a collect, and when we had finished he would stroke our heads affectionately. Mr Brown would congratulate him for his labour and his success, and would say, "You're doing much good here, Robyt, and you'll be rewarded for it." [2] If any of us happened, in Mr Brown's presence, to look discontent, or in any way to indicate that we were anything other than perfectly happy, woe to us when the generous man turned his back. Indeed, however we looked, the effort that it cost the old Soldier to look gentle, and the extent to which it taxed his vicious nature in Mr Brown's presence, gave rise to a reaction as soon as the reverend gentleman turned his back; and his bad temper would be worse than before. On occasions, people would allege to Mr Brown that the Soldier acted cruelly towards the boys, and the reverend gentleman would come to the school to discuss the matter with the master. The old Soldier would call the boy he was accused of cruelty towards to face Mr Brown, and ask him, with a clear indication in his eyes of how the boy was to answer, "Am I not a gentle master?" It was not fitting for the boy to contradict him, and Mr Brown would be satisfied that the whole thing was nothing but gossip.

And yet there were benefits in Robin the Soldier's school, at least what we boys saw as benefits. Every Friday afternoon, the old trooper would pick two of us out to be his servants for the following week. The job of these servants was to clean the schoolhouse, light the fires, and run messages. Under the latter heading came frequent visits to the Cross Foxes to fetch beer for the Soldier, and that each time without money. Until one got used to it, this task would be very uncomfortable, because Mrs Tibbett the landlady would make an awful fuss; and each time she would have to show the messenger the size of the old Soldier's debt, written in chalk hieroglyphics on the back of the cellar door. Mrs Tibbett was a fat old lady, the same width from top to bottom. Her face was always a reddish-black colour, and some said that she got that way through her constant protesting that she never touched a drop of alcohol herself. Anyway, the boys had a high opinion of Mrs Tibbett, as she held the same ideas as they did about the life and character of the old Soldier. I remember well how much pleasure Mrs Tibbett

---

[2] …in his amusing pidgin Welsh, which I have not tried to imitate.

took holding forth on her ideas of the master's shortcomings, how she would show us his account on the cellar door, and state her opinion that he would never be able to settle it. One time, I heard Wil Bryan remark to her that the old Soldier had a much bigger account than the one on the cellar door, which he would also never be able to pay. "What!" said the old lady, deeply shaken, "has he got a tab somewhere else?" But when Wil explained that he was talking of the great account on the day which is to come, she calmed down and said, "Ho! Well, that's up to him; every one of us must give our answer, and everyone will have justice. If he would pay my tab, he can take his chances then."

The most uncomfortable job for the servants would be to light the fire in the schoolhouse; because they had to gather the kindling for the purpose, as the hedgerows all around bore witness. I remember one morning when Wil Bryan and I had not so much as a twig to start a fire, Wil asked me seriously if I knew whether the master took his wooden leg to bed with him, and would it be possible to steal it? "Ah," said Wil, "that would kindle nicely!" I saw his face shine with satisfaction as he contemplated it. Poor Wil! He never got the chance to put his desire into practice.

But I was talking about the benefits. When one was a servant, he was not asked so much as to look at a book, and he was wholly free of reproof no matter what mischief he got up to during his service. Indeed, it was said that the master had once, some time ago, even smiled at one of the servants. I cannot ascertain whether this is a fact, since I never once saw a smile on his face except in Mr Brown's presence. Because of these huge advantages, on Friday afternoons we would listen like mice to find out to whom the comfortable service would fall. It was rarely that it came to Wil Bryan and me, because our parents were Chapel people, and we rarely went to Church except for when they shared out *bara brith* there. A visit to the church one Good Friday morning was the occasion for bringing to an end the career of Wil Bryan and myself at Robin the Soldier's school; and once I have related that circumstance, I shall, as I said, bid farewell to that Pharaoh forever. As I consider the circumstance that I am about to relate, I find it hard to understand my feelings about it. To some extent, I feel guilt about my naughtiness, but at the same time I can't suppress the chuckle in my breast as I recall my part in it. If this feeling is sinful, then I hope to be forgiven for it. Although I will be chronicling my own wickedness, it is impossible for me to pass over it, as it is an important part of my story, and because the incident was the occasion for terminating that amount of schooling which it was seen fit to give me.

It was Good Friday morning, and as there was no service in the chapel and the weather was too wet for us to go out to play, Wil Bryan and I went with the other children to church. I did not know that Wil had any intent contrary to innocence as we went, and he gave no hint to me on the way. Perhaps he was afraid that, if he shared his intention with me, I wouldn't agree with him. In the old church there was a big, deep, square pew that would hold twenty or more children, and into this went Robin the Soldier's scholars. Once the door had been closed on this pew, we couldn't because of its depth even see Mr Brown in his pulpit, and nobody could see us. The pew next to this was long and narrow, and in this sat Robin the Soldier, and him alone, the purpose being to terrify the children and stop them from being unruly. For the schoolmaster's comfort, Mr Brown had, in accordance with his customary kindness, had a hole cut in the bottom of the Soldier's pew, so that his wooden leg might poke through when he sat down, and the tip of this was therefore visible in the boys' pew. It wasn't just the schoolmaster's comfort that was accomplished in this way. For the boys to see the tip of the wooden leg tended to remind them that he whom they feared so much was close by, even though he was unseen, and this would keep them within the bounds of good behaviour. As soon as the service had started, I saw Wil staring contemplatively at what was to be seen of the wooden leg. Next, I saw him pull from his pocket a length of thin, but strong, cord. The cord had a slipknot already tied, showing that it was no sudden idea that had come into Wil's mind. Wil went down on his knees, and slid the knot gently over the tip of the wooden leg. Then he made me hold the cord, and said, "When you feel him bite, hold your grip," speaking of the wooden leg as though it were a fish. It wasn't fitting for me to disobey; and I wasn't long waiting for the fish to bite, because, according to the order of things in the Church of England, it was time for the congregation to rise to its feet, and the Soldier tried to conform; but we heard him falling in his seat like a piece of lead. In this position we kept him throughout the whole service. At the beginning he writhed and snorted like a bull in a net; but soon his voice was drowned out by the majestic sound of the organ. Wil and I kept hold of the cord until we were blue in the face. We were not assisted in this task by any of the boys apart from John Beck, who, without being asked, rolled up his sleeves and was of great service. Most of the boys enjoyed our cunning trick, and had to hold their sides, and put their handkerchiefs in their mouths, not to laugh out loud. Others looked terrified as they thought of the consequences, and the son of the woman who cleaned the church looked very uncomfortable. As the service finished, Wil told John Beck to take his knife and cut the cord within a foot of the tip of the wooden leg. After Beck had done this, Wil pushed the rest of the cord into his pocket in a second and said, "There he is now, like a hen ready to lay," no doubt referring to the practice of tying a string to a hen's foot in order to know where she will lay her eggs. Then Wil ordered all of us to go out in a leisurely manner, and with sober faces. As we went out, slowly and seriously, we saw Mr Brown on his way to the vestry, looking over the side of the Soldier's pew, and we heard him say, "Hello! Robyt, I thought you weren't here today." We didn't stay to hear or see more; but Wil insisted that he had looked over his shoulder when Mr Brown was in the act of entering the vestry, and he noticed that the reverend gentleman was pushing his pocket handkerchief into his mouth, and his neck and cheeks were as red as flame; and Wil believed that he was laughing, having understood what had kept the Soldier out of sight. And this wasn't hard to believe, as Mr Brown was a jolly fellow.

It was a tense time for us from then until Monday morning. We became conscious of the enormity of what we had done, and there was no doubt in our minds that Slate would give a full account to the master of the whole circumstance. There was much discussion between Bryan, Beck and myself; but we could not see one path of escape from the just punishment that we deserved. Monday morning came, and we had to go to school. Indeed, Wil appeared that he was keen to go, as he called for me earlier than usual. I wondered some of the time if he wanted to get the punishment over with; but at other times I thought he had some plan in his mind to avoid it, as he was particularly quiet and contemplative. As for myself, I was so terrified that my legs would barely carry me. Beck felt the same way. Seeing us so fearful, Wil said to us as we entered the schoolroom door, "Cheer up, it will turn out better than you fear." I couldn't see how he could hope for this; but it strengthened my idea that he had some plan to save us. The boys were all present, and for once were quiet and still, as if they were waiting anxiously for our arrival. After we sat down, Wil planted his eyes in Slate's face, and he blushed up to his fringe and turned his face away. Everyone understood the suggestion, but no-one said a word. In a moment, the silence was broken by the sound of the old Soldier's wooden leg pegging up to the school. The boys looked at Bryan, Beck and myself with anxiety and pity. I can't describe my feelings as the master's fierce face appeared and when I saw his eyes directed, the moment he entered, at the place where Bryan and I were sitting. But I still had a weak hope that Wil had a plan to save us. The old warrior, as Wil called him, went straight to his desk, recited the Lord's prayer as usual, but the response was very weak. As soon as he had said Amen, every eye looked towards him, and we saw him pull from his desk a brand new, strong cane. He furled up his right sleeve, spat on his hand, looked like a bloodhound at Wil Bryan, and directed his steps towards him. Instead of baring his neck in the customary way, Wil leapt to his feet, and the Soldier stood and commanded Slate to lock the door and keep the key. But Wil was not thinking of fleeing. Though his lips were turning blue and shaking, and his eyes like fire, he did not move his gaze from the old Soldier for a second. Wil's daring appearance caused the master to hesitate for a moment; but the next moment he rushed forward, his face pale with fury. When he was within two yards of Wil he raised the cane above his head ready to begin the beating; but before he had the chance to act on his intention, Wil, with one leap, grabbed his wooden leg, pulled it towards him just as suddenly, and butted his head into the old Soldier's stomach, which brought him down in one stroke. As I remember the circumstance, the sound of his head striking the floor is in my ears as though it were happening this minute. Wil turned on his heel and walked in a leisurely manner towards the door. Slate handed him the key, shaking, and was wise to do so. As Wil went through the door, he nodded to me and Beck to follow him. I refused to do so, because for the first time I thought he was a naughty boy. I have repented hundreds of times that I did not take his hint. Beck was wiser than I, and ran for his life.

For some time, the Soldier was shaken, but not wholly conquered. I have never seen, before or since, a man with a wooden leg trying to get up off the floor. I can believe it is one of the hardest things to do. But up came the warrior without anyone trying to help him. He looked like a beast in a slaughterhouse, upon whom an unsuccessful attempt had been made at dispatching it. He snorted through his nostrils audibly. I saw my folly in not following Wil Bryan out, and I leapt to my feet with the thought of correcting my mistake. It was too late. The next moment the cane was raining down on me from all directions—across my head, my neck, my back, my hands, my legs, and everywhere on my body. Night fell on me, and I lost all consciousness. I don't know for how long I was in this state. When I regained my senses, I felt like I was in a dream, and I was wholly unable to get up. I thought that the school was empty, and yet I could hear someone moaning as though they were dying. I thought I was hearing my own groans, and that I had been left by everyone to die. I made an energetic effort to turn my head, and I saw two or three of the boys standing by the open door of the schoolroom, looking very frightened. John Beck was one of them. I called to him; and once he understood that I was alive, he ran to me, and lifted me up to a sitting position. I felt that every joint and bone in me were coming apart from one another. After Beck had sat me up, to my astonishment, I saw the old Soldier on his back on the floor, his face turned blue, and my brother Bob, in his working clothes and as black as coal, with his knees on his chest, busily strangling him, as far as I could see. To my shame I acknowledge, as I must tell the truth, that I shouted with all the strength I had left, "Keep at it, Bob." When Bob realised I was still alive, he let go of the Soldier, and came to me and started to weep. He saw that I could not walk, and took me on his back, leaving the Soldier to come to himself whenever he saw fit. It appears that Beck, after escaping, had stood by the door to listen and to see what would become of me. He understood quickly that I was 'for it'. At that moment, who should go past, after working his night shift, but Bob my brother. Beck called to him that the old Soldier was killing me. There was no need for him to call twice. Bob raced into the schoolhouse, and I heard the boys who were eyewitnesses saying that they were certain that when he appeared, his face as black as a chimney, he was the devil coming to fetch the old Soldier. Bob caught the master beating me when I was already wholly unconscious, and he ran at him like a maniac, and brought him down with the same suddenness as had happened to him a few minutes previously. It was in this situation that I had seen them when I came to myself.

Well, this was not the end of the matter, because Bob and I and Wil Bryan were 'children of the *seiat*', and it was not possible for an event such as this to pass without drawing attention. But as I will have to refer to a couple of the godly old fathers who were in the *seiat* at that time, I will take another chapter to tell the story. If I intended for this history to be printed, I would write in more detail about the school of Robin the Soldier, for boys of these days to see the tremendous growth and improvement that has happened to our schools and their masters in less than half a lifetime.

10

THE SUBJECT OF EDUCATION

I remember very well what was going through my mind as I went home on Bob's back after the incomparable beating I had received from the old Soldier, and that was: would I have another beating from my mother, perhaps, once she heard about my mischief? I asked the question to Bob; and he reassured me that there would be no need to beat me again for at least a year. Although I was nursing my wounds, the idea that the punishment was over was a happy one. My mind turned to Bryan and Beck. Poor things! Their punishment still awaited them, if not from the old Soldier then certainly from their parents. I was indeed made a scapegoat for them in school, but the punishment was over; and I felt that by now I was more fortunate than they. Hasn't this been my experience at every time in my life? Doesn't the small ordeal that awaits me loom far larger than the big ordeal that has already passed? It didn't occur to Bob to ask me what harm I had done to deserve such a severe beating from the master; but that was the first question I was asked by my mother on arriving home. I had never hidden anything from her, and I told in tears the story of tying up the wooden leg in church. I couldn't help noticing that Bob enjoyed the account greatly, but it had a different effect on my mother; and Bob only just saved me from another beating. In any case, when my mother inspected me, and found the red wealds on every part of my body, she changed her tone dramatically, and showed clearly enough that she was my close relative.

I remember as clearly as if it were yesterday that I looked upon myself as having come through a great ordeal, and I felt satisfied because I had wounds on my body that ensured my mother's sympathy. But I was surprised how little disapproval she showed for the Soldier. That doesn't surprise me today; because her aim, no doubt, was to impress on my mind that I deserved the punishment. She said that I was a naughty boy, and she wept copiously, and I thought it was because I was so naughty that she was crying. I'm sure by now that it was because of the wounds on my body that she was shedding tears. She said many things that I can't now bring to mind; but I'm sure that she said this, "There is reason even in war—there's a difference between hitting a child and fighting against Boney—a wooden leg is only a wooden leg after all." But the most comforting thing I heard was that I'd had quite enough of school—that I had been in education for nearly a whole year, and it was high time that I thought about starting to do something. My mother said time and again that too much education harmed children, and had led many to the gallows. She added that she had never had a day of school, except for Sunday School, and that not a penny was ever spent on my grandparents' education and yet they knew 'what was what', and had taken hold of the Truth—they were unremarkable, respected by their neighbours, and had died in peace.

My mother was a lady of strong temper, and remarkably prolix. She must also have had an excellent memory, because she would always clinch what she was saying with a verse from the Bible, or a verse from the Vicar Prichard,[1] or the bard of the Nant,[2] although she seldom quoted the latter without adding, 'a pity Thomas didn't receive grace'. In the current circumstance, she directed the attention of Bob and myself to various of Solomon's proverbs while she hurriedly put on her cloak and large bonnet; and then she went out. Bob looked out through the window to see in which direction she went, and said, "Rhys, you'll see, Mam is going to put the Soldier through *drill*. Let's hear the story about the wooden leg again." I went over the story again, and I must admit that I could recite it much more freely in my mother's absence. I had only just finished when she returned. She looked quieter than when she had gone out, but much sadder and more mournful. After she had removed her cloak and bonnet, and sat down and dried her eyes with her apron, the following conversation took place—that is, as for substance, though as closely as I can remember as for words as well:

"Bob," said my mother, "leaving aside the trouble I had with your father, this is the saddest day that has ever come over me. I had hoped for better things of you, things pertaining to salvation. I had thought that you would be a succour to me. But as I had thought that the good seed was thriving, here are the tares appearing. An enemy has done this."[3]

My mother customarily, as I observed earlier, spoke in a scriptural vein. Although there was a chair close to him, Bob, according to the coal miners' custom, was sitting on his heels with his back leaning on the post of the mantelpiece, and in reply to my mother said:

"Well, Mam, what is it now? The enemy, or Satan, is always troubling you; and anyone would think to listen to you that the old fellow has no leisure to think or take any notice of anyone or anything except us as a family, because nothing happens from morning till night where you don't see some interference from the devil. For my part, if that's how things are to be, I think he should have a go at someone else, as I don't have any taste for his company; and I don't care if both his ears hear it. And another thing, I don't see anything about our family that calls for such particular attention from the devil as you ascribe to him; my opinion is that he must be neglecting his work with other people that are just as worthy of his attention as we are; after all, however clever he is, he is only finite."

---

[1] The Rev. Rhys Prichard, Vicar of Llandovery and ultimately Canon of St. David's (1579–1644), who wrote many popular Bible-based poems that were collectively known as *Cannwyll y Cymry* (*The Welshmen's Candle*).

[2] Thomas Edwards, from Llannefydd near St. Asaph (1739–1810), who wrote numerous short plays (known as interludes) under the bardic name 'Twm o'r Nant' (Tom from the Brook).

[3] Matt. 13:24–28.

"Bob," said my mother, "I'm sorry to hear you speak so lightly of such serious things. We are not ignorant of his devices, who like a roaring lion is walking about seeking whom he may devour.[4] The thing I most feared has come upon me. I have said many times that that newspaper, half of it is lies, would harm you; and yet you have your head in it all the time when you should be reading your Bible. When I was a young girl, no-one spoke of a newspaper except the Squire, and a few uncircumcised Englishmen, they of the revels and hunting-dogs. No-one who cared about their souls read anything except the Bible, Bunyan's *Pilgrim*,[5] Charles' *Dictionary*,[6] and Gurnall's book.[7] But now, alas, everyone has their newspaper and their English book, no-one knows what's in it. And what's the result? A nation without the fear of God, irresponsible, proud, greedy, thinking more about grandness than the matter of life—knowing more about every thief than the thief on the cross, and about every death more than the death which was life for the world. That's the fruit of it for you, Bob."

"You are mistaken, Mam," said Bob, "these things you talk about are not the fruit of reading newspapers, but the fruit of a corrupt heart; and the apostle commands, 'give attendance to reading'.[8]"

"Yes, my lad," said my mother; "the apostle commands that, but reading what? Not the newspaper, but the Holy Scripture, which is able to make you wise unto salvation;[9] and the same apostle says, 'meditate on these things, and give yourself wholly to them';[10] and how is it possible for you or anyone else to give yourself wholly to them when you daily have your nose in the newspaper? Look out, my lad, look out."

"The times are moving on, Mam," said Bob, "and you can't think that things will stay as they were when you were a young girl."

"Moving on!" said my mother in a loud voice. "Yes, quickly enough; but where are they moving to, I wonder. Are they moving closer to heaven? Is there more hunger for the means of grace than there was? Is there more listening to the Gospel and of walking after ministers of the Word? Do you see people these days in harvest time leaving their work in the middle of broad daylight to go and listen to a new man? I don't think so! Now they'd rather go to the concert and the competition to stamp their feet and shout 'hooray' and 'encore' after a comic song, than go to the sermon to shout 'hallelujah' and 'glory' for free grace. If that's moving on, I say they're moving backwards, Bob."

"The time you're referring to," said Bob, "the Gospel was new in Wales, and people were necessarily more interested in it; but by now we are long familiar with the truth; let's hope that there is no less true religion in the land."

"New! Do you know what you're talking about, say?" said my mother in a bit of a temper; "Isn't the Gospel as new now as it ever was, to those who feel their need of it? *Wonders from that costly suffering, fresh delights to understand, shall we find revealed through ages numberless as grains of sand*.[11] The Gospel is good tidings of great joy, and always will be. No, heaven help us if in a thousand ages we become 'long familiar' with it. And I'm surprised at you, Bob, speaking like that, a boy who has read so much. The Gospel wasn't new as a subject—it had been in Wales since time immemorial—but the people had received new hearts, new spirits,

---

[4] 1 Peter 5:8.

[5] John Bunyan's *Pilgrim's Progress*, which appeared in Welsh in 1688, just ten years after the publication of the original English version.

[6] Thomas Charles' *Scriptural Dictionary*, published in Welsh in 1810.

[7] Almost certainly a reference to William Gurnall's *The Christian in Complete Armour*, published in English in 1655 and in Welsh in 1794.

[8] 1 Tim. 4:13. [9] 2 Tim. 3:15. [10] 1 Tim. 4:15.

[11] Bob's mother interjects here with a line from a Welsh hymn *Mae'r gwaed a redodd ar y groes* (*The blood that flowed upon the cross*) by Robert Williams (Robert ap Gwilym Ddu) of Eifionydd (1767–1850). The hymn itself was in some ways a theme song of the Welsh Revivals, but has fallen into obscurity. I have never sung it, and at the time of translating the book, I knew of no English translation. Even so, the verses are moving enough to merit their own special epilogue at the back of the book. See page XXVI for the background to this verse, the original version and a newly commissioned translation of the complete hymn by Martin E. Leckebusch.

and a new taste for it through reading the Word, praying to God, and receiving the outpouring of the Holy Spirit. But now, as I said, people read their newspaper rather than their Bible, and have more of an appetite for a concert or an eisteddfod than the means of grace; and there's no room to expect a blessing and the progress of ministry while things carry on like this."

"You must admit, Mam," said Bob, "that there is more hearing of the Gospel now than there ever has been; we have more chapels and religious facilities, and there are more ministers preaching the Gospel than there has ever been before. At the time you're talking about, there were only a few poor ragged folk involved with the cause, and in general our preachers were plain men, ignorant and uneducated. But nowadays our best and most respectable people are religious, and our ministers more often than not are refined and learned men."

"You have said the truth, Bob," answered my mother, "that there is more hearing; and we should give thanks for that; but the point is, is there more believing? There is cause to fear—and I hope I'm wrong about this—that religion these days is more a matter of fashion than of life. Many, I fear, come to chapel not to see Jesus, as those Greeks of old,[12] but to be seen by others; and our congregation often looks more like a flower bed than a people who have come to hear the Gospel. 'Poor ragged folk', it is true, were with the cause at the beginning, as I heard your grandmother say, and as I saw myself to an extent; but they were, you see, rich in grace and heirs of life. How many of these respectable people, as you call them, are famous for grace and godliness, and a terror to the ungodly of the neighbourhood? Do you see the drunks and layabouts slinking into their hiding places when one of these respectable people appears, as I saw them doing before the poor ragged folk? And as for these grand chapels, they are very convenient, I admit; but do you know what? I often fear—and I hope I'm wrong—that there will be more thanks given in heaven for the barns and houses than for them. You have hurt me a bit,

Bob, by speaking so dismissively of the old preachers. You have, I see, like many people of these days, learned to talk down the Lord's servants. 'Plain and uneducated men' they certainly were; but don't you call them ignorant in my hearing, if you know what's good for you. They had been educated for the kingdom of heaven, Bob; and as for the Bible, they had it at their fingertips. Where will you find their equal these days?"

"Nothing was further from my mind, Mam," said Bob, "than talking inconsiderately about the old preachers. They were good and godly men, no doubt; but they wouldn't do the job in this age now that learning has increased, and congregations are so much more refined than they were then."

"Do the job!" said my mother, raising her voice, "do the job for whom, do you think? They did the job for God at that time, and heaven knows they'd do the job for us today. Do the job, indeed! There's nothing I'd like to see more than for one of them to have permission to try. If old Llecheiddior[13] had permission once more, you've never seen the trouble it would cause here. You know what? One of these old preachers would set the congregation on fire—respectable people and all, while a whole wagonload of these students were still fumbling for their pocket handkerchiefs!"

"You are always prejudiced against the students, and indeed against all education, Mam," said Bob, "but it's wrong for you to snipe; the best men that we have are superb scholars, and do their best for education, especially education for preachers. And what would have become of us by now were it not for our educated men, some of whom you yourself think very highly of?"

"Me against education, Bob? I am not, goodness knows. But I will say this, that there is no need to give high learning to poor children; and it's not education that makes a preacher, or

[12] John 12:20.

[13] Probably a reference to John Williams (1768–1825), from Llecheiddior near Garndolbenmaen in Eifionydd, a Baptist minister who served in both Wales and the USA.

else Dic Aberdaron, the greatest scholar the world has ever seen, would have been the greatest preacher. But heaven help us, with his cats and his filth. Education is good where it is needed, and if it has been sanctified by grace, or else it is a curse to everyone, believe me."

"Paul," said Bob, "your great friend, was a superb scholar; and he would never have been able to do what he did if he weren't such a good scholar."

"How can you prove that?" asked my mother, "The fact that he had sat at the feet of Gamaliel doesn't make him a great scholar. Don't think that, if you understand politics, then you understand your Bible better than your mother. It was his conversion on the road to Damascus that made Paul great; he wasn't great in anything before that, except as a persecutor, and neither you nor I would ever have heard of him were it not for that conversion. And I'll tell you another thing; Paul put a very small price on 'human wisdom', and if someone tried to make him a Doctor, or a Master of Arts, he'd say to them straight away, 'I determined not to know any thing among you, save Jesus Christ, and Him crucified'.[14] He preferred a thousand times the title Paul, a servant of the Lord, to Doctor Saul of Tarsus. Do you know what? I have no patience to hear you and others going on about education, education and education, as if education could make the mountains and the sea, and do the job in place of God's grace. Does education, I wonder, teach people to disrespect old people? Grace does not teach that, I'm sure of that."

"What are you referring to, Mam?" asked Bob.

"You know exactly what I'm referring to, I guarantee you. Was it the newspaper that taught you to beat up an old man who had lost a limb fighting for his country? Bob, I'm amazed at you. I never expected that you, a boy who has never had a day of schooling, would bring the cause into disrepute, and bring shame upon your mother. Go and ask the old man's pardon at once, for shame on you."

"Ask his pardon?" said Bob, "I shall do no such thing. If I

went a bit wild, I did no more than my duty towards him; and if I ever see the old Soldier or anyone else, were he as big as a giant, beating up Rhys as mercilessly as I saw today, I am not his brother if I wouldn't do the same as I did earlier, if it were in my power. Nature teaches me that."

"It is not the corrupt nature that is to rule you, my boy," said my mother sadly, "but the new nature. The Word says clearly, 'Not a violent man'.[15]"

"That's a verse for a bishop, not a collier, Mam," said Bob.

"Bob," said my mother, "your heart is hardened. I never thought that the newspaper and those English books had had such an effect on you. I'm glad by now, although I did it in haste, that I called on Abel Hughes to tell him the story before anyone else did, and urged him to have a talk with you in the *seiat* tomorrow night. If other people want to hide the disobedience and wickedness of their children, I do not. Pray for grace, my boy," and then she started to cry, and buried her face in her apron, which would always put an end to Bob's counterarguments.

Although it was broad daylight, I was sent to bed to recover from my injuries. As I couldn't sleep I meditated and imagined much about one thing that my mother had said to Bob, 'the trouble I had with your father'. What could that mean?

---

[14] 1 Cor. 2:2. [15] 1 Tim. 3:3.

11

WIL BRYAN ON ECCLESIOLOGY

After spending close to a night and a day in bed, with the aim of recovering from my wounds, I wasn't a great deal better when I arose. Rather, I felt as if I had been sleeping in starch, since I was so stiff whenever I tried to move. But however much pain I was in, the thought of having 'finished school' was more than enough to sustain me through the trial. My mother looked depressed and disheartened, and I noticed that she sighed often. I thought I knew what was troubling her, and I grieved in my heart that my mischief had brought all this trouble upon her. Even so, she was not cross with me, and the only difference in her behaviour towards me was that she was quiet and sad. She did not even ask me how I was feeling, lest that, I suppose, would make me think that the beating I received was all that I justly deserved; and yet I knew that she very much wanted to know.

I think, if I am not deceiving myself, that I have had since I was fairly young some skill in understanding subtle suggestions and inferences, and that to some extent this is still with me today. I remember well when a neighbour came into our house that my mother, lest I understand the conversation, would speak in parables, and mention that 'little pigs have big ears', thinking in her innocence that I did not understand that. But I knew very well that I was the little pig, and I could understand the conversation pretty well, although she thought she was speaking in Latin to me. My mother thought that morning that I didn't see her glancing secretively at me as I moved; but I did, even so, and I understood what was on her heart as well as if she were carrying it on her sleeve. Oh, how unworthy I was of the care, the concern, and the love which was in that heart towards me! I didn't know at that time about the thing that bore most heavily on her mind, namely the fact that the circumstances called for the discipline of the church upon her sons.

Sometime during the day, I understood that Wil Bryan and John Beck were standing around close to our house, and keen to see me. While my mother was baking a loaf, I went out quietly; and in the corner of the garden my two friends and I had a long and secretive conversation. Comparing notes, I learned that the story of the church and the school was public knowledge throughout the district—that Bryan and Beck had both had beatings from their parents—but which, as they confessed, was hardly worth a mention compared with the thrashing that I'd had. This made me think again that I had 'come through a lot', and I felt myself some sort of hero. I understood, further, that neither of my two friends were in school that day—that Beck had got permission to stay home until his father found time to speak to the master, and that Bryan, even though he'd been firmly ordered by his father to return to school, was playing truant. During the conversation, I made two comments that affected them greatly. One was that my mother had said I'd had quite enough of school. The two looked at me amazed and envious, as though they could not comprehend how such happiness was achievable for a mere human. After the usual expressions of amazement, Bryan said, "Rhys, I'd be happy for the old warrior to tie my hands behind my back and make me stand on one leg for an hour, and then break a new cane over my neck, if that would make the *gaffer* (his father) say the same thing to me."

Beck nodded to indicate that he would be happy to go through the same ordeal. Their amazement was no less when I told them that Bob and I were to be brought before the *seiat* that night. Beck, as a Church boy, didn't understand the implications of the terms '*seiat*', and 'to be brought before the '*seiat*', until Bryan gave him the following explanation. Wil had a particular ability to furnish a description of something that he thought he understood, and this is how he described to Beck the nature and purpose of a *seiat*: "Well you see," he said, "a *seiat* is a lot of good people who think that they're bad people, and they meet together every Tuesday night to run each other down."

"I don't understand you," said Beck.

"Well," said Wil, "look at it like this: you know old Mrs Peters, and you know Rhys here's mother—not that I'm saying this just because Rhys is here—but everybody knows that they are two good and godly ladies. Well, they go to the *seiat*, and Abel Hughes goes up to them, and asks what is on their minds. They say that they're very wicked, and guilty of I don't know how many things, and Mrs Peters often says this in tears. After this, Abel Hughes tells them that they're not as bad as they think, and gives them some advice, and says a lot of verses, and then goes to someone else, who then says the same thing; and so on, until it's half past eight and then we all go home."

"There's nothing like that in the Church," said Beck, "they don't have a *seiat*, and I've never heard anyone running themselves down there."

"That's where the difference is between the Church and the Chapel," said Wil, "You people in the Church think you're good when in fact you're bad, and the Chapel people think they're bad when in fact they're good."

"You're not telling me," said Beck, "that everyone who belongs to the *seiat* are good people, and everyone who belongs to the Church are bad people?"

"Everyone," said Wil, "who takes communion in the chapel are good people, although they think they're bad, and everyone who takes their communion in the church thinks they're good people, when more than half of them are bad people. Take the old Soldier: you know full well that he takes communion on Sunday morning to please Mr Brown, and then on Sunday night he'll be in the Cross Foxes drinking until he's too blind to find the way home. If he were in the Chapel, you see, he'd be kicked out straight away. But when did you see anyone being thrown out of the church?"

Beck wasn't given to meeting counterarguments; so Bryan went on to explain what was meant by being 'brought before the *seiat*':

"Well then," said Wil, "when someone who belongs to the *seiat* has done something wrong, because they're not perfect you know, someone else will go to the elders straight away and snitch on them; and in the next *seiat* after that Abel Hughes will call them to account. If it's somebody poor, like William the Coal, Abel will call him to the bench before the big seat; but if it's a great man, like Mr Richards the draper, Abel will go to him."

"Well, what will Abel do to him? Will he take him to jail?" asked Beck.

"No danger," said Wil, "Abel will investigate the matter, and will ask for one or two people to comment; and if he's sorry, and blames Satan like William the Coal does, and promises never to do it again, then they'll forgive him. But if he's like Mr Richards the draper, and refuses to say anything, they'll bar him from communion for three months, or maybe longer, or cut him out of the *seiat*. There's no harm in the thing, you know, but it's a bit of a bother; and I'd like not to have to go to the *seiat* this evening; but I must go, or there'll be a row at home."

Although I was some years younger than Bryan, I considered the *seiat* a much more important thing than he set it out to be. My mother had taught me so to think about it. But for that matter, Will looked lightly at everything, and this was his undoing. Even so, Beck's last words made quite an impression on me, which he put like this:

"Boys, I prefer the rules in Church to the rules in Chapel. Everyone who belongs to the Church can do what they like, and nobody will call them to account. People there mind their own business, and that's best, to my mind."

Bryan was normally zealous for the Chapel; but it was obvious to me that he inclined to the same opinion as Beck in this matter, and in conclusion he stated,

"It's like this, John; it's more comfortable in the Church, but safer in the Chapel."

As far as I can remember, this was the first treatment I heard of the 'nature of the Church', and it left a deeper impression on my mind than many that I heard later from more important persons of higher learning. I could not, however, look upon Church discipline in the way that Wil Bryan did; and I was greatly worried as I thought about going to the *seiat* that night.

The time arrived to go; and seeing Bob getting himself ready, my mother didn't think it necessary to talk to him about the matter. She and I headed off towards the chapel; but after going a step or two, my mother turned back, and I heard her say, "Bob, don't you be stiff tonight, I beg you," and then we went on.

As I recall that *seiat*, I can't help thinking about some of the old characters who were there, who have now, as old Mrs Tibbett would have said, 'gone to their fate'. There was Abel Hughes, of whom I have said something already. He was a godly man, powerful in the scriptures, and decisive in his mind. His only fault, as far as I know, was that he was a little severe. Then there was innocent Hugh Bellis, a humble and tender-hearted man, who would always weep during the sermon, and was zealous to forgive everyone, whatever bad they had done. Even those with the least respect for religion acknowledged that Hugh was very godly. There was Edward Peters, a careful and meticulous man with the books, but crabby and unpopular with the children, because he wouldn't let them leave halfway through the services. He never said anything in public except about the collection, or the seat money. But he had a good foundation, and had the trust of the church. There was Thomas Bowen the preacher: a lively, zealous, quick-tempered man—daily making mistakes and retracting his own words. There was Mr Richards the draper; a proud and attention-seeking man, always wanting to push himself forward, while everyone else wanted to push him back. There was William the Coal, a poor man, slight of body and mind, compliant and easily led. He was called William the Coal because his family since time immemorial had sold coal by the penn'orth. Every winter, when work was short, William would be zealous in the *seiat*; but when harvest-time came, William had a tendency to drink too much, and then he would be excommunicated. He was forgiven many transgressions, as it was believed he was not entirely like other men. I heard my mother say once that William had the root of the matter, but his trunk and branches were too weak to stand a strong cross-wind. I was of the same opinion as her, since William would always weep as he prayed; and I believed as a boy that anyone who wept while praying must be very godly, and that belief has persisted to this day. There was John Lloyd as well—I have unpleasant memories of him; a tall, thin, sharp-faced, thick-skinned, and tiresome man. He was very faithful in the services, and always finding fault with someone or something. 'The old scratcher', Wil Bryan called him. He was thought to be a great miser; and because of that he never came under church discipline, since his love of money kept him from drinking, and from attending any forbidden place. He was zealously opposed to tea meetings, concerts, or any gathering where it was necessary to show the King or Queen's head in order to gain admission. He spoke sensibly about thrift and self-sufficiency. His concern about the spirituality of religion was great, and he often said there was too much talk about money, and preaching about money. My mother tried to believe that he had the root, but feared that a worm was eating him somewhere, which made his leaves bitter. Ah yes, there was Seth as well, the innocent child, who I will have to mention again, as he was the occasion for a formative time in my life. And there were many others I could name, some of whom will be mentioned again.

There was an unusually large gathering in the *seiat* that night. Hardly anyone was missing. I have noticed ever since then that, when someone is to be disciplined, it is a very effective way of gathering the friends around. There is something in good people similar in its nature to that which, in other sorts of people, compels them to go and see a man being hanged. Wil Bryan and I sat together in amongst the children; and I was amazed at how he could be so calm. The meeting was started by Thomas Bowen, and I listened to him carefully in case he said something about me; but he did not. While Thomas was praying, Wil whispered in my ear, "If they ask us anything, let's say the same as William the Coal, that we won't ever do it again, and they're *bound* to forgive us." Wil said many things; but I was too anxious to take any notice of them. The children were heard reciting their verses by Abel Hughes; but when he came to Bryan and me, he passed over us without asking for our verses. The storm was beginning, and although I had my head down, so to speak, I knew that everyone was looking at me, and I felt their eyes burning through my velvet jacket. As I looked out from under my frown I saw Wil with his head up, and looking around entirely shamelessly. Once Abel Hughes had finished with the children, Thomas Bowen gave a general word, and urged Hugh Bellis to speak, and he made some remarks on the Sunday's sermons, declaring the blessings that he had received from them. Then Thomas Bowen asked whether anyone else had a word to say on the same subject, and Edward Peters rose to his feet to remind the brethren that the seat money was due. After this there was silence, and some conferring between Abel and Thomas Bowen. I heard Abel say, "You do it, Thomas," and Thomas say, "No, you do it, Abel."

I can see Abel now, in his velvet cap, rising to his feet, and looking serious and agitated. I would be glad if I could chronicle the words of that good and honest man as he delivered them, but I cannot. I remember him speaking of 'an unpleasant case'—of 'the children of the *seiat* behaving like children of the world'—of 'shaming the cause of religion'—of 'maintaining discipline', and so on. He talked at length, and severely; and then he named Bob my brother, myself and Bryan, as the offenders.

When Abel sat down, John Lloyd said that the church wished to know from the officers what was the nature of the offence. "Listen to the old scratcher," said Wil in my ear. Abel answered that he believed that John Lloyd knew very well, as did everyone, and that it would not be wise to go over the circumstances again. Then Thomas Bowen rose to his feet suddenly; and said something along the following lines:

"Brothers, boys will be boys, and we need to remember that we have all been children. I'm very sorry to hear of the trouble, and Abel Hughes has done well to bring the matter to our attention. But what can we do other than to give a word of counsel to the poor boys? Remember, brethren, that I am not talking about Robert Lewis now; he is of age and sense; but about William Bryan and Rhys Lewis, they are under age—young and innocent; and good smart boys they are, too. Who says their verses better than William and Rhys? It's a terrible pity to talk of these boys doing bad. Have you got anything to say, William, my boy?"

"I'll never do it again," said Wil.

"Good, my boy," said Thomas; "are you sorry for the thing that you did?"

"Yes," said Wil; and at the same time he pinched me on the leg so hard that I couldn't help crying.

"Do you say the same, Rhys?" asked Thomas; "but for that matter there's no need to ask Rhys—the tears are pouring from him. Abel Hughes, do you hear what the boys are saying? They are sorry for the thing, and they say they won't do it ever again; and what can we say better ourselves than to mourn the fault and determine not to do it again? What shall we do with the boys, Abel Hughes?"

"Do what you want with them," said Abel, in a surly voice.

"Well brethren," said Thomas, "we can't do better with the boys than to give them a word of counsel, and let them go home, as we have another more important matter to move on to."

After Thomas Bowen had given us some good and kind counsel, he said that we were to go home like good children. No sooner had he said the word than the children all ran out straight away. As soon as I had gone through the door, Wil Bryan grabbed my arm and gave me a *right wheel* by the side of the chapel. I felt cross with him, and asked why he pinched me so hard in the chapel.

"So that you'd cry, silly," he said; "I knew very well that you couldn't say a word, but crying did the trick, you see. Didn't I say they'd forgive us? But we must see what will become of Bob."

In the side wall of the old place of worship there was a door that opened on to the stairs of the gallery, which Marged from the Chapel House would go through to open and close up the building, and which therefore was unlocked that night. I understood in an instant what Wil's intention was, and I had to follow him, as he had some hold over me that I couldn't resist. Wil opened the door quietly, and closed it in the same manner. In the darkness he said, "Take off your clogs, and put them that side, and I'll put my clogs this side, so that we'll know when we come down." I did so, and Wil said, "Up we go now, as quiet as mice." And so we went on all fours, Wil leading, until we reached the clock seat, Wil's favourite place. In that place we heard Bob's whole case being handled; and I could, I think, recite it word for word; but for what purpose? The circumstances are too painful for me to dwell on them for long. Words were spoken like the sting of a sword, especially by John Lloyd. I felt furious with him, because no matter how guilty Bob was, he was a thousand times better a man than him. Although Bob had done wrong by attacking the old Soldier as he did, he was doing that in order to save me; and I knew that he had a big enough and sensitive enough heart that he would sacrifice his life, not only for me, but for anyone he saw being wronged. But as for John Lloyd, he didn't love anything except money, and his heart was no bigger than a spider's. Yet, this was the man who threw the dirtiest slime at Bob that night; and I'm afraid I have never forgiven him, because I think it was his spiteful words that made Bob so stubborn. I knew that he could endure Abel Hughes' sharp rebukes, and that Thomas Bowen's kind words, when he chastised him, would soothe his heart; but the poisonous jibes of this narrow-minded hypocrite hardened him and made him more stubborn; and Bob protested to the whole *seiat* that he had nothing of which to repent.

I'll never forget that half hour in the clock seat. I felt cross with Bryan because he was so jocular. While Bob's case was being heard, he carved his name in the seat with a knife and made comments on everyone who spoke, and that so loudly that I had to plead with him to be quiet lest we be discovered. I felt so much for Bob that I couldn't help crying; and Wil asked mockingly whether I had toothache. It seems strange to me now that my ideas about various people in the *seiat* where I was brought up were formed while I was in the clock seat. I could see for some time what the outcome would be, and I thought of what a dreadful blow that would be for my mother; because she hadn't imagined that Bob could be excommunicated. But no other outcome was possible while he continued to say that he'd do the same thing again under the same circumstances. Wil said several times while he was carving his name on the seat, that Bob was 'messing up': "If he did like William the Coal," said Wil, "and put the blame on Satan, and say he'd never do it again, he'd be all right, but if he carries on like this, he's *bound* to be kicked out." For all his levity, Wil's prophecy came true within a few minutes. Thomas Bowen did his best to make Bob apologise; but he did not succeed, and Abel Hughes tried the same thing with the same result. The officers and the church had to do their duty; and when Abel was on his feet asking for the vote to excommunicate Bob, the old man's voice was shaking, and his words were sticking in his throat. The vote was given, and Bob was no longer in membership with the Calvinistic Methodists. At that moment Abel Hughes bent down on his knees, and prayed in his prayer,[1] if ever anyone had prayed. I marvelled a hundred times after that, that his prayer for Bob was not answered.

Well, would the church have excommunicated Bob if it had known the consequences? I don't think so.

---

[1] The author makes deliberate use of a Hebrew idiom that looks as unnatural in Welsh as it does in English.

12

AROUND THE HEARTH

Whatever other gifts I lack—and there are many of those—I think I have cause to give thanks for a good memory. Indeed, I would not have begun this memoir if I were not conscious before beginning that writing it in my hours of leisure would be more pleasure than labour to me. As I turn up one event and another in my narrative, I find that every circumstance has its family and relations, which spring back to life before my mind. It's like a man looking over a packet of old letters: every letter has its unwritten family, and some letters make the man think of others that were burned, but that he can't burn from his memory. Some are read with satisfaction, others with solemn memories, and others disturb his whole nature, awakening feelings and ideas that he thought had long been lost, but which still live in the nooks of the mind and the crannies of the memory.

Although I reckon the night of Bob's excommunication among the darkest nights of my life, it wasn't without its bright side. The circumstances caused me to think carefully about what religion was, and what is it that makes up the importance and sanctity of church membership. I already had some idea that there was a big difference between religious people and 'the people of the world', as my mother called them; but this idea, I'm afraid, extended no further than that the former took part in the Lord's Supper once a month, and didn't get drunk or swear, while the latter could do what they liked because they didn't belong to the *seiat*. But somehow, that night, I began to doubt my ideas, and to think that there was something more to it than what I just named. I asked myself what Bob would do, as he was no longer a church member—would he get drunk occasionally? Would he swear and curse every now and then? Would he give up reading his Bible and other good books, and cause havoc in the house like Peter the drunkard? Though I couldn't make myself believe that. I asked myself as well whether Bob, being out of the *seiat*, would be a worse and meaner man than John Lloyd, who was in the *seiat*. That too was just as impossible to my mind. What was it then that made a man religious? This circumstance was also the occasion when I formed a high opinion of my mother's religiousness. Perhaps it was the conversation between her and my brother Bob that made me think thus. I will try to chronicle the conversation as accurately as my memory will serve. Of course, my mother didn't know that I had heard the whole treatment of Bob's case, and it wasn't fitting for her to find out that Wil Bryan and I had been hiding in the chapel loft. Every time that we as a family went all together to chapel, the last one to leave the house would leave the front door key under the water tub, so that the first to return could secure easy ingress into our castle. This was one of the family secrets. As I should have been the first to arrive, I rushed; and I had been sitting down for about two minutes before my mother arrived; and even though I was still out of breath, I tried to appear as if I had been waiting for her for a while, and commented that she had been a long time. "Every wait is long",[1] was my mother's only reply, as she hung her blue cloak and big bonnet on the nail behind the door. Bob must have been hanging around with his friends after coming from the *seiat*, as I remember that supper had been ready for some time before he returned. After waiting long, he appeared and looked sad and dispirited; and in silence he sat down, picking up a book to read. Not without great persuasion did he come to the supper table; and I soon noticed that neither he nor my mother had much of an appetite. As I'd had a weight lifted from my mind,

---

[1] *Hir yw pob ymaros*, a Welsh proverb for which I can't think of a better English translation than the literal one given here.

so far as my own church discipline was concerned, and because I saw it would be a pity for the food to go to waste, I tried my best to make as much of it disappear as possible. After supper, Bob returned to his book, and my mother shifted her chair closer towards the fire. I could tell from her body language that she was minded to begin talking; because she had a custom of pleating her apron as she was gathering her thoughts together.

"Well, my boy," she said eventually, "this is a pretty painful evening in your life and mine. Although I'm poor, I'd like it more than a hundred pounds if what took place tonight had not happened."

Bob normally talked a bit more grammatically than my mother, and in reply to her said:

"I don't see, Mother, why you must look at what took place tonight in that way. It will not change anything about me, as far as my character is concerned. Being in the *seiat* does not secure anyone's salvation, nor does being out of it ensure their condemnation."

"Rhys," said my mother, turning to me, "you'd better go to bed."

"In a minute," I said, and lay my head to rest on the table, pretending to sleep. I'm not sure that I didn't even pretend to snore. What a rascal I was! In any case, my behaviour put them off their guard.

"Bob," said my mother, "I hope that you don't mean what you are saying. You've been saying so many things lately, since you've been messing with those old English books, that I find it hard to think that you believe everything you say."

"Mam," said Bob, and I heard him put his book down on the table; "you know very well that there is no deceit in me, and there's nothing on earth I hate more than hypocrisy. I'd prefer a thousand times to be thrown out of the church for telling the truth, than to be allowed to stay in by putting on a mask and saying things I neither believe nor feel. I know that my excommunication is a hard blow for you, Mam, and I'm sorry about that; but if that's how the church sees best to deal with me, I'm quite happy."

"What, my boy?" said my mother, "you don't put any value on being a church member?"

"No, I don't," said Bob, "if I have to buy my membership through hypocrisy. You've never heard me speak about myself before, nor grumbling; but you know very well that neither you nor my father thought to give a day's schooling to me. I grew up wholly ignorant of everything except the Bible; I was sent to the coal mine when I should have been to school, and I was an experienced collier before I was sixteen years old. When I came to my senses enough to realise my need of education, I threw myself with all my energy in my leisure hours to learn English, without the help of any living soul, and with you complaining the whole time that I was using up candles. To say the least, I've been as faithful to the chapel as any of my contemporaries. I've been a Sunday School teacher since I was seventeen. I am not praising myself; but you know, since the trouble with my father, that I have worked hard, and done my best to keep a home for you and Rhys. I have quietly endured, in the coal works, many snide and hateful remarks about our situation at home, and that for the sake of you and Rhys; because what would become of you if I left home? You know that I've never spent any money on frippery; and all the money I've been able to spare I've spent on books, or given it to the church. Apart from that, I've been trying for years to share with Rhys whatever knowledge I've been able to impart to him, lest he, if it were possible, end up a poor collier like me. Seeing my brother being wronged and beaten up without mercy, I did what anyone with a grain of humanity would have done and rushed at the one who was treating him like that, and rescued him like David rescuing a lamb from the mouth of a lion.[2] But this was a great sin in the eyes of the *seiat*, and

---

[2] 1 Sam. 17:35

especially in the eyes of some individuals within it; and doubtless they will now feel very happy to have got rid of such a defiled creature as I."

"You know what?" said my mother, "you are sounding very much like a self-righteous man. You make me think of that man who started to pray in the temple all those years ago.[3] You sound exactly like him. There's as little of the publican in you after coming home as there was in the *seiat*. What has come over you? There's some strange stubbornness in you lately. Pray, my boy, for grace, so that you'll feel the cord[4] and see your filthy rags.[5] If you were standing in the dock at the quarter session, it would be as well for you to talk about your virtues; but when you stand before your Judge, the less said about them the better unless you call them by what Paul named them, 'as dung'.[6] You know what, Bob? I've been thinking for some time that there were some ideas in your heart that you didn't get from the Bible, and that has cost me many nights' sleep."

"You, Mam," said Bob with feeling, "know me better than anyone, and I must be accomplished in wickedness if my own mother holds such a low opinion of me. Doubtless I'm the worst rascal in the neighbourhood. Well, so be it."

"No, my boy, not so be it," said my mother. "As a boy who's good to his mother, there is none better than you in the six counties,[7] and I never had any trouble from you in that way; and I'm very thankful to you, and to the great King, for your kindness in working so hard to keep a home for your mother and brother. But it's your soul I'm talking about now. It doesn't matter all that much whether I get a bite to eat or not; but it is of infinite weight, my dear boy, that your soul, and mine, is under the care of the Holy Spirit. Blessed be His Name! He doesn't leave me alone, and I believe He's thinking of making something of me; but oh, that I could think He was saying something to you! Seeing you so cool about being excommunicated breaks my heart, my dear silly boy. Outside are the dogs[8]—outside is the evil one, and the storm. You have gone outside the circle of the covenant and the intercession—you've lost the shelter, dear Bob."

"It was the church's work to decide whether I was to be inside or outside of it; and it was the church that excommunicated me, not I," said Bob.

"No, my boy," said my mother, "it was your work; and you should have been ashamed of it. Your work in refusing to repent and confess your sin, like the Psalmist did,[9] caused the church to cut you out. How many times did Thomas Bowen, I saw it myself, plead with you tonight to admit your fault, but you refused? No, it was with great pain that the church excommunicated you; but what can you expect when you don't repent? It's hardly fitting for you to expect forgiveness from God or man without repentance.

"I can't conform with the opinions of old-fashioned people when my own ideas go against it," said Bob. "And what do you think Mr Brown the parson said to me today whilst speaking of the thing? He laughed at the whole thing, and said he hoped that the thrashing I gave the old Soldier would do him some good."

"Bob," said my mother, not a little heated, "don't you speak about the great doctrines of the Gospel as 'old-fashioned' in my hearing, if you know what's good for you."

"I didn't do that," said Bob.

"You said something very similar," said my mother. "Repentance is a fashion, you see, that you'll need to conform with, or you'll never enter Life. It's a fashion, Bob, that has made thousands into gentry for eternity. But I'll tell you when it will become *old*-fashioned: when the summer is over, and the harvest-time for the soul has passed. There will be many then who will turn to the old fashion when it will be too late. Pray, my boy, that you

---

[3] Luke 18:11–14. [4] See note in Chapter 4. [5] Isa. 64:6. [6] Phil. 3:8.

[7] Presumably an expression for 'the whole of North Wales': Flintshire, Denbighshire, Caernarfonshire, Anglesey, Merionethshire and Montgomeryshire.

[8] Rev. 22:15, 9 Psalm 51.

won't be one of them. And as for Mr Brown, what does he know? He's a fine one to advise young people. If I wanted counsel for my soul, I'd never go to him, because he'd probably be in a field shooting rabbits anyway. Every respect to Mr Brown as a kind neighbour, but Tomos o'r Nant spoke well of him and his sort. Although Tomos wasn't all he should have been, he hit the mark pretty well:

> 'There's no-one who should be respected as much
> As an evangelical church minister;
> And no-one is more accursed than he,
> If he is not led by God.' [10]

It would be a blessing if Mr Brown could have a double portion of the spirit of the old Vicar of Llandovery. As the Vicar would say to you, if I remember rightly:

> 'Repent as soon as you can,
> You'll harden if you delay;
> To prevent your heart from hardening
> God commands you repent today.

> To those truly repentant,
> God is faithful and gracious;
> But to those who are reluctant, spiteful and stubborn,
> God is cruel and furious'. [11]

And your conscience knows whether it's Mr Brown or the old Vicar that's got it right."

"Every respect, as you say," said Bob, "to the old Vicar; but I don't believe that God is 'cruel and furious' at any time, much less towards me for what I did to the old Soldier. The Bible teaches me that God is love."

"What?" said my mother, "you're not going to doubt the words of the godly old Vicar who knew his Bible a thousand times better than you do hundreds of years before you were born? You never said anything truer than that God is love. If it were not for that, it would be farewell to Life and to the election of grace, as I heard Mr Elias[12] say on the green in Bala—I have fond memories of him. Who could put it better? Better, indeed; who could put it a quarter as well as Mr Elias, about,

> '…the love that now
> Beats every love into submission'?[13]

But if you heard him speak about the justice of God and His anger at the ungodly, your hair would stand straight up on your head. If you're going to entertain ideas like that, Bob, there's barely a hair's breadth between you and Wesley.[14] No, my boy, the Vicar had it right—God is angry every day with the ungodly; and you know that better than I can say to you."

"I haven't got the spirit nor the inclination to argue with you, Mam," said Bob.

"I don't know about that," said my mother; "alas, I see you

---

[10] A stanza from Twm O'r Nant:
> *'Nid oes un i'w ganmol na'i berchi yn gymwys*
> *O flaen efengylaidd weinidog eglwys;*
> *Nac un yn fwy melltith na hwnnw'n fyw,*
> *Oni fydd Duw yn ei dywys'.*

[11] Some stanzas from Vicar Prichard:

'Edifara cynte gallech,	*I'r rhai ffyddlon edifeiriol,*
Ti ymg'ledi pan ddyhiriech;	*Mae Duw'n ffyddlon ac yn rasol;*
Rhag i'th galon ymgaledu	*Ond i't cyndyn cas gwrthnysig,*
Duw fyn it' repento heddy.	*Mae Duw'n greulon ac yn ffyrnig'.*

[12] Mrs Lewis would have been old enough to have heard John Elias, probably the greatest of the 'second generation' of Calvinistic Methodist preachers, who died in 1841.

[13] Curiously, the quotation comes not from John Elias or any other Mr Elias, but from a hymn by William Williams Pantycelyn:
> *'Wel dyma'r cariad sydd yn awr*
> *Yn curo pob cariadau 'lawr'.*

[14] …about the most insulting thing one could say to a Calvinistic Methodist at the time.

being quite a bit too high-spirited. I had some secret hope that it was a fit of stubbornness that had come over you in the *seiat*, and that your heart was better than your tongue; but I see that I was mistaken, and I see I've been at fault that I didn't sit down with you long ago to talk with you about your condition. All I can do is pray, my boy, for the Spirit of God to visit your soul." "Well," added my mother with a groan, "there's more need than I've seen for I don't know how long, for a revival of religion to bring down people's high-spiritedness, and bring them to their duties."

"When it comes," said Bob, "it will have much more work than that to do. It will have a load of covetousness and miserliness, things which pass nowadays under the name of thrift, to turn out of the churches. Hypocrisy, narrow-mindedness and a lack of Christian love, which nowadays are called piety, diligence and zeal for church discipline, will have the same fate that met me today. On that day—if it ever comes—it will be seen that some of the people who were crowing over my excommunication today have been overcome by the cancer of worldliness and profiteering, and sell Jesus Christ for thirty pieces of silver every day they get out of bed. When the day comes that you talk of, I expect that there will be a great crowd—some that I will be appalled to recognise."

"You're leaving one thing out," said my mother, "On that day, everyone will have their hand on the plague within their own hearts, and not picking at the faults of other people and justifying themselves. Peter, you see, didn't think for a minute about pointing the finger at Judas, who had betrayed, as a reason not to repent for denying. No, he went out and wept bitterly, and I'd like to see a bit of the same spirit in you, my boy." And my mother started crying, which, as I said before, would always bring Bob's counterarguments to a close.

Once my mother had let out her feelings, she took hold of the collar of my jacket and shook me energetically, unaware that I had been perfectly awake the whole time; and she never knew. After I had gone to bed, I thought a lot about what I had heard, and especially about the references that had been made to my father. But that night went past like every other. My mother's appeals did not have any great effect on Bob. After his excommunication, he did not often talk about religious things, nor about the chapel, even though he carried on attending the services. In the house he would be fairly quiet, and almost always reading, and he did not cease to share with me whatever knowledge he could. Well, what would I give tonight if there were nothing more unpleasant to say about him?

13

SETH

As I've mentioned before, I must say something about Seth, the simple-minded boy, as he was the occasion to form a critical period in my life. Seth was a strange character. I don't remember when I first came to know him. As I search my memory, I can't find anything about him except—Seth—the same size, the same appearance, the same age, always the same. If someone were to ask me when I first noticed the crabtree which was next to our house, and whether I could remember various stages in the growth of its branches, I'm sure I would have to answer in the negative. The only definite event that I remember about the crabtree is the day that the Squire decreed that it be cut down. And as the hard-hearted woodman applied his axe to the trunk and caused the chips to fly here and there, and as the old tree fell to the ground, I felt as though I was losing an old friend; I had eaten many a crab apple from its branches, and although they set my teeth on edge they were sweet in the absence of anything better. I have just this one image of the crab-apple tree until the day that it was cut down. It's the same thing with Seth. Up to the day he died, his story is just one period in my mind, with nothing in it except Seth: a boy with a bright face, fairly tall, thin and sinewy, his neck bent slightly, his chin small and almost lost in his neck, his mouth always half open; small, bright eyes, vacant but rather merry; his nose unadorned but never entirely clean, his forehead small and receding in a straight line towards the top of his head, which was long and narrow and bordered on to his long nape.

His parents were simple and innocent people, who lived in a tidy little house a short distance outside town. A shoemaker by profession, or rather a cobbler, as he never made new shoes, was

Thomas Bartley, Seth's father. Neither Thomas nor Barbara Bartley would have been counted as belonging to the intellectual elite. Indeed, they were both commonly regarded as being not quite the full yard; with Seth as the result. Neither Thomas nor Barbara could read a letter of a book; and neither of them ever went to church or chapel except at harvest thanksgiving. But I had heard with my own ears Thomas saying more than once that he had attended Sunday School constantly for four or five years, and he believed that if he had persevered for a few more years he would have mastered the A B C. I also heard him boast that he had listened from time to time to John Elias, Williams of the Wern and Christmas Evans;[1] but when asked what sort of people they were, his answer would invariably be, 'Dash it all; they were severe; very severe!' The two old dears Thomas and Barbara were remarkably innocent and happy. The sin that most easily encompassed Thomas was that he had a tendency to take God's name in vain, though probably not disrespectfully. He didn't hold with working on the Sabbath; and would never expect a blessing if he were guilty of that. But he saw no harm in spending many hours every Sabbath standing with his pipe in his mouth watching his pig eat, and calculating when it would be ready for the knife; how much it would weigh, and whether it would be wise to make black pudding or brawn out of it; whether it would be better to keep the offal or sell it, which neighbours was he obliged to send a rib to, and so on. Thomas did not think that there was any harm in the world for Barbara and himself to spend the Sabbath talking in this way; yet he wouldn't, even for a fortune, put his leather work-apron on for an hour on the Lord's day. My brother Bob was very fond of taking his shoes to Thomas Bartley for repair, so he could be

---

[1] These three were, according to the *Dictionary of Welsh Biography*, known collectively as the 'three giants of the Welsh pulpit': Elias (1774–1841), from Abererch near Pwllheli, was a Calvinistic Methodist; Williams (1781–1840), originally from Meirionydd but associated with Wern, just outside Wrexham, where he spent most of his ministry, was an Independent; and Evans (1766–1838), from Ceredigion but known for his ministries in Llangefni and Cardiff, was a Baptist.

'strung along', as he put it; and I saw him laughing until the tears rolled down his cheeks while telling my mother about the strange ideas that he had heard from him during these visits. My mother was often irritated by rheumatism, and I remember one time that she was suffering severely from this complaint as Bob returned from visiting Thomas. Bob reported the following conversation as the latest he had heard from the old shoemaker; and although my mother never liked frivolity, she couldn't help smiling because Bob so naturally imitated Thomas Bartley's way of speaking.

"How's your mother, Bob," asked Thomas.

"Very bad, Thomas Bartley," said Bob, "she's suffering very much with her rheumatism; she only gets a little sleep because of the pain."

"…dash it all! Dash it all!" said Thomas. "You know, Bob, I don't understand the Good Lord, look you; I don't understand Him at all. A woman like your mother, who's never done anythin' against Him, bein' tortured like that all the time; I don't understand Him, to be sure."

"You think too well of my mother, Thomas Bartley," said Bob. "She accuses herself often, fearing every day that she won't be saved in the end."

"Not saved in the end?" said Thomas. "What's the matter with the woman, say? I never heard of one false step by her; have you, Barbara?"

"I never heard, goodness knows," said Barbara.

"It's not likely," said Thomas, "that anyone else has either. Wait now, Bob, you're a scholar, and Barbara and I have often thought to ask you but we forget—doesn't the Book say that a lot of us will be saved in the end?"

"It talks of a great multitude that no man can number," [2] said Bob.

"To be sure! Weren't I sayin' to you, Barbara? And ignorant people

---

[2] Rev. 7:9.

do talk. I believe, you see, Bob, if we're honest, and pay our way, and live somethin' like we should, we'll all be saved. D'you want soles as well as heels on these? They're beginnin' to go; you better have 'em welted, too."

I heard Bob say many similar things. But I was talking about Seth. I have heard many times about those who are so unfortunate as to come into the world without being *compos mentis*, so to speak, that they have craft and cunning beyond that of other people. But there was nothing of that in Seth. I think he was perfectly innocent; and he had a remarkably kind and tender heart. Whatever was asked of him, he would do it if it were in his power, and he could not keep anything of his own without giving it to someone else. It seemed to me that his heart was always in the right place; but poor thing! His intellect was small. In truth, he was a child even though he was the size of a grown man. Whatever thoughts went through his heart, he only had the weakest ability to express them; his language was babyish and his words were few. Everyone in the neighbourhood knew Seth, and was kind towards him on account of his weakness, I suppose. Yes, even all of the dogs of the town and countryside knew him, and would wag their tails for him; and Seth would not go past one of them without patting its head, and greeting it affectionately in his own way. Now I think of it, he had one special ability, namely to be able to remember the names of dogs, horses and so on. He spent little time at home. Seth could somehow be happier anywhere than in his mother and father's house. If I happened to rise early, I would be sure to see Seth. If I was out late, Seth would cross my path somewhere. If there was some trouble in the town, one of the first people I'd see would be Seth. In every preaching meeting, concert and lecture, Seth would be one of the audience; because he had a licence to go everywhere, as no ticket was asked from him by any denomination or party.

He would be in every chapel service consistently, and would listen intently to every word that was said; but no-one thought he understood anything. By now, I doubt whether that was true;

because I remember noticing his face many times, as the preacher was speaking, that some spark of joyful understanding went over him. This wouldn't last more than a second, and it would leave his face as vacant and expressionless as it been before, and yet it was so different from his normal demeanour as to draw my attention. When he was asked what the preacher had been saying, he remembered nothing except the name Jesus Christ, or at least he couldn't express it. There's cause to believe that he thought highly of every preacher: nothing gave him so much pleasure as being able to hold the head of his horse, or show him the chapel house. When it was his turn to do this, he told all his contemporaries about it with great pleasure. Although Seth was, as I said, an adult in age and stature, children were his constant companions.

He came regularly to the children's *seiat*, and recited his verse just as the other children did. He invariably had the same verse: 'Jesus Christ is the same yesterday, today and forever'.[3] Neither my mother nor I, nor anyone else could find out who had taught it to him. The verse seemed to have grown up with him, and filled up his mind so that there was no room for any other verse, as it was always the same verse that he recited each time. I remember Abel Hughes one time in the children's *seiat* passing over Seth without asking him for it. Seeing this, Seth broke out in copious tears, and wouldn't be comforted. All we children were very fond of Seth, and most of us ended up crying with him. I for one, I remember well, was pouring forth, as it never took much to make me cry. Although Abel, as I have said before, was a decisive and self-possessed man, I never saw him in such a fix. He pulled some strange faces, and couldn't speak clearly. He eventually tried to mend Seth's feelings, but could not. I know that he felt terrible about what he had done; and as an atonement for his bad behaviour, Abel presented Seth the next day with a hymn book, and that healed all his wounds. That hymn book is the only thing that I ever remember Seth being able

---

[3] Heb. 13:8.

to keep for himself, and not give to someone else. He wouldn't have sold it for anything; he carried it to every service, and opened it near the middle when he sang; but, strangely, he almost always held it upside down. Seth had noticed that some kind people would show the right page to others that were alongside them, who couldn't remember the hymn number; and if he ever saw someone with the slightest hesitation, he went to them straight away, showing them his open book as if he were perfectly certain of it.

He would strike a strange pose sometimes during the worship, and this can't have been less than a challenge to visiting preachers; but the congregation were long familiar with it, and didn't notice. Occasionally, he would rise suddenly to his feet, then put his feet over the pew in front, put his right elbow to rest on his knee and his chin to rest on his hand, all without taking his eyes off the preacher. Seeing Wil Bryan, myself and others writing down the title of the sermon and the main headings, Seth had a strong urge to imitate us; and occasionally someone would jokingly give him a large piece of white paper and a pencil for the purpose. Then Seth would usually hold the paper in his right hand, and the pencil in his left, and wait anxiously for the preacher to announce his title; and then with great concentration he would scribble onto the paper the strangest shapes that anyone had ever seen. But he soon tired of this, and returned to his original pose of staring the preacher fixedly in the eye. As I remember his conduct during the worship, and also the fact that Seth would sit right by the preacher, I wonder that he never threw any of them right off their train of thought. There was something in Seth very much like the spirit of worship. I heard Marged from the chapel house saying that Seth would more often than not be waiting for her to open the door to the sanctuary; and once she had made everything ready and turned her back, Seth would go to the Great Seat; he would open the Bible, and make a sound as if he were reading; then he would go down on his knees, and say a lot of something that nobody knew, as Marged put it, if he knew himself. But as soon as someone came in to the chapel,

Seth would direct his steps quietly towards his usual seat.

Seth and I were great friends. Not because we were of similar mind, I hope. When my mother would not let me out to play, many times I saw Seth standing around outside our house for hours waiting for me. I don't know what it was that made him take to me so much; but I know for sure that when he saw me being wronged by other lads, it would grieve him sorely. As I remember how weak his health was, I feel ashamed to think how often he was my horse. If all were put together, I'm sure that he carried me on his back for scores of miles, and this wholly without complaint. If Seth was given a ha'penny or a penny, which happened often, he would consult with me every time what to do with it, and my advice was invariably to spend it. But I must hurry, as I have something more important to say about my connection with him.

I noticed one day that Seth was looking very ill, and coughing badly, and not at all inclined to play, although he did not complain. Indeed, I never heard him complain. The next day Seth didn't come out of the house. The day after that I went to see him, and I found him ill in his bed. As I first entered the room, he looked at me wildly; then his face brightened, he reached out his hand, and shouted "Rhys!" Within a couple of minutes, he ceased to recognise me, calling me other names. He spoke ceaselessly, but I couldn't make any sense out of what he said. Vainly his mother tried to keep him calm. He sat up in the bed, and pointed with his finger to an empty corner of the room, as if he were seeing something there that he couldn't describe. His appearance had frightened me; and my heart was nearly breaking with sympathy towards him, as I slipped quietly down the stairs. In the kitchen, Thomas Bartley walked back and forth in deep sorrow. The first question he asked me was whether Seth had recognised me; and when I answered in the affirmative, he was greatly comforted. But soon his anxiety returned, and he said, "The doctor says, Rhys, that he has a fever. Dash it all! Dash it all! Ask your mother, my boy, to pray for him a bit. Dash it all! What if I lose him!"

If Seth had been the most talented boy in the land, his parents could not have shown more care for him. My friend continued in the same condition for days. I visited him every day—sometimes twice a day. Wil Bryan and I were the only two of his old companions who were permitted to go into his room. It was rare for him to recognise us. I can't remember whether it was on the eighth or ninth day of his sickness when Wil Bryan came to our house late at night with the news that Seth had 'altered' and was calling for me. Although it was nearly time for me to go to bed, I had permission from my mother to go and visit him. On the way, Wil said to me, "I'm afraid, you see, that Seth is going to leg it;" by which he meant that Seth was about to die. Although Wil was speaking in this way, he was perfectly serious. When we arrived at the house, Thomas Bartley greeted us warmly and said that Seth was much better. My heart leapt with joy when I heard this. We went quietly up to the bedroom. Old Barbara, and her neighbour, were sitting on the edge of the bed looking quietly joyful. "He's been asking for you for a while," said the neighbour to Wil and me. Seth was lying perfectly calm, with a cheerful smile on his face. There was also some strange beauty in his appearance. Anyone who didn't know him would have taken him for a normal boy, as far as the look of him went. Wil and I were struck dumb, almost, by how different he looked from his normal self. I should have mentioned that Seth always talked about himself in the third person. For example, he didn't say when he was going somewhere, 'I'm going', but 'Seth is going to such and such a place'. And so, in every circumstance, he spoke about himself as if he were someone else. And we his companions had adopted the same convention when speaking to him. When Wil and I went into the room, Seth, having reached out his thin white hand to us and greeted us by our names, asked his mother and the neighbour to go down to the kitchen, and they went straight away. When we had the room to ourselves, I leaned over him and said, "Seth is better?"

"Yes, Seth is better," he answered, haltingly.

"Does Seth want to say anything to Rhys?" I asked. He looked at me cheerfully, with the sort of clear and understanding expression on his face that reminded me of the sparks I mentioned that I saw sometimes pass over his face in chapel. Then he recited the verse that I had heard from his mouth hundreds of times in the children's *seiat*: "Jesus Christ is the same yesterday, today and forever." There was something about the way he said it that made me believe that it came, not from his tongue, but straight from his heart. He continued to look at me as though he was expecting me to ask him something else, and I didn't know what to ask him. Eventually I said to him that Seth would be mended soon.

"No," he said, "Seth won't be mended. Seth won't play again with Rhys. Seth won't go to Abel's chapel again. Seth is going far away—away to… to…" and he pointed his finger up, as if he were struggling to find the right word; I suggested the word 'heaven' but that wasn't the word he was looking for, and eventually he spoke the whole sentence:

"Seth is going far, far away to Jesus Christ's big chapel."

That was poor Seth's picture of heaven—'Jesus Christ's big chapel'. I had for a while heard Wil Bryan, who was standing behind me, breathing in quickly through his nostrils as though he had a cold. I had seen, when we were in the school, the old Soldier smashing a cane to smithereens against Wil's back, and him not make a sound, or shed a single tear; but hearing Seth, our innocent old companion, talking about dying and going far away, was more than Wil could bear and he 'legged it', as he would have said, down the stairs leaving me alone with Seth. When Wil had left the room, Seth looked around and saw that no-one was there except for him and myself, and he said,

"Rhys, pray."

I understood his wish in a moment, and I didn't know what to do. I thought that no-one was to pray with the sick except for a preacher. He said to me again, with more earnestness in his expression,

"Rhys, pray."

I couldn't refuse; and I was glad by then that Wil had gone away, so that he didn't make fun of me afterwards. I went on my knees by the bedside, and prayed as well as I could. I don't remember now what words I used; but I know I asked Jesus Christ to mend Seth, and then my mind went blank and I had to resort to saying the Lord's prayer. When I asked for Jesus Christ to mend my friend, I know that the prayer came from the bottom of my heart, and at the same time I felt Seth's tender, light hand upon my head. He kept it there while I said the Lord's prayer. I stayed for a while in silence, to see if he would pull it away, but he did not. I felt it press more heavily upon my head. Slowly I felt it go colder and colder, and a strange shiver went through my whole constitution. I moved his hand slowly, and rose to my feet, shaking. His eyes were wide open, and looking into the distance, so it seemed. I spoke to him, but he did not answer; I called to him again, but Seth was too far away to hear. He was just an empty house, even though the windows were bright and clean. The innocent soul—I almost said sinless—had gone 'far away to Jesus Christ's big chapel', as he had said.

When I realised that he was dead, I shouted like a maniac; and the next moment his mother and father and the neighbour were by my side. I won't try to describe the scene, though I will never be able to forget it. It would be cruel to try to describe the wild and uncontrolled grief of parents without the mental or religious capacity to sustain them in a severe trial. I rushed home with a heavy heart. It was a bit of a way from Seth's house to ours, and I had to go by myself because Wil Bryan had already gone some time ago. It was a moonlit night and the air was clear, and the stars were shining and appeared very far away. I imagined that the moon was staring persistently at me, and the stars were nodding ceaselessly. The more I looked at them, the more I felt that they were looking at me. I asked myself whether Seth had gone beyond them, or whether he was on his way to them; how much time would it take to get to heaven, and would he arrive there before I arrived home, and a host of similar questions. It's strange for me to remember now, but something came into my mind that night that I was to be a preacher. Where the thought came from, or who put it there, I don't know; but I date my desire to be a preacher from that evening. Was it the hand of Seth, the retarded boy, on my head as he hung between two worlds, that first set me aside for the work? I often preach so poorly, that many would believe it if I said that was the case.

But I digress. I had two or three fields to cross on my way home. My path also went along the edge of the Manor woods. Although I was fairly bold, considering that I was only a lad, I have to admit that I was not without fears that night. But I hurried on, trying to keep my spirit up. When I came to the Manor wood, I saw something in the form of a man sitting on the hedge, precisely at the side of the path that I would have to go along. I hesitated, and my heart started beating so heavily that I thought I was not just feeling it but hearing it as well. It was late at night, and it would have taken as much courage to go back as to go on. I called up that amount of boldness that I had, and went on quickly. As I approached the man, I saw that he had a gun in his hand, and I decided in my mind that the man was the Manor's gamekeeper, whom I knew well, and my fear went away. The moon by now was behind the trees, so I couldn't see clearly; but when I came within a few yards of the man, I said in a loud voice, "Good night, Mr Jones." I was answered by a harsh and unpleasant voice.

"Wait, wait, Rhys Lewis! Don't walk so fast or you'll come across some of your relatives."

I stopped and saw that it was not Mr Jones, and that he had an old-fashioned double-barrelled gun in his hand.

"Don't be afraid," he said, "I won't shoot you *now*, if you do as I say. Sit down on this hedge so I can talk to you."

I obeyed, shaking. I thought that I ought to know the voice, but the man's form was completely strange to me. After I had sat as he'd commanded me, the man lay his gun to rest on the hedge, so close to me that I could see the two yellow caps shining. Before saying another word, the man filled his pipe, and lit a match. As he put the fire to his pipe, and the flame of the match lit up his face,

I recognised him; and I almost fainted with fear. I recognised in his ugly and vicious face the dirty and bad man, whom I had seen coming to our house late that night many years ago, and whom I called at the time 'the Irishman'. Quite a change had come over him since the time I first saw him; he now looked much stronger. He started to ask me in detail and authoritatively about my mother and Bob, and especially about the Squire and the gamekeepers. I kept nothing from him; because I was so afraid of him that my clothes were sticking to my skin with cold sweat, and it seemed that he derived great enjoyment from seeing me so scared. He kept me there for a long time, and let out various words that opened my eyes to the history of my family. I had my suspicions before; but now, I saw the whole thing clearly. The Irishman, for that was the name by which I knew him, was busily asking me questions and talking, when he stopped suddenly in mid-sentence. He took hold of his gun, and pulled his pipe from his mouth, listening intently. The silence was oppressive to me. In a moment, he pulled strongly at his pipe, as though he was afraid that the fire would go out, and listened intently again. I imagined that I heard the sound of feet walking quickly along the path that I had come along. The Irishman pulled his hat down tightly over his head, and then I heard someone not far away whistling low and meaningfully. Without saying a word, my strange companion leapt to his feet and leapt over the hedge into the trees. The same moment, I was like a frightened deer destroying the distance between that place and our house. A bullet could hardly have overtaken me. When I reached the main road, I stopped to catch my breath, and I heard a shot, then another, and shouting, and a commotion. I went on quickly; and very soon I met with my brother Bob who was coming to look for me, and I told him briefly what had happened. He charged me not to say a word to my mother or anyone else; and he added that the time had come for me to know what he had kept from me until now, and that he would tell me everything after we had gone to bed. He kept his promise, and I kept his command, and I've never said a word to anyone until today about what took place that night by the Manor woods.

Wasn't it appropriate that I said that Seth had been the occasion to form a critical period in my life? I knew so much more about my family by the following morning, and I'd like to hope that I was a much better boy.

14

WIL BRYAN

Seth's funeral was the first I had ever been to; and because so many changes have been brought in to funerals within the last thirty years, perhaps it would not be inappropriate for me to note a fact or two in relation to it. Around that time, the more intellectual Methodists of Flintshire were trying to teach people to do away with the foolish custom of drinking beer at funerals. I remember that I was in Thomas Bartley's house the evening before Seth was to be carried to his resting place, when Abel Hughes came to visit the grieving family. Abel tried to draw valuable lessons out of the sad circumstance; and it was obvious to me that Thomas and Barbara were cut to the quick by his teaching. Even so, when Abel referred eventually to the custom of drinking beer at funerals, stating his hope that Seth's parents would not uphold the custom, Thomas raised his head, and looked rather angrily at Abel, and said: "Abel Hughes, you don't think I'm goin' to bury my boy like buryin' a dog? No, there will be bread and cheese and beer for everyone who comes here, if my eyes are open."

Abel argued with him zealously, but his reasoning had no effect on Thomas Bartley, who said: "No, no, Abel Hughes, if Seth weren't quite like other kids, I'm not goin' to bury him with a cup of tea," and he rubbed his eyes in the sleeve of his coat.

He was true to his word. When Wil Bryan and I came early the following afternoon we saw on the table, half a cheese with a knife beside it, a loaf of white bread, an enormous jug full of beer, a selection of new pipes and a small plate of tobacco. We were received into the house by Thomas Bartley himself, and the first words he said to us were: "William, take somethin' for your head; Rhys, take somethin' for your head."

I didn't feel that there was anything wrong with my head; and I think Wil felt the same, because he looked at Thomas Bartley in surprise. Thomas knew that we had not understood his wish, and he cut a big chunk of bread and cheese for Wil and me, and filled a small glass of beer for us. I was amazed at how Wil drank the beer without pulling a face. I had quite some trouble swallowing it, and I felt its effects straight away. I felt on exceptionally good terms with every man, and I thought that my hands were very big and long, and I had a strong desire to either sleep or laugh, not being able to choose which. I knew that neither behaviour would be appropriate in such a place, so I put up an energetic fight against the effects of the glass, and I took no more 'for my head'. Various of the old neighbours had come to the funeral before us, and they were smoking alongside, and others came in after us. Each time someone came in, Thomas Bartley greeted them with the same words: "Take somethin' for your head," and then the new arrivals would head straight for the jug of beer, pour a glass, and cut some bread and cheese. I remember that everyone who came left their hats on their heads, and each one in turn would share old memories of this and that, without any connection with Seth's death. Almost everyone was smoking and spitting on the floor, on which white sand had been spread thickly. The jug was refilled many times. After someone had helped themselves to the beer, they would put the glass down in front of the man seated to their left, and turn the handle of the jug the same way. Occasionally someone would forget to do their duty in a reasonable time; and then someone bolder than his brothers would shout, "Whose is the handle?" which was a signal for the one at whom the handle was pointing to have a drink, or to turn the handle towards the person next to him. This went on for an hour and a half or two hours; and a few of them drank as much as they could safely hold, the expressions on their faces having changed. I remember now James Pulford the tailor, a small, thin, talkative man, whose face was usually as grey as death—that afternoon his face was as ruddy as any farm labourer I ever saw.

A few minutes before starting off to go to the cemetery, two men came in from the next room; and in their hands were pewter vessels similar in shape to those that are used to serve communion these days, but bigger. The handles of these jugs had been decorated with lemon skin. In one vessel was 'the hot beer', as it was called, but it would have been more appropriate to call it the boiled beer; and in the other vessel there was 'the cold beer'; and both of them were highly spiced. As soon as these vessels made their appearance, everyone pulled their hats from their heads, and in the midst of silence like the grave, the two men went around serving the two kinds of drink in exactly the same way as the Lord's Supper is served, and almost with the same reverence. What this meant, I didn't know, and I've never found out to this day. Having been through this ceremony everyone put their hats back on their heads, and the storytelling began again. Soon David the carpenter passed the plate round, and the men put in a shilling each, and Wil Bryan and I put in sixpence each, because that was the custom for boys. I should have said Abel Hughes had come in a couple of minutes before 'raising the body', as it is called; and when Thomas Bartley asked him to 'take somethin' for his head', he declined. When the time came to start off for the church, there was no-one among those who came to the burial who was accustomed to praying in public, apart from Abel Hughes, Thomas had taken so unkindly to him for refusing to 'take somethin' for his head' that he didn't ask him to officiate; and I saw him talking in the ear of David the carpenter, who was a very immoral man. When the body was put on the bier, everyone put their hat to one ear, looking as though they were listening to something that it had to say to them. The women were pulled from the other room to look through the windows, putting their pocket handkerchiefs over their mouths; and David the carpenter went down on his knees beside the bier and said the Lord's prayer as quickly as the wind, just as if he were counting twenty sheep.

Then they went in procession to the cemetery. Wil Bryan and I walked on either side of Thomas Bartley; I carried the evergreens, and Wil carried the sand to decorate Seth's grave. In the church, as Mr Brown galloped through the burial service, I noticed that several people had fallen into a deep sleep, among them James Pulford whose nose lay quietly in his waistcoat. After the service at the graveside, David the carpenter climbed onto a tomb to thank the neighbours on the family's behalf for their kindness in coming to the funeral. He added that Thomas and Barbara Bartley wanted to state their confidence that before long they would be able to pay the same kindness to every one here, and that the father of the departed would like them all to meet in the Crown an hour after the service. After decorating the grave, everyone at the funeral apart from Abel Hughes, Wil Bryan and myself went straight to the Crown, in accordance with the invitation. Wil also was keen enough to go, but he was afraid of trouble at home. While we were in the church, there was a houseful of female neighbours in the house drinking tea with Barbara, and my mother was among them. She went there very much against her will; but I heard her say that if she refused the invitation then Barbara would never speak another word to her. I don't know what was going on in the Crown but within a few hours I saw Thomas Bartley returning home between two neighbours. Although they were fairly quiet, I could see that there had been some disagreement between them over which side of the road it was best to walk; and soon after that I heard James Pulford go past our house singing,

'*By the banks of the Conwy on my way...*' [1]

If I were to print this, doubtless some would be amazed and disbelieving; but I know that others would bear witness to the accuracy of the description, and say that its main fault is that it is too short and doesn't tell the whole story. I have refrained from

[1] The first line of a poem 'Myfyrdod ar lanau Conwy' ('A Meditation on the Banks of the Conwy'), written some time after 1807 by a poet with the bardic name 'Pyll' (whom I haven't been able to identify), to be sung to the tune 'Earl of Moira'.

describing quite everything unseemly that went on in connection with Seth's funeral. O mercy, what reforms have taken place at funerals by now! And yet there is room for more. If the beer has been exiled, the tea and coffee, and ham and beef have taken its place. If some strangers come a long distance to attend a funeral, there is possibly some merit in preparing food for them. But what reason can be given for all the feasting at a funeral that is seen amongst neighbours? Some poor families are forced to prepare costly feasts, and that for people who live close by them. Maintaining this foolish custom is a cruelty to the poor, and wholly inappropriate, I think.

Once Seth had been buried, I had no close friend apart from Wil Bryan; and I became more convinced every day that my connection with him would not last long. Wil had an open and kind heart, and a lively and daring spirit; but from day to day the consciousness grew within me that he was not a good boy. He spoke disrespectfully about the strict rules of the *seiat*; and it was rare that he called anyone by their proper name. He had nicknames for almost everyone he knew. John Lloyd, as I said before, he called 'the old scratcher'—Hugh Bellis, the elder who often wept during the sermon, 'the old waterworks'—Thomas Bowen, the man who was so popular among the children, 'the old trump'—Abel Hughes, because he wore knee-length breeches and because his legs were thin, 'the old onion'. He had an 'old something' name for everyone. He never referred to his father and mother except by the names, 'the gaffer at home' and, 'the old pea-hen at home'. And I've noticed ever since then that my mother spoke truly when she said that there is an important defect in the character of a boy who is accustomed to call his father 'gaffer' or 'governor', or similar. I don't doubt that Wil's ability to give descriptive names to people would have been a particular talent if he had channelled it in the right direction. Some of the mischievous names have stayed with their owners to this day; but it wouldn't be good for me or anyone else to record them. I didn't particularly notice this tendency of

Wil's to give people names until he referred to my mother as 'the old Ten Commandments', which offended me greatly. When Wil saw that I did not like the name, he didn't use it again. But as I think today, I can't help but see some appropriateness in that name; because my mother was always giving us commands, and charging us to do this or that. When I remember that my mother was a quite astute woman, I'm amazed to think that she tolerated me having so much contact with Wil; but when I think about it again, it's not surprising at all. Never in my life have I seen a boy with the same ability to put himself on good terms with people. His cunning, his handsome and cheerful face, his strong and brave manner, his pleasant voice, together with a sharp and witty tongue, were weapons that he always used with purpose. He understood my mother perfectly. I heard her say more than once that when she felt low of spirit, a visit from Wil would go halfway to mending her. I saw her smile, and having to try hard not to laugh out loud at some of his amusing observations, when I knew full well that if I made the same comments, even in the same words, she would have boxed my ears. I know that she often felt that she went along too much with Wil's levity, and as if to allay her conscience she gave him good advice. The following conversation serves as an example of many like it:

"Well, dear Wil, you'll do a lot of good or bad in this world; and I dearly hope you'll have a bit of grace."

"There's plenty of that to go round, isn't there, Mary Lewis? But I never like to take more than my fair share of anything, you know."

"Don't talk lightly, Wil; you can never have too much grace."

"That's what the gaffer at home always says; but it's not a good thing, you know, Mary Lewis, to be too 'having'."

"Who is your gaffer, say?" asked my mother.

"The old hand at home; my father, you know," said Wil.

"Wil," said my mother, looking seriously at him, "I'm charging you to stop calling your father 'gaffer' and 'old hand'. I've never seen any good come of children who call their father or mother 'him at home' or 'her at home', or 'the old hand at home' or 'the old woman at home'. Don't let me hear you calling your father by those silly names again, remember."

"All right," said Wil, "next time I will call him Hugh Bryan, Esquire, General Grocer and Provision Dealer, Baker to his Royal Highness the Old Scratcher, and …."

But before finishing his story he would have to show a clean pair of heels, my mother following him with some weapon in her hand. But despite all his mischief, my mother did not feel angry towards him, and she frequently said, "That boy's a keen one; if he gets grace he'll be a noble preacher." This sort of comment created a bit of jealousy in me; because she never said that I would make a preacher, even though that was the chief desire of my life by then; and I knew that Wil did not imagine becoming a preacher.

I don't think that my mother thought any less of Wil than that he was just a mischievous boy, but this changed when he started to turn his hair off his forehead, or as it was called at that time, 'doing a Q.P.' When she saw the white expanse on Wil's head, and signs that he had put oil in his hair, his fate was sealed forever in her view. I was very sorry that my mother looked on this innovation as such a big deal, because I thought that Wil looked splendid in his Q.P. and I longed for permission to imitate it. I had long been fed up with the way my mother cut my hair, namely to put the big butter bowl on my head and cut around the edges, until I looked just like a newly built haystack. I saw that there was no hope of change in this respect; and I remember my mother making the following observations to Wil when she saw his Q.P.:

"Well, dear Wil, I had thought that you were a fairly good boy despite all your frippery. But I see that the devil has found your weak point."

"What's the matter now, Mary Lewis? I didn't kill anyone recently, did I?" asked Wil.

"No, I hope not," said my mother, "but you need to kill the old man."[2]

"Who do you mean, Mary Lewis? The gaffer at home? Dear me, no way, I won't kill the old hand. What would happen to me? I'd starve."

"No Wil, I don't mean your father, but the old man which is in your heart."

"An old man in my heart? There's no old man in my heart, I swear."

"Yes there is, dear Wil, and you'll know that one day."

"Well, when did he come into my heart, Mary Lewis?" asked Wil. "He must be very small, smaller than Tom Thumb."

"He was in your heart before you were born, and he's bigger than Goliath," said my mother, "and if you don't take your smooth stone from the river of salvation, and sink it in his forehead, he's sure to cut off your head with his sword."[3]

"How can I sink a stone into his forehead if he's in my heart? And how can he cut off my head with his sword?"

"You know who I'm talking about, Wil," said my mother, "The old man of sin is what I mean."

"Oh! I understand you now. Why don't you speak plainly, Mary Lewis? But isn't there sin in all our hearts, according to the old… to my father, at home."

"Yes, my boy," said my mother, "and it's coming out of your head as well with that silly Q.P." And my mother held forth at length and without reserve about the pride and wickedness in the custom of turning one's fringe off one's forehead. Wil felt the rebuke, and went away rather haughtily.

"Rhys," said my mother when Wil had left, "don't have much to do with Wil from now on. Pride has taken possession of his heart. I'm amazed at Hugh Bryan for letting him do such a thing. If he were my boy I'd have shaved his head, I would. There he is, I know,

---

[2] Romans 6:6. [3] 1 Samuel 17:49–51.

looking at himself in the mirror every day and feeding his pride. Thank goodness there has never been a mirror in our family until your brother Bob brought one here; and I'd have been glad in my heart if that had never crossed the threshold. Your grandmother used to say that people who look in the mirror see the devil; and I can easily believe that. I don't know what will become of this younger generation if we don't have a visitation soon," And my mother groaned from the bottom of her heart.

15

THE BEGINNING OF SORROWS

One day my mother said to me:

"You're beginning to be a big boy, and I can't afford, for all the world, to keep you to run around and play. Your brother had started in the coal mine before he was your age, and there are those younger than you who earn their living every day, I know. But what you can do I don't know, I don't know. It's an awful thing for you to have your head in the wind at your age, and your mother no better than a widow, if as good. You're not strong, that much is clear, or to the coal mine you'd be going straight away; you're not enough of a scholar to be a shopkeeper, and if you were, I have nothing to put before you. Where can I find five or ten pounds to apprentice you, I don't know? If ten shillings would put you into the best shop in town, I don't know where I'd turn my head to look for them. And yet you need to think of doing something to earn your living. Your feet nearly reach the floor, and you're like a dog, wearing the same coat on Monday as on Sunday; if you only earned enough money to put clothes on your back, that would be something. Food is so expensive, and your brother's salary so small, that it's all I can do to make ends meet, and set aside the occasional penny for the cause.[1] And you'd be amazed if you knew how much your mother has to worry and scheme to keep things on the level, because as Thomas from the Nant[2] would say,

'There are many ways to get Wil into his bed'.[3]

And if this strike that they're talking about in the works comes, I don't know what will become of us. So far, thanks to the great Provider, we've been able to pay our way, amazingly, although life has been hard. But I've never seen the good of keeping children too long without them starting to work; it just succours them to do wickedness.

I don't doubt I could persuade James Pulford the tailor to take you on. But he's a shiftless and inconsiderate man, and very often drunk; and I'm afraid that your soul wouldn't get fair play, and that's the main thing after all. I'd rather see you a godly chimney sweep that an ungodly Justice of the Peace. Perhaps you say that the children would shout after you, 'poor tailor, shoes without socks'.[4] Well, let them; they won't break your bones, and your back would be dry in all weathers, and you'd have a trade in your hand. I'd rather see you a tailor than a farm labourer. The weather, or something, stiffens and chills their souls as well as their limbs, I think; and being with animals all the time makes them remarkably like animals. I've never in my life seen people more listless, with less man in them, as your brother would say, than these farm boys. They're like slaves somehow, and too shy to lift their heads except in the stable and at ploughing matches. I felt pity for them the night I was in the Manor. It was a cold and wet night; and when the poor men came in for their supper, sopping wet, they went over to that long table, you know, by the window, far away from the fire. There were about six of them, I believe, and they came into the house, so quietly, and sat on the two benches on either side of the table with their heads down, looking out from under their forelocks as though they had been out stealing all day, not working hard in the wet and filth. And not one of them said a word. All I heard was the sound of them eating their soup, and that finished quickly. For about a quarter of a minute they looked out from under their forelocks at the husbandman; and when he gave the sign, there was a noise of feet and shifting benches, and

---

[1] The 'cause' is a common idiom in Welsh for referring to the Chapel.

[2] Twm o'r Nant again.

[3] 'Mae llawer sgil i gael Wil i'w wely'; nowadays the Welsh idiom equivalent to the English, 'there are many ways to skin a cat'.

[4] 'Teiliwr tene, clogs heb sane'—in Welsh, it rhymes.

out went the poor things in one row. I had pity in my heart for them; they weren't like men, somehow. And then I thought that two of them were members of the same church as Mr Williams, their master, and that one of the two, Aaron Parry, is an amazing man when he is on his knees. I didn't like seeing such a distance between the master and the workman. I can't believe that the Saviour likes such a thing.

But as I was saying, I wouldn't on any account in the world want you to be a farm labourer. I'm almost beginning to think that Bob your brother is right, and that a bit of learning is useful enough, so long as you don't have too much of it. If you'd had a bit more schooling, I'd put the boat out and ask old Abel to take you into his shop. It's not possible that after all the trouble he'd refuse me. But enough about that now. Thomas Bowen was saying to me, coming back from the *seiat*, that it's high time you were received as a full member, and I'd like to see you come forward if you've thought about the matter. You've memorised the chapter of the Instructor, I know, and have learned long ago the chapters in the Gospels that record the ordinance of the supper. But you need, my boy, to pray that your own mind be inclined towards it, so that you don't come forward unworthily. I'd be glad in my heart to see you apprenticed for a heavenly career before you're apprenticed for this old world. 'Being under the yoke while young is a hundred thousand times better than false pleasures'.[5]"

She said a lot else besides; indeed, my mother could go on in this strain for a whole day. It was obvious to me that the time had come when I would have to think about earning my crust. I had an older head on my shoulders than my mother realised, and I knew more about her struggles than she imagined. I felt my heart burn with desire to help her. We depended entirely, the three of us, on what Bob earned, and he, even though he worked hard,

---

[5] 'Mae bod yn fore dan yr iau, yn ganmil gwell na phleser gau'; a quotation from a hymn by Pedr Fardd (Peter Jones, 1775–1845).

barely had enough to feed and clothe himself, if he had fair play. The market for coal was quite lively, but there was a swarm of rapacious foreign officers and supervisors in the 'Red Fields' mine, pocketing, eating and drinking the profits while the poor workers and their families half starved. Bob was one of the oppressed; and it had been obvious to me for a while that his spirit was soured, and there was a righteous indignation building up in his breast that one day would burst forth. I understood from the talk of the miners' children that Bob was quite an important man amongst his fellow workers—he had been the chairman in a meeting that had been held some time before that, to consider whether it would be appropriate to ask for an increase in wages, and that he had spoken well. I felt proud of him, and not without cause; because he took a lot of trouble on my behalf. He never tired of instructing me in this and that, and I am more indebted to him than any man alive for the direction that my life took. It's true that after he had been excommunicated from the *seiat* he didn't talk to me about religion, nor about religious subjects if I didn't raise them with him. But whatever other knowledge he could share with me, as much as he could, he did not fail to do so. I had to promise him earnestly, many times, that I would not become a collier, even if I had to beg instead. Perhaps the insufferable oppression and mistreatment that he himself experienced made him ask that of me. But he didn't have to be so persistent; I didn't have the least inclination to go into the 'works'. His daily complaints about the hard work and oppressiveness had given me an irreconcilable loathing for the colliery.

Besides that, I was secretly nurturing the desire to be a preacher, and I thought that it was a great distance from the bottom of a coal mine up to the pulpit. Perhaps it's a foolish idea, but I thought that it would be easier to climb into the pulpit from anywhere other than the coal mine. No living creature knew about the desire that was in me, and I was terrified of anyone finding out. As I roll back in my mind, and try to explain to myself what the initial impulse was that gave me the desire to be a preacher, I can't by any means in the world give an account for it; and I'd be glad to know of the experience of others who have been in the same situation as me, if anyone has. I have to admit that it wasn't the true motivation, namely, a desire to do good and turn sinners from the error of their ways; because that, at the time I'm writing about, hadn't yet found a place in my mind. I tend strongly to think that it was an admiration of preachers, if not something worse, like proud ambition because I remember imagining myself as a big fat man (something I have never been), a full pulpit of a man, preaching fluently, and the people listening to me as though their lives depended on it, and talking about me and complimenting me after the sermon. I would be untrue to my story if I were to say that I didn't know something of religious impressions. After all the trouble that my mother had taken with me, it would be a near miracle if I'd had no impressions of that sort. I had known many times before that, of minutes of seriousness, of fearing sinning against God and dying ungodly. But I can't give an account of what created such an overpowering desire in me, and this when I was still only a young lad, to be a preacher. I regret to this day that I did not share with my mother the thing that was hidden in my heart, not just because she would have given every welcome and nurture to the desire, but also because I feel that I deprived her of the greatest pleasure and joy that I could have given to her in the midst of her bitter struggles. I know that it wouldn't have been possible for me to pour more joy into the cup of her happiness than to tell her of my decision to be a preacher some day. But I kept it all to myself. I am not flattering myself, nor doing anything other than stating a plain fact, when I say that at that time I was more serious than my contemporaries; and although I felt it to the quick when Wil Bryan mocked me by calling me 'the holy one', I was conscious that I had a purpose hidden from him, that he didn't understand and with which he didn't have the slightest sympathy. I took a particular interest in every preacher and

I never tired of talking about the 'order of preachers'[6] if I could find someone who would talk about it with me.

Through continued application, and with Bob's help, I was more of a scholar than my mother thought. I could read and write Welsh and English competently. I had for some time, on the instigation of John Joseph in the Children's Meeting, been writing out the texts[7] on the Sabbath, and as many as I could of the headings of the sermon. I remember being very annoyed with some preachers because they didn't specifically state their headings, and also that I was very fond of William Hughes, Abercwmnant,[8] because the headings of his sermons were largely the same whatever text he took. They were generally three in number, and ran something like this: I.) The object which is noted. II.) The action which is attributed. III.) The duty which is urged. When W. Hughes was giving his introduction, I could often see the headings coming, and had them written down before he named them. The old preacher had a custom that often caused me to be amazed that he was not held to account for it. Towards the end of his sermon, he would always say, 'One more word before I close', he'd speak another hundred words or so. He would say again, 'One more word before I leave you', and speak for five or ten minutes. He'd say the third time, 'One more word before I run off', and speak for a long time after that. I was amazed that he, a preacher, was not called to account for telling lies. Wil Bryan would often take this as an excuse to say things that weren't true. I was praised by John Joseph for being able to recite the sermon headings, and this pleased me greatly. Around the time I'm referring to, John Joseph established a meeting of young men for the purpose of teaching the basics of music and grammar; and very soon it became a meeting

---

[6] 'yr urdd pregethwrol'—the body of those with the status of preachers; roughly equivalent to what a Catholic would call 'the priesthood'.

[7] That is to say, the scripture verses that formed the subject of each sermon.

[8] There is no such place as Abercwmnant but thousands of William Hughes', so this character is clearly meant to represent the 'generic' Methodist preacher of the time.

for competitive recitals, for competitions in essay writing, and for debating religious subjects. The group included various members; but I am afraid to name them lest I have to give their whole stories. Wil Bryan was a member, but he rarely took part in the public activities. His favourite work was to make fun of our mistakes and shortcomings. Wil became bolder in this until he made himself abhorrent to the majority of the young men; and they decided, by any possible means, to get rid of him. Wil was the only one of the members who turned his hair off his forehead; and in one of the regular meetings, a resolution was passed that no-one was to be a member of the society if they were guilty of doing a Q.P.; and he was duly thrown out. Wil cared nothing about this; but to pay them back for the insult, he gave the society a nickname, calling it the 'Hair Down Society'; and like most of his nicknames, it stuck for as long as the society was in existence. Anyway, I and many others gained great benefit from the 'Hair Down Society'; it left impressions on our minds that have never been erased, and created in us a taste for religious and literary things for which I can't ever be thankful enough.

Soon after Wil had been excommunicated from the society, his name and mine, and others, were put before the *seiat* as applicants for full membership. Thomas Bowen the preacher pleaded our case. He was always zealous on behalf of the youth of the church, and very careful about leaving it too late before fully accepting them. He daily compelled parents to press the matter into the minds of their children, and to prepare them for the eventuality. On the other hand, Abel Hughes spoke of the care that was necessary to avoid, and the danger of, receiving people into full membership before they were mature enough in their experience and knowledge. As the preacher and elder were at two extremes in this respect, there were various disputes between them. Thomas Bowen had for a long time been talking of bringing us forward, while Abel Hughes counselled care and deliberation. In the end, Thomas Bowen won out; and one evening we were called to come forward to the bench in the middle of the chapel floor to be examined. My contemporaries and I were keen to come forward; but Wil Bryan would have preferred to have been left alone. No doubt he was afraid of the examination, since he took only a little interest in religious matters, even though for natural ability he was above any of us. If I remember rightly, there were six of us; and we sat at one end of the bench, and Wil at the other, and he looked nonplussed. Abel rose to his feet, and started to question me first. He pressed me quite hard, but I came through the trial better than I had expected. I knew from Thomas Bowen's expression, and the sounds he made, that my answers were satisfactory; because he smiled, crossed his legs, nodded to Hugh Bellis, and said "Ho!" or "Hum!" after each answer, as if to say, "Jolly good, indeed." Abel pressed on with the next two boys, and had the same satisfaction. Then he sat down, and urged Thomas Bowen to press on with the next three. Thomas Bowen rose to his feet, put his hands in his trouser pockets, looked satisfied, and before going on turned to Abel and said, "Well, Abel Hughes, were you satisfied? Am I not right, don't you think, that these boys are quite ready to be received. Haven't I been saying that for months? But we'll go on."

And so he went on, examining the fourth and fifth. I thought that Thomas was not questioning so hard as Abel had, and the boys answered easily. When he received a fairly good answer, he turned to Abel and looked in his face suggestively, as if to say, 'What do you think of that, then, Abel? Will he do?' Eventually it was Wil Bryan's turn to be examined, and Thomas said to him—"Well, William, my boy, you're a bit older than these other boys, and you should have been accepted a long time ago, in my opinion, but there are some who believe that there is a need for deliberation. I won't examine you hard, although I know that if I were to do so, you'd be able to answer perfectly well. Will you tell me, William, my boy, how many offices belong to the Lord Jesus as Mediator?" [9]

"Three," said Wil.

---

[9] The correct answer is indeed, 'three': Prophet, Priest and King.

"Ho!" said Thomas. "Three! Do you hear, Abel Hughes? Three! If Dr Owen himself were here, he wouldn't be able to answer better. These boys know much more than you think, Abel Hughes. The Children's Meeting and the other meetings haven't been in vain, you see. The boys listen and take in more than we think, you can be sure. I've always said that. Yes for sure, 'three'. Well, William, my boy, will you name them?"

"The Father, the Son and the Holy Spirit," said Wil. Various people laughed throughout the chapel. Thomas Bowen looked as though someone had hit him around the back of the head with a mallet, and he sat down in shame and disappointment, looking down at his shoes without saying anything except "Hum!"

"Go on, go on, Thomas Bowen," said Abel, playfully; but Thomas pretended not to hear. I don't know whether it was mischief or ignorance that caused Wil to answer as he did, because he was flippant enough and careless enough to be as guilty of one as of the other. I know that Abel Hughes thought it wasn't possible for Wil to be as ignorant as his answer suggested; and he spoke severely to him and, as a rebuke, urged the church to accept the five of us as full members, leaving Wil until he matured in his knowledge and experience. This was passed unanimously.

But Wil cared nothing for what had taken place. After leaving the meeting, he laughed heartily and said that he didn't want to be a full member, and at the same time he said, "It's a good job that the old hand and the old pea-hen weren't in the *seiat*," referring to his parents. That evening I came to feel more than ever that there was something very deficient in Wil Bryan's character, and yet I loved him greatly. No sooner were we out of the chapel than he took hold of my arm, and said, "Let's go to the colliers' meeting." I didn't know that such a meeting was to take place, but somehow Wil knew about every gathering of people. As I didn't think there would be any harm in going, I went with him.

It was an open-air meeting. It was a beautiful summer's evening, and as we approached the place we heard a great noise and shouts of 'Hear! Hear!' and 'Hooray!', and we saw there were hundreds of people present. When we arrived at the place where the meeting was being held, I can't describe my surprise when I saw that my brother Bob was addressing the people. My heart leapt, and I believed that whatever he was saying was perfectly true; because at that time I didn't believe it was possible for Bob to make a mistake. Wil and I pressed forward, and Wil started shouting "Hear! Hear!" before he understood a word of what was being said. I'll never forget how my brother looked. He was standing on a high pile of stones, with several of the main 'cutters' of the Red Fields around him, and a great crowd below him. He held his hat in his left hand, and reached out with his right. His eyes were like two lamps shining under water, his lips were shaking, and his face as white as chalk, forming such an incongruity with his beard and hair as if a snowball had been placed in a pile of soot. I remember being amazed at how Bob's face was so white as he spoke, when preachers' faces were normally red as they preached. I knew from the look of him that every bone, sinew and muscle that he had were stirred to their utmost, and I thought what an able preacher Bob would have made if the *seiat* had not excommunicated him for his minor transgression. I had never heard him speak publicly before, and I wondered greatly about from where he found all the words that flowed from his lips. The crowd before him laughed, groaned and cried; they were entirely in his hand. I think I could now report that which I heard of what he said; but what use would that be? It would have been good for him if he had not said a word that night. His subject was the oppression and hardship that the miners were suffering because of the corruption of the officials, and their inability to understand the working of the Red Fields. He proved to the satisfaction of his hearers that the *Lancies*[10] had no idea how to run a Welsh coal mine, and that they were oppressing the miners and damaging the interests of the owners. When he stopped speaking, there were loud

---

[10] i.e. the sons of the palatine county of Lancashire.

cheers from the crowd; and I ran home to tell my mother all about it—what a champion speaker Bob was.

My mother sat in front of the fire, pleating her apron. As I entered the house, she looked contentedly at me, and congratulated me on how well I had come through my examination. I hurried to give my account of Bob—what a splendid speaker he was—and how people were shouting their agreement, and so on. Instead of being proud as she heard the story, as I had expected her to do, her expression changed and her face wore such sorrow as was wholly inexplicable to me.

"Well, well," she said with a deep groan, "the sweet is never received without the bitter. Something tells me that trouble will come of this. The day of trouble is close. Oh, for grace to refrain from saying anything foolish!" And my mother retreated into a solemn meditation, continuing to pleat her apron and gazing intently into the fire.

By now I felt sorry that I had told the story to her, even though I couldn't tell how it had brought such sadness upon her. I went to bed feeling low of spirit, and that mainly because I could not understand the cause of my mother's sadness. It was late at night when Bob came home; and although from the bed I couldn't make out anything, I heard heated words between him and my mother, and to the sound of their voices I fell asleep. How true were my mother's words. While there were intemperate and wasteful sinners sleeping quietly on their downy beds in prosperity and luxury, with a continent's width between the wolf and their doors, the 'trouble' that my mother had prophesied about was already prowling back and forth outside our cottage, ready to knock on our door; indeed, and it knew that there was in that cottage one, at least, who feared God more than many. God knows that she never spent six of her waking hours without sending a prayer to Him!

16

THE DAY OF TROUBLE

It is with sad memories that I write this chapter; and if it were possible for me to give a faithful account of my life without mentioning what is related within it, I would do that, but I cannot. Now in cold blood, and at a more mature age to form a judgement about things, it's possible that I don't hold the same ideas now, about the events I'm about to describe, as I did at the time when they took place.

The Red Fields was one of the main workplaces in the neighbourhood where I was brought up; and it employed—including the young boys—a few hundred people. All of the owners, if I remember rightly, were English. At one time, all of the 'underground matters' were under the supervision of a simple and honest Welshman of the name Abraham Jones, a deacon with the Independents.[1] He was a thoughtful man with good common sense and a strong influence over the men under his care. Whatever disagreement arose among the men, the only thing needed was for Abraham Jones to arbitrate, and straight away everything would be quiet again. The secret of his influence was his particular acuity in seeing where the blame lay, and the total trust that everyone had in his honesty and faith. He proved himself in every way a bosom friend of the workers, because he knew very well what it was to be a worker himself. With him it was a matter of conscience to keep his eyes open to the interests of the masters from whom he received his wages; but that did not prevent him from daily considering the happiness and safety of the men whom he saw sweating and toiling every day amidst great dangers. He was considered one of the most

---

[1] That is, The Congregationalists, theologically identical to the Calvinistic Methodists but with a different church government structure.

capable coalmen in the land; and during his tenure in the Red Fields, everything went on well and there was not one disturbance worth remarking upon.

He had one great disadvantage with respect to his superiors: his English was very imperfect; and in their eyes this caused his story to be less straight than he would wish, and this troubled him greatly. He had noticed lately that one or two of the directors would take delight in examining him in great detail about the works; and although he had nothing to fear from this, the difficulty he had in expressing himself often placed him, or so he felt, in a very difficult position. He had been so tormented by these ordeals that he felt neither disappointed nor grieved when he was told one day in a directors' meeting that he had better leave, as they had an Englishman who would be likely to do his job better, and also be able to give a better account of the situation in the works. With this word, Abraham Jones felt a great burden falling from his shoulders, and in his own halting way he said to them before leaving, his breast swelling as he spoke "Gentlemen, I am pleased to hear what you say. If the man you are speaking about is able to keep the Red Fields works going on as smoothly and quietly for the benefit of the masters and the workers for six months as I have done for six years, he is surely a clever man." Then he took his hat, bowed to them, and went out. It was often said afterwards that he believed he must have had help from on high to speak English so well when departing from his masters. When Abraham Jones went back to the works, and told the men of the news, there was no small amount of grief and dismay. Many of the colliers would have wanted to state their feelings in words that would not be tolerated in the presence of Abraham Jones, in language not entirely parliamentary. But in his presence, such words had to be swallowed once they had come into the mouth; and they were so great and salty that they brought tears to the eyes, which ran down the cheeks leaving clean white streaks on the blackened faces, to show how pure were the feelings that gave rise to them. It was suggested, and widely accepted among the workers, that it was not any lack of ability or faithfulness on Abraham Jones' part that had led the directors to ask him to leave, but rather that they wanted to find a place for a friend of theirs who was in need of a crust. Whether this was true or not, this belief led the workers to hate their new supervisor before they had even seen his face. Neither the appearance nor the acquaintance of Mr Strangle—for that was his name—did anything to lessen, but rather increased, their antipathy towards him. He was a middle-aged man, short, pot-bellied and loud; and he carried in his person all the roughness, brashness and ignorance of his Wigan heritage. His language was crass and unpolished; and even the uneducated miners smiled to hear him say 'Ah' for 'yes' and 'mun' for 'must'. But his language was just a minor deficiency compared with his insufferable self-importance and utter disregard for everyone around him. He was nicknamed 'Bulldog' on his first day in the works; and indeed, as I recall his short dimpled nose, and his wide chin, I think that if he were to have claimed a relationship to that sort of creature then few would have doubted him. His own claims, though, argued against it: to take him at his word, he knew everything about everything, and had never made a mistake. In short, Mr Strangle was a coal mine in and of himself—main coal, hollin,[2] byeman, cutter, shelterer, shaft, chimney, engine house, boiler and all, especially the latter. But Bob said, and of course I believed that everything he said was true, that Abraham Jones' flannel jacket could oversee the Red Fields works much more capably than Mr Strangle. It is certain that nothing competed with

[2] These words seem to refer to the individual coal seams within the mine. For example, a contemporary source describes the geology of the local area thus:

'The Strata of the coal fields in the different parts of this parish are nearly the same consisting of Freestone and Shale of a saponaceous quality with occasional beds of Ironstone, Sand and Gravel. The workable seams of coals are four. The upper seam is called the *Hollin coal* from six to seven feet thick containing some portion of sulphur and therefore less valued, the second seam is three feet thick and called the *Brassy coal*, the third seam is three feet thick and called the *Rough coal*, the lowest seam is ten feet thick and called the *Main coal*; this last is of a superior quality for House purposes and for Breweries Distilleries &c; it is generally sought for in the Dublin market.' Richard Willett, A Memoir of Hawarden Parish, Flintshire, 1822.

the workers' opposition to Mr Strangle except for his own hatred towards the Welsh, and the Welsh language. He delighted to show his contempt for it, and he did everything connected with the works exactly the opposite way from how Abraham Jones would have. The result was that he soon pulled the works down on his head, so to speak, and hundreds of pounds' worth of timber was needed to prop it up. To summarise, as it would take me a long time to tell the whole story, the situation was so unsatisfactory that it was daily feared by the tradesmen of the town, and the neighbourhood in general, that they'd hear of a strike in the Red Fields works.

Something like these were the circumstances when the meeting of the colliers, that I mentioned in the last chapter, was held and when Bob spoke so excellently, as I had thought. The next day, when my mother was speaking with her neighbour about the meeting, I came to understand why she was saddened so much by my account of Bob's addressing the crowd. She was afraid that my brother would get himself into trouble. She said it was worth suffering a great deal of hardship for the sake of peace. In contrast, the neighbour thought that it was high time someone spoke out— the wages were so low that that it wasn't possible to keep a family, but she had charged her husband not to say a word, or to make himself prominent in any way at all. And I remember my mother making a comment of the following general import:

"So, Margaret Peters, you're keen for our Bob and others to fight the battle, and for Humphrey your husband and everyone related to you to be like those Danites who waited in the ships,[3] coming in for a share of the spoils once the war was over. There are many Danites in our days, as Mr Davies,[4] Nercwys, was saying."

Margaret didn't know enough Scripture to understand the

[3] Judges 5:17.
[4] Probably a reference to John Davies, a Calvinistic Methodist minister from Nercwys, near Mold, 1834–1879.

comparison; but she understood perfectly well that it contained a shot aimed at her, and she turned the conversation to another subject.

How soon were my mother's fears realised! When Bob came back from work that evening, he looked pensive. Once he had washed and eaten, my mother said to him,

"Bob, I know from the look of you that you've had bad news; have you had your notice?"

"Yes," he said, "Morris Hughes, James Williams, John Powell and myself are to leave the works next Saturday."

"Well, well," said my mother, "what will we do now?"

"Do our duty, mother, and trust to Providence," said Bob.

"Yes, my boy; but do you think that you have done your duty? I have charged you many times, have I not, to take care and not take such a prominent role in the trouble? [I thought of my mother's remarks about Danites in ships.] I know very well that you workers have cause for complaint, and that it's a shame that some Englishman has come from far away to take the place of a godly man like Abraham Jones who never caused any trouble. But you're only young; and why didn't you leave it to someone like Edward Morgan to speak nonsense—a man who has his own house, and a cow and a pig? It wouldn't make much difference to Edward to have his notice. But I may as well be quiet—it's too late to close the stable door when the horse has bolted; but it's what will become of us that is the subject."

"Mam," said Bob zealously, "that's not how you brought me up. 'Do your duty and leave the consequences to the Almighty' was one of the first lessons you taught me; and I intend to hold to it while there is breath in me, not only because you taught it to me, but because I believe it is a good rule. This is nothing except what I expected. Someone has to suffer before any good comes to the multitude; and if I and some others are to become scapegoats for the three hundred who work at the Red Fields, and if we can be the means to bring about their freedom and well-being, then all to the good. I haven't said one word that isn't the truth, and that which everyone in the works believes and feels, but they're too cowardly to say so in public. As I said, someone must suffer on behalf of the multitude; that is the great principle of God's government. Either the comfort or the life of some creature is being sacrificed every day to keep other creatures alive. As Caiaphas said, 'It is necessary for one man to die for the people, so that the whole nation is not destroyed'. The principle of the sacrifice of the cross is being acted out on a small scale every day, and ..."

"Stop your nonsense," said my mother, in a bit of a temper, "I can't bear to hear you speak. Are you out of your mind, tell me? Are you comparing the death on the cross with having notice to leave work, or with anything on this earth? Are you trying to tell me that that's anything like the Saviour's sufferings? If you are, it's time for you to go to the asylum as soon as you like."

"Steady on, Mam," said Bob, "I don't need to tell you, who are so familiar with the book of Acts, that I'm not the first to be accused of being out of my mind for being a bit zealous.[5] To set your mind at rest on the subject, please understand that I don't imagine to compare anything with the sacrifice on the cross in terms of greatness and intention, but only in terms of principle. Even if there is not a comparison to be made between the finite and the infinite, there is an analogy, and I'm talking about the analogy."

"Watch it," said my mother, "don't go throwing your long words at me. Keep to Scripture, and I'll follow you where you like; but none of these long words. I'm sure that 'analogy' isn't a scriptural word, and as far as I remember it isn't in Mr Charles' *Instructor*.[6]"

"I know, Mam," said Bob, smiling, "that you haven't read Butler on Analogy[7]..."

---

[5] Acts 26:24.

[6] The Calivinistic Methodist catechism, published by Thomas Charles in 1807.

[7] Analogy of Religion, Natural and Revealed by Bishop Joseph Butler (1736).

"Butler?" said my mother before he could say any more, "What are you telling me about your butler? That pagan who never goes to any place of worship except the Church, and who doesn't know about anything except carrying wine to his master? What do you mean by 'reading the butler'?"

This was too much for Bob, and he laughed loudly, which caused my mother to blush a little; and Bob had to explain himself quickly…

"I don't mean the butler at the Manor house, but Bishop Butler, a good and godly man. This is what I was trying to say, if you had let me—that life, blessing and well-being depend on sacrifice. Before it was possible for sinners to have life, the Son of God had to sacrifice himself. ['Now you're talking sense', muttered my mother to herself.] Before it was possible for that life to be owned by men, it was necessary for the apostles and a host of the best men in the world to suffer a great deal, and even lay down their lives. And there's something similar to this going on with a view at our natural life, with this difference, that the lesser is sacrificed on behalf of the greater. The cow, the sheep and the pig, and a host of other creatures, lose their lives to sustain the lives of you and me. And so on in every circle of existence that we know about. The same principle may be found in society. In the fight to promote justice and chase away oppression, some of the brave men involved in the effort are sure to be trampled and harmed under the feet of the oppressors, even when they are in retreat. Some from the Red Fields must fight before the oppression can be got rid of; and if I and some of my comrades must fall while sounding the trumpet, then so be it. The call to battle has gone out, justice is on our side, and some, even if not we ourselves, will benefit from the spoils of the victory which is sure to follow. With a bit of wisdom and resolve, I don't doubt that there will be a different face on the Red Fields within a few months. The only thing I fear is that some of the men may use unlawful means. Some of them are wholly devoid of sense, and governed entirely by their unruly tempers.

These, unless they are led by someone wise, will do more harm to the cause than can be imagined. But perhaps they will behave better than I fear."

My mother either couldn't be bothered or simply couldn't answer Bob, and all she said was, "Pray more, my boy, and talk less."

The warning that my brother, and the other men I named, had received caused a great deal of talk in the works and in the neighbourhood, and the coming Saturday was viewed with excited apprehension. Some feared that there would be violence amongst the workers if the warning were carried out; while others thought that the warning was just a bluff to try to frighten the workers into submission, and that Mr Strangle wouldn't dare to turn away the soberest and most skilful workers that the Red Fields had, without bringing trouble on his own head.

Saturday came, and Wil Bryan and I, and several other boys went to stand on the gallery[8] ready for when the men came up, to see what would happen. At just the same time, two policemen came with the same aim. They were two Englishmen. In due course the workers started to come up from the pit a cage at a time. As they came out, they went to the office to receive their wages, But instead of going straight home after receiving the money as they usually did, they waited on the gallery in clusters here and there, sitting on their heels. Whether it was by accident or design I don't know, but Bob and his companions, who were under the warning, formed the final load; and when they made their appearance at the mouth of the pit, with their pickaxes bound together, all the men who were on the gallery rose to their feet like a horde of demons. But beneath the blackness of their faces and the ugliness of their clothing there was many a warm and honest heart, although there was a murmur to be heard in their midst. Bob and his companions

---

[8] The Welsh word, 'ponc', refers to the type of rocky ledge that is often a feature of quarries and open-cast mine workings.

went into the office, and their re-emergence was awaited with quiet anxiety. There was no need to wait long; and when they made their appearance they looked totally unconcerned, and picked up their pickaxes and laid them on their shoulders, which was a sure sign that the warning had been carried out. In a second Bob and his companions were surrounded by the workers, who asked across one another whether they had been paid off. Morris Hughes motioned to Bob to speak, and he said the following—and I testify most solemnly that he said not one word besides what I report here; I won't yield to any man over the accuracy of my account of what I heard with my own ears:

"My dear fellow-workers, I and my companions have been paid off. We are saying farewell to the Red Fields, and must turn our faces elsewhere to look for work."

Before he could say any more, some of the men started to curse and swear, and the two policemen intervened, urging them to go home quietly; but they were pushed aside without ceremony, and Bob was urged to go on. He added:

"We are leaving you with a quiet conscience that we did nothing wrong; and we are confident that no-one would condemn us for stating publicly our conviction that we have been treated unjustly. You must now fight for your own rights without our help; but wherever we are, your comfort and success will be close to our hearts. I am well aware that there are before me scores of men who are older, wiser and more experienced than I, but allow me to give you a word of advice. Be sure not to do anything that you might be ashamed of. Take your lead from the wisest among you; and while fighting for your rights, do that as men who have sense, and as those who know that they will have to give an account of all their actions. I think, and my companions also think, that the best thing for you to do will be to put your grievances before the directors. In Abraham Jones' time, if any one of us had a complaint, he need only lay it before him and he would give his careful consideration to it; but I fear that it would be futile, by now, for you to appeal to Mr Strangle, because…"

Unfortunately just as the name of Mr Strangle was on his lips, the man himself came out of the office and looked contemptuously at the crowd. No sooner did he make his appearance than scores of voices cried out like a pack of hunting dogs. They rushed at him furiously, and he was carried away along the road to the railway station like a straw before a hurricane. The two policemen, with remarkable courage, tried to save him and free him from the hands of the furious colliers, and likewise did Bob and others. But as soon as he was freed from the grasp of one swarm of men, another would seize hold of him. One of the policemen, no doubt believing sincerely that Bob was the chief of the attackers, pulled out his staff and struck him on the side of the head till he fell. It would have been better if he had not, because the next moment he and his companion were lying wounded at the side of the road while Mr Strangle was being driven before the furious crowd at a speed wholly unbecoming to a man as fat as he was. I thought Bob had been killed, as he looked fully dead on the roadside and no-one except Morris Hughes stayed back with me to attend to him. I can't describe my grief when I thought that he was dead, nor my joy when after a few minutes he came to himself and leapt up on his feet. "Morris," he said, "our efforts are all in vain; the idiots have ruined our cause; we need to stop this if it's not too late." The two ran after the crowd, with me following them. It was with difficulty that Bob marched on, because of the effect of the blows he had received, and when he held on to the arm of Morris Hughes, who was a strong and sturdy young man, I could see that his legs were buckling beneath him. As we approached the station, I could see that the crowd had doubled in size. "Thank goodness," said Bob, "that the train hasn't come in, and perhaps we can stop the fools from forcing Mr Strangle to go away," But as we were within three hundred yards of the station we heard the train arrive, and a huge cheer from the workers. "Too late!" said Morris Hughes, "if it makes any difference." "Any difference?" said Bob, "I should think it does. We'll lose all sympathy in the country, we'll be looked upon as savages, some of these idiots will be carried off to prison and punished for their folly. We have lost everything, and I'm sorry in my heart that I've had anything to do with this!" And he burst into tears like a child.

The engine whistled loud and strong,[9] and the air was filled with mindless cheering. Then the crowd rushed, wholly undisciplined, towards the town. When they came to the place where Morris Hughes, Bob and I were standing, they wanted on all accounts to bear him on their shoulders and hail him as their hero; but Morris' strong arm prevented them, and he told them, "My friend could not bear for you to do that; but if you choose to listen, perhaps he has something to say to you." As the crowd showed a willingness to listen, Bob climbed to the top of the embankment and, resting his hands on Morris Hughes' wide shoulders, said:

"Friends, from the beginning of the effort to raise our wages and have better order in the Red Fields, I have taken a prominent role and have done my best to improve your circumstances. You know as well as I do that two or three of us, if we wanted to suck up a bit, could have made ourselves very comfortable at the Red Fields; but you'd have been no better off. After what has just taken place, I must say to you honestly, even if I risk being treated as Mr Strangle has been, that I am ashamed to have anything at all to do with you."

Bob was overcome by his feelings and could say no more, and the crowd scattered, some cursing, others murmuring, and others quiet and pensive. It is fair to say that among the excited crowd that had escorted Mr Strangle to the station, bought a ticket for him and placed him safely on the train, there were scores of men who wholly disagreed with the action but were utterly unable to hold back the folly. Before my brother and I arrived home, my

---

[9] A line from a comic poem by John Ceiriog Hughes (1832-1887), who wrote some 600 comic songs under the pen-name 'Ceiriog' and a volume of satirical letters under the pen-name 'Sir Meurig Grynswth' ('all-encompassing Sir Meurig').

mother had been informed of the events, with exaggerations, and was waiting anxiously for us. In any case, her mind was put at rest to a great extent when Bob reassured her that he had done his best to save Mr Strangle from being sent away. At the same time, I could not avoid seeing the signs of fear and unease on the faces of both of them. Bob did not leave the house that evening, but he was visited by his three friends who were paid off alongside him; and they spent some hours trying to guess what would be the consequences of the day's idiocy. Although my mother said nothing, I could see in her face a presentiment of something worse to come. The friends went away, and after that little was said in our house that evening. Bob pretended to read; but I could see that he wasn't turning the pages of his book, and I knew that he wasn't thinking of anything within it.

It was late at night, and we were just about to go to bed, when we heard the sound of footsteps approaching the house. In a moment there was a knock on the door, and before anyone had time to open it two policemen walked in. My mother's face went pale, and I started to shout as loudly as I could; but Bob commanded me to be quiet, and with difficulty I was able to overcome my feelings. Bob, with perfect self-possession, urged the officers to sit down, which they did. Although I never liked either of them, I must admit that they were good men, and not happy about the work they had to do that night. I was glad that they were Welshmen, so that my mother could understand what they were saying.

"I think," said Bob quietly, "that I understand your errand."

"Well," said Sergeant Williams, looking at my mother, "it's a very unpalatable task as far as I'm concerned, Robert Lewis, I assure you; but I hope that all will be well by Monday, Mrs Lewis," he said as he handed the warrant to Bob to read, to spare my mother's feelings. "Don't be frightened, it's merely a matter of form; we must do our duty, you know that, and as I said, I hope that everything will be put right on Monday."

My mother said nothing, but the shaking around the corners

of her mouth and the twitch in her throat made the state of her feelings clear. Bob leisurely put his shoes on, and the last words he said were, "Mam, you know where to turn; my conscience is clear," and he walked away with the officers. He wasn't twenty yards from the house when I heard raised voices and a struggle, as I thought; and in spite of my mother I ran out, and saw a terrifying fight between the two officers and two strange men. One of them was a big strong man, and he beat the policemen mercilessly. The other was only of average build, but he was skilled at the task in hand. I had no difficulty in recognising the latter—he was the same man who had detained me on my way home the night that Seth died, whom I had named 'the Irishman' when I had first seen him. I didn't know who the big strong man was; but I thought that his gait and demeanour was similar to that of my brother, except that he was older and stronger. The aim of the two strangers, it seemed, was to give Bob a chance to escape; and when they saw that he was not taking advantage of the opportunity, but rather helping the officers, the two ran away. When I returned to the house and told my mother what I had seen, she got up and locked the door.

We did not go to bed that night; and no matter how much I tried to control my feelings for the sake of my mother, nor how much she tried to hide her distress for my sake, we were both overcome by a touch of weeping during the night. The morning dawned— a beautiful Sabbath morning. We saw the people going to their various chapels, and as they passed they looked over curiously towards our cottage. Neither my mother nor I stepped across the threshold, and I heard her whisper more than once, "The day of trouble!" We ate very little. The day seemed to last a week. My mother opened the big old Bible dozens of times; but as soon as she started to read, her eyes overflowed, and she would look for a long time in the same direction in sad meditation. We saw the people go home from the morning service, but no-one called in. We saw them again on their way to Sunday School, and on their way home, but no-one turned towards our house. We thought for sure that someone from the chapel would call in to see how we were after the evening service, but no-one came, or as my mother put it, "No-one darkened the door through the whole day." We were anxious for someone to call, as we did not know how many people had been taken to prison, and my mother was afraid that Bob was the only one. The clock struck nine, and my mother said she ought to go to bed and try to get some rest; but at that moment someone knocked on the door, and I went eagerly to open it, and I saw two of the elders…well no, I saw Thomas and Barbara Bartley, who had not for conscience' sake been able to go to bed without coming to see how my mother was doing in her trouble. It would scarcely have been possible for two people more dissimilar to my mother in terms of inclinations and personality to come to see her, and yet we were glad in our hearts to see them. We had opportunity to pour out the grief that had been welling up inside us for the past twenty-four hours. Thomas and Barbara had been in the Crown, and had heard all the details about the trouble. They stayed with us for many hours. Now, as I recall the conversation that took place between the three of them, I think it was one of the strangest and funniest things I ever heard, though it did not seem so at the time. And were it not for the fact that this chapter is already too long, and the things I am going to relate in the next chapter are pressing on my mind, I would chronicle it; but I will refrain. Their visit was a great relief to us, and my mother and I could sleep that night without much thought that even bitterer things awaited us.

17

MORE TROUBLE

I can hardly persuade myself that I am writing the facts of my own life, and not the creations of a wandering soul. It was Monday morning, and my mother had been sitting contemplatively in front of the fire for hours, pleating her apron. I easily obtained permission to go to town to see what would become of my brother, and the five others who were taken to prison. The streets of the town were half full with people keenly waiting for the court to open. Before I had been in town for many minutes, I was found by my companion Wil Bryan. He always managed to find me. I soon came to understand that a lot of interest was being taken in me, as the brother of one of the prisoners, indeed the most important of them by some accounts. I met some of Bob's friends, who asked how my mother was, and each one gave me a penny. Wil said to me, "Take care of those pennies—they'll be right handy very soon." I didn't understand him, and I was too worried to ask him to explain; but I always gave him credit for being able to see further than I. In due course, I came across some more of my brother's friends, and I had some more pennies, as many as five. I had never been so rich before. Wil had one penny of his own, and he urged that we should consolidate our assets. I transferred to him my five pennies, as I didn't care about them because I was so sad; and my faith in Wil's honesty knew no bounds. No sooner did he have the coins in his hand than he slipped into a shop selling pork pies; and I thought he was going to spend our fortune on those items, not that I had any objection to him doing that. When Wil came out of the shop, I was disappointed to see him showing me on the palm of his hand a shiny silver sixpence as change for the pennies; and giving me a knowing wink, he placed it carefully in his waistcoat pocket. I was still in the dark about what

Wil intended to do with the sixpence; and I'm not sure that I didn't think he meant to use it to hire an attorney to defend my brother. I knew little at that time about the reasonable charges made by that honest class of men.

I was entirely in Wil's hands, for him to do as he pleased with me and my property, when I saw a big disturbance that was caused by the arrival of the Squire driving quickly in his carriage towards the court. He was the main Justice of the Peace. Before my friend and I could reach the place, the wide building was tightly filled with hundreds of people like me failing to gain admittance. On each side of the door were two policemen—the incarnation of authority—stating emphatically that every inch of the building was already over-filled. But Wil said in my ear, "We're *bound* to be able to get in." I didn't see how he could hope for that. In a moment, the crowd began to slacken a bit, and Wil and I pushed towards the vicinity of the policeman's blue coat. We had almost arrived at the door. Wil had to pull more than once on the lapel before drawing the attention of its owner. Eventually, the policeman turned his head; Wil spoke a few words in his ear, the officer opened his eyes in surprise as though he had just heard amazing news—the two shook hands, and the next moment Wil and I had been allowed in, while hundreds of strong men were left outside. But I knew that our joint assets had changed hands. The Americans talk about the almighty dollar! Well, I could write a book about the miraculous power of the sixpence. Wil had discovered as early as this that sixpence was the password—the 'open sesame'—to everywhere. In the present circumstances, I felt that my friend had sunk our joint assets into an excellent cause; and if they had been six shillings I would not have complained.

I soon saw that the policeman spoke the truth about the building being over-full. But Wil had no great difficulty to get himself and me into a convenient position in the hall where we could see and hear everything. He pushed me forwards like a wedge to open up the crowd, and when that proved difficult he said to those who were in the way, while looking very important, "Robert Lewis' brother;

Robert Lewis' brother!" and with these words the people opened a path for us to go straight through, just as if we were going to give evidence in the case. There was no end to Wil's craftiness. I knew that Mr Strangle had returned a few hours after being sent away; and he was one of the first people I saw in the court; and he looked sullen and vengeful. On the bench sat Mr Brown the parson, and the Squire. As I have remarked before, Mr Brown was a generous and kind man; but the character of the Squire was entirely different. He was a big, ungainly, masterful and unforgiving man. He felt, one would think, that everyone and everything had been created just to serve him; and it was believed that if the law allowed it, he wouldn't hesitate to hang a man for killing a pheasant. It was as if the harshness of his cruel nature had been watered—or perhaps, wined—too frequently, and as a result had grown out through the skin of his face, which looked like a lump of raw American beef. His face was decorated with an enormous nose, which twitched continuously, and through which its owner, when agitated, would snort like a war-horse. No-one ever determined what qualifications the Squire had for being on the judicial bench besides being a brazen Tory, a zealous Churchman, a rich man, and the fact that he wore spurs at all times except when in his bed. Even Mr Brown confessed that he was terrified of him; and I noticed myself that when that kind and respectable man was talking with him in the street he looked apprehensively and watchfully at the spurs, as if he were afraid that their wearer would suddenly jump on his back and ride him to hell, where the wearer himself was going quickly, alas. He appeared that morning 'in his element', as Wil Bryan put it. Having a few poor miners before him was a tasty prey, since he believed that they were all poachers. Those who wished to know, knew very well that only three of the six prisoners who were before him had taken part in the attack on Mr Strangle. Morris Hughes, John Powell and my brother had tried to restrain the folly. But Mr Strangle and the two policemen testified that these three were the leaders of the outrage; and although neither the supervisor nor the policemen understood a word of Welsh, they stated under oath that Bob had stirred up the action, because, they said, they had heard him name Mr Strangle when he was rushed upon by the workers. The prisoners had no-one to defend them, and that because of the stubbornness of my brother. He wanted no-one to defend him, and his example was followed by the others. The Squire accepted the testimony of the officers eagerly; and nothing was too bad for him to believe about the accused.

After he had heard the testimonies, he asked as a formality whether the prisoners had any defence to make. Of course, three of them had nothing to say, as they were quite guilty of the crime with which they were charged; and neither Morris Hughes nor John Powell was a very able speaker - especially in English. After a second or two of silence, Bob said that he wished to answer for himself—that he was entirely innocent of taking part in the assault on Mr Strangle, and not only that, but he had done his best to defend him, and that that was what he was doing when he was struck by the policeman. At this, the Squire smiled mockingly, and said,

"Do you expect the bench to believe such a thing as that after all the testimony that has been heard?"

"I hardly expect the bench to believe anything I say," said Bob, "because I am telling the truth; and if there were any point, I could call many eye-witnesses to state that I am telling the truth."

"Many that were committing the same crime as you, no doubt," sneered the Squire. "If we listened to you, you did nothing wrong at all; you never spoke an untruth. But we happen to know something of your story before today. We do, indeed. Sure, you want the masters to become workers and the workers to become masters. But wait a minute! We'll see soon enough how it pays to make speeches. We have heard about you before; and we know your family, young man, before today."

"My family have nothing to do with the accusation that is made against me today," said Bob.

"We say that it has everything to do with it," said the Judge.

"If so, you'd better fetch my mother here," said Bob.

"No," said the Judge, "You are quite enough; there's no need for these old women."

"For all I know," said Bob mockingly, "you need another one on the bench."

"None of your impertinence, young man, or you'll be made to pay for it," said the Squire furiously.

My mother had often counselled Bob to learn to hold his tongue; but the task was too hard for him; and the reason he gave for his inability was that it was a fault that ran in the family.

After the Squire had spoken a few words secretly with Mr Brown, who had a look of fearful obedience in his eyes, he said:

"The bench sees no need for remand; the testimonies are regarded as sufficient. The bench regrets that no more of the villains have been brought before it to receive what they deserve; but the bench is determined to make an example of those who have been brought before it. The bench is determined to show that the master is meant to be master, and the workers are meant to be workers. And the bench wishes to show the colliers that they are not to take the law into their own hands, and that suitable men have been put in place to administer the law. And the bench is determined to show that the law is stronger than the colliers, however many of them there be. And therefore the bench sentences five of you, namely Morris Hughes, John Powell, Simon Edwards, Griffith Roberts and John Peters, to one month of prison with hard labour, and Robert Lewis to two months of prison with hard labour, because the bench believes that he was the chief agitator. And the bench is confident that this will be a warning, not only to the prisoners but to others who ought to be in the same position as them, who are just as guilty, not only of creating disorder and breaking the law in this fashion, but even of poaching on the estates of gentlemen."

As soon as the sentence had been delivered, everyone in the court started to weave through each other like bees, and the sound of people going out, and talking, was so loud that I could hardly hear myself cry, which I did with gusto. Wil sympathised with me greatly, and did his best to comfort me. So deep was my distress that for a minute my friend could not find any way to assuage it. The next minute, he was struck by a sudden thought, and he offered to me his only possession, namely, his pocket knife; and he said with emphasis that he was giving it to me *forever*. I have the knife to this day; and although it isn't worth sixpence, I list it with the widow's mite,[1] and value it as the sacrifice of a heart that was full of unfeigned sympathy, and I would not part with it for anything. The level of interest in the prisoners was clear from the size of the crowd that by this time was outside the court, which was reluctant to leave until it had caught the last sight of them being taken to the county jail. I can confirm that the great majority of the workers in the Red Fields were sober, industrious and moral men; but in their midst, like in any large workplace, there were numerous men of worthless character, with a tendency to drink too much; and the pity is that the better class are often besmirched because of them. That morning the worthless men I mentioned had been crawling around the pubs, and were the worse in their tempers for that reason. But I see I am descending into unnecessary detail, which I promised myself I wouldn't do. The account of how some of the colliers fiercely attacked the police as they were doing their duty in taking my brother and his companions to the prison—how those offenders were arrested, tried, and found guilty—how the soldiers were called out, and themselves attacked and wounded—and how the soldiers, under sharp provocation, opened fire on their attackers, killing several of them, and so on—does not belong here, as it has nothing to do with my own story.[2] I can say this much: when the disturbance was at its height, the opinion of the majority, and in their midst some men of enlightened judgement, was in favour of the colliers; but when things had settled down, and there had been opportunity to view the circumstances dispassionately, the same people were forced to acknowledge the folly and immorality of the whole thing, and were forced too to feel the horror of what frightening extremes even sensible and religious people could be driven to when ruled by their tempers, and not by reason and grace.

I remember that I was afraid to go home because of the distress I thought my mother would be in because of the shame that had been brought upon us; because I knew that someone had already told her about what had happened to my brother. I feared it would be the death of her. But in this I was pleasantly surprised, and I am glad to remember that day as a proof of what true faith can afford to its holder in the day of trouble. As I was going towards the house, I met with two neighbours who were coming out after comforting my mother. I could see on my mother's cheeks the evidence of much weeping; but I was amazed to see her so comforted. The smile on her face was like a rainbow in the clouds after heavy rain, showing me clearly that God had not forgotten His covenant with her. I think I can remember precisely what she said to me that afternoon. Among other things, she said,

"Well, my boy, it gets worse and worse for us. But something tells me that it will get light soon. The darker the night, the nearer the dawn; and the tighter the cord, the sooner it breaks. The Lord, I believe, has a hand in this. The furnace must be made seven times hotter before the Fourth[3] appears. I didn't expect things to fall so heavily on your brother; but I don't think any less of him for it. I know that he is innocent, because he has never told me a lie, and there are men a hundred times worse than him walking free. Since he was a child he has been too ready with his tongue, and all the trouble I had with him was when he said too much of the truth. He was a bit too set in his mind, and that's the reason he left the *seiat*. But he lived better than many of us who profess. Who knows whether the Lord's purpose through all this is to draw him back, and to show him that he has lost the shadow and protection?"

I've always noticed since then that my mother, whenever her boy was overtaken by shame, just as when he was overtaken by death,

---

[1] Mark 12:42.

[2] The events described here reflected actual events in the Mold Riots of 1869. See the appendix at the back of this book for an account of this event.

[3] Daniel 3:25.

forgot all his faults, and delighted to bring his virtues to light.

"I find it hard to believe," added my mother, "that Bob is not a Christian. If he is not in the house, he belongs to the family, I'm sure, and perhaps from the distant land of the prison he will start to long for his Father's house.[4] How did he look, say? Did he look calm? And was he? It's amazing how he is able to take everything so quietly. I know what lies heaviest on his mind—and that is, what will become of the two of us—how we will get a bite to eat, because there was never a boy fonder of his mother than my silly boy!"

At this point my mother burst into tears, and I helped her in the work. After she had calmed down, she said.

"Do they have a Bible in jail, say? They do! I'm glad to hear it; but in any case Bob knows enough of the Bible to chew the cud over it for two months at least. What vexes me most is that I haven't seen him. It seemed cold for me not to go to the hall, but somehow I couldn't do it for the life of me. Do you think he'd get a letter if I wrote him one? You do? Well, I won't sleep tonight until I've sent a word to him. I'm glad that you're a bit of a scholar, because there's no need for everyone to know our business!"

Then I had to buckle down and write the letter. At my mother's insistence I wrote it down first on a blank page of my copy book "in case," she said, "we'll want to alter it." That copy is still in my possession, and perhaps I can do no better than finish this chapter by transcribing it. There's nothing special in its content; but what makes it valuable for me is the evidence in it of my mother's knowledge of the Bible. It is precious for me to remember that, as she was dictating the letter to me, that she didn't consult with the Word so much as once, even though each time she mentioned it she gave chapter and verse. I record it here in full as she dictated it, apart from a few corrections in her dialect where otherwise the meaning would be unclear.

"Dear Boy, I am writing these lines to you hoping that you are

---

[2] Luke 15:17.

healthy, as we are. I am feeling very mixed up and what d'you call it, and I know that you are the same. My complaint today is bitter— Job, Chapter Twenty-three, verse two. But who can speak and have it happen, if the Lord has not decreed it—Lamentations, Chapter Three, verse thirty-seven. I know very well that your mind will be troubled about us, as ours is about you; but I hope that you know where to turn, as you said that I would when you left the house on Saturday night. Call on me in the day of trouble, and I will save you, and you will glorify me—the fiftieth Psalm, verse fifteen. If I am not deceiving myself, I have had that promise fulfilled today. Dear boy, I am cruelly afraid that you will be downhearted and lose your health, because you have been put in jail unjustly. Perhaps it will be of some succour to you to remember those the scriptures mention who were put into prison unjustly like you, and whom the Lord showed afterwards that they did not deserve to be there. If you have opportunity, turn to the following places—Genesis, Chapter Thirty-nine; the fifth chapter of Acts, and the eighth, and the sixteenth. Remember as well that He was taken from prison and from judgement. Isaiah, Chapter Fifty-three, the eighth verse. You know the trouble I went through with your father: but today's trouble is quite different. I'm fairly sure that even if you made some mistakes you are quite honest, and that your conscience is quiet just as you said: and if this gives you something to think about, even though you're in jail, you are no worse in the sight of your mother, and I hope that you are no worse in the sight of your Redeemer either. At the same time, I hope very much that you will come to see now that you have angered the Lord of the house by leaving the *seiat*; and although I believe that you have never been a stranger to the great things of the Gospel, I am confident that I will see you, when things have settled down, turning your face towards the shelter. Dear boy, the wind is strong and the waves are rising; but if we come through this to call upon the Master to save us, all will be well. Read the eighth of Luke, and the eighth of Romans. If Morris Hughes and yourself can be together, it will do no harm at all if you sing a tune from time to time, like Paul and Silas did long ago, and I don't know of any better verse for you than one by Ann Griffiths,

> 'It's a great wonder to be still alive
> In such hot furnaces'.[5]

You know how it finishes, and who knows what blessing you'll receive from singing about the Man with the thresher in his hand. Will God make it thus? There's a parcel of things I'd like to say to you; but I must bring this to an end. Keep your spirit up; two months is not long, it will come to an end soon. Pray day and night; and if they stop you from reading, no-one can stop you from praying. In your mind you were enough of a boy before, except for one thing; but something tells me that you'll be a much better man after this trouble. We remember ourselves to you very keenly. This, in short, from your dear mother and brother,

MARY AND RHYS LEWIS."

After I had rewritten it and read it back many times to my mother, I placed it carefully in an envelope, and addressed it; but my mother insisted on writing 'haste' on the corner; and because she didn't have much faith in gum, she insisted also on adding red wax and placing the imprint of her thimble upon it. When all was finished, she looked calm and submissive before the order of Providence. How the incarceration of my brother affected our circumstances, and defined a period in my own story, will be the subject of the next chapter.

---

[5] The verse in question goes:

'Mae bod yn fyw yn fawr rhyfeddod,
Mewn ffwrneisiau sydd mor boeth,
Ond mwy rhyfedd, wedi 'mhrofi,
Y dof i'r canol fel aur coeth:
Amser canu, diwrnod nithio,
Eto'n dawel heb ddim braw,
Y Gŵr a fydd i mi'n ymguddfa,
Sydd â'r wyntyll yn ei law'.

'It's a great wonder to be still alive
In such hot furnaces.
But still more wonderful is that, being tested
I will emerge as refined gold:
A time of singing, a day of winnowing
But yet quiet, without fear,
The Man who will be my hiding place
Appears with his flail in his hand'.

18

THOMAS AND BARBARA BARTLEY

As I look back on my boyhood, I feel that it went past without me enjoying much of that careless exuberance that belongs to almost every boy, no matter what his circumstances. Even when I wasn't aware of need and trouble in my home, the puritanical precision of my mother placed boundaries on my play, numbers on my companions, and a measure on my fun. Some sort of knowledge about the 'fall of man', the 'two covenants', and such things, was drummed into my head when I should have been playing marbles. While my contemporaries were playing 'catch the fox', I was kept at home to learn parts of the great Psalm; and it's no wonder that I was a worse sportsman than anyone when I was in Robin the Soldier's school, and that even the girls would laugh at me. I wouldn't on any account want to say a disrespectful word about my mother, as I believe that her aims were as pure as a ray of light. But I fear that in her ignorance she caused my physical weakness, the sadness and depression that I am so prone to, which by now is like an illness. Before I could rejoice in the innocence of boyhood I had been well taught about the inheritance left to me by my father Adam, the ins and outs of my defiled heart, and the old gentleman who roams about like a roaring lion.[1] In a word, the dark side of human nature had been portrayed to me as being as ugly as the gifts of my mother could make it. The teaching had its effect on me; and by now I don't wonder that my companions at the time nicknamed me 'the old man'.

I was thirteen years old when my brother was imprisoned; but it wasn't as a boy of that age that I experienced the disgrace and

---

[1] 1 Peter 5:8.

grief of the circumstances. It wasn't the bitterness of a day and a night, to be healed the following day by the amusement of my playful companions. My spirit was filled with sadness, and a worm grew in my heart that even my faithful friend Wil Bryan could not slay. I can't easily describe my state of mind. It was a mixture of pure sympathy for my brother in his tribulation, a deep conviction of his innocence, and an increasing admiration for his character. I must confess that there was also wounded pride, a spirit of revenge, and a tendency to quarrel with the ordering of Providence. I know very well that I wasn't in an appropriate frame of mind, because when I heard the day after my brother and his companions had been taken away to prison that there had been terrible destruction among the Squire's game, I was very satisfied, though I wouldn't have dared say so to my mother. There was a palpable emptiness in our cottage because of my brother's absence, almost as painful as that which gave rise to it. Without him the home was like a body without the soul, and the lack of life within it was as obvious as the strange feeling one gets when one has been in a mill for some hours and the wheels suddenly stop. I felt the loss of his manly appearance, his sonorous voice, and his inexhaustible wit; and home was no longer a home. Although she didn't say so, I knew that my mother felt the same way. In the space of a day, the colour and form of her face changed. The last remnants of the blush of youth went away—never to return; and beneath her blue eyes trouble wrote its name in big black letters. Many times in the one day she went to the door, each time looking in the same direction, as though she were hoping against hope to see her boy returning. So deep was her conviction of his innocence, and the injustice of his imprisonment, I'm not sure that she wasn't expecting some supernatural intervention to free him. I don't know whether it was the force of habit, or something else, that caused her to prepare a meal for the three of us; but I saw her more than once, for example at teatime, putting three cups on the table, and then realising her mistake taking one away secretly, thinking that I hadn't noticed.

I could remark on many other small things that she did, which showed the daydreaming state of her mind. By now everything that was my brother's particular property had to pay tribute for his absence. She dusted his English books, against which she had previously had a strong prejudice; and she frequently turned their pages even though she couldn't understand a word of them. I think that at the time I was perfectly conscious of the state of her feelings, though I couldn't have put them into words. It wasn't a shallow disturbance, but a grief that delved into the inward parts of the soul, carrying with it all the painful connotations of that which caused it. It wasn't a hopeless sadness either, but one which seemed to span the distance between the depths of tribulation and a stable faith in the One who governs everything. She read much of her Bible and spoke comfortingly; but I knew that it cost her an enormous effort.

Just like the day before, Thomas and Barbara Bartley were the first to come to visit us, and we felt very grateful for their kindness. As I remarked before, they were two simple, innocent old people. They always appeared to me remarkably happy. Apart from the fact they were a well-matched husband and wife, there was a twin-like similarity of countenance and mind. Whatever Thomas said, Barbara would confirm with a nod of the head; and whatever Barbara said, Thomas would seal with a 'to be sure'. Their world was small, and so was their knowledge. Planting a peck of potatoes, and killing a two hundred-pound pig, were the two poles on which their world turned from year to year. It was as if Providence, when preparing the programmes for people's lives, had forgotten to put down any trouble alongside the names of Thomas and Barbara Bartley, with the exception of the death of their son Seth; and that looked like a mistake, which turned out in the end to perfect their happiness. Thomas was renowned as a mender of shoes, and was never short of work. He was also considered an outstanding neighbour. He was not a teetotaller, but he would never get drunk except on special occasions, such as the Monday after Whitsun when his club would walk together. But even then, Barbara would never admit that Thomas had got drunk, just that he'd 'had a drop'. They both believed that they had good hearts, and that living honestly was enough religion for anyone. No doubt they lived up to their profession; because Thomas and Barbara had never been known to harm anyone, nor had Thomas ever done dishonest work upon a shoe. What they possessed was not just legalistic and cold honesty, either. No-one was more ready to do acts of kindness, for which, it seems, they took credit as 'works of supererogation'. In passing, I must say that during my short life I have met many people of higher and more spiritual persuasions who would have done well to imitate the religion of Thomas and Barbara. Even so, this is what I was about to say—the two of them came to visit us in our tribulation, and we had a long conversation—too long for me to recite. The following few words will have to serve as an example of the whole. After they had sat down, Thomas said:

"Well, Mary Lewis, you are in a bit of trouble, aren't you? And I'm sorry for you in my heart." Barbara gave a nod, the meaning of which was 'ditto'.

"I am that, dear Thomas," said my mother, "and I'm very grateful for your sympathy. 'His way is in the sea, and His path is in the great waters'.[2] 'Clouds and darkness are round about Him'.[3] But He knows…"

"Steady on, steady on, dear Mary," said Thomas, "you're confused now. Isn't it to jail that Bob has gone? He hasn't gone near the sea at all—he hasn't been transported. You're here with your head in the dust, and thinkin' things are worse than they are. Dash it all! The boy hasn't been anywhere near the sea."

"I know that very well, Thomas; I was talking of the government of the Good Lord over the world and its circumstances," said my mother.

"Ho! You can say that, Mary," said Thomas. "Neither Barbara nor I can read, so we don't know much at all about the Good Lord; and to tell you the truth, we never mention him except by chance when someone has died or been killed, in case we make a mistake, you know." Barbara nodded her head to signify that her husband spoke the truth.

"I'm sorry to hear that, Thomas," said my mother, "we should all think and say much about the Good Lord, since it is in Him that we live, move and have our being.[4] This is what the Psalmist said, Thomas, 'My meditation on Him shall be sweet'.[5] And in another place, 'Evening and morning will I pray, and cry aloud; and He shall hear my voice'.[6] And if we were more like the Psalmist we'd be closer to being in our place, dear Thomas."

"Well in truth, Mary, Barbara and I try to live as close to our place as we can, don't we Barbara?" Barbara gave a nod of confirmation.

"I know that you are, as far as living honestly and unremarkably goes," said my mother. "But religion teaches us that we need something more than that before we can enter into Life, dear Thomas."

"Well, what can we do, Mary, besides livin' honestly? I've got a good heart, on my oath, and I'd rather do a kindness than not, if it is in my power—don't I Barbara? (Nod.) And I never stay angry with anyone, do I Barbara? (Nod.) And as for religion, I see you religious types being worse off than anyone. Here you are, Mary, you've been professin' for as long as I can remember, and always talkin' about religion, and the Good Lord, and the world to come and such things; and who has had more trouble than you? Anyone would think you had enough trouble with your husband—and now here you are again in trouble over your head. And there's Bob—one of the finest boys who ever wore a Blucher[7]—whenever he came to our place to get his shoes mended he was always talkin' about religion—and there he is today worse off than anyone.

---

[2] Psalm 77:19. [3] Psalm 97:2. [4] Acts 17:28. [5] Psalm 104:34. [6] Psalm 55:17.

[7] The technical term for a particular type of men's shoe, where the tongue under the laces is an integral part with the shoe upper and the lace-panels either side are sewn on separately; as opposed to the Oxford style, where the lace-panels are an integral part of the shoe upper and the tongue is separately sewn underneath.

I said to Bob—if that's what religion is—that I don't understand the Good Lord at all. I see you always in trouble and with your head under your wings."

"Religion doesn't promise to keep anyone from trouble, Thomas," said my mother, "and for all I know there's some truth in what you say—that religious people have more trouble than other people. 'You, who have shown me great and severe troubles',[8] as the Psalmist said. 'In the world you will have tribulation',[9] as the Saviour said. And Paul, in Acts, says, 'We must through many tribulations enter the kingdom of God'.[10] The great subject for you and me, Thomas, is for the oppressions to sanctify us, and for us to be able to recognise the hand of the Lord in all of them, and not let our spirits fall into excessive sadness."

"They tell me, Mary," said Thomas, "that there's nothin' better to raise spirits than—what do they call it—the thing they sell in the druggist shop—what's its name, Barbara?"

"Asipheta",[11] said Barbara.

"To be sure," said Thomas, "if you had a penn'orth of asipheta, a penn'orth of jaundice drops and a penn'orth of rhubarb tincture, there's nothin' better to raise the spirits, they say, Mary. I've never tried it myself—I had a drop to drink durin' the trouble with Seth, and it did me a great deal of good—I could cry much better, and I wouldn't be surprised if it helped you, Mary. Barbara wanted to bring a drop in her pocket for you; but I told her that you wouldn't take it—you religious people are so odd about things like that."

"I hope, Thomas," said my mother, "that by now I know a better recipe for raising my spirits than anything which is sold in the druggist or the tavern. In my mind, Thomas, there's nothing except the balm of Gilead, and the ointment of Calvary that can lift an oppressed spirit."

"Quite sure, but I hope it's not too expensive—the same thing doesn't cure everyone—I always say that, Barbara knows," said Thomas.

"You don't understand me, Thomas," said my mother, "what

I mean is this—the only thing that can lift an oppressed spirit is the sweet and precious promises of the Bible—a knowledge of God in Christ reconciling the world to himself, not imputing their trespasses to them [12]—and a resting of the soul upon the costly death on Calvary's hill. And I would have been very glad if Seth's death had led you and Barbara to come under the sound of the Gospel, and to seek comfort in its truths, and not to try to drown your sorrows with worthless alcoholic drinks, dear Thomas."

"You know what, Mary?" said Thomas, "if you happened to belong to the Ranters, you'd make a champion preacher. But I don't agree with you about the drink. I know that you know more than I do, Mary; but doesn't the Bible call it 'strong drink'?"

"Yes indeed, Thomas," said my mother.

"That's what James Pulford said; and the Bible wouldn't call it strong drink it if didn't strengthen a man," said Thomas.

"It's strong enough to throw you down, Thomas, if you're not very careful," said my mother, and added—"seriously, dear Thomas, haven't you and Barbara begun to think about the matter of your souls? You're beginning to get old; don't you ever feel the urge to come under the sound of the Gospel? Don't you think it's time the two of you asked about the Friend that you and I will need very soon now, or else be in misery for ever? I'm being bold with you, but you know I have your own good in view. My kind old neighbours! I think about you a lot, and try to pray for you. The Good Lord has been so good to you! You have been so healthy, so happy, and so wealthy over the years! Wouldn't it be a great pity, dear Thomas, for the two of you to lose out in the end? You would like, I know, to see Seth again, and be with him forever. Well, there's no doubt in my mind that Seth is in heaven: 'Though

---

[8] Psalm 71:20. [9] John 16:33. [10] Acts 14:22.

[11] A herb, Ferula assafoetida, related to fennel and widely used in Wales, until at least the 1950s as a cure for all sorts of ailments, but apparently largely unknown in England.

[12] 2 Cor. 5:19. [13] Isa. 35:8.

fools, they shall not go astray'.[13] You remember what he said to this boy when he was dying—that he was going far, far away to Jesus Christ's big chapel? And you can be sure that he went there. But Seth came to chapel, Thomas—he never missed a service, the dear silly boy! And though we never took any notice of him, and thought that he didn't understand anything, Seth was making his fortune; he found the precious pearl that was worth his life to him. There are more pearls, Thomas, in the same field; and you, my dear neighbours, must come to the means of grace, or I fear that you'll never be in the same place as Seth."

These last words of my mother's had an effect like electricity on Thomas and Barbara. Thomas looked at the fireplace in shock, big tears rolling down his cheeks and landing on his shiny cord trousers. Barbara rubbed her nose and her eyes with her checked apron, and she could barely stop herself from crying out when my mother mentioned Seth dying. My mother could see that the iron was hot, and she started seriously to use the old great hammer of Scripture with the skill that she possessed so fully. And for me to continue the metaphor, she turned their hearts around every way on her anvil; and it seemed to me that there was no part of them that my mother didn't hammer the living sparks out of. I'm not just saying this because she was my mother; and I'm not exaggerating to say that I never saw her, if she saw an opportunity to give a word of counsel or a Bible verse to those she feared were without religion, to let it pass. Just as in this circumstance, she forgot her own troubles in her keenness to say some word which was likely to stick in the conscience of someone that she thought 'careless about the matter of their soul', as she would say. As I consider how negligent I am myself in this respect, I am ashamed to remember that I am my mother's son.

I had been able to see for some time that Thomas was very uncomfortable, and keen to leave, and my mother took the hint. When she had finished evangelising, Thomas let out a heavy sigh, and rose nervously to his feet, and said, half choking,

"Barbara, we need to go home, look you. What have you got in the basket there?" Barbara took a big slab of bacon out of the basket, and offered it to my mother.

"Champion stuff, Mary," said Thomas, "it was fed on potatoes and barley flour—it never had any brewery dregs.[14] Don't mention it! Don't mention it! You're heartily welcome to it. Do you have potatoes? If you send Rhys over to us tomorrow, I'll give you some of the best pink eyes you've ever tasted—they're like fine flour."

"Dear Thomas," said my mother, holding the lapel of his coat, "you are always wonderfully kind; but will you be kind to your soul? Will you promise to come to chapel next Sunday? You'll never regret it."

Thomas looked at the floor; and after a second or two of silence, he said, "Mary, if the preachers spoke as plainly as you do, I'd come to chapel every Sunday; but to tell you the truth, I don't understand 'em—they talk about things I don't know anythin' about."

"Will you promise, dear Thomas, to come with Barbara to chapel? The light won't come on unless you come," said my mother, holding his lapel still tighter.

"What do you say, Barbara?" asked Thomas. Barbara gave a nod of approbation, and Thomas said, "Well, for sure we'll come. Good night, and God be with you."

After they had gone away, did my mother turn to the piece of bacon and praise it? I hardly think so! She'd had a more tasty feast, and she said joyfully, "I see it, Rhys! I see it now! Bob has been sent to jail to save Thomas and Barbara Bartley! 'His way is in the sea…' "

Well, it wasn't about Thomas and Barbara that I'd intended to write when I started this chapter, and I see that a man does not choose his own way in this, any more than in other things.

---

[14] Apparently a common animal feed to this day, with a vigorous international commodity trade.

19

ABEL HUGHES

Anyone who has paid any notice to men and their habits will have noticed, among others, the following three categories. Firstly: those who were once almost completely under the dominion of the devil and their own base instincts, but through some good fortune came under the divine influence of the Gospel and received mercy—'Old things have passed away; behold, all things have become new'.[1] Their tempers are subdued, their hearts are transformed, and their whole lives, if not their experience, are such as to say daily about the evil one, 'he has no part in me'. What heavenly beauty characterises this class of my fellow men! Secondly: those about whom there is no doubt that religion has had something to do with their hearts, nor that they have had something to do with religion, but there are obvious signs that their old master also has something to do with them. On particular occasions the cloven hoof comes into view. It looks as though both heaven and hell claim them. Yet, listening to them pray, or telling of their experience, it's as though the jury, if trying them for their life, would give them the benefit of the doubt. The important thing for them, and for me, to remember is that there will be no doubt about our characters on the great day which is to come. And here is the third class: those who don't have anything to do with formal religion in any way, and yet who exhibit in their lives many of its virtues. They are honest, guileless, without malice, and giving, kind to man and beast, and more ready to do hurt to themselves than to anyone else. As a general rule this class is not particularly intellectual, and appear to look at everything through their hearts. Their innocence is like a remnant of the cloth that our first parents were cut from. As I said, they are not religious in the theological sense of the word, and yet much of what is considered its fruit grows in them. They have not wounded their consciences with wanton acts, nor read and thought enough to create doubt and discomfort, and therefore they are relatively happy. To me there is a great beauty in this class of person; and on occasions I am envious of their situation.

To this last class belonged Thomas and Barbara Bartley; and perhaps it was their kindness to my mother and me, when we were in trouble, that caused me in subsequent times to view those similar to them with a particular degree of interest and admiration. When our family was in the trouble I have already described, I remember being very surprised at the indifference of the officers of the church where my mother was a not insignificant member, in contrast with the ready kindness and sympathy of Thomas and Barbara Bartley. And I couldn't help saying this to my mother. But she did not want me to develop a low opinion of the church elders; and in line with her normal style of speaking, she said,

"This is part of Providence, my boy. There's some reason that the brethren are behaving a bit distant towards us. Perhaps the Governor is keeping the best wine until the end.[2] If we are worthy objects of succour, the Head of the church will see to us in His own good time."

I didn't need to wait long to see that my mother was pretty close to the mark, because early the next day we were visited by the venerable old elder, Abel Hughes. I have had occasion more than once in this story to make mention of him. If it were his biography I was writing, rather than my own, I would have many interesting things to say about him. I flatter myself that I have followed the times reasonably well, considering my disadvantages. Yet somehow, old ideas that I formed when a boy have stuck with me in spite of everything. I would be ashamed to state them, but for the life of me I can't erase them from my mind. If some young man from an English town were to ask my opinion about this or that, I could state them freely

---

[1] 2 Cor. 5:17. [2] John 2:9–10.

and honestly; but underneath I know that there would arise in me very different ideas, which were formed long ago, which there is no way in the world for me to get rid of. One of these is my idea of an elder. Is not Theophilus Watkin, Esq., from the Upper Manor, the man who because of his unmatched ability to deal with the world made his fortune in a short time, who lives and dresses in accordance with his honourable status, who keeps a liveried servant—who takes his wife and daughters in full dress to all the main concerts—is he not a credit to the Great Seat of the Methodist chapel in Highways?[3] Is he not generous towards the cause, kind towards the poor in the church, hospitable and respectful towards ministers of the Word? It's true that he's never at the monthly meeting, and he's absent for most of Sunday School; but we must remember his status, and the circles in which he moves. He is zealous about the pastorate, and very humble and self-denying in church meetings, allowing the minister to do all the talking. But isn't he a worthy elder, and a great gain for the cause? No doubt he is, and I feel glad for him. There's Alexander Phillips (*Eos Prydain*[4]), the young man who sweetly sings, capably looks after the church's books, is always ready to arrange a concert, and is always well turned out—isn't he an excellent fellow? He's a bit quiet in the *seiat*; but it would be almost impossible for the brethren to organise a tea party, let alone a competitive meeting, without his valuable service. He's genial and merry, and enjoys a joke; but his behaviour is never unbecoming. All things considered, he is very useful for the cause; and he is considered by the congregation, and by myself, a good elder. Yet there is an old-fashioned idea that whispers to me that men such as those I have named do not measure up to the name of 'elder'. The pattern that this old idea holds before my mind is Abel Hughes.

This is the sort of man he was: a man of some age, tall and thin, wearing knee breeches, a dark-coloured coat and waistcoat, a black scarf wrapped many times around his neck, a wide-rimmed beaver hat, a low fringe, a carefully shaved beard apart from about half an inch of sideburn, his hair cut parallel to his heavy eyebrows, which looked down onto his serious face. That's one side of the pattern. Here's the other: a man mighty in the scriptures, thoroughly learned in and zealous for evangelical doctrine, faithful to the Monthly Meeting and the Sessions, ceaseless in attending the means of grace, fluent and original in his comments, fresh and spirited when on his knees, whether in the prayer meeting or opening a meeting on behalf of the preacher; diligent in exercising church discipline, with some tendency to be ill-tempered but yet possessing a tender and godly heart; his life blameless, opposed to any sort of vanity and flippancy, expecting everyone belonging to the church, even the children, to be serious. Such a man was Abel Hughes, and he formed within me my earliest notion of an elder, which remains in the depths of my consciousness no matter how erroneous it may be. My common sense leads me to believe that the ideal pattern for an elder lies somewhere between Abel Hughes and those various bearers of the title today who are nothing other than lodging-house keepers for the preacher and clerks for the church. Abel was seen by my mother as a man almost without fault, and I expect that was because their views of the world and its ways, and about religion and its doctrines, ran together and agreed. The two ate the same spiritual food and drank the same spiritual drink, and spoke much about experimental[5] religion. In the chapel as in the house they were unassuming and very homely; and according to the older custom they did not habitually address each other by the titles 'Mr' or 'Mrs'

I know very well that there was no-one my mother wanted more

---

[3] A real church located in Hawarden, between Mold and Chester, but it's not clear whether an actual Theophilus Watkin was ever an elder there.

[4] '*The Nightingale of Britain*'—a bardic name suggestive of his singing ability. Curiously, this same name had been adopted by the well-known opera singer Dame Adelina Patti when she was admitted to the Gorsedd in 1877, eight years before the publication of this book. There's no reference to an Alexander Phillips bearing this name outside the works of Daniel Owen, though he appears in another of Owen's books, *Enoc Huws*.

[5] Nowadays we would probably say '*experiential*' religion, that is, faith worked out in one's own experience, but the term 'experimental religion' has been in use since Puritan times and would no doubt have been the appropriate English phrase to use in Owen's time.

to see, in her trouble, than Abel Hughes; and nothing would please me more than to be able to chronicle in detail the conversation that took place between them during his visit, but I cannot. Even though I have an excellent memory, and I was a bit precocious at that time, I had to conclude that the conversation was very different from the one with Thomas and Barbara Bartley and most of it was over my head. At the same time, I'm not content to move on without trying to record some of the discussion; because my mother said some things about the value of a personal religion that have stuck in my mind. When Abel came into the house, as usual without knocking the door first, my mother looked at him rather self-sufficiently; but we could both see the moisture in her eyes, and the twitches in the corners of her mouth and in her neck betrayed the fact that it was taking all her strength not to burst into tears. Abel extended his hand, and said, "Well, Mary, how are you?"

"I'm wonderful, considering, Abel," said my mother. "I am 'troubled on every side, yet not distressed'; I am 'perplexed, but not in despair; cast down, but not destroyed'.⁶"

"I know, Mary," said Abel, "that you know where to turn for succour, whatever trouble comes to meet you, otherwise I'd have come sooner, more than likely."

"Well," answered my mother, "I hope that I don't need much nursing. I'm not like the woman from London House, staying away from chapel for weeks because the elders didn't look in on her when she had a bit of toothache. No, at my age, I wonder if I've at least learned to walk? But it wouldn't have done any harm, Abel, if you had looked in on me sooner, after all that has gone between us, although, remember, if you didn't come here for a month I wouldn't think any less of you. And indeed, Abel, I feel rather grateful that you didn't come, because if you had, I wouldn't have got the view I did of the

> 'One there is, above all others,
> Well deserves the name of Friend;
> His is love beyond a brother's,

Costly, free, and knows no end:
They who once His kindness prove,
Find it everlasting love!'[7]

You know, Abel, that Joseph drove everybody out before revealing himself to his brothers;[8] and I'm somewhat hoping that this trouble is just the cup being placed in the mouth of my sack[9] so I will be brought to know the Governor of the land."

"I'm glad to find you in the rich pastures, Mary," said Abel.

"Where were you expecting to find me, Abel?" said my mother; "not on the common, surely. After all this religion, it would be a terrible thing to be without any shelter on the day of the storm. If I am not deceiving myself—and I often fear that—I have nothing left worth mentioning except the pastures. As you know, Abel, I am without support, worse than a widow; and my boy, who was a support and a provider for me, has been thrown into jail,"—and my mother hid her face in her apron, wholly overcome by her emotions.

"In the Truth there are words such as this, Mary," said Abel, "'I have been young, and now am old; yet I have not seen the righteous forsaken, nor his seed begging bread.'[10] 'The Lord tests the righteous, but His soul hates the wicked and he that loves violence.'[11] 'Many are the afflictions of the righteous; but the Lord delivers him from them all.'[12] 'Light is sown for the righteous, and gladness for the upright in heart.'[13] I am sure, Mary, that light is sown for you, even though it is night for you now, and you will see it sprout and shoot in this world, even if you don't see it in its full maturity. Be comforted, and strengthen yourself in the Lord. He will deliver you from all your troubles."

---

[6] 2 Cor. 4:8–9.

[7] This is an English hymn by John Newton; the Welsh hymn quoted by Owen is a literal translation of this, but I have been unable to find it in any of the Welsh hymn books.

[8] Gen. 45:1. [9] Gen. 44:2. [10] Psalm 37:25. [11] Psalm 11:5.

[12] Psalm 34:19. [13] Psalm 97:11.

"I'm trying to be like that, Abel, as best I can," said my mother. "But to hear you talk, I can't for the life of me stop thinking about the words of Tomos o'r Nant.[14] I know that Tomos wasn't a religious man, but he said many good things; and I think it was he that said this:

'It is easy for the healthy while without hurt
    To say to the sick to take comfort'.

And yet I do feel very grateful to you for your comforting words; and I've been wondering and wondering why you didn't come here sooner, Abel."

"Not because I wasn't thinking about you a lot, Mary," said Abel, "I was sorry to miss you from chapel on the Sabbath, although I wasn't expecting to see you there under the circumstances. Bob wasn't a member with us, though he was more like a member than many of us. No-one had anything bad to say about his life, and he was acknowledged as one of the best teachers in the Sunday School. But these strikes are a very strange thing, Mary. They're things that have come from the English; they don't belong to us, and I fear that they will do a lot of harm to this country and to religion. We, as brethren, decided we should take pause. Bob was one of the leaders, and that was inevitable, since in terms of understanding and gift of speaking he is the better of any of them; and no-one doubts that his intentions were perfectly honest; indeed, there are many wise people who sympathise with the colliers, trying to gain an increase in their wages and struggling against oppression. But there's no-one with an ounce of sense in his head, not to mention grace in his heart, who can excuse them for attacking the steward and driving him out of the country. According to the first accounts Bob was one of those guilty of that; and had I run here to show sympathy with you, someone would have been

---

[14] Thomas Edwards, more usually known as 'Twm o'r Nant'—see footnote 2 in Chapter 10.

ready enough to say that we were at one with the rioters, and the greater cause would suffer, and the great Name that we bear would be blasphemed. I'm glad to be able to say to you, Mary, that no-one now believes that Bob was guilty, even though he is now suffering as though he were guilty. There are men who were eye-witnesses of the whole disturbance, who can tell the truth as well as anyone, who testify clearly that he and John Powell tried hard to stop the idiocy. I have other good news to tell you. The men have firmly stood against working any more for Mr Strangle, and the masters have paid him off and sent for Abraham the old steward; and he has agreed to take up the job again. The works will start again tomorrow. We as a neighbourhood are indebted for this to Mr Walters the solicitor who succeeded in getting the masters and workers to talk to each other, and acted as a translator and intermediary; and I understand that if this had been done in the first place then all the trouble would have been prevented, because the masters can now see that it wasn't without reason that Bob and his colleagues were complaining about Strangle. So you see, Mary, things aren't so bad after all."

"Well for sure," said my mother, "they'll release Bob from jail now after seeing that he is innocent, and the things he was saying were right."

"No, I fear, Mary, we can't expect that. When magistrates have made a mistake, they never try to put it right. They're like a man who, having told a lie, thinks the best thing he can do is to stick to the lie."

"Well, it's not possible," said my mother, "that Mr Brown the parson will be able to get into his pulpit and preach, if indeed he does preach, and about justice and mercy, whilst he himself has sat on the bench conspiring with the Squire to commit injustice."

"He'll preach—if indeed he does preach—as you say, just as usual, and perhaps better, Mary," said Abel.

"I'd defy him to preach any worse, if I heard him well, Abel," said my mother. "But where people's consciences are, I don't know. I often give thanks, Abel, that I am with religion, and not the Church of England."

The two went on for a while conversing about religion and its comforts: and I could see clearly that Abel's visit was a great blessing to my mother. She looked comfortable; and not least in making her so was Abel's declaration that no-one believed in Bob's guilt. But very soon my mother and I learned that it was not possible to live on a happy feeling. It was a long time to wait for my brother's release. Because the wages had been so low during Mr Strangle's time in office, my mother didn't have anything put away to live on. For about three weeks our friends were very kind to us; but as often happens in such circumstances, time wore the sharp edge of the sympathy away. There were still five weeks to go before Bob would be free. I'll never forget those weeks. Whether out of pride or anything else, I didn't confess even to my closest friend that I was suffering from the lack of food. I confess it now. I don't believe it's possible for anyone to imagine that situation without being in it. To enjoy perfect health, and yet to feel the stomach as if it were full of roaring lions without anything to satisfy them, is a state that I cannot describe; but I know from experience what it is to be in, many times. My mother had no tendency to complain, and she had some sort of foolish independence, without which we would not have needed to suffer so. I had inherited her weaknesses, and I did not disclose even to Wil Bryan that I was suffering from hunger. Yet I'm sure that he understood it; because I saw him many times going into his house, and bringing out a big piece of bread and butter or bread and meat, and having begun to eat it pulling a face, and saying that he didn't really feel like it, and that he would throw it away unless I wanted to eat it. The lions were roaring; and rather than see him throw it away, I would take it. Ah, Wil! You understood my proud heart as much as you understood my empty stomach!

My mother sold various small things that we could do without; but she made sure that the purchasers were strangers. I knew that she was terrified that the chapel people would learn that she was so much in need—but I don't know for what reason, other than that I've suggested, namely a foolish independence and pride. I think she was guilty of dissimulation two or three times; and I hope that under the circumstances it was excusable. When we didn't have a crumb to eat in the house, and after a long fast, we went to the house of Thomas and Barbara Bartley, on the pretext of congratulating them for starting to come to the chapel services, something I'll say more about later. There's no doubt in my mind that my mother was indeed rejoicing in her heart that the two old dears were coming to chapel; but there was a quiet understanding between her and myself that Thomas wouldn't let us leave his house without an excellent meal. We went there three times under various pretexts, and never once did we come away hungry or empty-handed. That trick is painful for me to recall now; and I hurry on, not touching many others which come vividly to my mind. But I can't leave out one incident without mentioning it. It was between breakfast and lunch, at least for other people it was; since breakfast time and lunch time didn't mean anything in particular in our house. We hadn't had anything to eat since about noon on the previous day. I felt weak and downhearted, but I tried to spend the time reading. My mother sat quietly and contemplatively. Eventually, she got up and put on her bonnet, then sat down again for a little while. She rose again, put on her cloak, and having thought for a while sat down again. I could see that she was in a turmoil of mind, and I heard her whispering; but I could only make out two words, namely, 'seed' and 'bread'. I didn't understand the significance of the first, though I felt great need of the latter. Within another minute or two, she rose to her feet purposefully, and fetched from the back room the arm basket that she used to carry things from the shop when Bob was working. I asked her where she was going, and she said:

"Well, my boy, there's no use in the world for us to be sitting here dozing. I can't hold out for much longer, you see, and they say that the dog who goes, gets. I'll go far enough that nobody will recognise me."

I understood her intentions in a moment, and my stomach turned within me. I put my back against the door and, weeping, told her that she couldn't go; and I added that I could hold out until the next day at least. It wasn't difficult to persuade her. She put the basket down, took off her cloak and bonnet, and after I had let my feelings out for a while, I felt that the need for food had left me altogether, and that I could manage for days without anything to eat. If any act causes me more satisfaction than any other, it is the work I did that day of stopping my mother from going out. If I had let her go, my faith today in God's promises would have been less. I can't describe the pleasure I have in the fact that she, despite her many trials, went to her rest without ever having begged. We didn't step over the threshold that day, and the hours dragged slowly. When night came, we heart a hard, quick knock on the back door, and the two of us rose at once to answer it. When we opened the door, there was no-one to be seen, and we were about to close it when we noticed something on the doorstep. It was a brown paper packet, carefully wrapped. When I took it into the house, we saw that my mother's name was written clumsily upon it. The writing was not unfamiliar to me. The package was like the heart of its sender, containing many good things, which made my mother's face shine. Yet there was a mystery to it that made her hesitate a little to make use of it. The next minute she said:

"David, you remember, one time when he was hungry, ate of the temple showbread, and the Saviour commended him for that.[15] And although we know nothing at all about where these good things have come from, I don't think we'll do anything wrong in using them."

As she didn't ask me if I could guess where the package came

---

[15] Matt. 12:4.

from, I suggested nothing to her. And if I had done so, I question whether she would have touched the contents, because I doubted strongly that the sender had acquired them by honest means.

Well, my pure companion! I know fairly well that you would share your last crumb with me; and though you said nothing to me about the package after that, nor I to you, I was as sure that you were the sender as I was that it had been from your hand that I had received the piece of bread and butter the day before.

20

THE PARISH PARSON

I have said that my mother possessed an independence of mind and a foolish pride; and if she were more dependent and apt to complain, neither she nor I would have needed to endure much need. I fear I must confess that I saw her once—only once—being guilty of impoliteness and of speaking to a man of status as though she were his equal, when in fact she was suffering daily need. I am confident that I will be forgiven by any friends into whose hands this memoir may possibly fall—the more so as by then I will be six feet under—for thinking that my mother was in fact the best mother in the world. But I would be a hypocrite, and not faithful to my promise of telling the truth, and the whole truth, if I were to hide her weaknesses. She was one of strong tempers and feelings, and I think that she was something of a champion at 'plain speaking'. It is my experience that a danger for people like her, even though they excel in honesty, is to forget the feelings of others, and to display a lack of refinement and good taste—characteristics that ought to adorn the character of every true Christian.

In a small and unremarkable town, the 'parish parson' is never an unimportant man. It frequently happens that there is an eagerness, perhaps an over-eagerness, to recognise the status of that fortunate man who lives in the vicarage. It's possible also that the security of his position, and the tendency of the parson himself to receive with good grace the honour given to him, and perhaps a little more, coincides with the man's own natural temper. Mr Brown was no exception to this general rule, and if anyone in my home town received less respect than he was entitled to, then it wasn't Mr Brown. He was a fat, double-chinned and generous man, and although I cannot on any account suggest that he 'walked according to the flesh',[1] yet he was in literal sense 'carnal'. He carried in his body the evidence that his stipend of seven hundred pounds a year had not been without blessings to him. And if I say that others took advantage of his comfortable circumstances, I'll only be stating what his memory justly deserves. He did not close his ears to the cry of the needy, and he did not button his pocket so that nothing would come out of it for the benefit of the poor and troubled. In him the widow and orphan found a kind friend, especially if they went to Church. Even though Mr Brown, like everyone else, felt that an elbow was closer than a wrist, the wrists—namely the poor Nonconformists—were not wholly forgotten by him. When they appealed to him for help, even if he couldn't see his way clear to contribute from his own pocket or from the money that had been left in perpetuity by the departed whose names were written on the walls of the church, he would without fail put a word in for them with some guardian or other for them to have a few pennies from parish funds. If anyone needed a letter of recommendation, to Mr Brown they would go to request it. No movement within the town, of any significance, was complete unless Mr Brown's name was associated with it. No matter how painful the rheumatism of the withered old man or crooked old woman, they were expected to take off their hats and tax their sinews to genuflect before Mr Brown when they met him. Those idlers who are always found at the street corners, of whom no-one knows how they make their livings, when they saw Mr Brown they would stop their jesting, hide their pipes in their fists and raise their hands to their hats as he passed. There was a respectability, a particularity, a charm, or something that I can't quite put a word to, all around Mr Brown at all times. I think that everyone at that time would have been as unable as I am now to put their finger on what that thing was. It was something in the air that affected everyone, yes, even the Nonconformists. I remember

---

[1] Romans 8:4.

Mr Brown once honouring the Bible Society with his presence; and when he appeared there was clapping and stamping of feet like never before. Some in their joy nearly lost their breath and forgot themselves. It's a fact that some Nonconformists, let alone Church people, shed tears of joy at the occasion. I don't doubt that the reason for this particular display of feeling by the congregation was their sincere love for the old Book, and to think that a man of Mr Brown's standing had been won over to pay homage to the Society, whose intention was to give 'a Bible to everyone in the world'.[2] In that meeting Mr Brown only spoke a few words (he wasn't able to, without a book to read from); but he was there, and that spoke volumes; and that fact caused some, who thought they understood the times, to hope that the Millennium[3] could not be far away.

And yet Mr Brown himself was a simple man; and if some others had received the adulation paid to him, they would have lost their heads. Even his greatest admirers acknowledged that he had one drawback, namely that *he could not preach*. His delivery was slow and painful; but like a wise man he took care every time not to weary his hearers with many words, and he had a custom when in his pulpit of turning the whites of his eyes upwards, which to some was 'as good as a sermon'. Apart from that, his weakness in the pulpit was made up for, and more besides, by the fact that Mr Brown was a Justice of the Peace. This latter office gave him influence over those who would never be found inside the walls of the church. When Ned the poacher met him on the road he would make sly eyes at Mr Brown; and it was easy to see on Ned's face that he felt guilty that he had such wide pockets inside the skirts of

---

[2] In Welsh the original, more elegant slogan was 'Bibl i bawb o bobl y byd'; the Society had been founded in 1804 by Thomas Charles of Bala.

[3] Nothing at all to do with the year 2000, but rather a future period described in the bible in Revelation Chapter 20, where Christ returns to rule on the earth for 1000 years, and during which Satan is imprisoned prior to final judgement. This period of earthly perfection, was much hoped for amongst the Nonconformists. Various theologies about the precise nature of this '*millennium*' were—and still are—deliberated amongst bible scholars and lay-people.

his velvet jacket. Drunken Tom also would often, when he was too blind to see anyone else, somehow see Mr Brown from afar, and after staggering for a second, while looking through his half-open eyes as if through fog, he would make a huge effort to walk in a straight line until Mr Brown had passed. If Mr Brown in his role as Justice did not come frequently into contact with these characters, on a Monday morning in the County Hall, he would not have had any influence upon them. Without going into any more detail, Mr Brown was a man of great influence in every circle; and it was said that he feared nobody except the Squire. I have to conclude that Mr Brown was a man fairly close to his place, otherwise my mother would not have had such a high opinion of him; since, as I have said more than once, her prejudice against people from the Church of England was fierce. Yet, as for Mr Brown, I heard her praise him on many occasions, though she was careful always to temper her praise with the words 'as a neighbour'. 'As a neighbour' only did she have a good word to say of him, but when she spoke of religion she did not hesitate to state her fears that Mr Brown had never 'tasted of the great things'. One time my mother made a remark about Mr Brown that I have never forgotten. When one day she was extolling the Methodist preachers to Margaret Peters, who was a Churchwoman, Margaret said, 'Our Mr Brown is a wonderful parson, but he can't do much of this here preaching'. My mother said, 'That is exactly the same thing, Margaret, as if you were to say that James Pulford is a good tailor, except that he can't sew'. Margaret must have felt the force of the comparison, since, as they say sometimes in the House of Commons, 'the subject was then dropped'.

As one might expect, the action of Mr Brown and the Squire in finding my brother guilty and sending him to prison added nothing to my mother's respect for the former, inasmuch as she believed that the Justices on that occasion had displayed judicial blindness and unforgiveable vindictiveness. Whether it was his care for us as parishioners, or a feeling of guilt for the part he played in sending Bob to prison, that caused the reverend gentleman to visit us in our distress, I can't be sure. I am very content to take the more charitable view of his behaviour and to believe that his intentions were pure and praiseworthy; and as I remember his visit to us, I am ashamed of the reception that he had from my mother, especially as I recall how respectfully he was treated by people in general. Perhaps I should say, although Mr Brown was a Welshman on his mother's side, his grasp of the Welsh language was very far from perfect.[4]

"Good morning, Mrs Lewis," said our vicar, blowing heavily through his nostrils, as if he was failing to find enough breath to fill the bellows within him, and drying the sweat that was pouring out of his red face and wide neck.

"Good morning," said my mother, tersely enough, without any genuflection or any sign of adulation, or even so much as inviting him to sit down. Mr Brown sat down anyway on an old chair that was near to him and which, like its contemporaries in our house was very frail. I expected that any minute it would collapse under its load, the more so as it was very uncomfortable and was squeaking like an old basket.

After a little painful silence, Mr Brown said:

"It is a lovely day today, Mrs Lewis?"

"The day is fine, Mr Brown; if everything were as fine as the day there would be no need for anyone to complain," said my mother drily, beginning to pleat her apron, which was always a sign that she had something on her mind that needed saying.

"How are you getting on with the way things are now, Mrs Lewis? Are you getting enough food?" asked Mr Brown tenderly.

"I'm getting on better than I deserve, and have had enough food to keep body and soul together; but I have no-one to thank for that except the One who feeds the rook's chicks, and who makes the sun to rise on the good and the bad, and the rain to fall on the just and the unjust,"[5] said my mother.

"You are doing very well, Mrs Lewis, to acknowledge the hand of the Good Lord," said Mr Brown.

"I hope I am; but as I acknowledge the hand of the Good Lord, I can't close my eyes to the hand of someone else as well. Those poor people of old who saw the hand of the God of Israel knew something of Pharaoh as well," said my mother, menacingly.

"Yes, Pharaoh was a very bad man, Mrs Lewis," said Mr Brown.

"Very bad indeed," said my mother, "and alas even if he was drowned, not all his children were drowned in the Red Sea; and there's cause to fear that some of his descendants, and those of Og, King of Bashan, continue to trouble the people of God to this day, even though the Bible says that Og had no children."[6]

"You know a lot of Scripture, Mrs Lewis," said Mr Brown, approvingly.

"I am afraid, Mr Brown," said my mother, "that like many others I know more than I act upon: 'Blessed are those who *do* His commandments, that they may have a part in the tree of life, and that they may enter in through the gates of the city'.[7]"

"We must all try to keep the commandments, Mrs Lewis, or we'll never be able to enter Life," said our visitor.

"We must," said my mother, "as a rule of living; but we'll never enter Life through keeping them. I know this much theology, that we were all shut in at Sinai,[8] and that if we are thinking of entering Life then we must look somewhere else for the basis of our hope. That's what the Bible and Charles' *Instructor* say, and I believe them, whatever the Common Prayer teaches; I'm not saying anything about that."

"You Chapel people know nothing about the Common Prayer. The Common Prayer is a very good book, Mrs Lewis, just like the Bible," said Mr Brown.

"I'm saying nothing about your Common Prayer, Mr Brown, but I'll say this, that the Bible is God's book, and I have no fear in

---

[4] Mr Brown's pidgin Welsh is actually very entertaining to read, but I'm at a loss how to translate it into English.

[5] Matt. 5:45. [6] Deut. 3:11. [7] Rev. 22:14.

[8] Mrs Lewis is in effect paraphrasing Galatians 4:21–31.

saying that the next book to it is Charles' *Instructor*, and if I live for 100 years no-one will ever change my mind about that," said my mother fiercely.

Mr Brown smiled at my mother's innocence, and said:

"Well, we'll let that be, Mrs Lewis. I like people to be zealous; but I was thinking about you, how are you doing while Robert is in jail, and are you having enough food, you and the boy here; and although you don't come to Church, I was thinking, Mrs Lewis, of giving some… some assistance to you, or having something from the parish for you until Robert comes back."

Mr Brown said these words kindly, and I don't doubt that he sympathised much with my mother and me in our hardship. But his words struck a chord in my mother's independent nature, that caused her to address him in a fashion that I thought was rude, and wholly inappropriate for a man of Mr Brown's status and respectability. I think I can remember what she said to him word for word:

"Mr Brown," she said, "I know of only One who can wound *and* heal,[9] and cast down *and* raise up; and if you came here with the idea of putting a plaster on the wound which you caused, your errand is in vain. A kick and a kiss is what I call that, Mr Brown. After you put my innocent boy in jail, it would be bitter for me to accept any help from you, whatever my hardship might be. Perhaps you'll say that I'm bold, and so I am; but I must say what's on my mind, and I'll feel lighter after saying it. I'm surprised at you, Mr Brown! I used to think well of you as a neighbour—but— if this mattered anything to you—you have gone down ten degrees in my estimation. I think I realise to whom I'm speaking—because as Tomos o'r Nant said,

> 'There's no-one who should be respected as much
> As the minister of an evangelical chu'ch;
> And no-one's more accursed than he,
> If it's not God who leads him'.[10]

And I do not think, Mr Brown, that God is leading you to socialise and co-operate with one like the Squire, a man who thinks of nothing on earth except his racehorses and hunting dogs and tackle."

"Mrs Lewis! Mrs Lewis!" said Mr Brown, astonished.

"Mary Lewis is my name, Mr Brown, a poor woman, and there's no need to address me as Mrs, if you please. But I'll say it again—it is not your place to be on the bench hearing every case clean or unclean. A priest has enough to do caring for the souls of his hearers, if that is laid on his heart, without going to meddle in other things; and if I were Queen I'd tell every priest, and preacher as well for that matter, what the Lord said on another subject—a subject that it would be good for you and me to think more about—'What have you to do with my laws?' [11]—and I would. Paul, before being converted on the road to Damascus, had a pocketful of summonses to throw good people into jail; but after the great conversion I'm sure he threw his papers over the hedge, and after that no-one ever heard of him putting anyone in jail—after that, he had much better things to do. And another thing, Mr Brown, I don't know how you expect to have blessing, nor are able to sleep at night, when you know in your heart by now that you have sent an innocent boy to jail—a boy—and I'm not saying this because he is my son—who has more in his head than many who think that they are something; and a boy—although he does not, alas, profess religion—whose lifestyle no-one can say anything against. I don't wish to hurt anyone's feelings—but my boy has never tasted a drop of alcohol, and he's never been to the Red Dragon playing hunt-the-scarecrow—or whatever it is you call it. Although my boy is just a common collier,

---

[9] Job 5:18.

[10] A stanza from Twm O'r Nant:
 'Nid oes un i'w ganmol na'i berchi yn gymwys
 O flaen efengylaidd weinidog eglwys;
 Nac un yn fwy melltith na hwnnw'n fyw,
 Oni fydd Duw yn ei dywys'.

[11] Psalm 50:16.

I think as much of him as other people think of their children who have been brought up in boarding school, and have been taught to dawdle, and to feed the pride and lusts of the flesh, so I do. And there'd be no need for anyone to talk to me about help from the parish if you, Mr Brown, and the Squire had not put my boy in the jail unjustly; and I hope that I will yet be kept from going on the parish, even if it is good for others to have the parish's help. But as for the Church, I'll never go there. As you know, I have been there from time to time for Thanksgiving meetings; but I must tell you frankly that I have never found anything for my soul there. I have always been a Methodist, and with the help of grace I shall always be a Methodist; and I will try to manage until my boy comes back without help from the parish nor the parson."

My mother delivered this address fluently and with energy, and her face wore an expression of withering scorn that I have never seen before nor since. Because I was continually afraid that the chair would break beneath Mr Brown, and I was very ashamed of my mother's boldness, I was dripping with sweat, and I was glad in my heart to hear her conclude her lecture. Mr Brown looked astonished and wounded, and not without cause. But he was not a man to defend even his own actions, if he knew they were unjust. My mother knew Mr Brown well enough to be confident of this. She knew as well, as it was commonly believed in the town that Bob and his companion John Powell had been put in prison unjustly, that no-one would be more aware of this than Mr Brown, who was never a stranger to public opinion. Mr Brown did not try to defend himself; and when he rose to his feet I felt a great relief, as I was sure by now that the chair would not collapse beneath him. Before leaving he said, in a rather surly manner,

"No-one has ever spoken like that to me before, Mrs Lewis; and perhaps you will need my assistance another time."

"I don't doubt," said my mother, "the first thing that you said, Mr Brown, because I hope that you have not put an innocent boy in jail before; and there's no harm in the world for you to hear some truth from time to time, and I feel better for having told it. And as for the last thing you said, namely that I will come to ask you again. I can only hope in the order of Providence for that; but if I ever come to seek your good mercy, you can be sure that I will have tried everyone else first."

Mr Brown went away under a cloud, and my mother said to me:

"I wasn't too severe with him, tell me?" And I answered that I was afraid that she had been too bold, and that she had hurt Mr Brown's feelings.

"Don't be silly," she said, "his skin is much thicker than you think. The Saviour and his leading apostles said much plainer things to the chief priests than anything I said. I know exactly where I stand, and I defy him to send me a summons no matter how great a man he is."

That evening Abraham, the steward of the Red Fields, came to our house to inform us that good and steady work was being kept for Bob ready for when he came home, and that any money she needed could be had now, and Bob could pay it back from his wages when he was able. After my mother had wept for a time and thanked him again and again, she told Abraham—who was a zealous Independent—the story of the parson's visit, which entertained him greatly, and as he left, Abraham gave to my mother a sovereign as a loan, and went away. My mother looked at the sovereign from every angle, like one looking at an old friend that one had almost forgotten, and she said:

"'A good man deals graciously and lends; he will guide his affairs with discretion'.[12] Do you know what? I had just about forgotten what this Queen looked like. I remember the time when I was very familiar with her, and I hope that we shall see each other more often. Long life and grace to her and her children is the sincere desire of my heart."

---

[12] Psalm 112:5.

21

CONVERTS

Time went by, as it daily goes by, and it brought with it, as mercifully it usually does, not only its troubles but also its comforts. Through the kindness of Abraham, the steward of the Red Fields, our cupboard was no longer bare, and by now the lions had ceased roaring in my stomach. As the time drew close for Bob to be released, my mother's face brightened; and yet I knew from her conversation and her behaviour that she was not without many worries about how he would look, and what effect his unjust incarceration would have upon his spirit, and a thousand and one other things that any responsible mother would ask under similar circumstances. John Powell had already returned; and although he could only report a little about Bob, as they had been held separately, my mother had, through detailed questioning, extracted enough from him to look forward with fear and anxiety to the day when my brother would return. Before that day arrived, two things happened that gave my mother great satisfaction. Lest I go on for too long (something that I say sometimes while preaching, even though I say every word that I mean to), I will barely touch on those two things.

The visits of Abel Hughes, that redoubtable old elder, to our house were such frequent events that I took little notice of them except on particular occasions, such as the one I have just chronicled. But I have good reason to recall one visit of his about a fortnight before Bob came back from prison. My mother and he had been talking for a while, and I was taking no notice of them, writing something at the table by the window because I had not forgotten Bob's advice to better myself rather than be forced to work as a collier; but my attention was captured by Abel's saying to my mother:

"Mary, it's high time that this boy here thought about doing something, especially the way things are with you now."

"I think exactly as you do, Abel," said my mother. "But what he can do, I don't know, because he isn't strong and he isn't much of a scholar."

"But he's a big boy to be doing nothing," said Abel.

"Precisely," said my mother.

"I could do with a boy in my shop now, if I were sure that Rhys would fit the bill," said Abel.

"Just the thing that I've thought dozens of times," said my mother, "but I've been afraid that Rhys isn't enough of a scholar. I know that he'll have fair play for his soul with you, Abel, and I don't think you'll have any trouble with him. He's a decent boy, all things considered. And it's a strange thing, Abel, the older I get the more I come to see the same thing as with poor Bob, that a little bit of education is a very handy thing, so long as you don't get too much of it; I hold to that."

"What are you doing here then, Rhys?" asked Abel, walking towards me, and he added: "You know what, you are writing very tidily; who taught you, say?"

"Bob," said I, humbly.

"Can you count? Can you do *simple addition*?"

I'm afraid I smiled a little mockingly as I answered, "I can do *addition*, *subtraction*, *multiplication* and *division of money*."

"What's he saying, Abel?" asked my mother.

"Oh, he's only saying that he knows how to count money," said Abel.

"Rhys," said my mother, looking disapprovingly at me, "I've never before caught you telling a lie. Do you want to break your mother's heart? Haven't I had enough trials, don't you think, without you going and telling a lie before my very eyes? The old saying is true enough, Abel, that no-one knows what it is to raise a child. I'll tell you honestly, because I don't want to deceive you;

no money has ever crossed his hands; and I wonder at you, Rhys, saying such a thing to Abel Hughes."

Many of the old Methodists believed, I think, that laughter was not 'fitting for the Gospel', and I don't remember ever before that time hearing Abel Hughes articulate his feelings in that manner; and he was so unfamiliar with the task that his laughter sounded more like a cross between a scream and a moan than anything else. But laugh he did, and he said,

"Don't get excited, Mary dear; Rhys is talking about the tutor's rules for counting money."

"Ho! So you say; I never knew that Mr Tudor had rules for counting money, even though I hear that he has plenty of money and takes good care of it. If he came here to count my money, he could leave his rules at home, goodness knows. But children these days know more than their parents, or at least they think they do. As the two of you understand each other, carry on."

And on we carried—Abel asking, me answering. Without flattering myself, I'm sure that Abel was surprised that I knew as much as I did, not having had much schooling to talk of, and that he admired Bob for the trouble that he had taken with me.

"I hope, Abel," said my mother, "that Bob hasn't taught him any evil. They have their English these days; and you don't know what's going on inside your own house."

Abel reassured my mother that Bob had done well to teach me these things, and to her this was a tasty morsel, and she said,

"I quarrelled with Bob a lot because there's too much of the book and the slate here, and not enough of the Bible; but I'm glad to hear you say that he hasn't taught him anything bad. And yet I hold to this, that there's too much of a tendency in the young people these days to neglect the Bible."

Lest I go on for too long, as I said, the result of Abel's visit that evening was an agreement between my mother and him that I would go on trial for a month in the shop—that I would eat at his table, and come home to sleep. This was one of the things

I referred to that gave comfort to my mother, as much comfort I'm sure as many a mother has had from the appointment of her son to a job with the government; and I know that a large element of her comfort was the fact my soul would 'have fair play', as she'd say.

The other thing that gave great pleasure to her was that Thomas and Barbara Bartley continued to come to the chapel services, and there were grounds for believing that the Truth was working something upon their minds. I have said that my mother and I would visit Thomas and Barbara frequently, and I have suggested that there was an understanding between us when we were suffering need, that we would not leave our neighbours' house hungry. Yet I would be very unfair to my mother if I let it be understood that this was her only or even her main intent; no, I believe that she felt as much interest in their salvation as Paul felt for the salvation of his people according to the flesh.[1] She watched carefully to see how the two would listen to the sermons on the Sabbath; and on Monday morning she'd go to them to search out how much they had understood of the Truth and what effect it had left upon their minds. I am strongly tempted to reproduce some of the conversations that took place during these visits; but lest some think that I were exaggerating the zeal and persistence of my mother, I shall refrain. As she cross-questioned them, and explained the truth to them in simple language, I heard Thomas Bartley say many times, "It's a terrible pity, Mary, that you didn't belong to the Ranters; you'd have made a great preacher."

The friends in the chapel understood perfectly well that my mother was the means by which Thomas and Barbara had been brought to the services; and great was their amazement and joy to see the two old dears—who, although living close by the chapel, had been their whole lives entirely indifferent to religion—at last being present at every public meeting. My mother said, "If the imprisonment of your brother has been the occasion to bring

---

[1] Romans 9:3.

Thomas and Barbara under the sound of the Gospel, and especially if it is the occasion to bring them to Christ, I'll never complain about the bargain; and I greatly believe, you see, that the Truth is working something upon the minds of my old neighbours, and I wouldn't wonder if Thomas and Barbara will have come to the *seiat* before Bob comes home. I think I'm as good a Calvinist as anyone I know, but the devil did a pretty poor job of farming with Thomas and Barbara; they're good ground for the Gospel, without the thorns and briars of jealousy and deceit, nor the swamps and bogs of fleshly sinfulness. In a manner of speaking, there is less work for the Spirit to do in making a new heart. Bob says a lot, as you know, about the ignorance and innocence of Thomas and Barbara, and makes fun of them a lot; and there's nothing I'd like more to say to him when he comes home than that the two have been saved. Perhaps you think I'm talking nonsense, with Bob himself not being in the *seiat*; but I cannot for the life of me think—not for the life of me, that Bob isn't one of us. And something tells me that he'll come to the *seiat* now; what do you think?"

I received a lesson that I will never forget from the case of Thomas and Barbara, namely that preachers who are thought of as being poor are much more of a blessing to certain sorts of hearer than those who are thought of as being great. I remember that Thomas and Barbara wouldn't gain much from the ministry of those whom my brother Bob considered his favourites, while the two would speak very highly of those who were rather looked down upon by him. This gave great joy to my mother, as she believed it confirmed what she had said many times to my brother, namely that not everyone could be Peter and Paul, and that many had been saved, even though it was not remarked upon, under the ministry of Thaddeus, else the Lord would not have called him to the work.

After a few days, while I was having breakfast, my mother said, "This is the last Sabbath that poor Bob will be in the house of bondage, and thanks be for that. And yet I'm almost afraid to see him come home, lest his spirit will have hardened under the regime. I wonder who will be preaching here next Sabbath? If Bob were at home today, I know he wouldn't pay much attention to our preacher. Bob has always tended to look down upon William Hughes, Abercwmnant. But I think that William has been sent, and I always have a blessing when I listen to him. And although no doubt we will have today, as usual, 'the object which is noted', 'the action which is attributed' and 'the duty which is urged', whatever they'll be, William Hughes will say something worth listening to and doing. I hope his Master will be with him, and he'll have an anointing, I'd say."

William Hughes came to his appointment. It is very rare for a minor preacher to break his appointment, except when he is minor enough to imitate the failings of great preachers. I remember well his text that morning—'Turn to the stronghold, you prisoners of hope'.[2] I thought that everyone was thinking about Bob my brother when William Hughes was talking about prisoners. The old preacher seemed unusually lively, and I remember that he was being listened to particularly astutely. I have the notes of that sermon in front of me now, and looking at them I see that he preached the Gospel purely and clearly. But amazingly, according to my notes the headings of the sermon were not as usual. Perhaps I was negligent in noting them down. They are as follows: I.) *The object which is noted—prisoners.* II.) *The gracious provision made on their behalf—a stronghold.* III.) *The duty which is urged—turn to the stronghold.* I remember that my mother was drinking it in so richly that I was continually afraid she would break out in praise, like I heard her do once under Cadwaladr Owen's[3] ministry, when Bob my brother was so annoyed with her that he didn't speak to her for two days afterwards. I remember Abel Hughes, in the middle of the sermon, rising from his usual

---

[2] Zech. 9:12.

[3] A Methodist preacher associated with a large revival in Caernarfonshire in the 1830s.

seat underneath the pulpit and placing himself right in the front of the Great Seat—which was always a sign that the preacher was saying something remarkable. Perhaps the reason that I took so much notice of Abel's behaviour was that I had heard my mother say to him more than once after we had had a powerful service, "Well, Abel, you had to get up out of your kennel today." It's proof enough for me that W. Hughes was preaching particularly well that morning that my notes are so imperfect; because it is my experience that, when a preacher is labouring through his material, I can write down almost the whole sermon; but when the preaching is good and lively, I forget my notebook and pencil and lose myself in what is being said.

As soon as we left the chapel, I noticed that Thomas and Barbara Bartley were waiting for my mother; and the three went homewards in serious conversation, while Wil Bryan and I walked behind. Although it was the Sabbath, I couldn't help telling Wil that I was going to be apprenticed with old Abel. Wil was struck with amazement, looked at me with pity, and said,

"Good bye, old chap! This boy (and he tapped his breast) would rather be an apprentice to a showman or a barber. Never again will you taste play or laughter. You'll never have anything except the *seiat*, and learning Bible verses; and within a month from today, I swear, you will have had to learn how to groan like an Irishman with toothache and make a face as long as a double-bass. You'll be fit to go to heaven any day. But before this boy (he tapped his breast again) would be apprenticed to the old onion, he'd go to be footman to the King of the Cannibal Islands. I'm sorry for you, Rhys; but as things are settled—fire away. But this chap (and he tapped his breast) would rather go to collect oysters at the summit of Moel Famau than become an apprentice to the old Ab."

I knew that Wil was stating his mind honestly, and when I said to him that I didn't take such a dim view of my future as he did, I was surprised at his answer.

"Listen to you, the old Hundredth! I think it's time for us to make you a preacher or an elder, I swear."

Wil little knew that nothing would be more desirable for me than for him to make me the first person that he mentioned, if that were in his power. To save myself from his mocking I kept that to myself.

When I arrived home, I found my mother humming songs; and although she didn't say much, I had never seen her displaying such a degree of inner happiness. I thought it was the 'stronghold' that the preacher had talked about that filled her heart; but I don't remember her saying anything about the sermon, other than that William Hughes "had felt his feet under him," which was a saying she had whenever a preacher had caught the hwyl. At six o'clock that evening William Hughes had another dazzling service, and my notes show the following: Text—'Come to me all who are weary and heavy laden, and I shall give you rest…'[4] Headings—I.) *The objects which are noted—those who are weary and heavy laden.* II.) *The duty which is urged—'Come to me'*. III.) *The precious promise to those who obey—'I shall give you rest'*. I don't remember anything particular about the sermon. In the *seiat* after the service, Abel Hughes asked as usual, "Is anyone here who has stayed on for the first time?" and I wondered how he could ask such a question when at just the same time he was looking at two who *had* stayed on for the first time. John Llwyd (he who was nicknamed by Wil Bryan 'the old scratcher') said aloud what everyone knew, namely that Thomas and Barbara Bartley has stayed.

"Ho! Go and have a word with them, William Hughes," said Abel to the preacher, and added, "You mustn't expect too much of them; they haven't listened much;" and then he sat down beside the preacher and whispered into his ear, as far as I could tell, whatever information about the converts that he could in half a minute. Somewhat reluctantly, the preacher rose to his feet, held his hands behind his back under the flaps of his coat, and walked as though it

---

[4] Matt. 11:28.

181

were against his will towards Thomas and Barbara Bartley; and as far as I can remember, the conversation went something like this:

Said the preacher, "Well, Thomas Bartley, I know nothing about you, and perhaps you yourself can tell us something of your background."

"I shall, for sure," said Thomas, "my mother and father were poor people, and I was the youngest of three children. They're all dead now apart from me; and I don't know of any relatives of mine except for one cousin who lives down in England, if he's still alive. A family that's ..."

"I didn't mean for you to tell your family history," said the preacher, "what I wanted was to know something of your experience. What caused you and your wife to stay here this evening?"

"Oh! Beggin' your pardon," said Thomas. "Well, I'll tell you. Barbara and I, these last few weeks, have been thinkin' quite a lot about comin' to the *seiat* here; and Mary Lewis was sayin' that it's high time we did, and that we'd never do a better thing; and hearin' you beggin' us so earnestly this mornin' to turn to the stronghold, the two of us decided to stay this evenin', because we knew very well you were referrin' to us." Barbara gave a nod of agreement.

"You did well," said the preacher, "and I have no doubt that the friends here are very happy to see you. It seems that you see yourself as a great sinner, Thomas Bartley?"

"Well, I'll say this, I've never been angry with anyone, as Barbara knows, and I've always tried to live honestly," said Thomas.

"I'm glad to hear that, not everyone can say so," said Mr Hughes; and he added, "but every one of us are sinners, you know, Thomas Bartley."

"Yes, yes," said Thomas, "none of us have done especially well; but I think that some are worse than others."

"Can *you* read, Thomas Bartley?" asked the preacher.

"I have some grasp of the letters, but no more; but I love to hear people read," said Thomas.

"It's a great loss not to be able to read, and it's a bit late in the day for you to think of learning," said Mr Hughes.

"I know that I'll never learn, because I don't have the wit in me, more's the pity," said Thomas.

"As you haven't listened much, and cannot read, you must, Thomas Bartley, give double diligence in coming to the services from now on," said Mr Hughes.

"If we live," said Thomas, "Barbara and I have decided to follow the services solidly, because the time passes much better than when dozin' at home. And to tell you the truth, Mr Hughes, we have great pleasure in the chapel; and if we'd known that before, we'd have come here years ago; but nobody asked us till Mary Lewis more or less forced us to come."

"What is it that gives you so much pleasure in chapel, Thomas Bartley?" asked the preacher.

"Well, I can't really tell you, but Barbara and I feel very much more what d'you call it since we started comin' to chapel."

"Very good," said the preacher, "but what do you think of the stronghold that I was trying to say something about this morning?"

"Well," said Thomas, "we thought you were speakin' about it very well, but we didn't catch exactly what you were sayin'; but Mary Lewis explained to us on the way home that Jesus Christ dying for us is the stronghold, and trustin' in Him for our lives is turnin' to the stronghold, and that's what I was thinkin' if I had been able to put it into words."

"Whoever this Mary Lewis is, she's pretty close to the mark on that," said the preacher.

"Yes, I'll vouch for her, Mary's a sharp one, you can be sure, Mr Hughes," said Thomas.

It had been obvious for some time, as I heard my mother say, that Mr William Hughes did not understand his customer; and after waiting a second or two he made one more attempt to get Thomas to the point, and said:

"Thomas Bartley, can you tell me, what need there was for Jesus

Christ to die for us?"

"Well, as far as I understand," said Thomas, "there wasn't anythin' in particular callin' for him to die for us except that He Himself chose to do so."

"Well, wasn't there anything in us calling for him to die, Thomas Bartley?" said Mr Hughes.

"Not at all, in my mind," said Thomas. "Perhaps I'm missin' somethin'; but I should think that no-one imagined that he would die for us, and that he took everyone by surprise, so to speak."

Mr Hughes looked again as though he had been thrown out of his saddle, and he turned to Barbara, and said:

"Well, Barbara Bartley, can you read?"

"Some grasp of the letters, just like Thomas," said Barbara.

"Well, say a word about what you feel," said Mr Hughes.

"Exactly the same as Thomas," said Barbara.

William Hughes walked back to the Great Seat, and he said, "Abel Hughes, you know these friends better than I do."

Abel rose to his feet; and though I was only a lad I knew that if anyone could work out whether a spark from the divine fire had descended into the hearts of Thomas and Barbara, Abel was the man; because I have never seen his equal, I think, for knowing the heart of a man, whatever character he pretends to wear. He said, his voice shaking with feeling:

"My dear old neighbours, there's no need for me to tell you that my heart rejoices to see you making a move towards the stronghold that we heard about so sweetly this morning. I hope, and for that matter believe, that your intentions in staying this evening are correct." "Friends," he added, turning to the church, "I feel that I have had a heavy rebuke here this evening; and I trust we all felt it, when Thomas Bartley said that no-one except Mary Lewis had ever invited him and his wife to come to the services. Let us be ashamed of ourselves, and repent. Well, Thomas Bartley, I will try to speak to you so that you understand me. Do you find any change in your feelings and in your mind lately, from where you were, say, three months ago?"

"A great change, to be sure, Abel Hughes," said Thomas.

"Well, say in your own way what that is," said Abel.

"You never saw a worse one than me for sayin' anythin', Abel Hughes; but before we started comin' to chapel, Barbara and I would never think anythin' at all about our end; but now not a day goes by when we don't talk about that. We think a lot about how it will be with us after goin' from here—whether Barbara and I will be able to be together, and will be comfortable."

"Splendid, Thomas!" said Abel. "What do you think you will need to make you comfortable, here and after going from here?"

"Well," said Thomas, "I can't say to you exactly; but I think it's trustin' in Christ, like Mary Lewis says."

"Don't change your mind about that, dear Thomas," said Abel, "you and I and every one of us will be safe enough if we only trust in Him. You have a boy, Thomas, who has gone to Him already, there's no doubt about that. Seth, though being so unaware, knew the Man, and I can't imagine anything better for the two of you, and for myself, than being able to say so clearly as Seth could where he was going."

No sooner had Abel mentioned Seth than big tears started to fall down Thomas' cheeks, and his account was halted—it wasn't possible to get another word out of his mouth. Barbara too wetted her checked apron with the same tears. Abel Hughes was a stern man, but he had a big heart; and when he wept, his tears, like the late rains, affected everything around him except the stones, and so they did this time as he was completely overcome. In a while he possessed himself once again, and asked for a vote of acceptance for Thomas and Barbara Bartley; but before anyone had a chance to raise their hand, John Llwyd asked, "Is Thomas Bartley a teetotaller?" ("Listen to the old scratcher," said Wil Bryan quietly in my ear.) In any case, Abel pretended not to hear, and the vote was passed.

I sat down beside the Great Seat. After the preacher had drawn the *seiat* to a close, I saw Thomas Bartley going up to Abel; and putting his hand in his pocket, he said: "Abel Hughes, is there any entrance fee to pay tonight?"

Abel smiled, and said, "No Thomas; you will have other opportunities to put something on the church book."

"To be sure," said Thomas, and off he went.

22

A VISIT BY MORE THAN ONE RELATIVE

If I had known before I began to write my memoir that it would grow to such a size, I doubt that I would have undertaken the task at all. Here I am having written twenty-one chapters—some of them long and narrow—and so far I've hardly sharpened my pencil. I've said so many things along and across that I don't remember if I've said what I feel writing almost every chapter, namely that there's far too much of 'me' and 'my mother' and 'my brother' and 'she said' and 'I said' and 'he said'; which, if the work were published, would doubtless make the reader feel sick. But what help is there? Inasmuch as I have started the task, I'm not happy to leave it unfinished, especially as I haven't touched on some of the main events of my life.

There's no point in beating about the bush or making a display of false humility—the fact is that my brother Bob was a hero among the workers of the Red Fields. Although his language, his lifestyle, and his habits were totally different from the majority of them, I'm perfectly sure that if they were to choose a king from among themselves then Bob would be the chosen ruler. It is a fact worth taking note of that understanding, purity of life and of behaviour, sooner or later, will earn the respect of the most worthless and ungodly men. Bob had been working in the Red Fields since he was thirteen years old, and no ear had ever heard a swear word descend from his lips. It was soon understood by his co-workers that he was a reader, and at meal times he was asked for news. He had an excellent memory and a fluent tongue; and when he was still only a lad, he would entertain hearts much older than his by the light of a Davy lamp in the bowels of the earth. When he grew to be a man, he found himself one of the leaders of his co-workers; and although he could not, any more than anyone else, govern an excitable crowd of colliers, yet he was generally looked upon as their counsellor.

During the time that Abraham was the steward, it was to Bob that he gave responsibility for the works when he happened to be away from home. No wonder, then, after Abraham had re-taken the job, that my brother's old companions looked with interest to the time that he would come back from the prison. Even though it was only a few days since I had started 'working' with Abel in the shop, the kind old man gave me a holiday to congratulate my brother on his return home. He was expected on the midday train; and since the early morning my mother had been excited and nervous, cleaning the house and preparing a welcoming reception for him. She said:

"I've been wondering for some time what we can give the boy to eat when he comes. They say that if someone who's just come out of jail gets food which is too heavy, they get sick. It strikes me that Bob is very fond of currant cake; and for him to have a treat, and something which won't weigh on him, I don't think he can have anything better than a cup of tea and some cake. If you'll run to the shop to get three penn'orth of the best flour, tuppence worth of baking soda, and a quarter of currants, I'll make it straight away."

I was very willing to do my part of the work, as my own tastes inclined towards the griddle[1] as strongly as Bob's. The table was laid, the cake had been baked, and the water in the kettle had been boiled and cooled down again many times over before the time came when the train was due to arrive. I was in the station at least half an hour before the time; and fair play to Wil Bryan, he was there before me. Very soon there were tens of burly colliers on the platform, their spirits and their voices high. Some of them petted me with their hands under my chin, others pulled my hair

---

[1] If what Rhys had in view were currant cakes made on a griddle, rather than in an oven, then they would almost certainly have been what nowadays go by the name of 'Welsh Cakes'.

and ears—with the best of intentions, of course; and others gave me pennies. I preferred the latter. Wil looked at the pennies rather enviously; but he didn't ask me for them as he had done on that previous occasion, when I had thought he intended to hire an attorney to defend Bob. This time, he appeared to be wondering what to suggest to me that I should do with my pennies; and he said, "It's a terrible pity that Bob doesn't smoke—or that money would be just right to buy a box of tobacco for him." As he couldn't suggest anything else, I must confess that I was inclined to sympathise with him. Wil made one other observation that I remember well: "There's one advantage," he said, "to a collier going to jail—they can't give him the 'county crop'—because I'd defy them to cut his hair any shorter than it was already." Wil made many other comments, which at that time I considered remarkably wise. By this time the number of colliers who had come to meet with Bob was very large; but I was surprised by the absence of his best friend, John Powell. While I was thinking how disappointed Bob would be that his old companion was not there to meet him, I heard the train coming in, and my heart started beating quickly, and Wil Bryan opened his mouth and started to make train noises. The bell rang, and the row of carriages came into view; and seeing it come so quickly, I thought it couldn't possibly stop; but stop it did. With the din of the steam escaping from the engine, coal being thrown onto the fire, boxes being loaded onto the platform, doors being opened and closed, people weaving past one another and speaking loudly, the station was in a wild hubbub. I looked everywhere for Bob. "All right," said someone, and away went the train again. The colliers looked disappointed, and Wil Bryan ran to me; and he said, "A mare's nest! Bob hasn't come." My heart fell within me, and I could hardly contain my feelings. The colliers tried to comfort me by reassuring me that Bob would come on the next train, which was due in about three hours. I went homewards with my head bowed sadly; and long before arriving at the house I saw my mother in the doorway waiting for *us*, and when she saw that I was coming on my own she retreated into the house. Her disappointment was bitter; but I told her that the colliers had assured me that my brother would come on the next train. The currant cake was not cut, and the kettle was refilled because the first filling had boiled away. I went to meet the train again, and I found that the workers from the Red Fields were there in greater numbers than before. I had a presentiment that Bob wouldn't come with that train either, and my suspicion was correct. By this time I had, so to speak, forgotten my own disappointment as I thought of what a blow it would be to my mother, whose heartstrings were pulled to such a tension that I was afraid they would break at the news. When I approached the house, she wasn't standing at the door as she had earlier; and when I went in she did not appear as disappointed as I had expected her to be. Before I said anything, she said, "I knew he wouldn't come; something told me. The furnace hasn't been heated seven times hotter[2] yet, it seems. I know that something has happened to him," and hiding her face in her apron, she let herself weep copiously.

I followed her example, and before long we both felt better. I don't remember us eating anything. My mother didn't care whether I went or not to meet the last train; but I went. I noticed that by now there were many workers from the Red Fields, who had been working during the day; and they looked newly washed, with their faces clean except for a little blackness near the corners of their eyes and on their eyebrows. I also noticed that a lot of those who hadn't been working that day were by now half drunk. The train came in, but did not bring Bob with it; and the class of men I just mentioned began to curse the train and almost everything else, especially the two Justices of the Peace, Mr Brown and the Squire. Wil Bryan tried to persuade me to stay for a while without returning home, as there were signs, he said, that there would soon be a row among the colliers that would be worth

---

[2] Daniel 3:19.

seeing; but when he saw that his words made no impression, he returned with me, and I know that this was a great sacrifice for him, as Wil was in his element when there was trouble. Wherever there was a disturbance, there if possible would Wil be. When we were together in Robin the Soldier's school, his favourite task was to get the boys to fight; and in chapel too, he liked hearing about a bad-tempered teachers' meeting a thousand times more than a good sermon. From the time when Wil had turned his hair into a Q.P., my mother had been very much prejudiced against him, and daily put me on my guard lest I be defiled. Wil understood that perfectly; and when he came to our house he took care to pull his hair down over his forehead before coming in. This had an excellent effect on my mother; and I think that it would have dispelled all of her prejudice had she not accidentally observed Wil in the act while looking out of the window; and he had a heavy telling-off from her for his hypocrisy.

But on the whole, as I have suggested before, Wil understood my mother perfectly, and he could handle her marvellously. When it suited his purpose he could speak almost as religiously, in his own way, as she. I don't think she was sorry to see Wil coming with me that evening. She had one or two neighbours comforting her, and no doubt she thought that Wil was offering some support to me. When we came to the house, Wil and I were amazed by how quiet my mother was, and Wil said in my ear,

"The old woman is holding up like a brick."

"I see," said my mother, "that you have bad news again. But it's only what I was expecting. Something has happened to him, or he'd have been home by now."

"Don't lose heart, Mary Lewis," said Wil, "I believe that Bob will turn up from somewhere soon."

"Neither you nor I have grounds to believe that, William," said my mother. "Tonight, you see, I feel the wise man's words coming home to me, 'Hope deferred makes the heart sick'.[3] And Job said when he was in trouble, 'You wash away the things which grow out of the dust of the earth, and you destroy the hope of man'.[4] 'And where now is my hope? As for my hope, who shall see it?'"[5]

"Well, wasn't the preacher saying last Sunday, Mary Lewis," said Wil, "that things had come all right for Job in the end, after all the humbug people said to him, didn't it?"

"He was, William," said my mother; "and if I have the same confidence in my living Redeemer as Job had,[6] it will be all right for me as well, you'll see."

"It's sure to be all right for you, Mary Lewis, because you're as godly as Job, I swear," said Wil.

"Don't be silly and blasphemous, Wil," said my mother.

"I'm speaking the truth from my heart," said Wil, "you are as godly as Job every day he got out of bed. And from what the preacher was saying about him, I see the two of you as very similar to each other. Job had a bad wife and you had a bad husband, but the two of you stuck to your colours, first class; and I'm sure the Good Lord won't be shabby with you in the end, you'll see."

"I beg you to be quiet, William," said my mother. "You should know that I'm not in the mood tonight to listen to your nonsense."

"Nonsense?" said Wil, and I know that he was being zealous and honest, "it's not nonsense at all. I bet—that is, I'll take my oath that it will be all right with you in the end. Didn't the preacher say about Job that it was testing him that the Good Lord was doing? And that's how it is with you, just showing what kind of stuff you're made of."

"William," said my mother to change the subject, "were there many colliers in the railway?" ('railway'[7] is what my mother called the station.)

"Thousands and thousands," said Wil.

"There you go again; there are only three hundred who work in the Red Fields," said my mother.

"Well, yes, in a manner of speaking, you know, Mary Lewis," said Wil. "I'm sure that there were just about a hundred there."

"I suppose neither of you happened to speak to John Powell? What did he think about Bob not being there?" asked my mother.

"John Powell wasn't there," we both answered.

"Not there! John Powell not there?" said my mother in amazement.

"He was working the day shift," said Wil.

"Who told you that, William?" asked my mother.

"Nobody, but that's what I thought," said Wil.

This caused my mother to pleat her apron and think long and hard. Eventually she said:

"William, would you mind running to John Powell's house, and tell him, if he's in, that I would like to see him."

"No sooner said than done," said Wil,[8] jumping to his feet. My mother followed him to the door, and said:

"It's very dark, William, and it's almost too much for me to ask you to come back. Rhys will come with you to find something out from John Powell, so that you can go home."

"Stand at ease, as you were;[9] if the darkness is very thick, I will cut it with my knife," said Wil, and off he went.

"There's something kind and decent in that boy," said my mother, "and I can't help liking him; but I'd like him better if he were a bit more serious and spoke a bit less English. I often fear that he will make you just like himself; and yet I don't think that there is deceit in his heart. Why didn't you tell me before that John Powell wasn't in the railway?"

Although it seemed like a long time to me, Wil came back soon with the news that John Powell was not at home, and hadn't been home all day, and this caused my mother once again to fall into

---

[3] Prov. 13:12. [4] Job 14:19. [5] Job 17:15. [6] Job 19:25.

[7] In the Welsh, instead of the proper Welsh word for railway (rheilffordd), Mary Lewis uses a very awkward-looking transliteration of the English pronunciation—'Rel-wê'.

[8] He said it in English, for added effect.

[9] Again, in English.

deep contemplation, so deep that she took no notice when Wil told me rather quietly:

"I called to tell the gaffer at home that I'd be staying with you tonight. We've missed some good sport. The colliers have been setting fire to straw effigies of Mr Brown and the Squire, and they were good ones too. There have been three good battles, and One-Eyed Ned has been taken to the roundhouse; but he fought like a lion with the policeman…"

Wil galloped along with his story, but I had no stomach to listen to it and I'm not inclined to re-tell it now. When he saw that I had no interest, he stopped; and the next minute he fell asleep and snored the house down, which caused my mother to wake from her reverie and say, "William, it's time for you to go home, my boy."

"Not going home tonight; told the gaffer," said Wil, and fell asleep again, and my mother started folding her apron again and stared thoughtfully into the fire.

I like silence. I don't know if there's anyone else like me, but I think it's something I inherited from my mother that I have this tendency to spend hours on end in the quiet of the night staring into the fire, while thousands of things that never existed, and will never come to pass, run through my mind. Despite every struggle against it, the tendency has stuck with me to this day. On many evenings I can spend a lifetime in a few hours. Among other things, I sometimes see myself married to someone whose name I don't know; I have children who fill the house with their noise; they grow up and are sent to school; I do my best to bring them up in the best possible way; I have all sorts of problems with them; then they leave home; and in the end their mother dies, and I'm a white-haired old man abandoned by everybody except my two sticks; and I feel cold, and the clock strikes one; and then I jump up on my feet and realise that I've been imagining it all, and that I'm a frozen bachelor, and then I run to bed. Before I close my eyes, I resolve that I will never again give free rein to my imagination, and it is harmful, if not sinful. The next evening I'll read until I get tired, and then say to myself, "Rhys, before you go to bed you'd better think about this or that, just for five minutes." No sooner will I have said that, than I start building castles in the air once again. I imagine for myself this thing, then that, and in this situation and then another situation for an hour, or two, or even three! Far be such a thing from me! And yet I enjoy it. I'm like a man who's a slave to alcohol, hating the habit from the depths of my heart, and at the same time finding the greatest pleasure in it; but always making up my mind to conquer it one day.

But to return. As I said, I like silence; and neither Wil's snores, nor the fact that something frequently came into his throat that seemed about to choke him, did anything other than in a sense add to the silence. Neither my mother nor I said a word; but I've thought since then that our imaginations, unconsciously, were running together, as our minds were so swallowed up by the same thing. I don't know how long we were in this situation for, but I remember well that I imagined tens of times that I heard someone walking across the yard towards the front door; and when they were a few steps from the door I would stop hearing them. Some of the times I was sure that they were Bob's footsteps, and I held my breath; but everything ended in silence. These imaginations were so sweet to me that as soon as I finished one I'd begin another; and if I hadn't seen Wil waking suddenly and my mother leaping to her feet, I wouldn't have known whether it was in my imagination or in reality that someone was knocking at the door. While Wil was waking from his sleep and I from my imaginations, ready to welcome Bob, my mother opened the door. But how disappointed we were! It was the man I hated with my whole soul that I heard saying to my mother,

"Well, Mary, how are you? It's been a while."

This was the one whom I named, when I first saw him, 'the Irishman', and the one who stopped me by the Manor woods on the night that Seth died. It's a strange thing that at every critical period in my early life, this man, whom I hated to see as much as the devil himself, was sure to appear. Wil knew in an instant who he was; as he knew almost as much about him as I did, since I couldn't, as I said earlier, hide more than a very little from my companion and he never betrayed my trust. When my mother understood who our visitor was, she straightened her back, and I saw that she had lost none of the pluck that she showed every time there was truly a need of it. She stood in front of the Irishman, as I called him, so that there was no way he could enter the house without violence, and she said to him:

"James, I have told you many times that I never want to see your face, and that you're not to come to this house."

Wil played with the poker, and the Irishman craned his head to see who was in the house; and he said as he saw Wil,

"Isn't that Hugh Bryan's boy?"

"Yes," said my mother.

"I thought that, by his nose," said the Irishman.

"What do you see by my nose—the smell of dead pheasant on you?" said Wil, angrily.

"William, be quiet this minute, or else," said my mother. I could see from the Irishman's face that nothing would give him more pleasure than to grab Wil by the throat; and my mother knew this as well. Wil played with the poker while sneering at his chest, and he said to me quietly, "Can I give him a whack?" All I'd have needed to do was to say 'yes' and Wil would have taken the poker to him that moment. But I warned him to take care, as the Irishman wasn't a man to mess with. Wil kept his grip on the poker, and kept his eyes on the visitor, as a chicken keeps its eye on a kite which is descending upon it, except that Wil did not fear the attack. I knew from the look on Wil's face that if the Irishman dared lay a hand on my mother, or tried to come into the house violently, he wouldn't seek my advice what to do with the poker. By now my mother was speaking to the Irishman so quietly that I could only make out a few words of what I heard.

I understood that my mother was pleading with him earnestly and with threats, that he should go away. I saw the Irishman turn his gaze towards Wil, and I heard him ask my mother, "Will he be able to hold his tongue after tonight?" I couldn't make out my mother's reply, as she spoke so quietly. Suddenly they both stopped talking; and I saw the Irishman turn his eyes towards the yard and suddenly turning pale; yet he didn't move from his place, and the next moment we heard the sound of footsteps coming towards the house. In the next few seconds I saw before me a guilty conscience causing its owner to tremble; and the next moment I saw a hand grabbing him by the neck and turning him around; and I heard a voice that hadn't sounded in our house for two months saying to him, "Hello, Gamekeeper! What do you want here?"

That was the last I saw of the Irishman that night; and Bob and John Powell walked into the house, closing the door behind them. I won't try to describe the joy of my mother and myself, since I'd be ashamed to see it on paper. However paradoxical it seems, the way that both of us showed our joy was through bursting into tears. Casting my mind back, I believe that the way Wil Bryan chose to show his feeling was much more reasonable. He walked, or rather danced, around the kitchen, whistling the tune of 'When Johnny Comes Marching Home', and running the poker back and forth across his left arm as if he were playing a fiddle. Wil had made a few circuits before my mother noticed that such ungodliness was taking place in her house; and she soon put a stop to his performance.

To my comfort, I couldn't see that the prison had made any difference to Bob's appearance. His face wore the same cheerful and determined calm that it always did, and there was nothing in his gait to suggest that he had lost a grain of his independence of mind. Hard work was nothing new to him, and perhaps that is what accounted for it. When my mother came to herself, she looked him up and down, and proclaimed that he was like the youths from the Exile who looked better after their 'hard rations'.[10]

197

Then she began to interrogate him; and when she asked how come he didn't come home on the midday train, John Powell answered,

"That was my fault. I understood that the workers were planning to make trouble and make an exhibition of Bob, and I knew that he wouldn't like that; so I went to meet him and kept him back until everyone had gone to their beds; but I knew I'd get into trouble for it."

When it was Bob's turn to ask for news, I expected that one of the first things my mother would tell him would be that I had gone to be apprenticed to Abel Hughes; but I was disappointed. And I'm not sorry about that; and I remember that her words were a great comfort to me that moment, because they showed clearly where her thoughts returned to, and what things caused the greatest joy in her heart. She said:

"The best news in the world that I have to tell you, Bob, is that Thomas and Barbara Bartley have come to the *seiat*, and there is every reason to think that the two have been soundly converted."

"And there was great fun with them," said Wil.

"Be quiet, if you know what's good for you," said my mother, "fancy talking about fun in the *seiat*. The two were a bit odd, as you would expect, you know, Bob; but in my mind the echo of the call was there clearly enough. And I have thought a lot, my dear boy," she added, sharing her gaze between the four of us, "about those words: 'The last shall be first' . It would be a hard thing, Bob, if Thomas and Barbara, despite all their ignorance and comedy, were saved in the end and we, the children of the Kingdom, were cast into outer darkness, wouldn't it?"

My mother spoke a lot in this strain; and I don't remember ever seeing Bob pay so much attention to what she said; and if my eyes weren't deceiving me, I think I saw his eyes moisten more than once that evening. My mother was so taken up in her theme that it didn't occur to her for a moment to offer my brother or his

---

[10] Daniel 1:8–16.

companion anything to eat. But it appeared that the two had been feasting somewhere before coming home; and my mother, at last, was thoughtful enough to put the currant cake in front of Wil and myself. I can say with a clear conscience that I speak the truth: if Wil and I, in every circumstance after that had done our duty so fully and perfectly as we did when faced with that currant cake that night, Wil would not be where he is now, and I would be a much more effective minister of the Gospel than I am. My mother commanded Wil and me to go to bed, and I felt myself perfectly happy; and according to Wil, at the last moment before he began to snore, nothing impaired his joy except the fact that I had refused him permission to whack the Irishman with the poker.

23

BOB

Months passed. The Red Fields works was prospering under the stewardship of Abraham, who by now had restored order. Although the price was lower, the profit was far higher than when the 'Lancy', as he was called, was supervisor, and the workers received a salary about which they had no grounds to complain. By now, the ugly words 'oppression' and 'injustice' were not heard in our house; and Bob was perfectly satisfied with his wages. Within a few weeks, every penny of the debt that my mother had incurred during his imprisonment had been paid off; and poverty and need had been exiled from our cottage. But was my mother happy? Bob's wages, as I said, were more than enough to cover our needs as a family, and my mother no longer had to worry how she was going to be able to pay her way. To me it appeared that Providence was smiling upon us, and that our tribulations had completely left us. It is true that there was one bitter thing that was always present in our consciousness, although no-one ever said a word about it; but by now it was an old story, not taken into account except in the way that original sin is, something that we can't shake off.

As far as I could see, the prison hadn't affected Bob's spirit much one way or the other. In his leisure hours he read constantly, and my mother said he was sure to damage his sight. He also came to chapel regularly as before; but despite many appeals would not re-engage with his Sunday School class. I must admit one other change in him, namely that he would no longer read the Bible in our presence. This caused great grief to my mother, as she feared sometimes that he was not reading it at all. Bob normally stayed up for some hours after my mother and I had gone to bed; but my mother took care, once the idea had occurred to her, to leave the Bible every night in a particular place on the table close to the window, so that she would know the next morning if Bob had had anything to do with it. What comfort she took from seeing in the morning that the Bible had been moved, and it became her custom to know every evening the exact position of the Bible on the table. Despite this change for the worse in him, I thought that Bob was more tender and loving towards my mother, more respectful towards her, and more willing to bear with her prejudices. But was my mother happy? I'm sure that she wasn't. The colour did not return to her cheeks, and the black circles did not disappear from under her eyes. In the space of three months she seemed to age ten years; and yet I believe that her colour would have returned and the black marks would have vanished if Bob had only said, 'Mother, I feel very uncomfortable, and I intend to offer myself to the *seiat* next Sunday evening'. But he never said that. My mother would often talk about the danger that tribulations would not just leave us in the same place, but push us further away from God, instead of softening our spirits and making us more consecrated and committed to religion. And Bob did not fail to understand her drift. But as he didn't make any acknowledgement that her remarks applied to him personally, one evening my mother cast subtlety aside, seriously pressing upon him his duty to re-engage with his religious profession; and he answered her, as closely as I can recall, with these words:

"You know that it's not my fault that I don't profess; I didn't throw the profession away, but the church took it from me. As far as I know, there is no difference between how I am now and how I was when I professed, except that I've been in prison; and that, I expect, doesn't add to my suitability to be a professor. And if I were to put myself before the church, the first thing that I'd be asked—or at least that I should be asked—would be, have I repented of the fault for which I was excommunicated; and I would have to answer that I have not, and never can; and the

church, or I, will look like _____[1]. The church alone is responsible
for the fact that I don't profess—if indeed having my name on the
seiat's book is the same thing as professing. But I believe that there
is a higher profession than that, and a far better confession of faith.
There are men—I don't say that I am one of them, lest you say, as
you have said before, that I am self-righteous—but there are men,
I say, whose highest aim is to know the truth no matter what direction
it comes from; men who are always feeling their way towards the
God of Truth, and who know what it is to lose whole nights of sleep
in painful and keen expectation for the light. They know what it is
to have deep wounds from doubt and unbelief, and yet they don't
give up searching for the balm that heals. I call these men the sons
of God, although some of them don't have their names on the book
of any *seiat*. I have deep respect, as you know, for many members of
the church as men who are honest, principled, godly, and zealous in
their own way for church discipline. But it seems strange to me that
they only recognise one class of sin. Are Robert Lewis and William
the Coal the only offenders? Can you explain to me why William
has been disciplined many times, but John Llwyd has never once
been rebuked? As far as I know no-one doubts the innocence of
poor William the Coal, and the sin which is ready to encircle him[2]
is that he forgets his head isn't strong enough to hold more than
two glasses of beer, and that he tends, after going beyond the mark,
to fall backwards or sideways; and in that no-one can or wants to
excuse him. But please, isn't there any rule to call a man to account
for his miserliness and mean-spiritedness? Are some men to be
allowed to sow the seeds of discord, to persecute their brethren and
misrepresent their characters—to chew their fellow members' heels
like corgis[3]—and to live constantly with jealousy and bitterness of
spirit, and to haul preachers and elders over the coals[4]—*just because
they are preachers and elders*? 'The thing which you are going to do,
do it quickly',[5] said Jesus Christ to Judas; and Judas obeyed the
command. But these people can't even come up to Judas' standard.
Every day they sell their Master for thirty pieces of silver, slowly,

thoughtfully, without any rush, and with no realisation, alas, that they will soon hang themselves and go to their own place.[6] And yet it appears that there isn't any rule of discipline for this class of men. Is discipline for William the Coal and me all that the church has? When William took too much drink, every letter in the rules of discipline cried out loudly for him to be excommunicated, even though, as Wil Bryan says, he blamed Satan for everything; and when I laid the old Soldier on his back when I saw him cruelly beating my brother, the letter and spirit of the rules called for me too to be excommunicated. Nonsense, I call this. In the Great Day which is to come—the day when the secrets of our hearts will be made plain, if I were compelled to stand in the shoes of either William the Coal or John Llwyd, I know which shoes I'd choose. You know that I'm as good a teetotaller as anyone in the church, and I think I grieve as much as anyone for the heartbreak that is caused by drunkenness. But I wonder, perhaps our God isn't just the God of teetotalism? Isn't he also the God of justice, love, civility and gentleness? The New Testament teaches me that he is especially that. But when did you ever see Abel Hughes—every respect to Abel, I believe he is a shining Christian—but when did you ever see him rising to his feet to ask for a vote to excommunicate someone for their miserliness, their hard-heartedness and their stubbornness? Who have you seen thrown out for setting people against one another? For criticising his betters? Or for the filth of his tongue? No-one, I know. Not because there aren't any who are guilty of such sins, you know as well as I do. It's a good thing that Paul didn't lend to me his authority with that coat that he left behind in Troas![7]

---

[1] The original text similarly leaves a blank here; perhaps for a rude word to be inserted by the reader's imagination.

[2] Heb. 12:1.

[3] The author naturally uses the correct plural form, *corgwn*, for what is after all a Welsh word.

[4] The text actually says, 'to kill and flay' them—but I have tried to find a similar idiom.

[5] John 13:27. [6] Matt. 27:5 and Acts 1:25.

[7] The author seems to have in mind both 2 Kings 1:13–14 and 2 Tim. 4:13.

You'd soon see that there would be others besides William the Coal and myself who'd be handed over to Satan!"[8]

My mother listened to him in total silence and self-control; and I was amazed at that, because I could remember the time when she wouldn't tolerate him going on in this vein for half a minute without attacking him fluently and relentlessly. Indeed, if Bob had dared to speak, like he did on this occasion, half a year ago, I expect that, even though he was a strong man, my mother would have boxed his ears. But now she listened carefully to every word he said; and if she were listening to his last words on his deathbed, her face could not have worn more care and grief. She looked to me like one who had lost her grip on her last hope, and as one who having been thrown down by disappointment was now trying to look quietly and resignedly into her fate. I was only a lad; but since I had been a child my mother had saturated me in religious ideas and theological terminology; and I think that I was as able at that time, as Bob held forth, and as I am now, to realise the depth of my mother's disappointment and sadness. I can follow and understand her words and feelings when she answered Bob in this way:

"Well, my boy, I never expected to live to hear you talk like that; and yet I must admit that I had feared it would come to this. I have tried to listen carefully to you in case I misunderstand and misjudge you. I can't ever tell you my feelings when you were taken to jail—falsely, I know, thank goodness. But many times in the middle of the night, when everyone else has been sleeping quietly, and I have thought of you, I have been afraid that my heart would break in two before the morning; and I think that, if I hadn't believed that your imprisonment was something that the Lord's hand would use to bring you back, my heart would have broken. But your words tonight have disappointed me greatly, and hurt me more than I can say. It's obvious that your spirit has gone away to a far country,[9] and I'm very afraid that you will be left to yourself. It's hard for me to believe that God's Spirit is not in some way working upon your mind. But remember, my boy, that there is the danger of grieving Him, and there is a limit to the patience even of the Good Lord. You've no idea what state you'd be in if He were to say, 'Let him be'. You were talking about some people whose chief aim is to know the truth; and I understand from your way of speaking that you bundle yourself with them. But what truth do you mean? If the Truth about God, about sinners, and about eternity is what you mean, I know you won't find that anywhere except in God's own Word. And here's what that says: 'If you remain in my word, you shall be my disciples, and you shall know the truth. The secret of the Lord is with those who fear him'.[10] And the same Word says, 'He who is not with me is against me, and he who does not gather with me, scatters'[11]. 'For whoever is ashamed of me and my words in this sinful and adulterous generation, the Son of Man will be ashamed of him when he comes in the glory of his Father with the holy angels'.[12] Who are these people you talk about who lose their sleep seeking the truth, with their names not on the *seiat's* book? I'd like to know where they are, because I never saw anybody who was up to much who wasn't in the *seiat*. I may as well speak my mind clearly to you, I believe that some ideas you've got from those old English books have addled your head. I was sorry to hear you use the language of backsliders when you were pointing out the failings of professors. I thought you were too clever to try to hide under the shadows of such things; and though I must confess that there is a lot of truth in the things you said, your conscience knows that a story like that wouldn't be worth anything before the Judgement seat. Cross yourself, cross yourself, my boy! I don't want to hurt your feelings, and I don't want for anything in the world to say anything that would drive you away; but indeed I would like to hear more echo of the publican[13] in you. I am trying to believe that there is no difference in your condition now

---

[8] 1 Cor. 5:5, 1 Tim. 1:20. [9] Luke 15:13. [10] John 8:31–32 and Psalm 25:14 (cf. Proverbs 3:32). [11] Matt. 12:30, Luke 11:23. [12] Mark 8:38, Luke 9:26. [13] Luke 18:9–14.

relative to when you did profess; and I can't say how glad I am that you continue to attend the services regularly and that you have not given yourself up to sin. But I want you to remember, my boy, that when a downpour comes the rain is heavier just under the eaves than anywhere. There is no *lander*[14] on God's house; and if you're not inside the house it's almost better to be far away from it. To drown alongside the ark is more bitter than anywhere else. It's your own business, my boy. In a manner of speaking it's nothing in the world to do with me; and yet it is something—as Mr Hughes, Llangollen, would say. I won't be here long for you—something tells me that. Between one thing and another I feel that I am nearing some land; and as I plumb I find that the depth is getting less every day. But the ship will go to shore much lighter if I could cast my worries about you into the sea. Between this Euroclydon[15] and that Euroclydon, I have been soundly tossed about recently; but the great Governor has seen fit to show me an inlet with a safe place to land more than once, and I have taken the hint that my soul will not be lost. I don't wish to live to grow old, because I know that I will only be a shackle upon the two of you. 'Although it is not so with my house before God'[16]—you know who I'm referring to—and I hope that God will visit his soul—'Yet he has made an eternal covenant with me'.[17] Rhys, I believe, is in a place where his body and soul will have fair play; and if I could only see you, Bob, as you were, it wouldn't matter to me how soon the call came. The eternal world is very strange to me, and I don't know what transformation I must go through before I enter it; but for now I cannot understand how I can be happy, even in heaven, without thinking that I have left both my boys zealous with the dear old Methodists!"

My mother dried her eyes with her apron, and, according to her old custom, began to fold it. When she referred to her departure, which we had never heard her do before, her words fell on my ear not as the complaint of someone suffering from depression but as the words of a prophet of God declaring the truth, and my heart jumped to my throat. I looked at Bob, and I saw that his eyes were wet. As I have said before, Bob was a difficult one to move once he had formed his ideas; but his heart was remarkably tender, and his love towards my mother was immense. If need be, he'd have died for her any day. I saw that his whole soul was stirred, and that he had to strive to govern his feelings, and I believe that both he and I at the time felt the same as those disciples did when Paul told them that they would see his face no more.[18] After being quiet for a moment, Bob said:

"I fail to understand, Mother, why you have to worry about me so much, and especially why you have to talk about dying and leaving us. You are not a shackle to me at all; and while I have strength and health, my chief pleasure is to keep you happy and carefree. Why are you crying? Do you see some deterioration in my character? What difference does it make to my condition if the church raises its hands, and if Abel Hughes writes my name in a book? I know that you don't want to be a hypocrite; and if you did, you know that I would never do that. It's as much a grief to me, I'm sure, as it is to you that we can't see eye to eye. But I say it again and you can think, if you like, that I am being self-righteous, that I hate hypocrisy with a perfect hatred. I can't say I feel this way or that way, unless I really do. I know as well as you do that it is a privilege for any man to be able to profess religion; but the church has dispossessed me of it; and what help is there for me! Perhaps you say that I have transgressed? I say that I haven't. Because I'll never believe that religion goes against the best feelings of human nature. If I saw tomorrow morning the strong oppressing the weak, and I felt myself stronger than the strong, I'd make him show his heels to the sun at that moment, and I'd go to work with my conscience clear that I had done my duty. And apart from that you must admit that heaven and its

---

[14] Of uncertain meaning; perhaps an architectural term.

[15] Acts 27:14. [16] 2 Samuel 23:5. [17] 2 Samuel 23:5 cont'd. [18] Acts 20:38.

207

population will be very thin if no-one is to go there except those who have their names on the *seiat's* book with the Methodists. I know that you are not so narrow-minded as to think that."

"Will you answer me one question?" said my mother.

"I'll answer a hundred, if I can," said Bob.

"Good," said my mother, "if you will answer two or three to satisfy me, I will feel perfectly calm. Do you see yourself as a broken sinner with no hope in eternity in and of yourself? Do you see the Lord Jesus Christ as a Saviour who is sufficient and suitable for you? Do you feel that you rest entirely on his merit for your life? And is your conscience clear that you are, as you are now, on the path of duty?"

I could see from Bob's face that he had been pushed into a corner. For a while he did not answer, and my mother looked into his eyes as if she were determined to turn him inside-out. Eventually he said, "You know, Mother, that not even many professors can answer questions like that clearly and unequivocally."

"What do you mean by 'unequivocally'?" said my mother. "Don't try to hide your meaning with words I don't understand."

"Well," said Bob, "we'll put 'unequivocally' to one side. I say it again that few even among the keenly religious could answer your questions clearly and without reservation. And I think that you can hardly believe that I will answer them positively. If I can do that when I am your age, I will be thankful. I have no desire to hide my meaning from you, and I must confess that I am in the dark so far, and feeling my way. I can say honestly that I am still groping; but it's as if spiritual truths are fleeing from me. I can assure you that the cry of my soul is, 'Light, light, more light!' On occasions I feel that I am having it, and that from above; but it is only as a flash of lightning, and it leaves me in more darkness still. On other occasions I find a different sort of light, which comes from below; and following it I find myself in swamps and marshes, and realise that it is just a corpse-candle.[19] What am I to do? I am not content to close my eyes and sit without hope in the darkness, because if

I did that I'd be like the devil, about whom Goronwy Owen[20] says,

'He loves to hide in the deep blackness'.

I do not love the darkness; I try to rub my eyes—and stand on tiptoe—and strain my neck to look for some sign of morning; but I see nothing except the night, spreading its black blankets over the vast bed of truth. I had resolved that I would never tell you about my state of mind, as I knew that it would only worry you; and I already regret that I haven't kept it all to myself; and yet I could not, with you questioning me. I know that you don't understand me. To you who are always living in the light, my words seem idiotic; but I assure you that they are spoken in truth and sobriety. I understand from the way that you have spoken for a long time that you believe I am unconcerned about religious things; but the Omniscient One knows that I am not so. And yet the future seems completely dark to me. I am sure that there is light somewhere; the denseness of the darkness itself proves that to me, quiet apart from the fact that I see you enjoying it all the time. Why it is being kept from me, I don't know. Every day I go down into the darkness of the coal mine, but I have my lamp there; but when I try to dig into the world of the mind and the soul, the darkness is just as great, but my lamp goes out. What have I done more than any other sinner to prevent the dawn from breaking on my soul? Perhaps you can tell me. I feel that I'm not like other people. I smile and laugh to be like my contemporaries; but my heart is always heavy, and my soul is groaning and crying. And how can I laugh heartily when I don't know when a big piece of coal will fall on me and sink

---

[19] In pagan Welsh folklore, the light of a soul as it leaves a dead body.

[20] Goronwy Owen (1723–1769) is regarded as one of the greatest Welsh poets of the 18th century; he was born in Llanfairmathafarneithaf, Anglesey, where he later served briefly as a curate before becoming a master at Oswestry School; later he lived in various parts of Shropshire before emigrating to Virginia in 1757 to take a teaching post at the College of William and Mary.

me into deeper darkness than I am always in? Perhaps you'll talk to me about praying; but aren't the yearnings of my soul a continual prayer? And when I put my desires into words they come back to me saying, 'no reply'. 'O wretched man that I am'.[21]"

My mother tried to look cheerful, and said, "Well, my boy, I'm afraid that you have a touch of melancholy. I always thought that no-one was troubled by that except for the old preachers; and I hadn't heard of it troubling any of them for a long time since old Michael Roberts, Pwllheli.[22] You have depression, my boy; you need to have some medicine and perhaps a change of air, they say there's nothing better. Sing a little, my boy, I'll help you," and my mother started to sing as well as she could:

> 'O powerful unbelief,
> You have wounded me!
> But in your face I'll still believe,
> That heaven's gifts are greater.'[23]

From that time onwards my mother changed her tune and her behaviour towards Bob. She spoke comfortingly and encouragingly, but Bob just shook his head, as good as to say that she didn't understand him.

I think it was about a fortnight after the above conversation that I was returning from the countryside after delivering a parcel from the shop—because during the first few months I was with Abel Hughes, most of my work consisted of running errands. The evening was pleasant, and I was very familiar with the road— I knew every house, hedge, wall, gate and milestone. I felt as though every tree was saying 'good night' to me, acknowledging that they knew me well from the days that Wil Bryan and I would go down this road to hunt birds' nests and collect nuts. As early as that night I was already, I think, a bit of a dreamer, and able to enjoy the romantic vistas and deep silence. For as long as I can remember I have preferred the countryside to the town. I always feel that the noise and bother of the town prevents one from hearing God speaking through nature; and the night, because of its silence, has a great charm for me. Perhaps people would laugh at my idea if they read it; but the truth is, I think it's very strange that policemen are not more refined and spiritual than other men. Think how much time they have to meditate in God's air in the deep silence of the night, 'the shining blue firmament' as John Jones Talsarn[24] says, above their heads, and everyone else fast asleep. Such an excellent opportunity to hold communion with God and nature, in the deep silence which is unbroken by anything except the occasional bark of a dog far away in some farmhouse. If it weren't for some of the other things that the job involves, I would like to be a policeman just to be able to stay out all night! But where am I wandering off to? I was, as I said, returning from the countryside full of happiness and high spirits, with no idea that anything uncomfortable might await me. As I neared home, I saw that people were running quickly towards town. I hurried, and soon came across an infirm old collier, who was also heading for town. I asked him why people were running. His answer was: "the damp,[25] my boy, in the Red Fields." I felt as though his answer had given

---

[21] Romans 7:24.

[22] A Methodist preacher, born in Llanllyfni in 1780 but lived in Pwllheli from 1802 onwards. Known as a remarkably powerful revival preacher, he is credited with the conversion of over a thousand people in a single sermon in Llanidloes in 1819, but he experienced a mental breakdown in 1836, from which he only recovered briefly before his death 13 years later.

[23] A lesser-known hymn by William Williams Pantycelyn:

'O anghrediniaeth mawr ei rym,
Ti roddaist imi glwy'!
Ond yn dy wyneb credu wnaf
Fod doniau'r nef yn fwy'.

[24] A Methodist preacher, poet and hymn writer, who lived from 1796 to 1857. He started to preach while working as a labourer on the A5 (as it is now), and as time went on he combined his preaching with work as a quarryman, a shopkeeper and quarry owner. Many of his brothers and sisters emigrated to Wisconsin in 1845, but he and his thirteen children remained in Wales.

[25] A general term used for explosive gas underground.

me wings. In my mind my feet did not touch the ground, but I was carried as it were by a whirlwind of terrors that were rushing through my heart. I left the main road, and made a straight line towards home. I leapt over walls, hedges and gates, and, which amazed me many times after that, didn't feel that there was any obstacle in the way. And I was so selfish! I didn't think of anyone except Bob. Was he among the ones who were burned? According to the time of day he should have been home by now, since his shift finished at seven o'clock. And yet it was only a few minutes after seven! If he had been burned to death, what would I do? If the fire had not touched him how happy I'd be! But what if it had burned his face—what a shame! I wondered if he might have lost one eye—how ugly he'd be! How many thoughts rushed through my heart while I destroyed the distance which prevented me from knowing all! Fairly soon I arrived within sight of our house, and I could see that Bob had come home. But what a state he was in! On a cart with straw in it, and two men, one on each side, holding him. I was at his side in an instant. I heard him moan as they carried him into the bedroom. My mother was as white as a sheet, but perfectly quiet; Bob was as black as coal, and burned to a cinder, but completely calm. His clear and understanding eyes had been burned clean out of his head—and yet he was alive. I wouldn't have recognised him out of all the people in the world. I saw Dr Bennett, the works doctor, in the room but he shook his head hopelessly. A tear ran down the doctor's cheek, and I was jealous because I could not cry. Trouble is sometimes so sharp and severe, that the normal signs which we have to show that we feel it refuse to serve us out of kindness. That is how they behaved to my mother and me this time. We could not cry. When someone, I don't remember who, had given him a mouthful of water, he appeared to revive a bit, and said clearly—"Mother."

My mother drew close to him and said, "Do you see anything, my boy?" (My mother hadn't understood at the time that he had lost both his eyes.)

"I do, mother," he said, "the light has come at last."

A few seconds later he added, in English, "Doctor, it is broad daylight!"[26]

The next minute Bob had left fear and darkness behind, to me and to others.

---

[26] In the foreword to the 1993 printing of the book, E.G. Millward argues that the light Bob sees here is the 'dawn of socialism breaking', following 'the battle of the workers against the oppression of capitalism; the battle of the social gospel for justice in this world'. Well, obviously.

24

MEMORIES OF SADNESS AND COMFORT

One of the most valuable privileges of rural and agricultural areas is that it is very rare for something to happen in them that suddenly plunges them into trouble and grief. It is not so in industrial areas. Sometimes the morning opens its tender eyelids on an area which is already awake and busy, and smiles on it happily, as a small baby in good health and spirits smiling at his mother, sitting by his cot as he wakes up. It sees hordes of colliers turning out of their houses with their lamps hanging from their belts. The sound of their clogs on the hard road, and uneven pavement, is music to the ears of many Welsh women I know, and rekindles the longing in the heart of many a young widow who comes to the door with a child on her arm, and another tugging at her apron, to watch them pass, as if she were still expecting John to come back. If you look hard, you'll see a strong and well-set man hurrying out of the house, and walking as if he is proud to be able to work hard to earn money to keep his wife and children; but before he goes many steps, a young lad, barefoot, bare chested, half dressed, and not entirely clean, with the remnants of the previous night's supper on his fat, round face, runs after him; because his father, in his haste, forgot to give him a kiss before leaving for work. Now, reminded of his negligence, he lifts him up onto his wide chest, and in spite of all the filth on the boy's face gives him such a smacker of a kiss that the whole neighbourhood can hear it, which causes the mother, who by this time is standing in the doorway, to laugh heartily. Do any of them think that this is the last kiss? The engine of work—the heart of the district—beats strongly and steadily. The smoke of the big chimney rises in fat, black clouds straight to the heavens; because the day is fair, and God needs the smoke (or so I thought when I was a boy) to make clouds out of it! Team after team,[1] wagon after wagon, is seen coming from the works laden with the best coal, with the wagon-man in his knee breeches, his whip on his shoulder, walking as though he has one foot in a ditch, turning his crooked eye towards everyone he meets to see if they have noticed his well-fed horses, whose tails he took so much care to plait the night before, and tied up with blue and yellow ribbons. The children play in the street and make fun of the wagon-man's bandy legs and the way he adds the letter 'y' to the end of his horses' names, such as 'Boxer-y' and 'Blaze-y'. Our man takes no notice. Everyone seems to enjoy peace and happiness, from the fat butcher who, between customers, snoozes in his chair in the shop appearing as though long meditation upon fat has made him ready for the knife himself, to the thin, grey-faced cobbler who is walking towards his house at a half-trot with his apron full of work for repair. Although it's still morning, the tidiest of the colliers' wives are in Mr Roberts' shop looking for some tasty morsel for their husbands; because what use is it for them to work hard if they can't have something appetising to eat? They earn an excellent wage, so why can't they have the occasional treat? The shops all have the appearance of doing well, and their owners use the morning pause to remove the dust and put everything in order. It is said that the old lady who runs the toy shop has an 'old sock'.[2] And little wonder—look at the boys of every size and age going to school; you can see them all in a row, with their slates hanging by a cord from their backs, with the previous day's lesson still written on them—from the young lad's strokes to the older youth's vulgar fractions—as I was saying, all in a row, with their noses flattened against the shop window, and each promising themselves a toy the next payday. What happy creatures!

But perhaps within the hour the news will come like wildfire

---

[1] The author literally means a team, or a yoke, of oxen.

[2] Implying a bit of money saved for a rainy day, and hence a measure of quiet prosperity.

that there has been a collapse in the mine, and such-and-such a number of men have been killed; or perhaps water has broken out, and such-and-such have been drowned, or trapped in the upper reaches of the mine! A wild and deep grief spreads over the neighbourhood. The lad who, on his way to school in the morning was looking forward to the next payday when his father would buy him a bat, finds himself orphaned by lunchtime. The strong and well-set man in his prime, who in the morning was lifting up his child, as he would a feather, onto his broad chest to kiss, comes home in the evening on a cart as a dead body. You simple men of Anglesey! What do you know of these sudden and heart-rending visitations?[3] When through the long winter nights you enjoy your coal fire—not peat—remember that what you're enjoying is often worth blood!

When the fire broke out in the Red Fields, which was the death of my brother and various others, there was of course not a moment of warning; and the community that was, a few minutes before, quiet and happy, was sunk into a painful and indescribable grief. Every worker had his 'Davy lamp',[4] and how the accident happened no-one knew or ever will know. But it wasn't how it happened that worried those who were bereaved by the accident— among them my mother and I—but the thing itself. My mother lost a son, who although a lad had been to her as a husband, and on whom she entirely depended for her livelihood; and she loved him much more than her own life. I know that she didn't worry too much about me; but not a day passed—not even an hour of the day, when her soul wasn't bound up with that of Bob. I lost a brother among brothers, to whom I feel indebted for almost everything I have in the way of education; and even now I feel sure that I'd be something completely different from what I am, were it not for him. If I tried to describe my grief when I lost him, I would make myself an object of ridicule to those who remember me. At the time, I envied my mother because I saw her bearing the trial so well, while I had become a useless sop. How precious it is to me now to remember her behaviour! If all the works of the Puritans, and everything that was ever written on behalf of Christianity, were put into one pile in front of me, and if I could take in all of their arguments, my mother's quietness and self-control in the face of severe testing is an infinitely stronger argument in my mind of the truth and Divinity of evangelical religion. Did she feel as much as other women who were bereaved in the accident, who shouted and lost all control of themselves? Yes, and much deeper, I believe. But she had some hidden spiritual strength to fall back upon, which allowed her to look at the most grievous event as a necessary verse in the chapter of her life, without which the meaning and sense of the text would be unclear. It wasn't physical strength that sustained her, because, to my dismay, that had for some time been fading quickly. In her foolishness, my mother believed that Bob was the best-looking boy in the neighbourhood, and she suspected every young girl who came to our house of trying to charm him. However, so great was the insult that the fire gave him, that she decided the moment his soul left him that she wouldn't look at his face again 'until the resurrection has polished[5] it up'. If she had known that 'polish' was an English word then I know that she wouldn't have used it, so great was her prejudice against everything English. When his coffin was taken into the house (yes, and that's a terrible thing in a cottage where there is no room to escape to and avoid seeing it), my mother gave a strict instruction to the carpenter to screw the lid down at once. She was too jealous lest anyone come to gawp at his ugliness. Isn't it true that when someone we love is overtaken by death—especially sudden death—the defects and weaknesses that they had in life are diminished in our sight? Remembrance only sees them in their best clothes. I was quite sure

---

[3] The author is here a little unfair to the island of Anglesey, which at Parys mountain near Amlwch had the world's largest copper mine and suffered its share of fatal accidents.

[4] Invented by Sir Humphry Davy in 1815, specifically to prevent fires in coal mines as a result of flammable gases being ignited by oil lamps.

[5] ...with the word 'polish' in English; otherwise the next sentence would make no sense.

that my mother had prayed much for Bob, and had worried a great deal about his condition, though there was nothing in his lifestyle to justify that except his taciturnity, and the fact that he was not a church member. But now, when there was nothing but his burned body laying quietly between four boards in the bedroom, she did not appear to be the least concerned about the safety of his soul, which was by now far away from us; because I remember well that after she had been silent for about an hour, folding her apron and staring into the fire, she asked me:

"What did he say," using the pronoun as if we had been talking about him a minute before, "what did he say, tell me, in English to Dr Bennett?"

And I answered, "He said that it was broad daylight."

"And what did the doctor say?"

"He said that he was starting to ramble," I answered.

"I thought that was what he said; and that's what Festus said to Paul[6]—'You are beside yourself'. 'The natural man does not receive the things of the Spirit of God, for they are foolishness to him; neither can he know them, because they are spiritually discerned'."[7] And she added, as though to herself, "Rambling, indeed! No danger of Bob rambling. But he was talking of the spiritual light—the thing he had been groping for, like he had said. 'At evening time it shall be light!'[8] Wonderful, wonderful! He had to lose both his eyes before he started to see![9] 'For judgement I am come into this world, that they which see not might see.' I would have much preferred it if he had professed; but I never believed he was without any religion. Abel Hughes always said that there was a better grain on Bob than on the half of us. But the thing which most quietens my mind is what Bob said about a fortnight ago—that he was not dismissive of the things of religion, and that the cry of his soul was for the light. And God said, 'You shall seek me and you shall find me, when you search with your whole heart'.[10] 'I did not say to the children of Jacob, "Seek me in vain"'.[11] 'Ask and it shall be given to you; seek and you shall find',[12] said the Saviour on the mount. I'd say that it's hardly likely that he is lost. I hope that I am not sinning; but I feel so sure that he is in heaven that, if I go there myself, as I expect, but find that Bob isn't there, that will be enough to spoil all my comfort."

Well, today I cannot but hope that my mother's belief was correct. If many a learned man were to read what I'm about to say, no doubt he would laugh at me. Let him laugh. But I believe that godly people, no matter how uneducated they are, have some spiritual perception and receive, though perhaps unconsciously, glimpses of the eternal world that the natural man is denied, and that he wouldn't understand even if he were allowed them. I know very well that my belief does not concur with the doctrine of some of the capable men of our 'enlightened' age—an age in which there are some who look at the religious as old-fashioned people, and at the Bible as a harmless little book, and who more or less promise us that soon, through their scientific discoveries, they will enable the schoolboy to write on his slate, between breakfast and lunch, all the secrets of nature—the secrets of existence, and the yearnings of the eternal soul.

Although my memories are fresh, I would not like, and do not intend, to linger around the time when that of my brother which was mortal was waiting to be forever hidden from my sight. If I were to try to give a description of my feelings at the time, perhaps it would be regarded by those who take the trouble to read this memoir as a lack of good taste. Although every family knows it, death is a stranger every time. It visits us without being invited, and it is never welcome. And the colder its welcome, the more likely it is to visit again soon. I know that I describe the experience of many when I say that the time when the body of a loved one is in the house, while we await the hour which by the custom of the land is seen as appropriate for him to be taken to his long-term

<hr>

[6] Acts 26:24. [7] 1 Cor. 2:14. [8] Zech. 14:7. [9] John 9:39. [10] Jer. 29:13.
[11] Isa. 45:19. [12] Matt. 7:7.

home, is very strange and alien. It's so hard for us to realise that the one who only yesterday was looking at us, speaking with us, eating and drinking, and walking around just like us, is now peaceful and cold, deaf and dumb. How cruel of us it seems to leave him in a room on his own! The weather is cold, and there's no fire in the room where he is. How hard! Do we feel that we are being unkind to him? Would he leave us like that? We know that he—the real he—is far away from us; and yet we are still conscious that he is in the room next to us; otherwise why do we speak so quietly, as if we were afraid of waking him up? How slowly the hours drag by! How unfeeling is the custom of the land, which forces us to shut out the daylight and make the whole period one long night, as if we didn't have enough of the night in our souls already! The sadness is all-embracing, and the urge to get everything over with is strong. What! Are we in a hurry to bury him? Oh, we are not, the dear one! But the time is long and tedious. We try to read; the eye looks at the book, but the mind wanders far away to some strange place. The slightest noise causes us to listen, and listen intently. Our ear directs itself to the next room. How similar the sound was to his familiar cough! Did he move? The whole thing is imagined; he and the room are as quiet as the grave! We fall into a sleep of short duration and when we wake we wonder if we were dreaming, and once again we go through the whole situation. Everything takes on a different form now. There is now no charm in life, praise, or profit. The things of this life are emptiness in our sight; and we're amazed that anyone can be so dedicated to things of the world, and especially that they can laugh; forgetting that we ourselves, a few days previously, were guilty of that, and after a short time will be as we were. How many resolutions we make! All of which will have been greatly compromised, if not completely forgotten, within two months. Death is an ugly black beast; but it throws a lot of light on things, even for the living. How much more for those it takes away?

The time when death has ploughed the soil of the heart, and

tribulation has softened it, is an excellent opportunity for the evangelist, and the man of counsel, to sow the good seed. The seed easily goes deep. Even if the soil hardens again, it's possible that the seed will sprout some day, that it will break out through the hard crust, and bear fruit, perhaps a hundredfold. The visits of friends from chapel to my mother and myself in our trouble were so blessed and comforting that I cannot give them a fair description, nor put a price on their value. I remember my mother saying that the next most valuable thing to her, after the great promises of the Bible and faith in God as the chief controller of all things, was the encouraging words of religious brothers and sisters. The number who came to comfort us was not small, and among them Thomas and Barbara Bartley were not the least faithful. They were so childlike, and their sympathy was so genuine, that you couldn't help but value it. But my mother could hardly help smiling at some of Thomas' simple and innocent questions, such as:

"Mary, d'you think that Bob has told Seth yet that Barbara and I have started comin' to the *seiat*? That is, if he's come across him yet, as there are so many of 'em there, aren't there?"

"For all I know, perhaps he has, Thomas," said my mother.

"Well, it's not possible," said Thomas, "that they won't come across each other sometime; two men come together more easily than two mountains, as they say."

After being silent for a minute, Thomas added, "Barbara and I were thinkin' about you a lot last night, Mary, and we couldn't see at all what on earth you can do now except come and live with us. There's as much space there as you could want, and a hundred thousand welcomes, aren't there, Barbara? We've made a space there for you already, and the two of you must come over tonight. You're not buryin' Bob for another three days, so why stay here breakin' your heart, isn't it, Barbara?"

Barbara nodded; and my mother said, "You are very kind and neighbourly, Thomas; but I couldn't think for a minute of leaving Bob here by himself, even though the whole thing is a fancy."

"To be sure," said Thomas; "I didn't think of that. No, no, honour bright; thinkin' about it, it would look a bit cold of you to leave him, specially as you have no fear. But we'll talk about this again."

"What have I got to be afraid of, Thomas? There's nothing here but the vile body—the empty house."

"That's not what I was talkin' about," said Thomas.

My mother understood his meaning. Thomas knew more about us than I had thought, and my mother tilted her head to acknowledge his thoughtfulness, and added, "There's a lock and a bar on the door, Thomas."

"To be sure, but you must come over in three days; we won't notice what you'll eat, any more than what a chicken would eat," said Thomas.

Three days passed, but my memories are dark and confused. We felt as if we were in a dream. There are two impressions on my mind that I can read clearly today, namely, that there were many people at the funeral, and that Wil Bryan walked alongside me with a bundle of boxwood under his left arm, and carrying in his left hand a cloth full of sand. I have a faint memory of Mr Brown's dry voice rushing through the burial service—and a clear memory of Wil Bryan on his knees beside the grave, scattering the sand over it and dressing it with the boxwood. I little thought at the time how soon he would be repeating the same task! In general, Wil was very talkative; but when he was in deep sympathy, he would always be silent. He didn't speak a word to me until we were halfway home from the cemetery; and I remember his comment well:

"Rhys, do you know what Bob would say if he knew that Mr Brown would be burying him? He'd repeat the last words of Bobby Burns –'Don't let that awkward squad shoot over my grave!' That's what he'd say, I swear." Wil was recalling Mr Brown's role as Justice of the Peace in wrongly sending Bob to jail, and I have no doubt that he was stating my brother's feelings to the letter.

The reader will remember—if I have a reader—that Thomas Bartley was a young believer. Old customs and ideas that didn't sit well with a religious profession often showed themselves in him. Although Thomas was very ready and willing to desert them, he felt that it couldn't be done without quite a wrench. On the day Bob was buried, Thomas asked my mother whether she was planning to get some bread, cheese and beer for people, and added that in his opinion the Brown Cow had the best drink, and suggested very clearly that he would bear the cost himself. While thanking him for his kindness, my mother took trouble to explain to Thomas how loathsome was the custom of feasting at funerals, and especially of putting alcohol on the table; and Thomas said,

"To be sure, Mary, you know best, you know more of the Bible than I do, and I'll always give in to you. But I thought it looks a bit cold not to have anythin' here for people to eat or drink."

My mother met the wishes of our kind friends half way, permitting Barbara after the funeral to make tea and to invite some of the closest neighbours to enjoy it, which went a long way to placate Thomas' conscience. After the neighbours had all gone home, and my mother and I, and Thomas and Barbara were left alone, after a little conversation Thomas said,

"Now, Mary, you have to get out of here. What will you do here, breakin' your heart? It's never been good for people to live on their own. You've seen how comfortable we are over there. It will save Barbara and me comin' over here for you to explain things to us. You know what? I'd like it as much as to hear a sermon, to have you over there; and like I said, we won't notice what you'll eat, any more than what a chicken would eat."

"I don't know how to thank you enough for your kindness, Thomas," said my mother; "but since you mentioned it the other night, I have decided to accept your kind invitation, on the condition that I can pay for my lodging for as long as my money holds out. I have a bit put aside, and I'll get something for the things here, and perhaps that will be enough for me while I live."

"We'll settle things like that again," said Thomas, loading his pipe.

I was shocked. I didn't imagine that my mother would condescend to accept kindness even from Thomas Bartley until circumstances compelled her to. I knew that independence of mind, and a terror of being a burden to anyone, were clear aspects of her character. While Barbara was helping my mother to put on her blue cloak and big bonnet, the reason suddenly came into my mind why she accepted Thomas Bartley's invitation so readily: she was afraid of our old visitor.

Within a few minutes the four of us were on our way to the Twmpath—for that was the name of Thomas' house. I can remember this minute the order in which we travelled—not unlike a train: Thomas leading like a locomotive engine, the smoke from his pipe whirling in the night air—me at his heels, and my mother following me, like passenger carriages, and Barbara, who was rather fat, like a luggage van at the back, swaying a bit like the back end of a train often does. The four of us were quiet, with the exception of Barbara, who was troubled by rheumatism, giving the occasional groan like a luggage van whose wheels needed oiling, and Thomas like a locomotive giving the occasional whistle in the form of, 'Are you coming, ladies?' Of course, I am describing the journey as I look at it now, and not as I saw it at the time. The thought of leaving the old house that I was born and raised in, where I had spent many happy hours and with which all my memories were tied up, filled my heart with sadness. That was the first night I had spent away from home. I always saw the Twmpath as the very pattern of cosiness and happiness; and our welcome there was true and without pretence. But when I went to bed, the bed that Seth had died in—and which was much more comfortable than my bed at home, there came over me such a wave of longing for the old house, for Bob, and for the old days, that I had to put my head under the bedclothes and push the sheets into my mouth to stop myself from crying out. In the morning my mother knew from my swollen eyes how I had spent the night, and a groan made it as far as her throat but she choked it before it could come out. We could see that Thomas was making an effort to stop us from being heavy-hearted, and to keep our minds off our troubles. He took us out to the yard to see the pigs and chickens, speaking constantly. My mother paid attention to everything he said; but I knew that she did not find his conversation edifying, as it ran something like this:

"Mary, these are the best pigs I ever had for comin' along. I don't give a fig for a pig that isn't greedy. These would eat the trough if they didn't get their food on time. Him over there, without the tail, is the master of the trough. I always raise two—because they come on much better like that—one to slaughter and one to sell. I never give India honey to 'em, because then when you put the bacon in front of the fire it goes to nothin'. Potatoes and barley flour is the best stuff to feed up a pig if you want good bacon, and boil up some nettles sometimes for them as a change. There's nothin' better for a pig that's lost its appetite than givin' it some boiled herrin' in its food. What good is there in brewery dregs for a pig? None at all. You know what, Mary? I'd never eat bacon if I had to buy that American bacon. How d'you know what they've been eatin'? They say that pigs in America eat blacks who have died in the forest, and I can easily believe that. Hello! Cobyn, is that you? There's a cockerel for you, Mary! If that white feather weren't in his tail, he'd be pure game. Look at his breast! It's like a lantern. There was a time, before I came to religion, that I wanted to trim his comb; but somethin' tells me that that wouldn't be right, somehow, because it would be like tryin' to improve on what the Good Lord has done. I don't find that these game birds are terribly good layers, but just that their eggs are richer. Barbara (shouting loudly), is breakfast ready? Ho! That will come soon. Fowls are things that really pay, Mary, so long as they can feed well. Did you ever see how fond of them you are gettin'? They look so cute when they turn their heads crooked. Well, let's go back to the house, to see what the old woman has for us. I don't know how you feel, but I feel I could eat worms' heads!"

After breakfast I set off for the shop, and my mother came with me for a little bit so she could talk privately to me. Putting her hand on my shoulder, she said to me, "I can see from your face that you've been fretting. You must buckle down, my boy. The two of us, you see, must submit but not give up.[13] You are only starting off in life, but I am pulling towards the end. If you are a good and obedient boy—and I believe you will be—God will look after you. Concentrate on pleasing your master, and by pleasing your master you will please God. Soon I'll come to speak with Abel Hughes about having you sleep over there, as it won't pay for us to be bolder than is appropriate with the kindness of our friends. You can come here every night after closing the shop to look in on us, if you choose. The only thing that troubles me is the fear of having to ask for help from the parish. But perhaps I'll be saved from that yet. I have a bit set aside, and perhaps that will last as long as I do."

I tried to say something that was on my mind; but my words stuck in my throat, and all I could do was burst into tears. My mother held my head to her chest; and when I had cried out my grief, she dried my eyes with her apron and said, "There you are, now—off you go, and remember what I told you."

And so I went, and so I did, I hope. On the way I couldn't help thinking of the terror my mother had of having to ask for parish help, and I lamented the fact that I, because of age and circumstances, could not provide for her. It was only a few months since she had spoken so freely and independently to Mr Brown the parson, declaring her confidence that she would never need the help of 'either parish or parson'; and I have no doubt that that altercation between her and the parson was raw and bitter in her memory. I was fairly sure that she would much prefer to fall on the mercy of the general Relieving Officer of the children of trouble—Death—than to make amends with Mr Brown; and I feared that something in her voice and her words that morning showed that that was her prayer!

---

[13] In Welsh, 'ymostwng ond peidio ymollwng'—a powerful turn of phrase that doesn't come through well in translation.

AN ELEGY IN PROSE

Before I draw the second period in my story to a close, and before I say anything about the period when I found myself alone and realised that I was beginning the battle of life, I must say something more about two or three characters who have already had no small mention; one of them in particular.

Throughout the season that my mother was staying with Thomas and Barbara Bartley, she received the greatest kindness and the best care that she could expect or wish for. Her main task while in the Twmpath was preparing the two old dears to be received as full church members; and that was no small enterprise. She took several weeks to coach them, so to speak, before she felt confident enough to encourage Abel Hughes to call them forward for acceptance. When this came about, there was a lot of entertainment to be had in the *seiat*. Their answers were simple and original, and they caused some to laugh and others to cry, and some to laugh *and* cry. The constraints I have set myself do not allow me the time to give a full record of that *seiat*. In answering some questions, Thomas would look towards my mother doubtful and half afraid, like one sees boys looking to their fathers as they recite their verses in church meetings, and he referred to her more than once in so many words as the authority on doctrine. On the whole, Thomas gave general satisfaction as to his knowledge and his suitability to be accepted. Barbara did not come through with quite the same level of satisfaction. It was hard to get any more out of her than that she thought and felt 'just the same as Thomas'. It was clear that Barbara saw herself as a duplicate of her husband, and so long as Thomas had answered correctly then it was unnecessary to waste time with her. The two, as I observed in a previous chapter, went together and thought together precisely, with the same level of similarity and unity between them as between two loops on a piece of string. Now that I bring it to mind, I would almost go a step further and say that they had the same consciousness, and there was more of identity than individuality in them. They were like a clock with two faces, which always showed exactly the same time of day. On the strength of Thomas' answers, Barbara was also accepted unopposed into all the privileges of the church; and when they went home that night, arm in arm like a pair of nuts, they felt very happy, their hearts swelling with the honour. My mother had looked forward to this with great interest and anxiety, since she saw Thomas and Barbara as her special pupils. I know that she felt happy that her labour, her teaching and her prayers had not been in vain.

This was the last time that my mother was in the chapel. As I suggested before, her health had for some time been failing, and her strength diminishing. 'Through this Euroclydon[1] and that Euroclydon', she would say, she had been 'tossed soundly, lately'. Her unravelling was hastened by Bob's sudden death. She realised that the stick she had leant upon had broken, and that she had neither the strength nor the health to earn her living. She had a terror of being dependent on the kindness of her friends, and especially of the parish charity; and she appeared to me as one who had raised her finger to death and was beckoning to it. Death had no sting[2] for her, and her heart and meditations had been beyond it for some time. She was not greedy for money; and I believe that she saw the little that she'd saved while Bob was earning a good wage, and that which she received for the furniture of the old house, like the sand in the hourglass, and like the measure of her remaining lifetime. Occasionally a kind woman—and I see all women as kind to a preacher—will boil an egg for my breakfast on a Monday morning before I return home after an appointment;

---

[1] Acts 27:14. [2] Hosea 13:14, 1 Cor. 15:55-56.

and as I see her watching the sand in the glass I always think about my mother. She looked in exactly the same way at the little money that she possessed; and I was conscious that, when the last penny left her purse, so she would leave also. She did not suffer much pain in her last days. She went to bed to die, just as you sometimes see a woman in a station going out of the cold wind into the waiting room to wait for the train, and looking towards the door as if she is tired of waiting. Yet she was herself, quiet and self-controlled. The old Bible with its loose pages was always open beside her on the bed, as if (for me to continue the analogy) she was looking for her ticket; and she died with her glasses on.

Well, my old mother; I am sorry in my heart that I am no poet. If I had the muse, I would sing you a magnificent elegy—an elegy that would carry in itself the proof that it had been crafted in the workshop of my heart, whatever defects it might have. Although I'm not of the elect poetic order, I am not content to move on without trying to pay the tribute which is due from me to your memory—even though I must do that in poor prose. Is it something effeminate, and a sign of weakness, to be too fond of one's mother? If so, then I am very effeminate and weak indeed. I don't know when I began to believe of you that you were the fairest, the most lovable, and the best among women. Trying to go back as far as I can, I almost believe that I had this idea in me when I came into the world; there doesn't seem to be a beginning of it, as far as I can see, in my mind. It wasn't the fruit of observation and reason. If it were, it could have been different. I felt that I was closer to you than you were yourself, and I knew that that was how you felt towards me. Didn't I know your face years before I knew my own? And if I were to look this minute at both of our faces in a mirror, yours is the one I would recognise first. When I was a child on your arm by the lakeside, and when you tried to direct my eyes to my reflection in the water, I knew your face, but not the other one. What care, what trouble you took with me! Before I could speak, you understood my needs and my wishes. When

I was unwell you could not sleep nor rest; when I was healthy and vigorous you were in your element. You taught me language, even though you did not understand its grammar yourself; and it took you years of labour to do that, and did not take a penny of salary. It was the dear old Welsh tongue; you did not know any other language, and you did not think that it had an equal. You printed its letters onto my memory when my heart was young and tender, and I could not, if I wished to, erase them. I love to remember now that one of the first lessons in spelling you gave me was, 'I, and e, and s, and u'.[3] You were uneducated, and as a result your prejudices were many and strong. You could hardly believe that there was anything worth knowing outside of the Welsh language, nor any religion worth the name except among the Calvinistic Methodists. Though you were one of the most avid readers of any woman I know, you could easily have counted all your books on your fingers: the Bible, Charles' *Dictionary*, *The Instructor*, the Hymnary, the works of Gurnal, *Pilgrim's Progress*, and *The Welshmen's Candle*.[4] Yes, I must add two others, however comically inappropriate alongside these, namely the Almanac of Robert Roberts, Holyhead,[5] and the works of Twm o'r Nant.[6] That is the sum of your books; but every one of them was stained with your thumbprints as you frequently communed with their words, and every corner of their covers was like Mal Milk-and-Water's[7] dog, balding at the ears. Your books did not get to lie long on the shelf in the dust and dirt; when the need came, you found the time to read and meditate upon them. You furnished your mind with their contents, so that at any time you could pour big sections of them from your memory as the need arose. And you were as familiar and at home with the grand passages of the Books of Job, Isaiah and Revelation as you were with the list of festivals and holidays in the Almanac and its rhymes, '*Eira gawn oddeutu'r llawn*'.[8] Considering your religiosity, I was always amazed how much pleasure you had in the work of the bard of the Nant, even though he wasn't approved of by the Methodists. One of those contradictions of character, I expect. I know that you read with relish the heavy blows that the famous satirist gave to irreligious parsons and oppressive stewards. Was it Twm who gave you such a prejudice against the Church of England? I have cause to think that you believed the bard had a return to faith before the end of his life, and I heard you scores of times reciting these lines from his work: [9]

'My handmaiden, my conscience,
Who is mine because of his amazing blessings,
told me your story,
That you are the greatest Prophet,
Whose deliverance is in Samaria, a good thing to seek;
In every way silence my complaints,
And let me not babble of Abana and Pharpar,
The disappointing rivers of my own barren land;
Turn me to the open Jordan, the waters of the Son of Man;
There is nothing that can clean away the filth of my life,
But the blood of Jesus, the one who

---

[3] Iesu, the Welsh name for Jesus.

[4] All these were referred to in Chapter 10, except for the Bible, the Hymnary and *The Instructor*. The Hymnary would have been that of the Calvinistic Methodists at the time, and *The Instructor* was a catechism published by Thomas Charles, the author of the *Dictionary*, in 1807.

[5] An annual publication by Robert Roberts, a scholar of astronomy and geography whose 650-page textbook *Daearyddiaeth* (*Geography*) published in 1816, was as comprehensive a survey of the field as any at the time. He published an annual almanac from his own press in Holyhead from 1824 till his death in 1836, whereupon it continued as an annual publication bearing his name until 1888.

[6] See note in chapter 10.

[7] Presumably some well-known local character.

[8] '*We'll have snow around the time of the full*' (presumably implying 'moon', or perhaps 'year').

[9] The first half of the verse refers back to the story of Naaman the Syrian captain approaching the prophet Elisha, as related in 2 Kings, Chapter 5, before comparing the healing of Naaman's leprosy in the Jordan to the cleansing of a sinner in the blood of Christ. In Welsh of course it rhymes and scans (see the appendix at back of book).

Went through death, wilting on the wood of the cross.
Oh! Let me, even though I sin, oh God,
take shelter in your pain.
You did not give, gentle Jesus,
Your precious blood in vain for a wounded world'.

But the book that you were most at home in, and feasted
your mind upon, was the Bible. You never tired of reading it and
speaking of its truths. I don't believe you ever once doubted for a
second that it was Divine, the true Word of God. I remember that
if Bob happened just to suggest tentatively that there was an error
in the translation of some verse, it would drive your jealousy into a
white heat. Though you were fond of the Reverend _____ ,[10]
weren't you almost cross with him when he said in a sermon that
there was a need to alter slightly the phrasing of a verse? And didn't
you say about him to Abel Hughes afterwards, that you were afraid
that much learning was driving him mad?[11] I know that the main
reason that you weren't over-fond of the 'students' was that one
of them once said that his text was rendered better in the English
than in the Welsh; and I remember you saying crossly that you had
no patience to listen to apprentice preachers trying to change the
Word of God. Your ignorance caused you to speak so, but perhaps
you will have credit in heaven even so, because it was your zeal for
the Bible, and your love for every verse and word in it, that caused
you to be so jealous. And no wonder. Wasn't the Bible *as it is* the
source of all your comforts? Weren't its promises *as they are*, word-
for-word and letter-for-letter, what sustained you in every trouble
and hardship. If anyone had succeeded in shaking your faith in its
literal inspiration one bit, it would have been over for you! You
had put your trust so completely in its truths, and loved them so

---

[10] Strangely, while he often makes reference to real contemporaries by their names the author still resorts occasionally to the annoying Victorian habit of putting a blank where the name ought to go.

[11] Acts 26:24.

much, that I can easily believe what Thomas Bartley said about you, that at the last moment before you died you were looking through your glasses at your Bible with all its loose pages as though you were unhappy to leave it, and eager to take it with you!

The circle of your life was small; you knew next to nothing about the world in the proper sense of the word. You could not imagine its size, its busyness, and its wickedness. Your road was narrow and your hedges were high; but you succeeded remarkably to walk down the middle of it, without once, as far as I know, falling into the ditch. But however narrow your road, I am certain that it led to Life, just like the small stream leads to the sea as surely as the wide river. As was your road, so was your mind: narrow, but straight. You knew as well as anyone that the Saviour was a Jew after the flesh; but you believed, in spite of that, that he was more of a Welshman than anything else. And in this you were right; because doesn't a believer of any nation feel that the man Christ Jesus belongs more to his own nation than to any other? And isn't this a clear proof of his qualification to be the Saviour of men wherever they are found?

As you won't read what I have written about you until I, like you, have crossed over to join the majority, so to speak, I feel I can speak the truth without being hindered by shyness or pretension. You were put together with strong faculties and especially with an outstanding memory; and if you'd had a good education in your early years, I don't doubt that you would have been a notable character. Uneducated as you were, it was rare for anyone to deceive you. And yet once you were deceived greatly; and if it were not for that then this hand would not be writing this summary of the story of your life—I would not exist. You were deceived by the one who should have been your leader and guide—by the one who won your heart and your love when you were a young (and, I believe, beautiful) girl. You were deceived by the one who should have been most faithful to you—by your husband—by my father. And no wonder. He was, I hear, a strong and good-looking man.

He wasn't a believer. He tried to talk to you; but you wouldn't listen to a man without religion. He started to attend services; but for what purpose? In the end he became a member in the same church as you. He could, now, talk to you—tenderly and religiously. The vicious hypocrite! He was sharp-tongued as you were, and in that the two of you were alike. Oh, how he admired the preachers; what pleasure he got from the chapel! He was a new man outside, but there was a legion of devils in his heart.[12] Yes, you listened to him! And 99 per cent of girls would have done just what you did. You married him on a fair and lovely day in May—in a shower of presents and good wishes from your friends. But after that—yes, after that! Only you and God know how much you suffered, and what trials you went through. About whom am I talking? About my father—about my own father—the rascal! And I was glad that when you died you did not see his face or hear his voice. On a noteworthy night in my own life I saw once his shape—only his shape—in the darkness, in the company of another whom I hate with my whole heart.

Well, my dear old mother! What a mercy it was for you to have religion of the best sort when you were a young girl. His filthy and devilish tempers could do no harm to your faith in God! When you were covered in bruises by his cruel fists—and the thought that you were ever like that makes my heart bleed—you were still able to pray for him! Many times you could not go to chapel because you had a pair of black eyes. The inhuman villain! My flesh creeps, and my muscles tense when I think of what you suffered. How fortunate it was for you, Mary Lewis, when his wickedness developed to the extent that he had to flee the country. He nearly killed you many times, and never thought of escaping, and he never imagined that the authorities may take him to jail. But when he came close to killing someone else, infinitely less worthy than you in character, the whole land was after him, and every policeman

---

[12] Mark 5:9.

tried to bridle him. Thank heavens! You never saw him again after that; and you didn't even want to hear his name. I have already referred to your poverty and need, and all you went through in connection with the imprisonment and sudden death of Bob; but there was not, as far as I know, disgrace or guilt or corruption in connection with these. What shame, what distress and hardship you suffered before I came into the world, when your house was a den of cruel and unruly poachers—who neither feared God nor respected man—no living creature knows, and you have never said except very sparingly. From what you said to me, I wouldn't know a hundredth part of your troubles. I was a relatively big lad before I knew anything for sure about your story, apart from what I had gleaned from the suggestions and insinuations of my enemies. The only thing I knew for sure was that you had some dark past; and Bob was the first to enlighten me—and that in bed on the night that Seth died—after I had told him about the man who caught me by the Manor woods, and what he told me. I have asked myself the question many times whether it was possible that you had a grain of love for the one that had brought such misery upon you. Oh, the love of women! Wasn't one of the last things you said to me: "If ever you and your father come face-to-face with one another, try to forget his wickedness and if you can do some good for him, do it. He has an eternal soul like you and me; and by now it makes little difference how he behaved towards me, but it is of infinite importance for him to be saved. If you ever see him—and who knows whether you will—try to remember that he is your father. I myself forgive him everything, and I am trying to pray to Him whose forgiveness is eternal life to do the same thing."

Wil Bryan said well, in his own way, about you—that you are like Job, sticking to your colours first class. I wouldn't finish soon if I were to relate all the exhortations and encouragements you gave me in your last days. I haven't forgotten that some might say I am exaggerating your virtues. The fact that you're my mother makes that possible. Here, I will just chronicle some of your last words to me—the ones which were of help to me throughout my life:

'If you are called to suffer in this world, do not complain, because it will make you think of a world in which there is no suffering. Don't make your home in the world, or dying will be more of a job for you than you think. Test everything against the Word of God, especially yourself. Take the Bible as a weather glass for your soul; if you lose the taste for reading it, you can be sure that there isn't fair weather awaiting you. Pray to be able to live godly, but don't expect to be able to live to grow old in case you need to die young. Try to have a religion that no-one will doubt, and you yourself won't doubt it. One of the worst things on earth is a weak religion; it will stop you from enjoying the things of this world, but won't help you to enjoy the things of the next world. Try to have a religion whose canvas will wrap someone besides yourself. If you can be the means to save just one soul, you'll push further into heaven after you die than if you were worth a hundred thousand pounds and hadn't done that. You can't expect to receive a penny from your relatives; but you can be the richest in grace in the land if you try. No-one would have heard of Abram unless he was wealthy in something better than camels. You will have three enemies to fight with: the world, the devil, and you yourself, and you'll find that you yourself are the hardest to conquer. In the war, make sure that you have all the weapons—prayer, watchfulness, and the Word of God. You're sure to lose if you don't have all three. If you have power to conquer your enemies during your life, you'll only see the backs of their necks when you come to die. I am going to leave you, and I have confidence in the Lord that I am a vessel of mercy. You'll find in the purse in the pocket of my black gown just enough money to pay for burying me. If you ever have it in your hand to do some kindness to Thomas and Barbara, don't forget their kindness to your mother. I would like it as much as anything if you had a bit of a gift for preaching, and an inclination towards that. But there's no help for it. Try to be useful for religion in whatever circle you find yourself. If I can see you from the other world, I'd like to see you a chapel elder'.

At the time, I didn't imagine that this would be your last command to me. The next time I saw you, Barbara had done the thing that death had left undone, namely closing your eyes. You had gone away, in Barbara's words, like 'blowing out a candle'! It was obvious that death was not cruel to you, because it left a cheerful smile on your face—a smile like that of a child dreaming in its cradle. The more I looked at you the more you smiled, as if you were trying to tell me that you were happy. Your cheeks were unwrinkled and as white as snow, and across your nose there was a blue line—the mark your glasses made when your blood cooled. At your side there were three hearts beating quickly and longingly as they realised they would not hear your voice again; and three consciences forced to testify that you had done all that was in your power to purify them and set them on the road to Life; and although your lips didn't move we imagined we could hear you saying:

'I have fought a good fight, I have finished my course, I have kept the faith; henceforth there is laid up for me a crown of righteousness which the Lord, the righteous judge, shall give me at that day: and not to me only, but to all them also that love his appearing'.[13]

Your life was troublesome; there were times when you really were poor, but the crowd that came to your funeral showed that there were others besides me who saw something in your character worth admiring. Wil Bryan never in his life had as much scolding as he got from you; and yet his testimony about you on the day you were buried was that 'you were a stunner of a woman'. Thomas and Barbara Bartley are now old people, but they still haven't stopped talking about you; and although Barbara has only a 'grasp of the letters, just like Thomas', she hasn't given up on Sunday afternoons putting your glasses on her nose and turning the pages of your old Bible, as if she were trying to imitate you.

---

[13] 2 Tim. 4:7–8.

26

VANITY AND VISION

Time is a famous old doctor; he outdoes all his fellows in the twofold and indispensable qualifications of his calling—the ability to make well and to put to death. With the latter he has an assistant, older and more experienced than himself—namely the devil. When I found myself homeless, without a mother and worse than without a father, I thought that no earthly comfort had been left for me, and that nothing in the world could charm me. I thought too that nothing would be easier for me to do than to follow my mother's counsels to the letter. I felt that there was not the slightest inclination in me towards anything else. My career was clear before me, one which was to be serious, meditative and religious. All my hours of leisure were to be spent reading good books, especially the Bible. No meeting place was to have any influence over me besides the chapel—the old chapel where my mother and Bob had spent their happiest hours. When I looked back, I had to acknowledge that I had been more imprisoned under my mother's care than any other boy in the neighbourhood. By now, though, I thought that my mother had been right, and I decided to keep within the old boundaries; because at the time I felt that they offered me the most freedom, and fully met the only appetite that I had and the chief wish of my heart. My greatest desire was to reach a position where I could be useful to religion; and my old boyish idea of being a preacher revived in me. Indeed I didn't see many obstacles in my path to reaching that state. All I'd do would be to follow the natural inclinations of my mind, and fulfil the best wishes of my mother. Besides that, my character was spotless, and I was determined to keep it that way; there was to be no gap or turn in my straight path. But how deceptive my heart was! I can imagine Time furrowing his old forehead, and his experienced assistant laughing in his sleeve. Was it possible that in my nature there was a heap of corruption that had never been disturbed?

'*Siop y Gornel*'[1]—the establishment where I was apprenticed—was one of the oldest institutions in the town; and my master—Abel Hughes—was considered a diligent, fair and shrewd man. It was a general drapery shop, but its main goods were cloth and woollens, which were always of the highest quality. In those quiet days, it was rare for the shop to be busy except for when there was a fair; and I don't believe that Abel Hughes worried that there were only fairs four times a year. Yet there was a good and steady business being carried on in *Siop y Gornel*. Those who frequented it were old customers, whose families had dealt there since time immemorial. They were country folk mainly and most of them were Methodists, because at that time the verse, 'Do good to all, especially to those of the household of faith'[2] was fashionable. As I said, Abel Hughes kept the best materials, and sought a reasonable profit on them. He did not oversell them, and he never dropped the price; and if a customer didn't like them, then he encouraged them by all means to leave them alone. I never once heard him claim that this or that product was worth a penny more than he was asking for it. Lies were not such a common thing in commerce in those days, as to force a man to declare anything on oath. I don't believe that Abel Hughes ever spent a penny on advertising; the only thing he ever sought from a printer was billheads. The window of the shop was small, and its glass was in small panes, around a foot square, because plate glass was not fashionable at the time. What window dressing there was could easily be completed within an hour; and that task was necessary about once every fortnight. The shop was fairly dark even at noon on a bright day, and the aromas

---

[1] 'The Corner Shop'.

[2] Gal. 6:10.

of moleskin, cotton cord and velveteen were so thick that I felt I could cut them with my scissors. When a customer came in, the first thing Abel would do was to offer him a chair and engage him in conversation. That is where the customer would be for half an hour—sometimes and hour, or more than that. But very often he would buy a valuable parcel, and most transactions ended with the customer going into the house for a cup of tea or a spot of lunch. Very little business was conducted after sunset; and although there was gas in the shop, only one jet was lit, to show that the shop was not closed. One book, which was long and narrow, served as both daybook and ledger; and when a customer paid his account, there was no need for anything except to place a cross in the book in the customer's presence to serve as a receipt. There was nothing about the way that business was conducted, that one couldn't easily imagine Noah having practised before the flood if he had kept a shop. Yet Abel Hughes was doing well and making money. What would become of him if he kept a shop these days? Yes, these days—when people fight for customers any way—it doesn't matter to them which way—and when winning a customer, and making money, is for many people as important as eternity, and eternity no more important than a yard of grey calico. In those days the chain had not yet been cut from the collar of greed; and tradesmen kept within the bounds of their own trade, and lived neighbourly, and didn't try to outsell each other and cut each others' throats. There was no ambition to make an impression, or over-keenness to throw one's neighbours into the shade. If they could get into a position where they were protected from worry—if they could be 'comfortable' or have 'a little put away in an old sock', they felt satisfied. And there was nothing in the outward appearance of those who had reached this happy state that distinguished them from those who had not. It was something to believe, rather than to perceive, that so-and-so was a wealthy man. Very rarely did anyone give a display of plenty and then after a few days go broke, leaving his creditors to pull long faces at their folly in trusting him. Even more rarely was anyone seen after deceiving their neighbours and spoiling them of their goods—yes, deceiving and spoiling is what I said, not failing despite trying to deal honestly—even more rarely, I said, were such people seen walking through town with their heads held high, bearing public office, and appearing in a better position than they had ever been, nor taking their place in the Great Seat or the pulpit. Alas such things are not unknown in these days.

But that is what I was asking—what would have become of Abel Hughes if he kept a shop these days, assuming that he too wasn't corrupted by the times? Well, he'd have had to go to the workhouse; and I believe that's where he would choose to go rather than conform to the greed, deception and high-handedness of the age. I know that he wouldn't flatter—I know that he wouldn't lie—he would never pretend to be selling things for less than he had paid for them himself; he wouldn't grab a customer by the neck and drag him into the shop; he wouldn't persuade anyone to buy anything that they didn't need; he wouldn't force a smile; in a word, there would be no monkey business; and therefore it would be in the nature of things that he would have to, heaven knows, die of hunger, or go into the workhouse, as I said.

In *Siop y Gornel* there was an assistant named Jones. In passing, I've noticed since then that there is an assistant named 'Jones' in almost every drapers shop without exception. I have a good memory of Jones, Abel Hughes' assistant. I can see him before my eyes this minute standing behind the counter, the shiny tips of his scissors poking into view from his waistcoat pocket, and the pins in his left lapel like the children of a showman doing tricks, trying to show how far they could go above their centre of gravity without falling over. Jones was a small, limp man, and caused one to think that Providence had ordained him to be either a tailor, or a mender of umbrellas. He had an abundance of hair on his head, each hair lying down and appearing to be the same length, like a pound of candles. His head had despoiled his cheeks, leaving them entirely smooth; but in order to indicate his gender, nature had planted a little tuft of hair on his chin and allowed a little more to grow here and there on his upper lip, much as might be seen on the lip of an elderly woman. Jones didn't exactly wear a moustache; rather, his lip hair wasn't worth taking the trouble to cut, and paying a penny to shave it would be a waste of money. His nose was shiny and bluish-red, misrepresenting the sober character of its owner. He had a way of folding his arms as if they were in his way, and as if he could do much better without them. His feet were wide, flat and floppy, and as he walked they turned outwards terribly, as though they were determined to go in opposite directions. His feet always struck the onlooker as though they'd had a bitter argument, which they would never forget despite every effort by the mediator, namely Jones. Summer and winter Jones looked the same, as if he were about to freeze, and that he'd like nothing more than to sit by the fire to warm up. I never saw him offended, no matter what was said to him. There was just one thing that Jones really hated, namely, a busy day, and the night before a fair he couldn't sleep a wink. What he liked most was to be out of everyone's sight, standing behind a pile of cloths like a monument to the winter, his feet turned outwards like the feet of a round table, his arms hanging down like the arms of a doll, and his eyes opening and closing like a cat in front of a fire, thinking of nothing and doing nothing. To him this was heaven. Jones was one of those creatures that nature favours by not indicating their age, and who represent the opposite of its behaviour towards cows' horns and horses' teeth.[3] If a stranger were to come into the shop and see just his back, he'd conclude that he was a second-year apprentice; if he saw just the side of his face behind a pile of cloth, he'd think he was Abel Hughes' sister; if he saw just his feet, he'd think he was an eighty-year-old man; if he saw him all at once, he'd be at a loss how to address him—whether 'my boy', or 'granddad'. I said

---

[3] The point being of course that both cows' horns and horses' teeth can be used to estimate the animals' ages.

that Jones always looked the same, but I need to take back my words. Someone who studied him closely, as I did, could see that the weather affected him greatly. Although he was so small and insubstantial, wet and cold weather would cause him to shrink like Welsh wool, except that unlike the wool he did not swell in one direction as he shrank in the other. No doubt Jones' intention as he shrank was to avoid the weather, and in this he succeeded well. When the weather warmed, Jones would go for a walk now and again, and then he began to thaw; and because his mouth was always half-open, the air would get into him and fill him out a bit. As with everything, there was another side to this, namely the effect Jones had on the weather. In the winter, when a customer came into the shop, the freezing appearance of Jones, with his nose and hands blue with the cold, would cause the customer's teeth to chatter and make them think about material for a warm outer coat. It was a fact Abel Hughes couldn't deny that Jones could sell more material for warm outer coats than anyone ever saw. How could one account for this? Because he was a perfect refrigerator.

Even so, people sometimes asked why Abel Hughes kept such a one as Jones in the shop. The reason was, I think, that Abel was a kind man, and he knew that Jones and his wife had to eat to live. Abel was a just man, with his honour beyond doubt; but the salary he paid Jones was very low, perhaps a third of what is paid to shop assistants these days. And yet Jones had the cheek to get married, and I hear that the two lived happily, but were wise enough not to add to the population, since Abel Hughes had said that one Jones was enough for the world, and Jones believed him about this as everything else. Jones' wife was a large and ruddy lady; and when they walked together, I won't say they looked like a cow and a calf, since that would indicate bad taste on my part; but I'll say this, that beside her Jones looked like a lion's provider; or, to be more tasteful, Jones bore the same relationship to his wife in terms of size as a boat does to a ship.

Why have I written so much about Jones? Because he provided

occasion to excite and bring out my own wickedness. You daily hear exhortations to parents not to let their children play with crafty and insolent playmates. I think it is just as important not to put them amongst those who are too innocent and simple. The temptation to mischief is stronger with the latter kind. If our first parents had not been so innocent, I question whether the devil would have paid so much attention to them. When we see childish innocence in someone who has reached adulthood, the temptation to offer them the apple is strong. I hadn't been in Abel Hughes' shop for many days before I saw that I could put my fingers in Jones' eyes, and buy and sell him whenever I wanted. From standing on his toes (pretending it to be by accident, to hear him squeal) to persuading him to use a special material to help his whiskers grow; my schemes where many, and I would never have thought of them if Jones were not so passive. This, of course, was after time had worn away my grief, and its helper that I mentioned earlier had thrown a wet blanket over my good intentions. Jones was in fact able to read, but I never saw a book in his hand besides when in Sunday School. His head was as devoid of knowledge as a potato. He was amazingly gullible—almost nothing was unbelievable to him, and when Abel's back was turned I told Jones strange and terrible things. My reports were a mixture of things I had read in books and things I imagined myself, but Jones believed every word. I didn't think at the time that I was doing anything wrong, since if Jones were not so gullible it wouldn't occur to me to put my imaginings before him as though they were facts. Besides that, I thought that the careful and faithful attention Jones paid to every word I said was a great opportunity for me to practise my gifts. I would be ashamed to list all of my tricks on Jones, and it wouldn't be to the benefit of the reader. I'll say this again, that Jones provided occasion to awaken something in me—I don't know what I would have called it—and I wouldn't at that time have called it sin. It was something not taught to me by anyone, and I knew that my mother would not have approved. It was something, I think, that had always been in me, and yet never awakened before that time. I thought sometimes that it was a kind of talent; because I sometimes fancied I heard someone saying '*Bravo*, Rhys!', but it was not my conscience saying that—it said something else. And it wasn't my mother's spirit that said '*Bravo*', because when I went to bed and shut my eyes, I imagined her scowling at me. If I'd known that it was one of the enemies my mother had talked about that was saying '*Bravo*', would I have listened then? Well, listen I did, sure enough; and I went from bad to worse. But to what purpose should I chronicle my bad deeds? I humbly hope that they have been crossed out from the book of remembrance.

I feel myself wholly unable to describe this time of my life. In a way I was my own master. When I first went to Abel Hughes, I was—because of the ordeals I had been through—a sad, serious, unplayful boy, and I earned his trust and good opinion straight away; and he believed, I know, that there was no need for him to keep an eye on me. His sister—Miss Hughes—who looked after his house, was a pure-minded old lady, kind and religious; and my status as an orphan gave me a place in her heart immediately. Whenever she and I had a *tête à tête*, and when I told her about the hardship I had been through, her eyes filled up with tears; and often she would go to the cupboard and bring me an extra piece of pudding, or some other delicacy. I saw that it was important for me to make an ally of her, and I fully succeeded. Abel Hughes did not say anything in the house except for what was necessary and for edification. Miss Hughes was no exception from her sex. She liked a chat. I made an effort to make it appear that I took a particular interest in her stories and trifles—even though something in me quietly said '*fiddlesticks!*' She liked to hear as much as I knew about everything and everyone. Small indeed was my store of knowledge; but when it ran scarce, I never hesitated to ask for help from my imagination, which was very lively indeed. I won Miss Hughes' favour and that paid me back well. If Abel ever thought I had transgressed, Miss Hughes would come forward to prove that I did it in ignorance. If something in my character was not as clear as Abel would have wished, Miss Hughes succeeded in a moment to polish me up as brightly as gold. Jones too was very useful to show up my virtues. Miss Hughes had no patience to talk about Jones except as a means to show my superiority to him. How did I feel? What did I think about myself? I thought that I was a very different boy from what I had been when my mother was alive. I thought that Miss Hughes did not know the whole story about me. I couldn't help thinking about the difference between Miss Hughes and my mother. I think my mother could see more through an oak table than Miss Hughes could through her glasses. Was I a naughty boy? Who would dare say that? It was true that neither Abel nor his sister knew the half of it. And why should they? If my mother knew everything about me, yes, even my thoughts, so it seemed to me, there was no need for Abel and his sister to; and someone kept saying '*Bravo!*' Who said '*Bravo*'? I don't know; but I felt somehow that I was my own master, and that I could turn Miss Hughes around my little finger. It's amazing to think, and I'm ashamed to remember how bold I was with her. I never hesitated to flatter her. She asked me once what I thought her age was (she didn't know that I had seen her date of birth in the family Bible, which was kept in the cupboard, and which showed that she was just about to turn sixty). "Well," I said, "although you look young, Miss Hughes, I wouldn't be surprised if you're forty." She laughed, and said that I wasn't very good at guessing. I had heard my mother say that Miss Hughes had never had a proposal. Despite that I said to her, "I know, Miss Hughes, the reason why you never married." "Well, let me hear your reason," she said. "You didn't want to leave the master," I answered. "You're pretty good at guessing," she said, and gave me two pennies and charged me not to say anything to Abel.

Had I changed or had Wil Bryan? Wil said to me:

"You know what, Rhys? Now you're just like any other boy. I won't ever call you the 'Old Hundredth' again. Once I was just about to give up on you. Once you went to the old Ab, I was thinking that your hair would turn grey before you were seventeen, and I was expecting that you'd start shouting out Amen! and Hallelujah! in chapel, like your mother used to. I'm not speaking lightly about your mother, mind; far from it. Amen and things like that were quite right for your mother, but there was no reason for her to try to turn you into an old man before you even started wearing a hat. Things like that aren't *true to nature*,[4] you know. Look at the big cat and the kitten; the big cat is quiet and looks sad, while the kitten jumps and tumbles and tries to chase its tail as though it were crazy. Or look at the mare and foal; you see the old mare—when she isn't working—standing in the middle of the field without moving a step for anything in the world, apart from shaking her head a bit when the flies buzz her ears; and she looks as downhearted as if she were contemplating her end in the knacker's yard, and you'd swear sometimes that she was sleeping on her feet. But watch the foal: how it prances about with its head in the wind, lifting its tail and kicking at nothing, and if anyone walks past along the road it will run along following him the other side of the hedge with his Neigh! Neigh! as if he wanted to see everything, because you know the world is new to the foal and the kitten. Well it's just the same with old people and young people. Though your mother scolded me frightfully, I thought as much of her as anyone alive—I swear; but as for keeping you, as she did, as though you were in a clock case, there was no reason for that, it wasn't *true to nature*. She may as well have made you wear a nightcap, or breeches and leggings and a beaver hat, and send you every Saturday to William the barber to be shaved, as take all week, as she did, to starch and iron you ready for Sunday. *Not true to nature, Rhys, at least that's Wil Bryan's way of putting it.*"[5]

I must tell the truth that, regretfully, I was inclined to think at

---

[4] Wil Bryan's catchphrase, invariably (as here) stated in English.

[5] Wil puts this whole sentence in English.

the time much the same as Wil, and we were better friends than ever. By that time his people were my people, and his things my things. Wil was no stranger in *Siop y Gornel*. When Abel Hughes went to a Session or a Monthly Meeting, he wouldn't return for a day or two, and it was understood that when he was away Jones would sleep with me in *Siop y Gornel* to deter thieves. In these circumstances, it wasn't difficult to persuade Miss Hughes to let Wil spend the night as well. Wil was amazing at creeping up Miss Hughes' sleeve. He told her funny stories, or sang English and Welsh songs to her. Wil was delighted to have an invitation to *Siop y Gornel*; indeed, he would 'stuff himself' as he said, when he realised that Abel was away. His main aim was to have a bit of fun with the 'genius', as he called Jones. My bed was small and narrow, and I remember Miss Hughes saying once to Wil, "Well, William, are you going to sleep here tonight? I don't know how the three of you are going to fit into that little bed;" and Wil replied, "Splendidly, Miss Hughes; Rhys one side and me the other, and Jones in the middle like a tongue sandwich." "It's you who should be in the middle if you want to be a tongue sandwich," said Miss Hughes. "One up to you, Miss Hughes," said Wil, "but according to your plan there'd be more tongue than bread." Miss Hughes was rather puzzled that her brother Abel wasn't very fond of Wil, because she thought he was a funny boy and good company. Abel didn't know that Wil was in the habit of visiting *Siop y Gornel* when he was away. One time that Abel was at the Bala Session, something happened in his house that nearly brought Wil and me into the hands of the law. I wouldn't mention this if it weren't important for my story. I'll relate the foolish event in a few words. After Wil and I had bidden goodnight to Miss Hughes, and gone to the bedroom, Wil thought it would be fun to put Jones on trial for killing a creature that there's no need to name here. Wil acted as prosecution and judge, and I acted as the jury, and I found Jones guilty, and Jones was sentenced to hang. Poor Jones enjoyed all of this greatly. Above the door there was a big nail for hanging clothes on. Wil tied some string to the nail and made a noose out of it. He made Jones to stand on a footstool, and put the noose over his neck, and Jones laughed. Without us noticing, and entirely by accident, the footstool overturned. For a few seconds we thought that Jones was pretending to choke to amuse us; but fortunately I noticed that the stool had turned over, and there was a gap of two inches between Jones' feet and the floor. I'd never had such a fright in my life, and in a second I had cut the string with my scissors, and Jones fell to the floor in a faint. Wil was no less frightened, and shook like a leaf. We laid Jones out on the bed, and I can't describe my joy when I heard him start to breathe heavily. My conscience burned like a bonfire when I realised that I had come within a whisker of ending the life of one of the most innocent creatures in the world. When Jones came to himself and saw my fear and grief, he looked at me kindly and said that he forgave the two of us everything; but that did not quiet my conscience or my fear. As soon as Wil obtained a solemn promise from Jones that he would not breathe a word about the event to any living soul, he went to bed and within five minutes was sleeping soundly. I couldn't sleep. For some hours Jones would fall into a restless sleep, and then wake up suddenly and afraid; and this happened many times. Hundreds of thoughts went through my mind that night, and I felt as if I were going through some important change. The room was dark and the night seemed long. I thought it couldn't be long before the dawn, when very suddenly I found I could no longer hear my two companions breathing. It was as if they were both dead. The silence was devastating and oppressive. At the same time, I could see the room becoming lighter, but it wasn't like daybreak—it was faster and, as far as I could feel, quieter and more tender, like the approaching glow of an angel's face. The light grew greater and greater, but it wasn't coming in through the window; it seemed to be entirely inside the room. By this time every object in the room was illuminated, and the light continued to get brighter, and it was so lovely that I felt my eyes getting keener and bigger as I looked at it. Was I dreaming? I can't be sure; but I believe I was fully awake—as awake as I am this minute. The light reached a climax that I can't convey any impression of on paper, and I've never seen anything in my life that I could compare it to. In front of me in the midst of the light that was overpowering, and yet soft and tender, I saw my mother sitting on a chair—not any of the chairs that were in the room, but the old oak armchair that she used to sit on at home. I didn't notice what she was wearing, because I only looked at her face; which, although it had all of its particularities, was a thousand times more beautiful than I had ever seen it. I wasn't afraid, but I felt a little guilty. She didn't look either cross or pleased with me. "Come here," she said. I jumped out of bed and fell on my knees before her, and I put my face in my hands and on her knees as I used to when saying my prayers before going to bed. "My boy," I heard her say, "I told you about the three enemies, and about the armour, but after all the trouble I took with you I'm afraid that you don't have any religion, and that you know nothing of the great things."

I felt that she had gone away before I could say a word to her, and I felt my forehead coldly on one of Abel Hughes' chairs. I leapt to my feet, and saw that the dawn had started to break. Was it a dream? I don't know. But thank God I never forgot her words!

27

DAYS OF DARKNESS

If any particularly diligent friends have followed me as far as the previous chapter, they will no doubt laugh at me and call me superstitious. I can't help that. I've only touched lightly upon the period in which I left the good road, lost my religious impressions and despised all I had learned from one of the most godly women who ever lived. Have I done this because my memory of this period is dim? No, but because my thoughts and actions were too ugly and distasteful to relate. Forget them indeed! That would be as difficult as to forgive them. Only God can do the one or the other; and even to Him, I expect that forgetting them is unspeakably harder than forgiving them; and if He Himself had not said that He would do that, I would think it impossible. Humbly and thankfully I do my best to believe the Word of the always-truthful God; but what a jolt He would have had to give to His omniscience to bring that about, I cannot imagine. If I am writing nonsense—Oh great Forgetter, forget this too!

Was I a church member at this time? I was, sure enough; and coming regularly to the Lord's table every month. And, as far as I know, none of the godly old brethren had any concerns about me; not one of them ever spoke to me particularly about the quality of my spiritual life, of the state of my religion. Remembering my own story makes me fear and tremble to think what is the spiritual state of hundreds of young people in our towns who, like me, were brought up with religion since their childhood. To keep their godly old mother happy, or to avoid the rebuke of their strict masters, they come regularly to the services—and take part in the Lord's supper—because they have come of age; but what more do we know about them? They can go for weeks at a time without looking at a Bible—they can live a totally prayerless life—they can be visiting lawless places, full of degeneracy—they can be feeding on filthy and corrupt thoughts—and they can be reading books which, if they were printed in hell by the light of the flame that never goes out, could not be more damning for their souls; and what would we know about it? Don't they come to chapel? They do, and thank goodness for that. They come under the sound of the eternal Gospel to please their old mother; and who knows, perhaps God will show mercy to them! But are we sure that the services aren't a burden to them? What interest do they take in biblical things? Don't they consider them rather dry? If only we could be sure that they had lost one—just one hour of sleep over the things that will determine their eternal fate! The shapely, beautiful, lovely girl—the best suited of all to work in a bazaar—if only we could be sure that your heart skipped as much over your fate as it did over the idiocy in the penny dreadful we saw you buy the other day. Isn't there some estrangement, some distance that there should not be, between church officers and the boys and girls who are nominally under their charge? Isn't it often the case that the only thing we know about them is the fact that they come to chapel? I know that the difficulty is bridging this estrangement without damping their spirits and driving them further away, without seeming to interfere, or without forming some type of confessional. I also know that the fact that I was guilty of the things I've referred to, while at the same time keeping my church membership, does not mean that others are guilty of the same. But please, who were my partners in crime? I must tell the truth: church members like myself. I'm glad to recall that they were few in number. If I were printing this story, I would direct a few simple questions at the consciences of boys in our churches, such as these: 'John Jones' or whatever your name is, 'leaving God out of it, would you want your mother to know how many chapters of the Bible you read from one Sunday to the next? How often do you pray, and what sort of prayers are they? Would you have any objection to her knowing where you go after closing the shop, or leaving the office? When you're with your friends, what do you think? Would she recognise you—not by your voice, but by your words? Would she believe that it's her son? Would you like your father to know what you spend your money on, and where every penny of it comes from? How much money would you want to let him see the book that you placed under lock and key in your box the other night? If he knew as much about you as you know yourself, what would he call you? A hypocrite, perhaps? Does the idea you have of yourself correspond with the idea that you know the "old folks," your parents, have of you? After doing many things that you know neither your parents nor the church you were raised in would approve of, haven't you said to yourself many times, "When I go home it will be all right, because I've got a letter from a church elder saying:

'To the Calvinistic Methodists
Dear Brothers, this is to inform you that the bearer, John Jones, is a member with us at the church of Taking-everything-for-granted. Grace be with you. Amen'."

To the pure all things are pure; and perhaps the one who has been guilty of a great deal of impurity tends to think that impurity is more common than it is in reality. In any case, I know one who attended services consistently because he didn't dare not to for fear of displeasing his master. This one did not absent himself from the Lord's table so much as once; but if his master, who was an elder, had known his true character, he would have thrown him out of the church without ceremony. That one was myself. My mind was defiled, my heart was hard and cold, and my conversation—when out of earshot of the 'brethren'—was inappropriate, to say the least. I wasn't unfamiliar with the words of the Bible; but I used them in jest and levity, to make people laugh and to try to be witty. I believe that this was the chief means of hardening my heart.

I remember now a saying of my mother's, that using the words of the Bible in jest causes them to lose their edge for the purpose for which they were intended. 'The same as that old axe, you see', she would say, 'we've used it to cut coal and to do odd jobs, and for everything else; and now if we try to cut some firewood with it, it won't do anything to the wood'. Her words proved true in my case. Without flattering myself, I think that at that time I was fairly quick on the uptake, and I wasn't lacking in skill to put my thoughts into words succinctly and powerfully. I don't know if it was this that created in me a love of arguing; but I know that I was always ready to do so, for which reason Wil Bryan called me 'Quick-to-fire'. I would always tend to take the doubtful side of the subject; because my aim was not to find out the truth, but to beat my opponent, even under a handicap. In time this custom caused me to devalue the essential distinction between true and false, and good and bad. With innocent and less able companions, I was able to make a better argument for the false than they could for the true; and like an idiot I started to admire myself and think that I was someone. I went to chapel regularly, as I said; but I rarely found a preacher who satisfied me because few of them, or so I thought, had anything 'new' to say to me; and I thought I could find holes in their arguments and errors in their language. By this time I had given up taking notes, as I didn't think it was worth the trouble. I enjoyed the Sunday School, because I found opportunity there to show off my gifts. Dear me! I've often thought what a kindness it might have been to me if Evan the butcher, who because of his size was nicknamed Daniel Lambert[1] by Wil Bryan—what a kindness it would have been to me, I say, if Evan had taken me behind the old chapel and given me a good thrashing with his ash cane, and then dumped me head first in the water butt. It would have been good for me, and for many like me.

---

[1] A Leicester man who died in 1809 weighing 52 stone, and became proverbial for his size and weight.

I am describing the period of my folly sparingly, as I'd be ashamed for anybody to know just how much an idiot I was. Although I was, because of the upbringing I had, reasonably familiar with the truths, or rather the facts, of the Gospel, I was as unfamiliar with their spiritual blessings as any pagan.

This was my condition when, as I mentioned in the previous chapter, I nearly sent poor Jones to give an account of himself, and when I saw the vision, if vision it was. It doesn't matter what name I give the thing, whether dream or vision; I am sure that it was the occasion to form a period in my story—a wonderful period that I have given thanks for hundreds of times. As I said before, hundreds of things went through my mind that night. The words, 'My boy, I'm afraid that you don't have any religion, and that you know nothing of the great things' were like a hot iron through my heart. I felt that every word was true, and I was in a pitiful state. I had been in the habit of appearing to be what I was not; and I tried to continue that by appearing happy and carefree, but I failed. I lost my appetite, and Miss Hughes urged me to go and see the doctor. Many times she said to me, "Rhys, I don't know what to think about you. You eat no more than a bird, and I'm almost ready to suggest that you have some wormwood tea. What's wrong with you?" She didn't understand my sickness. I made a great effort to shake my misery away by mixing with my old companions, and joining in their amusements; but all that did was to add coal to the fire that was burning in my conscience; and making an excuse that I wasn't feeling well, I left them, and got into the habit of staying in after closing the shop.

To avoid having to talk to Miss Hughes I pretended to read voraciously; but I hardly knew what I was reading, as my mind wandered here and there, returning daily to brood over my own unhappiness. Everything appeared to me with a new aspect. Before, God, sin and the world to come were just words to me; but by now they were living things, and the terror of them touched and moved every nerve in my soul, if I can be allowed to speak in such a way. Before, the *seiat* was just a sort of club, which I happened to be a member of; but now I looked on the church as a gathering of spiritual people, a chosen breed, of whose nature, food and sustenance I had no knowledge. Although my name was on its book, I felt there was a huge gulf between myself and its life and character. I turned things over in my mind for hours on end. I tried carefully to put myself before me, and put myself through an examination—what's the matter with you? Are you beginning to lose your senses? What wrong have you done that other people haven't, and more besides? But I remembered in a moment that my mother had told me these were the devil's questions, and I found no comfort in them. I looked back, and tried to persuade my memory to find some things from the past that were in my favour; but my conscience ran ahead, and found far more things to throw me down, and my memory lost heart and left my conscience to have its own way. I thought that all the faculties of my soul were conspiring together against me. In secret I read much of the Bible: but I felt that it was talking about some other people, and that its promises were for someone else; and I found no light for myself, although that was my great purpose in reading it. Every hour of the day and night, especially when I was on my own, I had an uncomfortable sense of the presence of God closing in on me; but when I tried to pray to Him, it seemed like He was leaving me and fleeing away. I'll never forget one evening in my bedroom, when I was possessed by a Catholic temptation. I had been meditating sadly until my candle was almost burned out, and a feeling of total and utter loneliness came over me. I felt that God had no sympathy for me; that He was angry with me. None of my friends knew of my feelings, and if they had then they wouldn't have understood me, or been any help to me; and I felt that neither good nor bad angels would have any interest in me. I was alone, so I thought, in the big wide world; and my soul froze within me, and no beam of warmth came from anywhere to thaw it. Suddenly I remembered my mother. Surely she who loved me so much had not forgotten me; and oh the folly of it, I fell on my knees and prayed to her. That was the straw that I clutched at that night, rather than drown. Needless to say this did me no good, and I immediately saw how silly it was. I wasn't ignorant of the way of salvation, as it had been made clear to me from my childhood; but I felt that it was meant for others, and that I myself was outside of its scope. I wondered if my familiarity with the Gospel made me unable to see its hidden spiritual meaning, and that I was doomed to stay in the outside porch neither in the world nor the church. I tried to nurture high thoughts about Christ, and His sympathy with fallen mankind—of his love and pity towards sinners; but at the same time my heart felt cold, my affections frozen; and my mind put a stress on sayings such as, 'My sheep hear My voice',[2] and my efforts were in vain. I was in this state for some weeks; and I remember that it wasn't particular sins I'd committed that troubled me the most, but a feeling of general and continual defilement, and a painful exile from all things spiritual and supernatural. I had been so hypocritical in my prayers for so many years that I was afraid to say too much. One time, I recall, my prayers were something like this: 'Great Jesus, Son of God, I've talked a lot of nonsense before You for so many years, that I am not surprised that You have left me to myself. You know, for You know everything, how bad I have been. No-one except You and I know my whole story. If You won't forgive me, I plead with You not to say anything about me to my mother, nor to Bob, nor to anyone. Although I want to, You know that I don't love You or even know You, and I'm afraid that You are angry with me for ever. Let me live for a little while longer. Amen.' At other times they would run like this: 'Jesus Christ, to stop You from being even more angry with me, I am going on my knees again tonight; but I have no more to say to You than I have said hundreds of times before, apart from the fact that I'm losing my health. But You know it all,

---

[2] John 10:27.

and there's no need for me to tell You. Amen.' Although I didn't dare go to bed without getting on my knees, I remember that sometimes I was possessed by a feeling of daring and defiance, similar, I suppose, to that felt by lost souls; and my prayers, if you could call them that, were of this character: 'O Saviour of sinners! What more can I do? I have called to You hundreds of times, but You are not listening to me. I read Your sermon on the mount tonight, and it condemns me for ever. But why did You say, "Ask and it shall be given to you, seek and you will find?"[3] Haven't I asked and sought? If I weren't afraid of sinning against You more, I'd almost think that You aren't as good as Your word. You know that I am a bad boy. Who called You the friend of publicans and sinners? Wasn't it those who called You a glutton and a drunkard? I am a great sinner, but You are no friend to me. Do you distinguish between sinners? Do you have favourites? What use is it for me to read the Bible? It has nothing for me, and I get no pleasure out of sinning. If You're determined not to listen to me, then at least leave me to sin in peace. You even let the devil do that. If I'm going wrong, why don't You help me to understand? If You put me in hell, I'll tell everyone for ever that You turned me down as a seventeen-year-old boy, even though You'd said, "Whoever comes to me I will never cast out."[4] If I sinned against the Holy Spirit, the unforgivable sin[5], then You know that I did it in ignorance. My heart is like a stone, and I can't change it. Although I want to love You, I can't. But You know that I hate the devil and his demons with a perfect hatred; and if You put me in their midst, I will never speak a word to one of them—not ever, even if they put a hot iron on my lips. O! Have I gone out of my mind? I hope I have, because You show mercy to madmen. Do with me as You see best. Amen!' No ray of light came to me by reading or praying, and partly I gave it up. I gave up reading the Bible and praying in the mornings. I failed, though I tried, to give up making some semblance of prayer before going to bed. I felt that this was too hard. And to this day I feel something similar. It is easier to forget

God in the morning than in the night. I believe I'm not alone in thinking this, because I remember more than once sleeping with irreligious companions who would never get into bed without first going on their knees, even though it wouldn't occur to them to do so on getting up. The feeling of dependence and responsibility is greater in the night than in the morning. How foolish! In the morning we feel more able to look after ourselves than we do as we go to sleep. Having given up reading the Bible, I turned to reading humorous books; but I couldn't for the life of me find anything humorous in them. To me they were like the tricks of a clown to a man on his deathbed.

I believe it was around then I became convinced that only a man who has a sound heart and a great deal of godliness can truly appreciate humour, and that only he can really laugh without there being poison in its root. Foolishly enough I kept all my trouble to myself, and I continued to look inside myself instead of looking outwards. I don't think that anyone, except one, guessed that I was in such trouble; and I wouldn't have imagined that one had guessed, especially as I had little to do with him at that time, unless I had one day received the following note from him:

'Dear Rhys, I rather think that you are in want of a *sackcloth*. I can lend you one. The *ashes*, of course, you can have anywhere you like. Glad to tell you that this chap is up to the knocker. Yours truly,

Wil Bryan'[6]

I understood that he had figured out my reason for staying in at night, and avoiding his company, and I was afraid to see him for fear that he would tease me. At the same time I envied him, as Wil's parents were just casual and unassuming worshippers; while the care that was taken with me, and the religious education

---

[3] Luke 11:9. [4] John 6:37. [5] Matt. 12: 31–32.
[6] The whole of Wil Bryan's note is written in English, except for the words 'sackcloth' ('*sachliain*') and 'ashes' ('*lludw*').

I received, made me look upon my responsibilities as infinitely more serious than his. Wil's note added to my unhappiness. Almost every day I was told off by my master, Abel Hughes, for not being cheerful with customers. He said that I was getting worse rather than better. This made me hate the shop. I did not despise Jones any more: rather, I envied him, as I thought that he was virtually without a soul. Bit by bit I fell into a state of fecklessness, confusion and depression. The devil tried to whisper to me that religion was stupid, that the Bible was just a collection of legends, and the cause of all my troubles was indigestion. But at the same time I remembered my mother's life, her integrity, her faith, her joy in the Holy Spirit, her peace and composure in the worst tribulations, her sense of happiness and exultation, and her immeasurable perseverance in the valley of the shadow of death; and neither the devil nor all the atheists in the world could take me away from that. I felt a great longing for her. I knew that I had tried my master's patience a great deal, and there was nothing he liked about me except the fact that I stayed in after shutting up the shop. If I went on an errand, I'd forget it, and have to go back to ask again what it was. Behind the counter I was confused and awkward, and often made mistakes about the prices of things. My behaviour caused Abel to be tired and cross with me; but I knew that Miss Hughes did the best she could on my behalf. One day Abel called me aside, and told me that he was very disappointed in me. He had thought, he said, that I would turn out to be a good, lively and able boy; but he was sorry to see that I was getting worse and worse, and he said, "Indeed, you're not worth your salt." I felt that he was telling the truth, and at the time I didn't open my mouth to argue with him; but his words affected me greatly, and I decided that I would no longer eat a piece of his bread, as I had not earned it. What was left in me of honour had been stirred. My intention was to leave and to cast myself at the mercy of fortune. In those minutes I didn't care what would become of me. Supper time came, but I refused to sit at the table. There was too much iron in Abel's constitution to ask me a second time; and Miss Hughes understood that there had been words between Abel and me, and she didn't enjoy her supper much, since she loved me very much. I thought that there was something dry and stiff about the way that Abel held devotions that night and I knew that Miss Hughes was not listening to him. For me, it was a night to remember. I felt that Abel was correct in saying that I wasn't worth my salt, and yet I felt I was being unfairly maligned; and I decided to clear my name before leaving, or at least reveal my situation. After devotions Abel sat as usual in his armchair, and began to smoke. For a while no-one said a word. I felt stubborn, strong, and decisive, and yearned for an opportunity to begin speaking. After waiting a long time, during which I think all three of us felt rather ungodly, Abel asked me in a steely tone whether I was intending to go to bed that night. I said that I was not, until I could tell him the reason why I had been so clumsy in the shop, and so unhappy and sour of spirit. Then I began to tell him of my troubles. No sooner had I started, however, but I was overcome by my feelings and began to weep freely. In my trouble, in all my fears and in my despair, no tear had run down my check since my mother was buried; but as soon as I opened my mouth to tell my master my story, the dam burst and for a while my words were drowned by the flood from my heart. There is such power in *telling* experience! I have rarely met with a kind woman who, if she sees a strong lad weeping from his heart, will not do the same herself. Miss Hughes was kind. The weeping was a great blessing to me—not only as a sign to me that my heart was not as hard as I thought it was—but also because it enabled me to compose myself before telling the whole story to Abel Hughes. I didn't hide anything from him, nothing at all; I didn't even hide the one thing I am holding back here, something that concerned him personally. I am holding it back here in obedience to his command, as he said—"Do not tell anyone else; because if it comes to men's ears, although God will forgive you, it may be held against you for as long as you live." He said this to me the following day, but we're still talking about the evening. I knew that I was dealing with someone who was every inch a man, and this gave me confidence to confess all my faults and tell of all my feelings without restraint. I believed that, after he had heard my story, he would sympathise with me, excuse my failings, and set me on the right path. I knew well that there were thick walls around his heart, but once I was allowed in I wouldn't be cast out lightly. He listened intently, but I failed to get the impression that he sympathised at all. Indeed, he looked cheerful, as if he was taking pleasure in my sorrow. When I had finished my story, this is all he said,

"Ho! Fine! If that's how things are, go ahead. You'll feel better soon."

"Abel," said Miss Hughes, "is that all you have to say to him? You are hard-hearted."

"There's no need for you, Marged, to tell me anything about my heart. I know more about it than you can ever tell me, goodness knows," said the honest old Calvinist.

"I'll say this," said Miss Hughes, "you should help the boy a bit, and give him a word of advice."

"Don't you know, Marged, that the One who began a good work in you will finish it?[7] It's not good, you know, to pick someone out of the pit too quickly. And I'll tell you something else: if the Lord opened the wound, the Lord himself will come to dress it in his own good time."

"What I mean is that you should tell the boy that there's a dressing to be had, or there's not much point you being an elder," said Miss Hughes.

"I'll vouch for him. He's not some half pagan coming to the *seiat* for the first time, like Thomas Bartley and others. You can't say anything to him that he doesn't know as well as you do. When his fever becomes hot enough, he knows exactly where to find the

---

[7] Phil. 1:6.

Physician. The best thing for him tonight is to have supper and go to bed," whereupon Abel refilled his pipe.

Although I had little comfort from Abel that night, I felt that he looked at me in a new light; and with the urgings of Miss Hughes, aided by the call of my own stomach, I took a little supper and went to bed—not to sleep, but to ponder over my situation. By now I no longer intended to leave, and my whole mind longed for some light on my situation and my future. I intend to recount where that light came from in the next chapter.

28

MASTER AND SERVANT

Making a full, unreserved, unrestrained confession—cleaning out every dirty corner of one's conscience, even in the presence of someone else, gives some sort of power to the confessor. Opening the doors of the heart and throwing them wide open so that fresh air can flood in is healthy for the soul. Making someone else, as it were, participate in our consciousness is like putting one end of the load upon their shoulder. Why are we so keen to hear that a condemned murderer has made a full confession of his crime? One reason is because we know it will make him stronger to face his terrible fate; and perhaps there is another that we don't want to recognise, namely a quiet wish to bear some of the burden of his conscience. He who makes a thorough confession of his sin—even if the sin is as black as hell—comes to feel something of the strength of a man who tells the truth. He strikes the devil on the forehead, and raises himself in the hierarchy of life infinitely higher than the hypocrite. A father can use the cane with relish on the back of a boy who is a sneak, but a naughty, mischievous boy who confesses his misdeeds with an open heart brings rheumatism to the shoulder, and can delay the punishment—perhaps forever. Why does God wish to hear us confess our sins? Is it because he doesn't know about them? No, but because he wants to hear us tell the truth, even if that truth is as ugly as treason against himself. There are natural sneaks, and there are spiritual sneaks, but one is as repellent as the other in God's sight. Tell the truth even if you'll be crucified for it, is his command. The truth, even in its ugliness, its hardness, and its enormity, is more acceptable in his sight than the hypocritical lie, even when it is dressed up with groans and tears. To the hypocrite and saintly faced he says, 'Well, if you love the darkness, if you prefer to live in the caves of your own making, I'll make sure you get a place fitting for your taste, where no ray of light will ever come except what comes from the *inverted lamp*[1] of your conscience'.

After I had effectively turned myself inside out before my master, although my condition was no more hopeful or my future any clearer, I felt stronger; I felt that I had scorned the name of a hypocrite, and had mustered enough courage to tell the ugly truth about myself, and if I had to go to perdition, I would not go there under heaven's banner. Eight o'clock the previous evening neither Abel Hughes nor his sister knew the first thing about my wickedness and the sins I was guilty of. The following morning, as I went downstairs after a sleepless night, I realised that the two of them knew just about as much about my situation as I knew myself; and yet I felt I could look them in the eye more straightly, more honestly, than I had done for years. What gave me this confidence? One thing, I felt that I was no longer a sneak. Another thing, I believed that the two were truly religious, that they loved God, and therefore that they loved man even when in the gutter. If I hadn't been sure in my mind that they were religious, would I have made the full confession that I did before them? I don't think so. If I had mistaken Abel Hughes' true character, into whose hands might he have delivered me after I had confessed my sins? Heaven knows. Abel Hughes! Your name is sacred in my mind and in my heart! Your righteousness and strictness were as sharp as Sinai itself; but your heart of hearts was saturated with the forgiveness and the propitiating blood of Calvary. I knew whom I had believed in, albeit with fear. At breakfast time I was amazed at the civility and kindness of Abel Hughes and his sister. I felt humbled and very unworthy of such kindness; and my feelings nearly overcame me and the food nearly choked me. I couldn't help thinking that there was something divine in the forbearance and kindness of godly

---

[1] The words '*inverted lamp*' are given in English; I have no idea what one of these is.

people. That morning, when Abel led devotions, I thought that there was an unusual anointing upon him; I was genuinely thrilled at his praying, which hadn't happened for a long time. At the same time I felt unhappy and defiled, and I decided I'd ask Abel to excommunicate me from the church at the first opportunity he had, though I believed he'd do that whether I asked or not.

Shortly after I had gone to the shop that morning, Abel came after me, and after casting his eyes over an invoice he asked Jones to check it, and added: "Jones, if anyone asks for me, tell them that I'll be here presently; but don't come to fetch me, as I have some business to attend to. Rhys, you'd better come and help me." Then he went into the parlour, and I followed him. After we had gone in Abel locked the door, and told me to sit down, and he sat down opposite me. My heart pounded like a bird caught in a trap, and I was afraid that I had mistaken my master's true character and had been a fool to confess all my faults to him. Yet I wasn't sorry for doing that, whatever the consequences would be. These things, and many more, flashed through my mind in a few seconds. For a moment or two before he began to speak he looked me in the face seriously, and I tried to look honestly into his face. Before he spoke a word, I thought that I could see, behind the seriousness of his expression, a background of mercy and forgiveness. By the way, I think that many good men, just like bad men, have two faces. Beneath the harsh frown you can often make out the tender, merciful face of the man underneath—just as you can see the devil standing on his head behind the smiling face of the hypocrite. I felt that I could see the kind man behind the darkness of Abel Hughes' face as he began to speak as follows:

"Your mother, who I'm quite sure today is in heaven—she and I were great friends; and I promised her, before she died, that I would take care of you and do my best for you. She thought highly of you—too highly, I fear; but I'm sure she thought that you were what you should have been after the care that she had taken of you; the religious education that she gave you and all the prayers she made for you. When you were telling your story last night I felt very grateful that your mother is in her grave. I don't know if I've ever met anyone who could possess themselves patiently in the bitterest trials in the way that your mother could; and as you know, she had plenty of them. But I firmly believe that if she had lived to see your decline—and she'd have been sure to see it, as she was more sharp-eyed than I—that would have been more than she could bear; it would have broken her heart. I remember her now how she would say to me, with her face cheerful, about how she was helped to forget all the trouble she had with your father, and her poverty and hardship, by seeing you growing up the way she would have you; how you would learn your Bible verses without being forced to, and were able to recite parts of sermons when you were still a small boy. When you weren't in earshot, she could talk about you for an hour at a time; and she sometimes asked me whether I thought that you might make a preacher one day. If she were alive today she would have preferred a thousand times to hear that you had died of famine by the roadside than to hear about your backsliding. But she was spared it all, and went to her grave believing that her only son wouldn't shame the teaching that she gave to you. Well, my boy, I must say that I have been very much deceived by you. But I believe that you have made an honest confession. Take note of that—*I believe you*. If you were to think that I don't believe you, it would do you much harm. I'm quite sure that you have told me the truth; but have you told the whole of it?"

"Yes, everything, I think," I replied,

"Fine. Have you told anyone else besides my sister and me?"

"No, not one word to anyone living," I replied.

"Better still. You have made a clean breast, as they say, and I don't see that any good will come from you telling anyone else. It could be held against you for as long as you live; because it often happens that a man's old transgressions are brought back to him by his fellow men, years after God has forgiven them. If I didn't know something myself of the corruption of a lost man's heart, perhaps I would look differently at the things you confessed to me. But I know something about struggling against temptation and being defeated now and again; and I hope that I know something of coming through the struggle victorious. Perhaps some would say that my duty is to throw you out of the door, announce all that you've done wrong, and excommunicate you from the church; and perhaps they'd count me as merciful for not doing anything beyond that. I don't intend to do the one or the other. Why would I do that? I myself am a great sinner. I was thinking last night, after you had gone to bed, what if we all made full and detailed confessions, what strangers we'd be to one another. I was thinking as well how small the real difference is between the best and the worst of us. Tell me honestly, now—I know at least that you'll be honest—have you declared an eternal war against the devil and the corruption of your own heart? Are you determined with God's help to be victorious or to die in the attempt?"

"I have nothing to hide," I said. "I hate myself, but I have no-one I could love besides myself. I hate my actions and my bad habits, but I find no pleasure in anything else. The truth is that I have no love for myself nor for anything outside myself, which is the same thing, I'm afraid, as saying that I hate everything."

"So," said Abel, "there would be no point in me giving you the advice that is given to everyone every day—the things you've heard hundreds of times from the pulpit and in the *seiat*, and the things which, to a large extent by now, I fear, have become meaningless both to those who say them and those to whom they are said. But have you ever before felt the way you have felt these last few weeks? Try to recall."

"No, I'm sure," I said.

"Fine. Do you remember a time when you felt fairly happy, when you enjoyed attending the services in chapel, and could go to bed at night without being plagued with fears or with the accusations of your conscience?"

"I certainly do; I was like that for many years," I said.

"Now," said Abel, "can you tell me what constituted your happiness at that time? Was it your own holiness? Or was it because you'd never thought about yourself at all? Or was it because you knew God, because you'd had a glimpse of His divine majesty, His perfect holiness, His hatred for every kind of sin? Was it because you had felt His infinite love in giving up His Son to die for us, and because you had laid your soul to rest on His atonement and His sacrifice, and because of that were enjoying the peace of the Gospel? Was that what was making you happy?"

"I don't know," I said.

"Try to think; I'll wait a minute or two while you consider," he said.

"I think," I said eventually, "that what made up my happiness at that time was a total lack of proper consideration about myself, together with the fact that I had not understood a single great truth about God and His doings. In other words, now that I think of it I believe that my happiness was based on ignorance about myself and about God."

"Exactly so," said Abel. "But one more question. You remember, don't you, a time when you weren't guilty of the things you mentioned last night? Fine. When you started to do them, I know that it was the least sinful of them—if I may use such a term—that you did first, wasn't it? Now when you did the first of them how did you feel? Did you feel that you had taken some completely new road, or that you were on the same road as before but that it was getting worse? Did you feel you had made a right-about-face, as the volunteers might say?"

"No, I don't think so," I said. "I think I was on the same road throughout, but that it got worse as I walked along it."

"I guessed that's how it was," said Abel. "Now, according to your own account, don't you see that there is more hope of your salvation today than there has even been? Even at your best times, you had never noticed your state as a sinner, nor had any inkling about the God that you appeared to worship. Your ignorance was the stronghold of your happiness. You were on the road to destruction since you were born. But now here's God in his mercy raising up a storm upon you and throwing a tree across the road, so now you have to turn back to the crossroads and take a completely new direction. And look, *this happens in the life of every man who is saved.*"

"How am I to do that? I'm afraid that God won't listen to me," I said.

"Have you tried Him? Have you told Him all about your old road, and asked Him to point you to the new road?" said Abel.

"I've asked Him hundreds of times for His direction, but I haven't told Him my whole story. Why would I do that? He knows it better than I do," I said.

"That's where you have gone wrong," said Abel. "According to your reasoning, there'd never be any need to pray at all, because He knows the deepest and most secret thoughts and wishes of the heart. But remember, He won't hear your prayer or mine while we hide anything we know about ourselves which is blameworthy without telling Him of it. I don't mean publicly, but in secret in your room. You can be sure that that publican[2] had gone through all the particulars before he went to the temple; and I don't believe that He would have listened to the prayer of the thief[3] in so few words if he weren't so pinched for time. No good ever came from half measures. Open your heart before him, and make a detailed and full confession of your sins. You mustn't worry about tiring Him by going on at length, because a thousand years with Him is as a single day. Although He hates sins, he doesn't mind hearing a sinner name them, if his heart is repentant, and if he has a deep desire to have forgiveness for them and complete salvation from their influence."

Abel waited for a minute at that point as if he were anxious to know whether his words were having any effect on me. And indeed they were affecting me greatly. I felt deeply, but I was unable to say more than this to him: "I'm grateful to you from my heart, master; but my sins are great and very many."

"Yes they are," he said, "much greater and more numerous than you have yet imagined; and so are my own sins. Both of us—all of us, for that matter—are in the same unfortunate boat. You have, I know, read more than that is usual for boys these days, and I'll tell you something of my own experience, since talking about experiences is what we're doing. I've never said anything about this in the *seiat*; and if you live to my age, you'll have experiences as well that you won't ever talk about in the *seiat*, nor to your closest friend, and you'll have feelings that you can't put into words even to yourself. When I was a young lad, a little older than you, the incarnation of the Son of God appeared to me to be unreasonable, too unlikely and too momentous for me to believe. I didn't have the religious upbringing that you had. But I'd had a little bit of day school, and I liked reading and thinking. Despite that, I wallowed in the worst of sins. Occasionally I would go to hear the Gospel preached. I would take some interest in the preacher. I was like that Zacchaeus[4] climbing into the top of a tree to see the preacher and the congregation; but unlike him, salvation was not coming to my house. Eventually the Revival came—the great Revival[5] that your mother spoke about daily, when she and I, and hundreds of others were convicted of our sins. In the terrible view of my own sin, which I had at that time, I saw the reason for the incarnation. And if you've ever noticed, you've never met anyone who's had a clear sight of the awfulness of their own sin but who doubts the

---

[2] Luke 18:10–14. [3] Luke 23:42. [4] Luke 19:1–10.

[5] Owen is writing in around 1885, so he could be referring to the great Revival of 1859 when an estimated 100,000 people (out of a population of not much more than 1 million) were converted across Wales in the space of a few months. On the other hand, bearing in mind that the events of Chapter 17 probably refer to the year 1869 when the author was probably already 7–8 years old, one would have expected Abel's conversion to have happened long before this. It may be that Abel is referring to some smaller event which was later overshadowed by that of 1859, since local revivals of various scales were a feature of Welsh life throughout the late 18th and early 19th centuries.

incarnation. People who do doubt it have slack ideas about sin, without exception. Call to mind the older religious people—the people of the great Revival, as your mother would call them. Have you seen the like of them for the strength of their love for Christ? Love which overcame every obstacle set in front of them? What was the reason for this? They were people who'd had the sort of view of their sinfulness which is not often had, I fear, these days. But this is what I was referring to: if you have had a sight of your condition— and I believe you have, to some extent—aren't you beginning to see the reason for the coming of the Son of God in the flesh? Don't you see that there is something in your hopelessness and the depth of your misery which shows that His coming to the world was not in vain? Solomon, as you will remember,[6] thinking about the smallness and pitiableness of mankind, rather doubted that God could dwell with man on earth. But for my part, I don't see that anything in man except his terrible misery could stir the bowels of His infinite pity, nor could anything be else grand enough to be worthy of His appearing in the flesh apart from that. I'm now an old man and an old sinner; but I prefer that name to that of an angel; because I feel that I'm an item, that I'm part of the reason that caused God as it were to come out of Himself. This, my boy, is where your salvation will come from if you are ever to be saved. To me the existence, sinfulness and misery of man is inexplicable except in the light of the accursed death on the cross. Only in the darkness that stretched from the sixth to the ninth hour[7] do I see what light and hope there is for a man to have about his condition. It is the old story, you see, that I have to tell you; but without it, the land wouldn't have enough asylums to hold its madmen. And there's no other story worth telling to someone in your state—nor any other name under heaven[8] that it will pay for you to hope in. Have you ever wondered at the silence of God? If you haven't, you're sure to feel something about it one day. When I was a young man, thinking about this would trouble me a lot. I would walk around at night on my own, especially if the night was moonlit.

Looking at the stars and the moon would make me sad. I'd think how far away, how old, and how quiet they were. They were in the sky, just as they were when my father, my grandfather, and my great-grandfather looked at them. I would wonder at the thought that many generations who now lay in the dust had looked at them just as I was, just as they were in the time of the Druids, in the time of Paul, in the time of David, Moses, Abraham, Noah and Adam. And yet they always were so quiet! I thought about the immense experience they must have! And yet they never said anything to me to quieten my troubled mind. In vain I asked what was beyond them; all they would do was to wink at me quietly, and make me feel uncomfortable and doubtful, with thoughts I could not articulate even to myself. Many times I looked up for a long time, expecting to see or hear something unusual, but it was in vain. Everything stayed the same. And if you and I went out tonight when it is late, we'd see everything just as it was when Isaac was meditating in the field.[9] Well, thinking about this sort of thing would make me feel sad. Something in the depths of my soul was 'looking for a sign'. I remembered the story of the pillar of cloud in the day and the pillar of fire at night,[10] and I thought that there was some reason in that—something that a man could see and be sure of. I remembered about Joshua in the valley of Gibeon commanding in the name of God that the sun should stand still,[11] and it obeying, and I thought that there was something noble in that; something that could give assurance to a man's troubled mind. And then I would ask myself why there had been nothing of that sort for centuries, and that ages and ages had passed in the most deafening silence. I felt somehow that God had gone away from home and left everything empty and quiet; and sometimes I felt a strange longing for God to come marching back from the distant regions where he was hiding, so that I would be willing to

---

[6] 2 Chron. 6:18.   [7] Matt. 27:45.   [8] Acts 4:12.   [9] Gen. 24:63.   [10] Ex. 13:21–22.
[11] Josh. 10:12–13.

witness another global flood, whatever my own fate would be in that. What was this discomfort in my mind? Well, I believe that the longings that are native to the soul of man for knowing God, and knowing his mind and purposes with respect to man and his future, had been stirred within me. But this is what I was referring to: I never had a moment's quiet or satisfaction in my mind until I believed with my whole heart the great truth about God's appearing in the flesh. And although I knew the story already, I hadn't believed it, at least hadn't believed it for real, until I came to feel the depth of my own defilement, and became conscious of my growing and indeed unmeasurable capacity for misery. Without a belief in the coming of Jesus Christ in the flesh, there is nothing but the silence of the grave everywhere; there isn't a clear answer to one of my dissatisfied soul's questions. But the life, teaching, death, atonement and resurrection of our Saviour defy the soul to ask any question that they cannot answer.

Now, my boy, I won't ask whether you know the story; I know that you know it as well as I do. But have you believed it? Believed the whole of it, without question and forever? I don't expect you to say yes. I don't put much faith in this believe-in-a-minute stuff that some people talk about. My own experience tells me that no man gains it without hard study, deep and continuous thought, and more and more prayer. My great hope is to set you on the right road to begin seriously the work of seeking the help of the Spirit to direct you properly. And if you seriously stick at it, the day will come when you'll be grateful for the misery that you're in today, when your eyes are opened to see the love of Him who remembered us in our lowly state. Do you wish to ask me anything?"

"I feel, Sir," I said, "that I wish to ask you many things, but I can't put them into words. I feel some great need, but I can't explain it, and I'm not sure I even know what it is. I had been thinking that no-one had ever felt the same way as me, but you have told me much of the story of my own heart. I'm aware of an emptiness that needs to be filled, and that the thing that is to fill it is still far away. How am I to fill my need, and find the rest that you have found?"

"The heart of man by nature," said Abel, "is desolate, empty, and once it has been woken up it longs every day. But there is a danger—especially for a man who has read and thought a bit—a danger, I say, for him to start living on the dreams of his heart, and to think that that is religion. Take great care against that. In many cases this is the religion of the sceptic; because as a rule you don't find them amongst the uneducated, ignorant classes, but amongst the bookish and contemplative types. How can this be? Well, this is how I see it. Reading and thinking make their heart wake up to their need, and to start asking questions of itself, and once it starts asking questions then it has plenty of work to do. The sceptic keeps on asking questions to himself, without getting an answer to any of his big questions. To begin with his questions are the main thing, but in the end it is his inability to answer them that becomes the main thing. Eventually he becomes comfortable with this, and sometimes even boasts about his ignorance. As it is to his own heart and understanding that he appeals, he is forced to sum up his whole credo in three words—*I don't know*. I don't pretend to be a philosopher, but I'm sure that I have a restless heart and soul that is always asking questions. Well, if I couldn't find higher ground and a better credo than that contained in *I don't know*, I'd be the most pitiable of all creatures. It would be better for me to be an elephant, or an ass, or a monkey, than a man. If I were sure in my mind that the most I would ever be able to attain through searching and meditating would be *I don't know*, then I'd raise my hat to every ass I met, and say to him, you are blessed. But thank God! We have revelation. To me there are two obvious facts. One is that once it has been woken up the human heart never stops asking questions. The other is that the experience of the cleverest men who have ever lived in the world has been that the only answer the heart can find to its own questions is, *I don't know*. Now, if the Bible is able to answer the deepest and

275

most complex questions of my heart—if it can explain to me my existence, my sorrow, and my future—if it can direct me to the One who can quieten the distress of my soul—then I believe that this book has come from God. If not, then why has no-one created anything like it, or indeed, better than it? I challenge any man, any nation, indeed, the best and brightest of every nation working together, to create anything like it, without being indebted to the Bible itself for the pattern and the materials.

"But where have I wandered off to? What I was talking about was the danger of you living on the dreams of your heart, and thinking that that was religion. Some people turn in on themselves with solemn, sentimental meditation, and moans and tears are their highlights. That's not religion. Religion is something more practical than that. Religion is a constant going outside of yourself. 'The kingdom of God is within you',[12] sure enough; but its going forth[13] is like its Author, from eternity. You'll get more good for your soul in one day looking to Christ and trying to do his commandments than in a hundred years looking inside yourself. You know what? When you lose yourself in your desire to do the most ordinary duties of life as a service to God, that is when you are most religious. By serving a customer from behind the counter, diligently and in the best way you can, do you know that you're pleasing God as much as if you were on your knees in your own room? In the midst of our dullness, our ignorance, and our darkness, there are some things we are sure of. You are sure in your mind that telling the truth is the right thing to do; tell the truth, then, in every situation. You are sure that living honestly is a good thing; therefore live so honestly that your own conscience can't point a finger at you. Remember that anything that resembles shabbiness or meanness is hateful in the sight of God; and the more like a gentleman you behave, the higher you will stand in His sight. Try to keep your heart as clean as God's own; and you'll find out soon—indeed I think you've

---

[12] Luke 17:21. [13] Micah 5:2.

found out already—that you can't do anything as you should do it without His help and direction. Every effort on your part to live a godly life will stir up the part of your nature that is contrary and defiled, causing you, I hope, to go to the only One who can give you help to overcome it. Try to believe that God sympathises deeply with you in your defilement, your darkness, and your weakness; otherwise He would not have sent His Son to die for you. But believe too that He doesn't have any sympathy for you when you give in to your weaknesses. Only when you are fighting against sin energetically does His sympathy and His strength run into you. At the beginning of your religious life—and I believe that only now are you seriously beginning it—I want to imprint it deeply into your mind that religion is not something that comes and goes. You know that there are some in our *seiat*, like William the Coal, who frequently fall into sin, and then have deep feelings during the sermon, and weep in the *seiat*, and put the blame on Satan for their sins, like I heard that mischievous boy Wil Bryan imitating him do. They think that the feelings during the sermon, and the weeping in the *seiat*, are true religion. I don't know what to make of them. I hope that God has some byelaw that will save them. No, my boy, the bitterest tears in religion don't come after falling; but in the effort, in the war, is where the strong crying and tears ought to be. Well, perhaps I have talked too much to you. You have, as you know, sinned against me; but I forgive you from the bottom of my heart, as I believe that you are sorry for what you did. If I who am beset by weakness am able to do that, how much more will He who is infinite in His pity delete all your sins, if you are truly repentant? Now, go to your work like a man, and remember, from now on I will expect you to take it in turns with me to keep the family devotions."

Abel unlocked the door and walked out, and I felt as if I were in a dream, but not so dark as many of the dreams that I'd had. I was frightened by Abel's last words, but from now on I looked upon him not as a master, but as a father.

29

THE CLOCK CLEANER'S ADVICE

I had light and blessing from the conversation that took place between Abel Hughes and myself in the parlour. I saw that it was possible to be brought up with religion from one's childhood, to take an interest in chapel things, to find some measure of enjoyment in the Gospel ordinances, yes, even to be of some service to it, yet without ever waking up to the big questions of life. I also understood from Abel's words—and to this day I've never had cause to think he was mistaken—that there is a particular time in the life of every believer, whether he has had a religious upbringing or not, when the spiritual light shines into his mind and makes him look at himself and at everything else in a completely new way. I understood too, and had learned from experience, that the more a man looks into himself, the deeper he plumbs the depths of his own heart, the more will be his sorrow and hopelessness, and the less able he will become to be any good to himself or anyone else; and that the only cure for one who has truly been woken up to his situation, and who has realised that there's nothing but darkness and terror in the depths of his own soul, is to settle his mind on the glorious person, perfect life, and atoning death of our Lord and Saviour Jesus Christ. I remember an observation which Abel made a while after our talk in the parlour. 'If you are troubled with biliousness, do you expect to get better by staying in your bedroom looking at your tongue in the mirror, and thinking how ugly the scale on it looks? I don't think so. I know you'd be sensible enough to go out and have a walk along your usual paths; and if that won't do the trick, you'll get some of your friends together and climb up Moel Famau to have a look at the wonderful Vale of Clwyd; and I'll guarantee that the fresh air of the old hill will shift every bit of bile from your stomach, and you won't turn your nose up at dinner when you return. Well, it's just the same thing with religion. I've said to you many times that no good comes from looking too much inside yourself. Go out to the highways and fields of the Gospel. Gather your friends together to climb the hill where the dear Lamb suffered under the iron nails; and you'll see that you'll be healthier, purer and lighter in spirit. You know what? There's a lot to think about in what old Dr Johnson said: "Gentlemen, let's take a walk down Fleet Street." Johnson had many memories full of refreshing charm about Fleet Street; and when he was fed up with himself and with the company he kept, he'd say, "Gentlemen, let's take a walk down Fleet Street." There have been hundreds of times when the old Doctor's saying has done me as much good as a verse from the Bible. Oh, the Gospel has its Fleet Street for the believer, full of charm, full of bittersweet memories. Scores of times when I've been fed up with the shop, sick of grey calico at a groat per yard and brown Holland for ten pence, and that sort of stuff, scores of times I've left it all to visit your mother or someone else and take a walk down Fleet Street. When going to a church service old Johnson's words are as often as not in my mind, "Gentlemen, let's take a walk down Fleet Street."

I tried to follow my master's advice, and to some extent I succeeded to stop being like a chicken sitting on a gate with its head under its wing. I set about forgetting myself, and thinking more about Christ and His words, and to look at the bright side of the Gospel. I was surprised that I hadn't understood before Abel had pointed it out, how that this was the secret of my mother's happiness. "Remember your mother," he'd say. "Do you know anyone who had so many troubles? And in spite of them all did you ever see anyone who enjoyed so much real happiness? Where did her happiness come from? From looking inside herself? I don't think so! She had learned to look at the One who is worth looking at. I always thought that the greater her trials were, the greater her happiness. Her poverty only made her think more about the riches that there are in Christ, and the filthy treatment she had from your inhuman father just made her feast on the gentleness and love of the Saviour. Don't be cross with me, but the truth is that, whenever I heard your mother was in trouble I would chuckle to myself and say, Well, here is another feast for you, Mary Lewis! You know what? You ought to be a strong boy, because you had a noble mother. I never saw anyone who could live so entirely on the resources of her religion as she. In a manner of speaking, she had no business dying when she did. She wasn't old, and she didn't have any disease. 'Abel,' she said to me when she went to live at Thomas Bartley's, 'there's no reason, is there, for someone who has everything to become a burden on the parish? I won't accept a penny from the parish, that's the truth of it.' She didn't either, as you know. I've thought much about her. When she saw that she'd soon need to depend on the charity of the parish, it had the same effect on her as the husks did on the prodigal son.[1] I imagined that I heard her say, 'Hold on, Relieving Officer! That food is an insult to my family; I will get up and go to my father's house.' I think that your mother wanted to die in order to prove the truth of the promise that the righteous will never be left destitute.[2] Thomas Bartley thought the same as me, although Thomas, I know, didn't understand the philosophy of the thing. I heard him say that he'd 'begged with her like a cripple' not to die, but dying was what she wanted. I don't commend your mother for that. But there's something, you see, in religion of the best sort, which makes one terribly independent of this world and its stuff. Try to get a religion like your mother's."

I've already said that Abel spoke with me little during the first few years that I was with him; no more than was necessary, between master and servant. But after I had made a clean breast to him, his behaviour towards me was completely different. His kindness and tenderness were without limit. At every opportunity he would talk freely, as a friend. After closing the shop, he would daily bring some subject or other to my attention; and after asking me about it, would discuss his own thoughts freely and clearly. He would talk about books he'd read, and note their strengths and weaknesses. He'd talk about the old preachers, and describe their appearance, their clothes, and their ways of speaking. He recited parts of their sermons, until I'd often lament the fact I hadn't come into the world sooner. It was as if Abel had decided to tear down every barrier, and destroy all formality, between him and me. Since I was a young lad, I'd had a great respect for him, and I saw him as the pattern of what a church elder should be; and his *condescension*[3] in taking such care of me, and all the trouble he took to teach me and make me familiar with religion and with general knowledge, together with his free and unassuming kindness, made me love him, and feel completely happy in his house. Miss Hughes was delighted that I was the occasion for making her brother so talkative and sociable, rather than being, as she put it, 'with his nose in a book, or his head up the chimney, the whole time.' In a word, the old bachelor had had a son in his old age, and this gave him the tongue and the heart of a father. Happiness started to smile at me again; and I took a new interest, deeper and more genuine than ever before, in the things of religion and in the ordinances of the Gospel.

But I was uncomfortable because I hadn't behaved properly towards my old companion in mischief and wrongdoing, namely Wil Bryan. I hadn't told him specifically why I had been avoiding his company; and I felt that this wasn't proper, or worthy of what our long-standing friendship deserved. I decided that I would take the first opportunity to tell him that my mind had undergone a

---

[1] Luke 15:16. [2] Psalm 37:25.

[3] Modern English seems, as far as I can tell, to have no word that corresponds to the original meaning of this word–a selfless voluntary humbling of the greater in order to do good to the lesser. It would certainly have been the correct translation of Owen's word, '*ymostyngiad*', at the time it was written; its meaning in modern English has changed, to something more or less the same as 'contempt'. No new word has come in to represent the original idea, which is of course deeply unfashionable in any case.

complete change, and that I was now trying with God's help to be a good boy. Something in my heart whispered, 'Can I, perhaps, win Wil over to make the same decision?' I can truly say that nothing on earth would have been more desirable to me than to be able to persuade Wil to leave his ways; because I could not hide from myself the fact that he was an ungodly boy, even though he was some sort of a church member. My heart cleaved to him like that of Jonathan to David,[4] and the thought of breaking my connection to him pained me greatly. He had a wide and generous heart, and I couldn't forget his kindness and faithfulness to me in times past. As I said at the beginning of this story, there was a great difference between our situations. I was a poor and needy boy, and Wil lived in plenty; but he never showed even in appearance that he was conscious of the difference. Scores of times he kept the wolf from my door; and he did this with the sort of unconscious finesse that left my feelings unhurt, because he knew that I had a proud heart. When in school I was a weak little boy, while Wil was strong and vigorous; and his strength was always available to me to keep me from harm. Was it proper for me to forget this? Was it right for me to break my connection with him? And yet I was sure, after all I had been through lately, that I couldn't maintain contact with him without damaging my soul. I couldn't bear the idea of Wil thinking ill about me, and I decided to reveal myself to him at once. At the same time I was afraid of this, because I knew that Wil was much more able mentally than I; in truth he was full of natural talent; and this made me lament even more that he wasn't on the right track. I thought uncomfortably, what if he makes fun of me? Well, if that were to happen, I decided to patiently suffer being roasted by him. I was keen that when we met it should appear entirely accidental. And so it was in fact, because I met him at a time when I wasn't expecting to. He wore his usual cheerful smile, and I could see that my behaviour towards him had not impinged in any way upon his good nature. He reached out his hand to me and said, "Hello! Old thousand years! How are you, it's been centuries. I was just thinking that you'd gone to heaven, but I thought you wouldn't go without saying goodbye to your old chum. Honour bright, now; is it a fact that you've had a revival—revelation—or whatever it is they call it? You know what? I'm ready to go to heaven or join the army—I don't mind which—because I'm completely fed up with things at home. There's been a terrible row there this week, and about almost nothing; and I'm not minded to put up with much more humbug."

"What was the trouble, Wil?" I asked as I walked with him, and he replied:

"You know that old eight-day clock in the kitchen at home? Lately it's been in the habit of losing time—*a fault, by the way, not entirely unknown amongst other orders of superior creatures.*[5] I believed that I could fix it if I had the chance, although I had never tried to clean a clock before—because you know that I'm no slouch at that sort of thing. Anyway, the old folk went to a fair in Wrexham—*with strict injunctions that Wil in the meantime should diligently apply himself to weighing and wrapping sugar, which occupation the said Wil considered unworthy of his admitted abilities; and the said Wil, following his more congenial inclination, betook himself to clock-cleaning, thinking that thereby he did not waste valuable time by putting the timekeeper to rights.*[6] But it was more of a job than I'd thought, you see; because as I pulled it into pieces I had to make notes of where every part came from and where it belonged. After I had cleaned it all, and put a bit of butter on every wheel, screw and bar—since there was no oil in the house—it was well into the afternoon, although I had skipped lunch to save time, and it was high time to put the thing back together again before the gaffer came home from the fair. *So far—good.* But when I set about putting the old eight-day back

---

[4] 1 Samuel 18:1.

[5] In the original, Wil Bryan says these words in English and Rhys adds a comment, 'I cannot be held responsible for the correctness or otherwise of my friend's use of English'.

[6] Ditto, and likewise other text in this passage which is written in italics.

together and consulted my notes—you never saw such a thing—
I was just like Mr Brown the parson and couldn't understand my
own notes. But I learned this—a man who's going to clean clocks,
just like a man who's going to preach, should be able to do it
without notes. You can't believe how much trouble I had. But you
must remember that I was *labouring under great disadvantages*,
because all the tools I had were a knife and a farrier's hammer.
I was dripping with sweat for fear that the old Pilgrim's Progress
would come home from the fair before I finished putting the clock
back together. *However*, you see, I worked like a *black*, and I got
it together somehow. But I had one spare wheel, and I had no idea
where on earth it went, or what to do with it, so I put it in my
pocket—here it is, you see (and Wil showed me the wheel). Well
you see, I put the old eight back in its place, and I wound it up
and the first thing *my nabs* did was to chime for all it was worth.
It chimed thousands and thousands of times, and the sound of
the bell echoing round my head made me feel quite strange; it
made such a row that I was afraid the neighbours would think
that that the Squire's daughter was going to get married! After it
had chimed as much as it could, the next thing *my nabs* did was to
stop dead. So long as I swung the pendulum myself the old eight
went all right, but as soon as I stopped pushing so it stopped too.
And to tell you the truth, I laughed until I was rolling around—
I couldn't have helped it even if someone was about to kill me.
*So here endeth a true account of the clock-cleaning. But wait a
bit.* Not long after, the old pilgrims came back from the fair, and
the first thing the mother did was to look to see what time it was.
I'd tried to guess what time it was, and put the hands fairly close
to that. But the old woman noticed that the clock had stopped,
and she said, 'What's wrong with this old clock, William?' 'Has
it stopped?' I said. 'Yes, by the looks of it, two hours ago,' she
said, and gave the pendulum a push. I was dying to laugh. 'What's
wrong with this old clock?' said the old woman again, and gave it
the sort of shake you've seen people give a drunken man sleeping

on the side of the road. So that I'd have an excuse to laugh, I said, 'I think it's got a knot in its guts, like the Squire's *hunter*, and we'll have to either shoot it or open it up'. But then the maid came in and told straight away that I'd spent the day cleaning the old eight. Well, you never saw such a row. My mother went crazy, and the gaffer was furious. I firmly believe that the old hand would have liked to give me a beating, but he knew that he couldn't. *And Wil went to his boots.* The next day they sent for Mr Spruce, the watchmaker, to get the old eight-day to go; but I knew he wouldn't be able to, because there was one wheel in Wil's pocket, and Wil had his *revenge*. '*Give it up*', said the old mainspring. But when this chap has the old people's backs turned for six hours, he's *bound* to do miracles on the old eight-day. Well, there we are, I've told you my story. But *honour bright*, is it a fact that you've been born again?"

"Wil," I said, "don't you think it's time we turned a page? I can't say to you for sure that I've been born again; but I'll say this, that my mind has undergone a remarkable change lately. Now I look at everything in a different way, and I'm sure that I'll never find amusement in our old things again. Hell, the world to come, and the things of religion, have been in my mind all the time for months, and although I've tried to drive them away, I can't. I've wanted to be able to tell you that I've decided to be a good boy, if I'm helped to be so. And there's nothing in the world that I want more than for you to make the same decision. You have always been a great friend to me; and if our ways of life become so different that we have to part from one another, that will be very painful for me. You know as well as I do, perhaps better, that it won't do for us to go on as we have been—it's sure to end badly. Don't you think about that sometimes, Wil?"

"Go on with your sermon—say, 'And we observe, as our second point'," said Wil.

"It's not a sermon, Wil, but a friendly chat," I said.

"Well, even if it's not a sermon, I've heard many worse," said

Wil. "But seriously now, I had spotted a while ago that you had gone along that line, and I said to you, didn't I? And to tell the truth, I wasn't surprised, because there's this religious nature in your family—barring your father—*no offence*, mind. If I'd been raised the same way as you, perhaps there'd be a bit of religion in me; but you never saw less of it than there is in my house, except on Sunday. Although I'm not *quite a pattern of morality* myself, I think I know what religion is. If I didn't know your mother, and old Abel, and the old *waterworks*, and some half a dozen others, I'd think for sure that the whole *pack of tricks* was nothing but a load of hypocrites."

"It's not right for you to speak lightly about your parents," said I.

"I'm not speaking lightly about them," said Wil. "It's about their religion that I'm talking, and a man and his religion are two completely different things. As a *man of business, clever at a bargain*, as a man for making money and making sure that a chap has plenty of *grub*, the *gaffer* is A1. But I'd swear that he can't say two verses properly, any more than I can. He never looks at the Bible except for two minutes on a Sunday before going to Sunday School. And the Bible he had as a present when he got married is still good as new. Nothing like your mother's Bible which was in pieces. But I'm quite sure that if the *daybook* and *ledger* caught fire tonight the old hand would be able to copy them precisely tomorrow morning. *It's a fact, Sir!* Do you think I don't know what religion is? It's giving four shillings a month for my mother, and four shillings for himself, and a shilling for me, regularly on the *seiat's* books. But do you think I believe we're getting any credit for it in the *ledger up above*? *It's all in my eye*, boy. I know how things ought to be really, even if I don't do them. If the gaffer can make his conscience *shut up* like that, I'm *wide awake* enough to know that we can't *cheat* the Good Lord. I know as well as anyone else that you need to live religion 365 days a year, not just 52. My mother and father would be real *honorary members* of religion if there were such a thing; but there isn't, I know, and so it will be *no go* for them in the end."

"Your responsibility is much greater, Wil, since you know what you ought to do, and haven't done it," I said.

"Do you think you're telling me anything new?" said Wil. "I knew that when I was a *kid*. But I'm talking about the kind of upbringing I've had, and what I've seen at home. It is enough for a pupil to be like his father. There's a verse like that, isn't there?"

"Like his teacher,"[7] I said.

"*Quite so*," said Wil, "it's an odd thing that I can never say a verse properly: but I know hundreds of *comic songs*. But as far as religion is concerned, a father and a teacher are the same thing; and perhaps it said father in the original, as they say. *But to the point at issue.* I know what a professor ought to be on a Sunday, and on a Monday, but I've seen so much *humbug, fudge*, and hypocrisy, that it's made my heart very hard, and filled my pocket with wild oats, and I need to sow them, you see. You know what? I'm ashamed to be in the *seiat*. Everyone knows that I'm not fit to be there, and the Good Lord knows that my father forces me to go, and that he's *just* as fit to be there as I am. There's no more true religion in our family than there is in a milestone, nor as much even, since at least that lives up to the purpose it was made for. You know that I'm not a *bad sort* by nature, and I'm amazed that I'm as good as I am. I sometimes think that if I was a son to someone like Abel Hughes I'd be—well, how can you know what I'd be? But, '*to be or not to be, that is the question*', said Shakespeare, and I say, '*What is, is, and there's an end of it*'."

"You're making a mistake, Wil," I said. "You know that you can and should be something other than what you are. You have clear talents, and it's a shame for you to use them in the devil's service."

"You'd better put a *stop* to it right there—you can't tell me anything new," said Wil. "It would be nothing but that same old

---

[7] Matt. 10:25.

hypocrisy to say that I had only the head of a turnip. But with religion, you see, a head without grace is good for nothing: and grace isn't something that you can buy in a *shop* as if it were a pound of sugar. It has to come from *head office*, or not *at all*."

"Why don't you go to *head office* to ask for it, then?" said I.

"I knew what you'd say," said Wil, "but that's *easier said than done*. Something tells me—I won't say it's Satan, because William the Coal puts plenty of blame on him—something tells me that I haven't had my *innings*. Old Abel or someone has bowled you out, and I'm glad of it. But for the time being I'm still in; and perhaps someone will shout *well caught* or *spread eagles* about me some day. I hope they will, because I don't want to carry my bat out, you know. I'd like to get religion but only if it's the proper sort. *Beware of imitations, is a motto for every man*. Perhaps you think that Wil is harder than he is. *Hold on!* I'm not *quite* like the iron of Spain yet. You've never seen me cry, have you? But many nights when I can't sleep, and something in me tells me that I am a bad boy, I've had *many a good cry*. But by morning I'll have hardened again, and something tells me that I have let out *private apartments* to some little demon in my heart, and that he's become my master, and I've never had any help from my father or my mother to turn him out. I'm fairly sure that it was to him that your mother alluded; but the 'old man' she called him. The Bible talks, doesn't it, about some bad sort of them, which don't go out without prayer and a meal?[8] Well, I can't pray for the life of me—it's not possible to get into the mood for that at home—and I won't sham it. And talking about a meal—I give him dozens of meals every day. I swear he's as fat as mud. But to tell you the truth, I'd like to put him on one meal a day and starve him. I've noticed a fair bit about *human nature*, and I know that you were feeling shy about meeting me. You thought that I'd make fun of you. *Far from it*, I'm glad in my

---

[8] Wil is thinking of Matthew 17:21, '*But an evil spirit of this kind is only driven out by prayer and fasting*', but he's got his Welsh words mixed up: he says '*un pryd*', 'a meal', instead of '*ympryd*', 'fasting'.

heart for you that you've been converted. You want to be a preacher, don't you? There's no point in you shaking your head, you'll be a preacher. I knew when you were a *kid* that that's what you'd be. That's what your mother wanted you to be, and if she asked the Good Lord, He'd be *bound* to *oblige* her. Perhaps you'll find this hard to believe, but I swear that I've felt uncomfortable many times at the thought that I've harmed you. But now that you've been converted you'll be a better preacher than if you had kept on the *straight line*. You know that no-one can play *whist* without knowing how many cards are out. You never saw any of these *milk and water* boys—boys who've never done a thing wrong—who were anything *extra* as a preacher. They don't know the *ins and outs*, you see. They preach well, but nothing *extra*. Mark what I say: if you hear a man preach especially well, and if you find out anything about him, you're *bound* to find that at some time he's been off the *metals*. Didn't Peter go off the *metals*? Yes he did, and he smashed the *engine* to dust and ashes; but he made a stunner of a preacher after that. He was the boss of all of them, wasn't he? Well, if you want to be a preacher—there's no point shaking your head, you're *bound* to be one—I'll give you a word of advice. This may be the last *chance* I get, because if there's not a *change of policy* at home soon this *chap* will be saying, 'Adieu! My native land, adieu!' You're cleverer than me with the scriptures, but perhaps I've noticed some things you haven't, and I can give you some advice that you won't get in the Monthly Meeting. Well, remember to be *true to nature*. After you've started preaching, don't change your face and your voice, and your coat, before a fortnight is out. If you do, I'll be *bound* to point out that you're a humbug. It's God's work, I know, to change your heart; but if your mouth and voice change, that will have been your work. And there's no need for you to—they're fine as they are. Don't try to be someone else, or you'll be no-one. You know what? There are many preachers like *ventriloquists*. When he's at home he's just like himself, but when he climbs into the pulpit you'd swear that he was someone else, and that the someone else is worse than him, because he isn't *true to nature*. Don't sing as you're reasoning, as if you were out of your mind; because the fact that you're in the pulpit doesn't give you a *licence* to be stupider than you'd be anywhere else. If you sang as you were reasoning with someone in the street, or in the house, or before the *magistrates*, you'd be taken straight to the asylum. Hearing a preacher tuning up as though he were in a *concert*, and the next minute breaking it up and speaking as if he were someone else, makes me think that the whole thing is a *dodge*, and makes my heart as hard as stone. When you pray, don't open your eyes. I can never believe that someone is godly if they look to see what time it is while they're praying. I've seen some do that, and they spoil the pudding for me. When you're a preacher—and you're *bound* to be—there's no point shaking your head—don't pretend to be more godly than you are, or children will be afraid of you. You know what? There was a preacher *lodging* in our house the last Monthly Meeting, and I was terrified of him. He was perfectly healthy, and he ate well, but he groaned all the time like he had toothache. It was just as if he had a coffin-lid on his chest the whole time, and I felt as if I were at a funeral while he was there. I swear I'd have been less afraid of the Apostle Paul or of Jesus Christ if they had come to stay. He wasn't *true to nature*, you see. If you want to put on *airs* like that yourself, save them for when you're in a house that you're paying the rent on. Remember to be *honourable*. When you're lodging somewhere, remember to give sixpence to the maid even if you don't have another sixpence to spare—or she won't believe a word of your sermon. If you smoke—and all the great preachers smoke—remember to smoke your own tobacco, or they will grumble about you after you've gone. You know that I'm fond of funny things; but if the sermon is serious, don't tell funny stories after going back to the house, or someone will think that you're a sham. I like a preacher who's *true to nature* in the pulpit and in the house; but a preacher who's just made me cry in chapel, and who after that makes me laugh in the house, spoils the sermon for me. When you preach don't *beat* too much around the *bush*; come to the *point*—hit the nail on the head and have done with it. Don't talk too much about the law and those sorts of things, because what do I and my *sort* know about the law? Come to the *point*—Jesus Christ. If you can't make every *one* in the chapel listen to you, give it up as a *bad job*, and carry on selling *calico*. If you go to *college*, and you will, I know, don't be the same as the rest of them. They say that the *students* are all the same—like a lot of *postage stamps*. Try to be an *exception to the rule*. Don't let the elders announce you as 'a young man from Bala'.[9] Preach so that they'll announce 'Rhys Lewis' without saying where you come from. When you're in *college*, whatever else you learn, study *nature*, *literature*, and English—because they'll pay you for their board one day. If you get on well, and you're *bound* to, don't swallow a *poker* and forget your old *chums*. Don't wear glasses to try to pretend that you've studied so hard that you've lost your sight, and to have an excuse to fail to recognise your old *chums*, because everyone knows that that's all a *fudge*. If you're ordained, don't start wearing a white dog-collar the very next Sunday. If you never wear one, it won't matter, because I'll never believe that Paul and his *chums* wore one—they wouldn't have had time to wait around for it to be starched. Never break an appointment for more money, or you'll make more *infidels* than Christians. Whatever you do, don't be a miserly preacher and make yourself a mean man. *Honour bright*! I hope that I'll never hear that about you: but I'd rather hear that you've been out on a *spree* than that you've become a miser. I've never seen a miser change, but I've seen many people sober up. It's *stranger than fiction* to me—if you go out on a *spree* just once, they stop you preaching; but if you become the biggest miser in the land, they let you preach

---

[9] Bala was the location of the Calvinistic Methodist theological college in North Wales, opened by Lewis Edwards and David Charles in 1839. It closed, and was converted into a church youth activities centre, in 1968.

just the same. *Old fellow!* Don't you think I'm giving you fairly good advice, considering who I am? The Monthly Meeting will give you advice about how to pray and that sort of thing; but it has no courage to give the advice that I'm giving you. *Give us thy paw, and wire in, old boy!*"

And so Wil went away without me being able to get a word in edgeways.

30

THE POACHER

I thought I knew my friend Wil Bryan thoroughly. I'd had every chance for that. He was so free and open-hearted, that I thought there was no difficulty in getting to know him. But in the conversation that I related in the previous chapter I saw that there were layers in his character of which I had not previously been aware. I always looked at him as the pattern of health and natural vivacity—like one whose talents shone out, even though they were never cultivated. He wasn't a great reader but whatever he did read, he took in its meaning and spirit with one draught. He was too lazy to take trouble over things but seemed to be able to do everything without any trouble. Everything that he saw and heard—except sermons—was recorded in his memory as if by shorthand. He was a sharp and detailed commentator upon everyone and everything around him; or, in his own way of speaking, he would '*spot*' something every day, and rarely be far off the mark. Returning from various places, I would be amazed how many times he would '*spot*' things that I hadn't noticed at all, and it was no wonder that in such circumstances he would call me Bartimaeus.[1] I was often jealous of his ability to see things as they were, and not as they appeared to be. I always sensed that he had a natural talent to spot deception and fraud, or, as he called them, '*humbug*' and '*fudge*'. His clear-sightedness and ability to say things as they were, and that in a few pointed words, had made an impression on me for years, and caused me to admire him. Even so I felt, as he confessed himself, that he had been bad for me, because many times, when I thought I'd had some good

---

[1] The blind man whose sight was restored by Jesus in Mark 10:46.

from a sermon or an address by someone or other, Wil would spoil the good impression by pointing out some '*humbug*' that he had identified. Although I could trust more in his honour, and count more upon his kindness, than anyone else at that time, I was convinced that he was wholly unfamiliar with deep feelings and completely indifferent to his own condition. After I had decided to reveal my intention of being a good boy to him, I had expected, as I said earlier, that he would turn around and mock me without mercy. But I was disappointed. I was surprised to see him rejoice that I had been converted, as he put it, and say that there was something at the bottom of his heart that longed for the same thing. He didn't, as he said, intend to 'carry his *bat* out' in the game that he was playing. In the loneliness and quiet of the night a voice rose from the depth of his heart, 'Wil, why are you a bad boy?' But, as he said, he never had any help from his parents to 'cast out the evil spirit'. Poor Wil! I often thought that if he'd had a religious upbringing—if he had seen something in his own home besides worldliness and the worship of the golden calf [2]—he could today be an adornment not just to his neighbourhood but to his nation. In the most thoughtless of us there is some sort of duality. Though corruption is uppermost, there is something in the depths of the heart that tips its hat towards the good—towards the truth. I know of a drunken man entirely oblivious to the things of religion. Yet, when he received a letter from his son—who had left home—describing how he had been received into full church membership, he was so overcome by his feelings that he had to flee into another room, out of his family's sight, so that he could weep out his joy. Such homage to religion! Whether on the throne or not, it is generally agreed that virtue is best. In the midst of all his levity and mischief, Wil Bryan had his serious hours, when his conscience demanded to be heard, and his soul yearned for help in turning the evil spirit out. I would never have imagined that such thoughts could find a place in his heart, if he himself hadn't confessed it to me. When one friend tells the secrets of his heart to another, it often happens that that draws out other secrets just as deep.

I don't know what made Wil think that I wanted to become a preacher, because I'm certain that I had never mentioned anything about it. When I was a small boy, it is true that I liked the idea of some day being a preacher, but I never said anything about that to anyone; and for some years after that, my lifestyle was anything but consistent with the idea, my youthful passions having completely erased the idea from my mind by the time I had reached an age of reason. When Wil had protested that I would become a preacher, nothing was further from my mind. At the time I was in too much trouble over my condition, and what I believed myself, to be able to think about anything else. Yet I must confess that Wil's words— 'there's no point in shaking your head, you will be a preacher'— stuck in my mind. He spoke the words with such certainty and authority that I asked myself whether Wil, like Saul, was among the prophets.[3] I chased the thought away but no sooner had I done so than it came back to me again. I remembered the strange and wonderful feeling that had come over me the evening that Seth died, after I had tried to pray by his bedside—as if something had told me while returning home that night that I would be a preacher some day. But also I couldn't help remembering how mischievous, sinful and irreverent I had been for so many years after my mother had died; and I could imagine unclean spirits laughing cynically at my elbow and asking, 'Who do you think you are to think about preaching? You who have broken every commandment a thousand times over!' There were scores of boys in my neighbourhood who knew about my old antics. I thought how they would laugh in their sleeves if I dared to talk preaching; how they would recall my old tricks as I preached, and as I would remember them if I saw my contemporaries amongst my hearers! What, me preach? Impossible! But how could Wil say so definitely that I would be

---

[2] Exodus 32. [3] 1 Samuel 10:11–12.

a preacher? He knew more about me than anyone else at home; indeed, he knew more about my faults; and yet he'd said, 'You're *bound* to be a preacher!' Impossible, I said to myself, since I'm not sure of my own salvation or about my credo. Anyone who's thinking about preaching should first of all be sure of his own salvation. I was not so. I chased the idea away once again; because it was impossible, I thought, for that ever to take place.

Weeks went by; and somehow I found that I didn't like wearing light-coloured clothes—not because I was thinking of being a preacher, but because black clothes somehow seemed more appropriate. I had light-coloured clothes as good as new in my cupboard, but I didn't wear them because I didn't like them. I decided that the next time I bought a coat, I'd get one a bit longer, but not as long as a preacher's coat lest anyone should think I wanted to imitate them, since nothing was further from my mind. I took a particular interest with books that touched on theological topics; and it surprised me a little that my contemporaries did not have such a taste for them as I did. I remembered the time when I tended very much to criticise preachers, and to pick holes in them; but lately I was struck by how flawless they seemed, and how they could carry out their work so well. Before, I would hate to see it become Abel's turn on the rota to provide accommodation for preachers; but by now, I would long for it, and spend as much time as I could in their company. Nowadays I can't help laughing at my innocence. I looked at Abel Hughes' diary as a sacred book—too sacred for me to be able to ask to see it, although I was dying to know who would be coming to preach with us in the months to come. And when Abel happened forgetfully to leave it on the mantelpiece, the temptation to take a hurried look at it was too much for me to bear; but after I had done so, I felt the sort of guilt that I expect a Jew who wasn't descended from the priestly line must have felt if he had looked inside the Ark of the Covenant![4] I'm sorry to say that I haven't managed to maintain the same respectful feelings towards the diary; because later on

I found out that there were some things in it that one couldn't always depend on, and looking at it at the end of the year that there had been as much 'fairing' in it as there had been fairs,[5] and that the moon had changed less often than some of the 'promises'. But to return. I loved to see every preacher who came to stay with Abel Hughes; but best of all I liked the younger ones, especially the students. Why so? Well, because I could be more bold with them, and ask them some questions, such as, how old were they when they began to preach? Did they find it hard work? Did they start on their own initiative, or did others persuade them to do it? And so on. What end did I have in mind by asking these questions? Was I myself thinking of starting to preach? Nothing was further from my mind, or so I thought. And if I secretly started to think about it, then remembering my family's shame—that any minute might have been brought up in the most painful way—was enough to quench for ever every thought or wish that could have been in me to be a preacher. And remembering my feelings at that time also brings to mind the event that I'm now going to relate.

In the neighbourhood where I was raised there was a remarkable man who was known as 'old Niclas' or more often, 'old Nick'. The name was not inappropriate for him because according to my boyish imagination, there was a strong family resemblance between Niclas and his namesake. He was tall, stooped, wiry and strong. Even though he was, at the time I am referring to, and old man, old age had not softened or relieved the severity of his appearance. His curly hair was too stubborn to turn grey, and his cruel face was too decisive for it to wrinkle. I believe that Niclas would have

---

[4] All except the priests who were the direct descendants of Aaron, the brother of Moses, were expressly forbidden from touching or even seeing the Ark of the Covenant and the other items which were kept in the Sanctuary; see for example Numbers 4:19-20, 1 Samuel 13-20.

[5] Apparently a reference to the practice of some preachers to change their engagements if they could get a higher speaking fee elsewhere, or to chapels cancelling engagements if they found that a more famous or respected preacher was in the area.

gone crazy if he had lost one of his teeth. When he walked around he always looked down at the ground, and he laid his hands in the small of his back, under his coat; and he took no notice of anyone except through the corner of his villainous eye. Children were terrified of him; and if a child was crying, or refusing to go into its house, its mother would be heard to say, 'Wait here, my boy, old Niclas is coming!' and that would put a stop to the crying and cause the child to run for its life into the house. Although my mother had never used Niclas to threaten me, I was very afraid of him; and I remember that, whenever there was a group of us boys playing, if we saw Niclas coming, we would hide out of his way as quiet as mice until he had gone past. Wil Bryan did not believe that Niclas was a man. Wil said that he was something between a gypsy and the devil. Niclas did not have any contact with his neighbours; and as far as I know, no-one lamented that. As he wasn't a native of the area, his background was a complete mystery to everyone. At the same time, many terrifying stories were told about him, which were believed absolutely by the credulous and superstitious—as no-one could disprove them. It was widely believed that he was from a noble family, as he was very rich. I remember that my mother's opinion of him was that he had sold his soul to the devil, and still lived off the bargain. I fear that my mother had too great an opinion of the devil's financial resources. But if accused of this, she would reply straight away that the love of money is the root of all evil,[6] and it wouldn't be surprising if the devil had an old sock in his possession with a bit put away. In any case, it was certain that old Niclas was not poor, since he lived in his own house that been purchased for a great deal of money. This house, called 'Y Garth Ddu',[7] stood in a particular clearing about half a mile outside the town, bordering onto the estate of the Manor. Around the house and garden there was a high wall, which had been built

---

[6] 1 Tim. 6:10.

[7] Literally, 'the black hill'.

after Niclas had taken possession. That which could be seen of the building had an ancient look about it, and ivy had grown up to the level of its roof, rendering its windows wholly useless. A newcomer would think that the house was uninhabited; and this idea would be confirmed by looking at the acre that belonged to it, which hadn't been grazed or harvested for many years. Nor had a foot stepped in it, apart from the occasions when Niclas was seen walking by the hedge with his gun under his arm, looking down as if he was searching, not for birds, but for moles. Since the time that Y Garth Ddu had been in Niclas' ownership, no-one was known to have set foot within its walls except for its owner and an unremarkable old woman called Magdalen Bennet, or as she was commonly known, Modlen Y Garth. Even the tax collector never got further than the door that was in the outer wall. As Niclas did not have anything to do with his neighbours, whatever transactions with the outside world as were necessary took place solely through Modlen. She bought his food, and the few clothes that he needed, and his weekly newspaper. Many attempts were made to get Modlen to reveal some information about Niclas' circumstances and lifestyle; but the only answer the old woman would ever give was, 'Well, that's asking'. All that could be got out of Modlen, even by her best friends, about how Niclas spent his time was that he tended his garden and shot house-sparrows. As Modlen did not like questions about Niclas, and because she was a good customer, shopkeepers didn't think it wise to pester her. Yet they couldn't help wondering at the power of his stomach, if he was able to eat all the food that was bought for him; and to think of the amount of powder and shots that were bought for him, it was a wonder that a single house-sparrow in the whole country had escaped with its life. It's likely that a story by Modlen had given rise to the widespread belief that Niclas had a magnificent garden, worth seeing; and many people lamented at how such a fair place was (in their imaginings) wasting its beauty in the same way as the flower in the wilderness that the poet spoke about. Niclas' hermit-like life, and the secrecy surrounding him, were by now so familiar that no-one talked or thought much about him; and it was generally believed that there was some flaw in the sanity of the odd man of Y Garth Ddu. This latter belief, together with the fact that shots were often heard within the garden walls, safeguarded Niclas from any needless interference from his neighbours.

There was not much communication between me and Wil Bryan for some months after the conversation I recorded in the previous chapter and, to his credit, I must say that this is due more than anything else to his determination not to do me any harm. By now I had no-one in particular as a friend except Abel Hughes, but he was an old man. I spent most of my leisure hours on my own; and the more I read and thought about things, the more the big questions of life weighed on my soul. No sooner would I have found light on one trouble of my mind, than I would be in the middle of another; and I can hardly say that I ever conquered my sadness except for short periods of time. Many times I lamented the fact that I had no friends my own age who shared the same inclinations, whom I could tell of my trouble; because whenever I found myself in confusion, or if I found light on some matter, I would be overcome by a longing to tell someone and I longed for someone who would listen. I was never strong in health, and my natural tendency to stay indoors was very harmful to me. On fine evenings my master, Abel Hughes, would force me to go out for a walk. One evening towards the end of May, I remember clearly that after closing the shop I voluntarily went out for a long walk in the countryside. As it was a particularly clear and pleasant evening, I took the zigzag path along the banks of the Alyn, and I went past several office clerks who were enjoying themselves fishing. When I felt that I had gone far enough, I thought I could return more quickly by taking a different path. I crossed two fields; and remembering that I was trespassing by doing so, I came to the main road that went past the Manor. As I approached that ancient seat—although I had no respect for its owner, for reasons that I have already recorded—I enjoyed its

environs, and drank in its atmosphere with relish. I felt, if I can be
allowed thus to speak, that there was some majestic innocence and
godliness in the tall, shadowy trees either side of the road; and that
verse about 'the trees of the Lord'[8] came to my mind with a new
and profound meaning. No wonder, I thought, that Wil Bryan
went on so much about *nature*. I don't know if anyone else feels the
same, but for as long as I can remember, a feeling of solemnity has
come over me whenever I have been in the presence of tall, thick
trees; perhaps it's something that I as a Welshman have inherited
from the old Druids. Perhaps the feeling is more common than
I imagine, since the inspired writers often mentioned the cedars
of Lebanon with respect. Perhaps some people would laugh at the
idea, but I think there is more of God to be felt in a wooded land
than in a bare and barren one. Anyway, that night in the silence
that was broken by nothing except for the barking of the Manor's
big dog, and the sound of my feet on the hard road, I had a sense
of being strongly defended as I walked thoughtfully between the
two rows of strong tall trees on either side of the road, like God's
grenadiers. When I reached the place where the trees were thickest
and shadiest, where the late evening light was almost completely
excluded, I saw a tall man coming to meet me, walking slowly, with
his head bent down towards the ground. As we came a little closer
to each other, I saw that it was old Niclas; and I must confess that
I felt my flesh begin to creep. I hadn't seen him for a long time, and
there was something in his appearance that befitted the solemnity
and loneliness of the place; I lost completely the feeling of being
defended, that I had enjoyed a minute before, and the shady trees
no longer looked like *grenadiers* but like big ugly cloaks offering
their assistance in covering up a terrible murder. With a shaking
hand I buttoned up my coat, which covered over an even-more-
shaking heart, and I walked quickly. "Good night, Mr Niclas,"
I said, as boldly as I could. But Niclas did not answer a word,

---

[8] Psalm 104:16.

and he did not raise his head. After I had walked on a few yards, I looked back and saw Niclas going on slowly. I thought how silly I was to be afraid; because it was obvious to me by now that poor old Niclas was quite harmless. I left the main road and took the path that led past his house, which I reached within a few minutes. I couldn't resist stopping to look at the old building. I thought how silly it was of the people in the neighbourhood to connect its owner with such frightening and groundless rumours. In all my days I couldn't actually remember hearing of Niclas saying one coarse word to any of his neighbours. It couldn't be denied that he had an odd way of life; but as far as the facts themselves went, no-one could say that Niclas wasn't an innocent man, after all. If he chose to make himself a recluse and a byword for everybody else, he had a perfect right to do that, as he hadn't harmed anybody. I thought as well that there was something charming about being mysterious, about the hermit's life, and that Niclas, it seemed, found pleasure in it. At the time, I felt a great curiosity about the house, especially as its owner was away. I would have loved to see the garden, which I'd heard so much about. The garden wall was not too high for me to climb. I decided to have a go. I had just begun the task, when I felt a strong hand grab me by the collar, and give me such a shaking, that I can't compare it to anything other than a terrier grabbing hold of a French mouse. It was old Niclas' hand.

"A thief, isn't it? A thief in the house of Niclas y Garth Ddu! Rather bold, isn't it?" said Niclas; and he gave me another shake that nearly shook my soul from out of my body, and added:

"Who are you? What are you? Where do you come from? Speak! Say your prayers! Or by _____ I'll tear you limb from limb!"

Had he not been holding me by the collar like a cat holds a mouse in its paws, I'm sure I'd have fallen down with the fright. I tried to speak but my mouth and tongue were as dry as dust, and I couldn't say a word. I was sure that he was going to murder me, and I couldn't shout for all the world. A hundred thoughts went through my heart: a painful death, the world to come, my condition, my mother, Bob my brother, Abel Hughes, and everything connected with them rushed through my mind; and if ever I prayed, I did then. All this went through my mind within a quarter of a minute, while I was looking in terror at the vicious, devilish face of old Niclas, and while I was unable to utter a word. After a few seconds he slackened his grip on me, but he did not let me go; and I saw from this face that he was half satisfied with the fright he had given me; and he said again, in a voice that was a little gentler, "Who are you, and what do you want?"

I don't know how, but suddenly I felt my tongue loosen, and I could say shakily, "I'm not a thief, Mr Niclas. I'm Abel Hughes' apprentice; and I wanted to see your garden, truly, I swear."

"Want to see my garden, do you? Modlen has been prattling, I know, that the garden is worth seeing—indeed, worth seeing? If the old witch doesn't keep her tongue still, I'll shoot her dead, so I will. And every lad I find climbing the garden wall, I'll skin him alive, and feed him to the dog—that will save me buying food for him. Want to see the garden, do you? Well, you'll see it, because it is worth seeing. Ha ha! Come in."

With one hand Niclas kept hold of me, and with his other hand he pulled a latch key out of his pocket and opened the door that was in the wall, and led me in, and closed the door carefully behind him. After doing this he let me go, and commanded me to follow him into the garden. How great was my surprise when I saw the famous garden! It was a perfect wilderness; from the look of it, I don't think Niclas had taken a spade to it for years, and apart from the path around it, it was covered with weeds and brambles. Some of the trees had died and shrivelled, and the rest looked as if their hearts were broken for want of care. Despite this, Niclas took me around the garden, showing me the various types of fruit, flowers and trees, using the classical names, and talking extensively about them exactly like a dedicated gardener might have done. Then he laughed coarsely and mockingly, and said, "The garden is worth seeing!" After he had finished his classical palaver over his weeds, brambles and thorns, he started to talk incoherently like a madman, something like this, as nearly as I can remember:

"Who is Niclas y Garth Ddu? (He spoke about himself in the third person.) Where does he come from? Who is he related to? How does he live? You'd like to know, but you can't. You think that Niclas is a fool, and he is a fool too. Who was the father of Niclas y Garth Ddu? David Niclas, Esquire, a great man, a wise man, a merchant, a miser, an idiot. Did he starve his wife before Niclas y Garth Ddu was born—no, after he was born? Who saw the mother of Niclas y Garth Ddu die? How much did David Niclas, Esquire, merchant, miser, idiot, pay the doctor for not saying anything? Where did David Niclas, Esquire, merchant, miser, idiot, send Niclas y Garth Ddu to be brought up? Did he offer a hundred pounds to poison him? Did he offer two hundred pounds? When did David Niclas, Esquire, merchant, miser, idiot, understand that Niclas y Garth Ddu had no brain? How much did he offer the schoolmaster to kill him with Latin? Did he offer a hundred pounds? Did he offer two hundred? Did David Niclas, Esquire, merchant, miser, idiot, try to kill Niclas y Garth Ddu twice? Did he try three times? Did David Niclas, Esquire, merchant, miser, idiot, have a stroke once? Did he have a stroke twice? Did he have a stroke three times? When David Niclas, Esquire, merchant, miser, idiot had the last stroke, did Niclas y Garth Ddu sit on his chest and wring his neck? Did he do that once? Did he do it twice? Can't you answer? Haven't you got a tongue? Where did Niclas y Garth Ddu get his money from? How did he get money? Would he have had any money if he hadn't sat on the chest of David Niclas, Esquire, merchant, miser, idiot? How much did he get? Did he get two thousand? Did he get five thousand? Did he get ten thousand? Don't you hear? Won't you answer?"

"I need time to consider, Mr Niclas," I said.

"Consider?" he said. "Never consider, or it will make your head weak, you won't be able to sleep for a week, for two weeks, for three weeks. You'll have to walk all night if you consider. Never consider, or it will make your head weak. Can't you speak? Are you deaf and dumb? I had a deaf and dumb cousin—he was always considering, and he died in the asylum. They wanted Niclas y Garth Ddu to go to the asylum, so they could have his money. What do they do in the asylum? Nothing but consider. Do they consider for a week? Do they consider for a year? Won't you answer? I'll wait for you to answer."

We were close to a tumbledown summer house; and Niclas went into it and took out a double-barrelled shotgun, then continued his rambling.

"Do you see this? What's it good for? Will it kill once? Will it kill twice? Here, take it and shoot me. One barrel at a time, mind. No, wait, first I'll shoot you in the head with one barrel, and then you can shoot me in the chest with the other. Toss up to see who gets to shoot first! Heads or tails? Who will shoot first? Wait for me to consider! But I shouldn't consider or it will make my head weak. Why does Niclas y Garth Ddu keep so many cats? To chase the evil spirit away. Sometimes the spirit of killing comes upon me, and I have to kill someone. Who will I kill? If I killed Modlen, who would fetch things for me? What do I do? Kill a cat, and tear it to shreds, and then the evil spirit goes away. What if the cats refuse to come? Then what do I do? I shoot that old tree, like this."

Niclas let out the contents of both barrels at the base of the old tree. For some time I couldn't make out whether this strange old creature was a fool or a knave; but as he went on with his palaver, I became convinced that he was a knave of the first order, or as Wil Bryan would have said, a perfect humbug. It had been clear to me for some time that he was trying to make me think that he was a madman; but there was no hint of madness in his face, and I could see that he was watching me constantly to see if his act was frightening me. I had for some minutes been entirely in control of myself, and had no more fear of him than if he'd been a sparrow. After Niclas had let out the two shots, I saw a short man coming from the house, and coming towards us, to ask, it seemed, what was going on. It was obvious that the man's appearing was as unexpected to Niclas as it was to me. When he arrived alongside us I recognised him, and he recognised me. "Hello Rhys!" he said and extended his hand to me; but I refused it. "Niclas," he said, "do you know who this chap is?" Niclas shook his head. "The old Pal's kid" added the new arrival. Niclas opened his eyes in surprise, and in obedience to a nod from his companion he went into the house.

"Rhys, won't you shake hands? How did you come here, say?" he said once Niclas was out of sight.

"Uncle," I said, for it was no other than he, and there was no-one I hated more ever since I first saw him and named him 'the Irishman'. "Uncle," I said, "if I shook hands with you, I expect mine would wither at that moment. I hate you with all my heart. Let me out of this accursed place."

"What's wrong with you boy? Why are you so unfriendly? Why do you hate me?" he said.

"Why?" I answered, "you know very well. You were the cause of all the misery that my mother and I endured; you led my father astray; you taught him to poach; you were with him when he did the thing that made him have to flee the country. Why do I hate you, indeed? Because you caused my mother more trouble than anyone in the world, except my father. How many times were you in our house, disturbing what comfort we had? How many times did my mother give you the last shilling she had to get rid of you? And how much more trouble would you have caused if you hadn't been afraid of Bob?"

"Bob was a fool," he said. "Didn't your father and I give him the chance to run away the night he was taken to jail? But he didn't want to run, and he went to jail like a halfwit."

"Don't you call Bob a fool," I said. "Bob would have hated to accept help from two scoundrels like you and my father. Uncle, tell me the truth, if you haven't forgotten how—where is my father? Is he hiding in this accursed hole? Tell the truth for once in your life."

"No, your father is in a much warmer place," he said.

"Where? Speak clearly, and tell the truth. Where is he?" I asked a second time.

"How can I tell you?" he said, "I've never been to the grounds where your father is now. All I can tell you is that he has kicked the bucket, and it's a shame that you have no crape on your hat,[9] and you a Methodist."

To my shame, I must confess that my heart leapt with joy, and I said, "Are you saying that my father has died? Don't deceive me—tell the truth for once."

"Nothing was ever truer," he said. "You know that he was fond of a drink, and the two of us were a bit lucky—he got too much money, and was too free with the whisky, and he had a stroke. I had told him many times to be careful; there was no use talking to him. He kicked the bucket in Warwick. At the time I happened to be, as it were, in Leamington for the sake of my health, and I went for a walk in Warwick and happened to bump into your father. I took care of him while he was alive—he was staying in an old tavern—and I emptied his pockets after his last breath. He didn't want to die at all, because he knew they were all teetotals in the other world. But it was his own fault, because I warned him to take care. The Union paid to bury him, because I was just a friend, as it were, you know."

"If you are telling the truth," I said, "that's the best news I ever heard; and if you had died with him, I'd be perfectly happy." This comment only made him laugh, and he said:

"Well, when I die you will be my closest relative, and you'll come into all the shooting grounds—and they are very big, reaching from Warwick to the Reined[10] in Denbighshire. You know what? The spirit of Twm o'r Nant looks after one end of the estate, and the spirit of Shakespeare the other—your father used to say they were the two head keepers. It's no wonder you want me to die, so

---

[9] A crape, or crêpe hat, was commonly worn at this time as a sign of mourning.

[10] I have been unable to find what this refers to: possibly a geographical feature.

that you can say, 'I have my Uncle James' estate'."

"Stop your nonsense, and let me out of this accursed place," I said, and I walked towards the door that was in the wall.

"Wait, what's the hurry? How is the old roundhead treating you? Do you have any objection to me paying a visit to you on the sly when I'm hard up? I see that you're a bit of a buck, and perhaps you'd like your Uncle James to come and look you up from time to time? Do you have such a thing as half a crown to spare? Where did you get that watch from? Now I remember, how much would you give for the pawn ticket for your father's watch, for you to have something to remember him by?"

I must tell the truth no matter how ugly it is; I was possessed by a strange and inappropriate spirit, a spirit that would have liked to strangle the rascal! But I was able to control myself, as was no doubt better for me, and I said, "Open the door, and let me out."

"You haven't paid for the gate," he said.

I was my mother's son, and I gave him all that I had at the time, two shillings.

"Thank you," he said, "and I'll see you again when you are more flush," and he took the latch-key from his pocket and opened the door.

Once I had my feet outside the door, I turned and looked at him purposefully, and I said to him, "Uncle, you must understand that now I have you under my thumb. I have discovered your lair—the hole that you are hiding in—and if you ever show your face to me again, or if I hear that you have been seen in the neighbourhood, or of anything that you have done, remember I will tell the police everything."

"What!" he said, "you're going to split? Are you going to dribble over your own clothes?"

"As sure as you live," I said.

"Look here," he said, "you'll never see me again. So do your worst, you proud chick," and he tried to spit in my face as he closed the door in my teeth.

I went home happy. The great burden that had always pressed on my mind had fallen away. And yet I couldn't help asking myself, had my uncle told the truth? I knew that he was more practised at telling lies.

31

DAVID DAVIES

He is a happy man who can look back on his life and say—with his conscience testifying that he is telling the truth—that he has behaved in every circumstance as he should have done according to the light that was in him. Where does that man live now? If we give fair play to our consciences, I'm sure that most of us will say that we haven't always behaved properly according to our own ideas of moral obligation. I'm sure that even a few of the philosophers, who searched deeply into the subject and wrote much about it, would recognise that that they did not act entirely in accordance with the clear and exalted ideas they had of their duty. It happens sometimes that someone has such a clear view of what is right that he feels proud of it, and stands the more upright as he contemplates his own orthodoxy. But the circumstances of this world are hateful old things; and what wonder is it that a man sometimes behaves a bit differently from his credo, and finds that that other system which is called 'convenience'—if that's the best word for *expediency*[1]—fits better with his wishes as he interacts with the events of life? It is one thing to have an orthodox view, and another thing to behave at all times according to that view. But thank heaven! There are still in this world some men who try to live every day in accordance with their convictions, let the consequences be what they may.

As I have sworn myself to telling the truth about myself in this story, I must confess against myself that I have not acted in every circumstance in accordance with my own idea of what was right. After the sudden and unexpected meeting with my uncle, the first question that presented itself to my mind was, 'What should I have done?' My conscience answered immediately, 'The path of duty is clear. Go to the police at once, and tell them what you saw'. But something told me that he was no fool who put these words together—'*Circumstances alter cases*'.[2] I thought that there was no harm in pausing to consider, and contemplating the matter thoroughly before deciding what to do. Something suggested to me again that it might be wise for me to consult with a man wiser than I—for me to tell everything to Abel Hughes, and listen to his advice. I didn't like this suggestion; and I decided to take a few hours at least to contemplate the matter before deciding upon a course of action. I went home and early to bed, to have leisure to think about my discovery. And I must confess that, the more I thought about the matter, the more ground was gained by *expediency*. One by one, personal considerations demanded their voices be heard; and pure, clear, unselfish duty was slowly pushed into the background. Who was this man that I called, when I first saw him, 'the Irishman'? He was my uncle—the full, red-blooded brother of my father. What sort of man was he? One of the craftiest, laziest and most corrupt scoundrels ever to have trod Welsh soil. He was so despised in the eyes of my mother and Bob that they did their best, as much as they could, to keep me in total ignorance about him. The night that Seth died—when I met the filthy wretch by the Manor woods, and when I came to understand his relation to me—that night Bob, when he saw that he could keep it from me no longer, told me his full story. Even when he was a young man, Bob said, work was a hateful thing for him. When honest people were about their tasks, he would be in bed; and when they rested, he would be searching about the countryside. He'd never work, and yet managed to live, eat and drink—especially the latter. Where did he get his money from? He knew, and his neighbours had guessed. They believed

---

[1] To clarify what's going on here: the author has been searching for the best Welsh word to represent the English term 'expediency', and hits on the word 'cyfleusdra', usually translated 'convenience', as his best attempt before giving the English word as well.

[2] Quoted by the author in English; the phrase itself is a legal term dating from the late 17th century.

that the game of the Manor estate had had to pay its tithe to the support of my uncle James. Although he knew what it was to have free board and lodging at the county's expense more than once, his skill at avoiding the clutches of the police and the gamekeepers for so many years was remarkable to everyone who knew him. My father was a skilled worker, but he too was prone to drink and to spend many hours sitting in the pubs. Drunkenness begat laziness, and laziness begat poverty, and poverty begat sons and daughters—harshness, sourness, short-temperedness and cruelty. With such a brood, who can describe my poor mother's life before I saw the light of day! What a feat it was to live a religious life with such an atrocious brute as my father! I have already noted briefly some of his cruelties towards my dear mother; though I can't help thinking of them here, it is too painful a task for me to describe any more of them.

My uncle James had little trouble, so Bob told me, to snare my father into his own wicked ways. Before long the two of them were regarded as professional poachers, and it was amazing how they managed to escape the arm of the law. This was attributed to my father's herculean strength, and it was said that the gamekeepers were terrified of him. My uncle James, as I've mentioned already, was slight; and yet had cunning, deceitfulness and daring well beyond my father's. The destruction they wreaked upon his property caused the Squire to dance with rage, and he changed his gamekeepers often. At last, he found two men who weren't afraid of their own shadows. Scotsmen, they were. But before they had worked on the estate for a month, they both lay wounded. For some days it was doubted that one of them would survive. From that day onwards, two of the district's residents, uncle James and my father, disappeared from view; and despite much searching they could not be found. All this happened before I was born. By this time my mother was 'worse than a widow', as she put it herself; but Bob said that this was the best thing that ever happened to her. I have already described briefly the hardship which she went through before Bob was strong enough to support us as a family; but this hardship was as nothing to her by comparison with the anguish of mind that my father's ungodly state caused her, and the constant fear that he would come again to visit us, or be captured. This fear would be revived and intensified by my uncle's furtive visits, which my mother took to indicate that my father was not far away. These visits took place without exception at bad times, and on dark nights, and went on until Bob was strong enough to stop them—and their intent every time was to take whatever money my mother had. For days after each visit, my mother would be sad and silent. I don't think she mentioned my uncle's visits to anyone except Thomas and Barbara Bartley; and I have no doubt that it was to save her from these undesirable things that the two kind old neighbours persuaded her to come and end her days with them at the Twmpath, and nothing else would have persuaded her to leave her home. For years I had flattered myself that the neighbourhood had almost forgotten my father and uncle, since no-one ever mentioned their names to me; but my sense told me that it was their civility, and their respect for my mother's godliness while she was alive, that caused them to behave towards me as if nothing shameful had happened in my family at all; and not a day went by without me thinking how easily the whole history of it could be resurrected, and then I would have to hide my face in shame. Whenever I was seized by enthusiasm for the idea of being a preacher, the thought that any minute my father and uncle might be hauled from their hiding-places into the light of day would quench that enthusiasm straight away. Yet wholly unexpectedly, as I have said, I'd had the news of my father's death and that, if the report was true, it had happened far away from home. Think how miserable one's family situation must be for him to feel joyful when hearing of the death of his father! But there's no point in me hiding the fact: I rejoiced greatly. I felt like one who had been released from a dank, dark prison into freedom and fresh air. And yet I was confused, and my conscience was telling me that I wasn't acting straight. On the one hand I had discovered that Niclas was deceiving his neighbours, and that his life was not so hermit-like as he pretended it was. To say the least, he was harbouring at least one character who was wanted by the law. It was within my power now to strip Garth Ddu of its false aura. I asked myself, 'Should I do that?' And my conscience answered straight away, 'Yes you should, without delay'. Beside all that there was my uncle. I knew that he did not deserve to be a free man. His offence—*the* offence—was now old; but that didn't make it any the less. The law that sought him was in force every bit as much on that day as it had been when the act was committed. There would be no difficulty in finding him guilty, because the two gamekeepers he half killed were still alive, and in the Squire's service. They would identify him at once. Although the offence was eighteen years old, all I'd need to do would be to whisper half a dozen words in the Squire's ear; and his anger against my uncle James would burn white-hot at that moment, and he'd spare no expense to get him into prison. The wretch was my uncle, my own father's brother, but he deserved no tenderness at my hand on that account; because I could attribute to him most of the hard times that I had endured. He ruined my father's character and shortened my mother's life. My idea of justice told me definitely that my duty consisted of telling all I knew about him to the police; and there was something in me—probably revenge—that told me it was an excellent opportunity to pay back the old fox for all the misery that he had caused me and my family.

That was one side to the question; but there was another side. The man who would have the most pleasure from my revelation would be the Squire; and I didn't care to add a grain of sand to his happiness. He was the one who had sentenced my brother Bob to two months in prison without a shred of evidence that he had in any way broken the law; and had eviscerated my father in the public court. I had not then, even if I have now, forgiven him for his meanness and injustice. Ever since the day that Bob was wrongly imprisoned, I had a deep hatred towards every policeman, however irrational that was; and my sympathy would always be with the prisoner, despite myself. Wil Bryan had also created in me many years ago a strong prejudice against the police with his phrase, '*pettifogging Bobbies*'; and therefore I didn't care to give any satisfaction to the police. Besides that I was aware that in my home—like in every neighbourhood—there was a fair bit of sympathy towards the poacher; and he wasn't looked at in the same light as those who broke other laws of the land. If some people admired my selflessness in handing my uncle over to the authorities, the majority would still look on me as a traitor, and as one, to use my uncle's phrase, 'dribbling over my own clothes'. More than that, if I were to share my discovery, the thing that I had feared most over the years would come upon me in one deluge. Although my father was dead, if my uncle had told the truth, all his misdeeds would be brought up again and be the topic of conversation in the Smithy, in the Cross Foxes, the Crown, and in every home; and the old neighbours, in answer to the questions of those not aware of the circumstances, would have to say that it was the father of Abel Hughes' apprentice that they were talking about. The children in the chapel, with whom I had been labouring hard of late, would be amazed that the man on trial was my uncle, and that my father had died as bad a man as he. That wouldn't make me feel good. I thought too that if I gave information to the police about my uncle's hiding-place, ten to one they wouldn't catch him; the likelihood was that by now James Lewis was far away, and old Niclas would say that I had made the whole thing up. Under those circumstances, I would just have resurrected all the old stories without anything in particular having been accomplished, besides making many people believe I had simply been making fun of the police. But the thing that most affected my decision was remembering my mother's last words: 'If ever you meet your father, try to forget his sins; and if you can do him some good, then do so'. I believed that the spirit of this command applied just as much to my uncle; and I believed too that if my mother were in the same circumstances as I, she would not have placed my uncle into the hands of the authorities. She was a good woman; and why couldn't I be a good boy and keep the secret to myself? I decided to be quiet, and I felt fairly sure at the time that there was no danger of my uncle showing his face to me again. Whether my decision was wise or not will be revealed later if I am able to finish this autobiography.

It's not difficult to keep a secret when the one keeping it will have the most harm from it being revealed. Keeping one for the sake of somebody else is the challenge. Not even the devil tempts a man to reveal what will cause ridicule to him and his family. This is his reserve fund for the time to come. The man who refuses to lend his tongue to report the faults and shames of his neighbours, when telling them will do no good, convinces the world that he will one day be a citizen of the land where there is no such thing as finding fault, and where the angels will not object to his being considered one of them. A few days after the things I have recorded here, I was flattering myself for my shrewdness; but I must admit that I didn't have that happy feeling that a man enjoys after doing what is right even though it goes against his own interests. It comes from the same family as the feeling that a worldly man gets after striking a good bargain. But God knows that I had in me a desire to do what was right, although I lacked the moral strength to do that at the cost of dragging myself into shame and unhappiness, and undoing the programme that I had been quietly forming in my mind. It would have been good if this were the only time that I had given in to expediency. I've heard, and I'm not sure that I haven't said it myself more than once, that doing one thing that the conscience can't say Amen to acclimatises a man to doing other things of the same kind. Is this true in all circumstances? It wasn't so with me on this occasion. My act of considering self-interest and my own happiness at the cost of neglecting my duty stirred up my whole moral nature to greater efforts and greater determination to fulfil that which I thought I was bound to do. But perhaps that was just an attempt to make up for my sin. I tended strongly to believe my uncle's story about my father's death, and I felt lighter in my spirit and freer to do what I could in the cause of religion. I had an excellent master, and I was free to attend all the meetings that took place in the chapel. I wasn't slow to make use of the freedom. Poor Jones was never keen to go to chapel, and wasn't as happy anywhere as he was when in the shop. Jones appeared to me like a well-trained sheepdog: he knew one thing very well, and only one thing. He knew how to measure and to fold cloth and put it away; and if Abel had pointed to a pile of cloth and said, 'Jones, lie down there', he would have obeyed happily; and wouldn't have moved from there, I'm sure, unless Abel spoke to him or whistled for him. This opened the way for me to go to every service and meeting. I think Abel believed that there was no point in sending Jones to chapel, as that would be no better than trying to make a negro white using just soap and water.

There had been so many changes in the chapel since the last time I mentioned it in this account! Noticing changes always makes me sad, and makes me think how short is a man's life and how soon we will all have given our places over to others. To a thoughtful man I don't think there is anywhere like a chapel to impress this lesson on his mind. If one went away from home for only a couple of years, how struck he would be by the changes which had taken place in the congregation of the chapel! He would see so many strange new faces as he looked around, and there would be so many old faces that he'd fail to be able to find. How he would wonder to see the greying heads of some of his acquaintances, and the bald heads of others. And perhaps he would not notice his own head following the same fashion. If I remember rightly it was when I was aged between nine and twelve that I last mentioned the chapel in this account. How different it looked when I was eighteen years old! Every face was new in the Children's Meeting. John Joseph, the old leader, was in Australia by now, and Abel Hughes, because of old age and because he couldn't put up with all the trouble over the Sol-fa, had stopped going. Who led the meetings now? Wil Bryan called me 'the kids' boss'. Alexander Philips (*Eos Prydain*) took care of the music. The Literary Society, which had been baptised 'the Hair Down Society' by my old companion, and which had done a great deal of good for many in its time, had long ceased to be. It was Sol-fa that killed it, unintentionally of course. By now it was almost impossible to get the boys to learn grammar, write an essay, or take part in a theological debate; they thought these things were far too dry. Their only interest was the Sol-fa Society. This had several advantages over the old Literary Society. It was felt to be easier to sound 'doh' together than to mutate a verb on one's own, and that sight-singing was more useful in this world, and maybe even in the world to come, than being able to understand justification through faith. Besides that, the Sol-fa Society was founded upon wider, deeper and more liberal principles than the old Hair Down Society. It embraced all of humanity—young, middle-aged and old, male and female. The latter of these undeniable advantages was particularly significant; for, under particular circumstances, changing one letter could turn the singing meeting into one of a totally different nature, and yet one which would give satisfaction to both sexes.[3] So, if a meeting had been spent in the key of 'la', it could very easily end in a different key altogether. The benefits that followed from this society were many and obvious. Under the regime of the old Literary and Theological Society, the young men were shy, lacking in confidence and really too humble, as if they knew nothing. But when they came under the influence of the Sol-fa Society, they learned to hold their heads up high like men, and show the world that they knew 'what was what'. At that time they came to understand that they were men, and that they needed to act like men, and make the gentry understand that they no longer had the monopoly on wearing gloves and rings. The society had a big impact on the history of the neighbourhood, and that in a very short time. Soon the old custom of young men carrying their Bible to chapel began to disappear, and the Tune Book took its place. It's true that the occasional old woman, who knew no better, would get cross at seeing the latter book take the place of the former; but it's never wise to stand in the way of progress. Like every other change, the way of doing things that I have been talking about here had great opposition from the old-fashioned people. My master, Abel Hughes, though a shrewd man, was a bit of a Tory when it came to new things; and sometimes I'd see him refuse to turn the Sunday evening service into a singing meeting, and he made a decisive stand against practising musical items on a Sunday in preparation for the National Eisteddfod. I heard him with my own ears saying that singing was not more important than preaching, and that the Tune Book must not have more attention than the Bible. He opposed too the practice of asking preachers to 'keep it short' to give more time for the singing. Although *Eos Prydain* would give him dirty looks, Abel refused to stop slurring his notes, or singing out with all his energy words like:

> 'He was led up to Calvary's hill,
> And nailed to a cross by His will'.[4]

If Abel had lived for a few more years, no doubt he would have learned new things. When I saw the marvellous effects of the Sol-fa Society, I joined it enthusiastically. I was a member for a month; and I learned not only that my voice was not promising, but also that I had neither the wit nor the patience to master the secrets of the art. And to tell the truth, I felt a bit ashamed, because I found that an eight-year-old boy, who had given me the most trouble in Sunday School trying to teach him to spell, was the best sight-singer of all. I saw that there was a danger that he'd lose all respect for me in Sunday School; and as Wil Bryan would say,

---

[3] The author is making a pun on the similarity of the Welsh words '*canu*', to sing, and '*caru*', to love.

[4] '*Ei arwain i Galfari fryn, A'i hoelio wrth groesbren o'i fodd*'; a line from the hymn '*Wrth gofio' i riddfannau'n yr ardd*' by Thomas Lewis, 1749–1842.

I legged it. I'm sorry now that I didn't stick at it to master the Sol-fa; as it's obvious to anyone who pays attention to the signs of the times that very soon this will be an essential skill. No doubt the age that is dawning will see, in the Ordination meetings at the Session, the questions from the Confession of Faith giving way to the blackboard and an examination about the Sol-fa; and by popular demand from the churches, it will be unimaginable that anyone should qualify as a minister of the New Testament unless he can explain in detail the difference between the major and minor keys. I regret missing the chance that was available to me at that time; and now I am too old to learn.

But I see that I'm letting myself comment too much, and there is a danger, if anyone reads these lines, that they will think that I'm joking. There were many other changes in the chapel; and not least was the absence of many of the old brethren for whom I'd had great respect when I was a lad. Edward Peters, whom I mentioned before, the ill-tempered man, careful with the books, who had been housebound for some time; but who never went to bed on a Sunday evening without first knowing how much the collection had been. In case I forget to mention this later, his last words before dying were, 'Remember that quarter of the Seats[5] is due next Monday night'. He was a coconut; his outer shell was hard and rough, but he had the sap of true religion in his heart. Hugh Bellis, the man who often wept during the sermon, and who Wil Bryan called 'the old waterworks'—he had left 'the children of tears and groans'[6] and had crossed over in full sail to the joy of which no-one can speak while on Earth without weeping very sweet tears. Of the old elders, no-one was left besides Abel Hughes, and my whole heart said, 'O King, live forever!'[7] David Davies, who came to us from another church, was already an elder, and he was recognised as such when he arrived. I will need to mention him again. Thomas Bowen, the preacher, and great friend of the children, about whom there is much I'd want to say if time permitted—he had left us, and everyone who knew him believed he had gone to the same land as Hugh Bellis. John Lloyd, the man who was always finding fault and whom Wil Bryan called 'the old scratcher' was still among us. Wil had some time ago changed his title to '*chapel nuisance inspector*'. Thomas and Barbara Bartley, who kept coming faithfully, were polishing their religion. By now they were the two originals in the *seiat*; and whenever Abel felt that the discussion was dragging along slowly, he would turn on his heel sharply and ask, "Thomas Bartley, what is on your mind tonight?" and it was rare for us not to have something that would be fun. Thomas would only describe his experiences, but they were very often funny, and the more so as he was what Wil Bryan called '*true to nature*'. I must give a few examples before finishing this story. I've already mentioned William the Coal a few times, who tended to get drunk and to put the blame on Satan every time. By now William was too old to 'follow the harvest', and therefore he was fairly devout. I remember that Abel used to say about William, that poverty was essential for the godliness of some people. Although Abel was a zealous Calvinist, he was very liberal in his ideas about some things. I heard him say once that he hoped that when death came to William the Coal, it would find him poor: "Because," he said, "poor William is very godly when his pockets are empty." I'm mentioning these characters, and these only, because I had occasion to mention them before.

The number of elders at this time was three—namely Abel Hughes, Alexander Philips (*Eos Prydain*) and David Davies. There never were three more dissimilar. Abel, as I have described, was a thoughtful old man of deep convictions, widely read in Welsh and English, one to whom preachers paid tribute for his wisdom in the

---

[5] At this time each Calvinistic Methodist chapel had to pay a 'seat levy' to the denomination in order to finance schools, buildings and evangelism.

[6] This phrase was put within quotation marks by the author as if it were a quotation, but I have been unable to find a source for it.

[7] cf. Nehemiah 2:3, Daniel 2:4 and many other places where Babylonian or Persian monarchs are addressed.

Monthly Meeting, and of undoubted godliness. *Eos Prydain* was a young unmarried man, capable and committed to the singing, lively of spirit, and popular with the young people. He had given his best years exclusively to the study of music, and he succeeded in making himself a master of the art. I have rarely seen his equal for organising and performing a concert. His faithfulness with the worship in the chapel was 'exemplary', according to the old people. His lifestyle was without blemish; his only fault, if a fault it was, being that he would sometimes turn the pages of his hymn book during the sermon, and purse his lips as though he were whistling under his breath. David Davies was a middle-aged man, a monoglot, brought up in the countryside, religious, sensible, zealous—a man of one book, proving the adage, '*Beware of the man of one book*'[8]. There were two main things that David Davies had; his religion and his farm. He knew no more about politics than did Abel (not Abel Hughes, but Abel the son of Adam). He had two masters, God and his landlord. To the latter he gave the appropriate respect, to the former he gave his whole heart, and both found him a faithful, honest and careful servant. He would have had more money in the bank if he didn't spend so much of his time and energy making himself a purse that would not grow old[9]. He cared more about a church member who backslid than about a sheep who went astray from his farm. When three of his cattle died of an epidemic, he thanked God that he still had others just as good as them; but when a godly sister from the *seiat* died he would be in mourning for weeks. He did not enjoy the potato blight, but a season of dullness in religion would worry him much more. He was thankful from his heart for an abundant harvest, but he rejoiced much more in a religious revival. He only consulted the barometer occasionally, whenever he remembered; but never a day went by without him consulting his Bible about the weather that awaited his soul—whether there was fair or stormy weather in store for him. The world and its busy affairs were almost as distant from him as from a man in a ship in the midst of the sea; but David Davies had a compass, and was certain of the port that he was sailing towards. He was a man of deep feeling, and I never heard him laugh; but he wore on his face the unconscious smile of a man with an unfettered conscience; a smile which the devil is not fond of. Sometimes one meets people who have an effeminate woolliness about their religion, which makes one think they would be less religious if they were more enlightened. David Davies was not such a man. He took the Bible as the chief study of his life, and the Bible itself was his main commentary upon it. As he read a part of the account of Jesus Christ's life from one evangelist, he showed me that every word that the other evangelists said about the same part were fresh in his mind, and he could quote them from memory. I admired him hugely, and wondered that a man who understood no English could understand the Bible so well. Perhaps, after all, I had such a high regard for David Davies because he took so much notice of me, and took me with him to hold meetings in people's homes, and it was he who first encouraged me to 'say a word'. I was eighteen years old, and was already secretary of the Sunday School, and had opened the school in prayer many times; but had never 'said' anything publicly. Coming back from one of these meetings, David Davies took hold of my arm and said, "Rhys, the next meeting will be in Thomas Bartley's house, and I'd like you to say a little bit about a chapter. You will, won't you? The friends will be glad to hear you. 'Do not tire of doing good, as in due course we shall reap if we don't lose heart'[10]. You have a week to prepare, and you will, won't you?" His words shot like electricity through my heart. I said something that was appropriately humble, as I thought, but I didn't say "no, I won't." Perhaps it would have been better if I had said "no, I won't," or "I'd rather not," as I will show in the next chapter.

---

[8] A saying of St. Thomas Aquinas later popularised by John Wesley; the meaning is that a man who knows one book thoroughly is a formidable opponent and not to be tangled with, particularly where that book is the Bible. Often rendered in Latin, '*Cave hominem unius libri*', the author here renders it in English.

[9] Luke 12:33.   [10] Gal. 6:9.

32

A MULTITUDE OF COUNSELLORS[1]

In the intimate memories of most people there is almost without exception a place for an old house. I myself love to remember the *Twmpath*—the house of Thomas Bartley—with its cosy kitchen, its ancient black furniture, its big settee, its pewter plates, and its wide inglenooks, in which I sat hundreds of times. Everything about that kitchen is in my mind at this moment—even the joints of bacon that hung from the ceiling, and the trays of onions, and the grey wormwood wrapped in old newspaper. Hanging from leather straps on the wall there was an old policeman's truncheon, which was painted blue and red, probably before the 'bobby' was born. And I remember Wil Bryan looking at it once and asking, as if to himself, "*I wonder how many a poor fellow was knocked over with that very weapon?*" In the time between when I would go there hand-in-hand with my mother—when my chief entertainment was lighting Thomas Bartley's pipe for him—up until the time when my mother's spirit departed there for another world, my memories mount higher and higher. Being able to say with certainty that even the meanest cottage has been a nursery for heaven endows it with a grandeur more magnificent than a palace, whose grand rooms have seen only feasting and pleasure. Seth's innocent soul was, as far as I know, only the first to go to glory from the Twmpath: but I'm sure that he was not the last. When one member of a family leaves home, it's a great thing to know which country he has gone to; and if the land is a particularly good one, it's very likely that the whole family will wish to go there too. It would have been hard to persuade Jacob to move to Egypt if Joseph hadn't been there already.[2] Thomas and

---

[1] Prov. 11:14, 15:22 and 24:6. [2] Genesis, Chapter 46.

Barbara, as my mother said, were more prepared to listen about the other world once Seth had gone there to live; and they looked at the prayer meeting that met in their home as an opportunity to talk about that colony. As I've mentioned, I had already been taking part in these meetings for some time, to Thomas Bartley's great satisfaction, who told me that I could read 'like a parson'. It was no doubt a thing of wonder to Thomas, who had nothing but 'some grasp of the alphabet', that any young person could read at all.

The fact that it was in Thomas Bartley's house that the prayer meeting took place, where I was expected to 'say a word on the chapter' at David Davies' suggestion, was a pleasant thought for me. All through the week, almost nothing else occupied my mind. I was in a bit of a quandary about which part of the scriptures I should take as my subject. At one time I thought that one of the parables might be appropriate; but after thinking a little about the chosen parable, I saw that I had virtually nothing to say about it, and I thought it would be more appropriate to explain one of the miracles, and take some lessons from it. No sooner had I settled my mind on one of the miracles than some obstruction made me think that I was once again mistaken. I thought it would be easier for me to say something about a verse than a whole chapter; but that would make it look as though I was trying to become a preacher straight away, and it wouldn't be appropriate to do such a thing. If David Davies had pointed out some particular part of the Bible that I could prepare to speak about, I think I could have done something with that. I remember feeling for the first time then, something that I felt many times after that—namely, how easy, trouble-free and effortless it appears to be to speak sense about a verse or a chapter when you hear someone else doing it, and yet how difficult it is when one tries to prepare something similar oneself. After hearing a sermon with nothing particular in it, you sometimes hear someone with little ability of their own saying, and no doubt believing what they say, 'I could have preached better than that myself'. Try, my good man, and you'll see that you can't, nor even as good; after all, why do you have so much trouble writing a letter to your aunt, and why are you ashamed of it when you finish it? Do you know as well, my good man, that that which reads most naturally and simply, or which slips over the lips of the speaker most smoothly, is often that which has cost the most labour? But that's what I was saying: for some days I kept changing my text, failing to find any part of the Bible that I felt I could say something about, no matter how simple it seemed before I started trying to do it. When I was forced by time to choose my text, I went for it seriously—I read every commentary that was within my reach, I wrote down every word that I intended to say, I memorised it all, and as I rehearsed it, I kept a close eye on how much time it would take me to deliver, lest it be too long or too short. By the time the night of the prayer meeting arrived, I felt that I was pretty much ready for the task, and fairly confident that I would make a good impression on the minds of those friends who happened to be present. I saw the occasion as being very important for me, and the key to my career as a preacher. In my mind I imagined many things being a direct result of my work in making a few remarks on a chapter in Thomas Bartley's house. I may as well tell the truth—I thought that because no-one else knew what was to happen besides David Davies and myself, I would take some of them by surprise and they would talk as they went home, saying things like, 'Well, didn't that boy speak well about that chapter tonight? He's got the makings of a preacher, mark my words. I was amazed', and others would say, 'I wasn't so surprised, because he's always had a bit of substance to him'. And I imagined a lot of other silly things. Apart from David Davies, I felt I had no need to fear any of those who normally attended the home prayer meetings; and David was always so kind to me that I wasn't afraid of him either, and so I didn't feel nervous at all. Wil Bryan rarely came to the prayer meetings except for when he could not, as he put it, be *better employed*, and therefore I did not expect to see him there. And if he were, what difference would it make to me? Wednesday evening came, and I went there full of…

well, full of something. I was a little bit late, in order to be more like a modern preacher. A brother was reading, and the room was fairly full. I sat down by the door. When I lifted my head, Thomas Bartley gestured towards me to move further in. I gestured back to say I was fine where I was. If my nod were anything to go by then I was a nobody, although I felt myself to be someone that night. I felt a sort of pleasure in false humility. Thomas carried on gesturing to me, and I obeyed in order not to draw attention to myself. When I got to a position where I could make some use of the candlelight, who did I see sitting in the corner but Wil Bryan. When I looked at him, he winked at me in his particular way—only using about a tenth of the width of his eye, but full of meaning. A big lump rose in my chest at that moment; and I felt that the devil must have sent Wil to that meeting, as he hadn't been to one for many months previously. For the first time, I felt afraid. As the brother prayed, I wasn't listening to him. I tried to pull myself together as best I could, and gather my thoughts; but in spite of this the lump in my chest increased, and came closer and closer to my throat. I wasn't at all afraid of Wil, or so I thought, and yet I would have much preferred it if he wasn't there. David Davies called on another brother to continue the meeting, and as we sang a verse my legs started shaking terribly, and there was no point in me reasoning with them or asking them to stop. I was comforted by the thought that I hadn't made any arrangement with David Davies for him to ask me to say anything as he called me forward, lest I appear to be taking the initiative too much. I thought perhaps David wouldn't think to do that; and if so, I decided that all I'd do would be to pray. This thought gave my legs some strength, and the lump in my chest shrank a bit. The second brother finished praying; and David Davies said, "Rhys Lewis, come forward my boy, to pray and say something about a chapter." My hopes were dashed, and I went forward with the intention of doing as well as I could. As we sang a verse, I had no choice other than to look at Wil Bryan or shut my eyes. I understood his expression as well as if he had been speaking to me, and saying, "Didn't I tell you that you were *bound* to be a preacher?" I read out the chapter that I intended to talk about, and I hardly recognised my own voice as it was so hoarse. When I started to 'say something', every thought and word of what I had intended to say flew from me, and I haven't seen it again from that day to this. I saw the room begin to darken and everyone seemed smaller and further away than they had when I went forward, and the candle looked as though it was about to go out as, indeed, my own breath was. The next thing I remember was hearing David Davies praying loudly and vigorously. By this time I felt my insides being eaten up with shame. The castle that I had built for myself was in pieces, and my poor heart was buried under the rubble. I knew that I was the object of the pity of everyone in the room— something which is withering for an ambitious spirit. I was longing for the meeting to end, so I could escape to somewhere out of everyone's sight and bury all of my hopes in peace. I had just one thing to take comfort in, namely that no-one except David Davies knew that I hadn't been entirely off-the-cuff in trying to speak, and even he didn't know just how much trouble I had taken to prepare. As soon as the meeting ended, I skulked away quietly and quickly without looking at anyone. But it wasn't possible for me to escape my old companion. Wil had caught up with me before I reached the main gate, and he said:

"Well, *old fellow*, I think I can translate your feelings pretty well tonight, and I'm sorry for you in my heart, I swear. You weren't *quite up to the occasion*, and despite a *split fair*, you had a *break down*. But don't break your heart—*never say die*. It's your own fault; you shouldn't have tried speaking off-the-cuff—because very few of the *dons* can do that *on the spur of the moment*, as they say. If David Davies had any sense he'd have given you a day or two's notice so that you could prepare. Isn't it enough to daunt the best of men to be asked *there and then* to explain a chapter? If you'd only had two hours' notice you'd have been able to say something tidy enough, I'd swear; but as it was, there'd be nothing else to expect apart from you making a fool of yourself. When I heard David asking you to come forward, I took it for granted that there was an *understanding* between you; but I saw in a moment that there wasn't; so I was surprised to see you attempt it when you hadn't known anything about it until that minute. I never saw such a pity. I'd be glad if I knew as much Scripture as you do, and I think you're not short of common sense; but you're lacking one thing very much, and that's *cheek*. What's the Welsh word for *cheek*, do you know? It's not the same thing, remember as impudence,[3] although it's a close relative of that. *Cheek*, as I see it, is one of the *fine arts*, and something every man should cultivate *to a certain extent*. I'm not sure if I can make my meaning clear to you. How shall I put it? Well, *cheek* isn't as *vulgar* as impudence, it's of a higher *order*. A mule can be impudent, that is, not shy; but you'd never say that a mule was *cheeky*. A dandy cockerel can be *cheeky*, but no-one would say that it's impudent. *Cheek* includes *self-confidence* even when there's nothing to be confident about. I'd like to be able to make this clear to you; but just like you were in the meeting, I'm *labouring under great disadvantages* because I haven't prepared. I'm not saying that *cheek* is a good thing in and of itself but because it is a means of obtaining other things. It's not as bad as *humbug*, and it's not as girlish as *affectation*. Many good men have lived and died without the world knowing anything about them because they didn't have *cheek*, and many have gone to the *top of the tree* with nothing except *cheek* to thank for it. *Cheek* takes it for granted that you don't know of a better man than you yourself unless you see *sufficient evidence*. If you see a man with a *retiring disposition*, you can be sure that he won't come to much in this world. He'll do all right in the next world, because the Good Lord, doesn't He, puts a *value* on humility because he knows that humility is a *very rare thing*. But as we're in this world, and not in

---

[3] In his search for a Welsh word for 'cheek', Wil has hit on 'wynebgaledwch', translated as 'impudence' in the dictionary but literally 'hard-facedness'.

the next world, I maintain that *cheek* is something to be cultivated *to a certain extent*. You have to remember that ninety-nine per cent of men are *duffers*, and in most *cases*, *cheek* will do the job in the absence of talent or knowledge. I'm not suggesting, mind, that you don't have talent, *honour bright*. Between a man with talent but no *cheek*, and a man with *cheek* but no talent, I'd put three to one on the latter. Just think of the two travelling salesmen who call at my place: there's Mr Davies—a sensible man, quiet, wearing the same clothes every time, and understands the *grocery trade to the T*. He never tells a lie, and when my father tells him there are no *orders* for him he takes it straight. Then there's Mr Hardcastle—a man with no more in his head than in the head of a mouse—but he has a new suit every three months that has pockets everywhere—cuffs, collars and rings all over the place—he won't take no for an answer, and it's impossible to insult him. He's learned about *twenty set phrases* before leaving home, half of them lies, and he says them the same way every time, and he's sure to get an *order* from my father because he's *cheeky* and my father's a duffer. You know what? When the gaffer's not at home, I sometimes give a *thundering good order* to Mr Davies out of pity for him, and because he's *true to nature*. But as for Mr Hardcastle, I could spit on his white waistcoat. After all, Mr Hardcastle is the man for this world, where the *majority* of shopkeepers are *duffers*. But that's the *point*: if you want to get on, you have to cultivate *cheek*. The Bible gives us examples of this, if I remember rightly. I have to confess that I'm not an *authority* on the Bible, and if I go wrong, perhaps you can correct me. Isn't it admitted by the learned that John was a cleverer man than Peter? But who was the leader? And who was first with everything? After he had really messed up that time *just* think of the *cheek* he must have had stepping forward to preach in their first monthly meeting, and everybody knowing what he'd done! That's the worst *cheek* I've ever heard of, I swear. If John had done anything so *shabby*, he'd have had too much shame ever to say anything again—and think what a loss that would have been.

Then there's that woman from Samaria coming to Jesus Christ to ask him to mend her little boy (I knew that Wil really meant the Canaanite woman[4])—she wouldn't take no for an answer, and because she had *cheek* she got what she came for. You know what? I think that woman would make an excellent *commercial*—she'd never have come out of a shop without an *order*. Speaking without preparation like this, I'm afraid that I won't be able to make myself clear enough about what I mean by *cheek*. You know that you can't do anything if you're *nervous*—but *cheek* is the *perfect cure* for *nervousness*. To cultivate *cheek*, note the following things: don't ever blush. I've noticed with you that if you happen to say something silly, or if you've made a *mistake*, then you blush right up to your ears like a girl. Don't ever blush, because that's not *manly*. If you've made a *blunder*, look just as if you've done the best thing in the world, and nine out of ten people won't know you've made a *blunder at all*. *Cheek* includes being *cool*. In public meetings don't ever sit by the door—make sure you're at the front; and when you stand, stand on your toes, because you're not especially tall, any more than I am. Make a *point* of everyone knowing that you're there. Speak as often as you get the *chance*, or even more often than that; and to be ready for that make sure that you've got twenty or so *set phrases* that will do the job *with slight variation* on any subject, in case you've got nothing new to say. Whatever, make sure you speak. You know what? Before today I've seen many a dull man rising to his feet and making a good observation by *sheer accident*, and making a name among the *duffers* as a *man of genius*. Before and after every public meeting, make sure that you shake hands warmly with the *reporters*, and keep your dignity at the same time. You'll never lose. I've heard that some report themselves—don't ever do that—something like that isn't *true to nature*. I know very well what's going through your mind—that I'm talking about *the way of the world*—but you'll see *by and by* that there's more of this going on with religious things

---

[4] Matt. 15:21-28—and it was her daughter, not her son.

than you'd have dreamed. You're *bound* to find that there are two things against you: for one thing, you don't have a strong voice; and another thing, as far as I can see, there's no hope that you'll ever be fat because there's no history of gluttony in your family. You'll see that this will work against you. Think now of a thin man saying something in a squeaky voice—falsetto, as these singers say—and a fat man, *regular through bass*—saying exactly the same thing in *double eff*—which will have the biggest effect on the *duffers*? I tell you that the *double eff chap* will be taken for a great man, and the *falsetto chap* for a *snob*. By the *duffers*, I mean, mind you, not by the wide-awakes. But I see that I'm not sticking to my subject. The point is, *cheek*. You know as well as I do that in this the English beat us Welsh. You never hear an Englishman saying that he can't do this or that; according to him he can do anything, and the *duffers* believe him. You sometimes see a John Jones—who's a *really good sort*, if only he knew it—touching his hat, as though he is pleased to see John Bull eating his bread and cheese. What is the *grand secret? Cheek!* Do you get the point? The man who lacks *cheek* appears worse than he is, and the *cheeky* man looks better than he is. Don't think I'm being *inconsistent*; I'll say again that I despise *humbug*, and I like a man to be *true to nature*. But there's a danger of a man who lacks *cheek* appearing less than himself. Note well: make sure you have *cheek*, but make sure you have something better besides. *Cheek* is very *handy* and will make the grade with many; but if you don't have anything better then you're *bound* to be found out by the *wide-awakes*. *At all events*, that's what *yours truly* thinks. Remember what Lord Brougham[5] said: '*What is the first secret of eloquence? Preparation. What is the second? Preparation. What is the third? Preparation*'. Never attempt to speak publicly without preparing, until you have cultivated *cheek* and learnt a lot of *set phrases* that will suit any circumstance—*with a slight variation*, as I said. I'm not *quite square* with the *governor*, otherwise I'd invite you home for supper; but under the circumstances I know I can't come up with the *demands of ordinary etiquette*. *Cheer up*, and don't look so *down in the mouth*. And now—*so long.*"

It was just as well for me that Wil little knew that I'd had a week of notice to prepare, and that rather than comforting me his words threw me into a furnace. I was glad when he left, and I went home without expecting that another furnace would be waiting for me there. My supper was on the table, and Abel was smoking in his armchair—both of them as if they were expecting me. Miss Hughes had gone to rest because she wasn't, as Wil would have put it, *up to the mark*. While I was eating my supper, I felt grateful that Abel didn't know about my breakdown, and I felt uncomfortable to think that he would be sure to hear of it, and soon. Then Abel started to ask me about the prayer meeting—who was there, what sort of meeting we had, who took part etc. I answered sparingly, but guessed from the half-joking smile on his face that someone had ran before me and told him all about my failure. Eventually he said, "How did you get on with saying something about the chapter?"

"Someone has told you," I said, and without being able to say any more, I was overcome by my feelings and despite my best efforts, broke out in tears and wept freely. Once I had quietened down, Abel said, "What's the matter with you? All I know is that David Davies encouraged you last week to prepare something to say in the meeting tonight. What has happened? Why are you in such a state?"

I told him all about my utter failure, and he said:

"Don't worry; it will be a blessing to you as long as you live. I remember two lines of an old, artless English poem: [6]

> *'There's many a dark and cloudy morning*
> *That turns out to be a sun-shining day'.*

---

[5] Henry Peter Brougham, first Baron Brougham and Vaux, 1778–1868; Lord Chancellor and inventor of the Brougham Carriage.

[6] From 'The Banks of Sweet Primroses', a traditional song.

Tell me, are you thinking of preaching?"

"I've been thinking about it, but I'll never think of it again," I said sadly.

"Don't be silly," he said. "I never saw a good cartsman who hadn't at some point thrown his cart over, and perhaps injured himself and his horse. You and I had many falls before we learned to walk. You'd never have learned to swim if you'd broken your heart the first time your head went under the water. The first step towards a useful life is often a false step, and the greatest success often begins with failure. I had guessed for some time that your mind was set on preaching; and that's the reason I've allowed you so much freedom to go to every church service and meeting. If I didn't think you had some suitability for the task, I would have told you long ago. If you have set your mind on it, don't let anything stop or discourage you. You couldn't have chosen anything better or more honourable. If I could have my time again, I think I would pray day and night to be given the inclination and ability to be a preacher. As I see it, there isn't any station in life comparable to being a preacher for having the chance to be really useful. The word 'preacher' has had a great charm for me for as long as I can remember. Perhaps it's a weakness; but I prefer the title of 'preacher' to that of 'parson', 'minister' or 'pastor'. The word 'preacher' suggests to me the pulpit, the conventions, the powerful influences that have conquered Wales; and the name has some anointing that isn't suggested by those other titles. Don't misunderstand me now. The words 'minister' and 'pastor' mean something desirable to me, and 'parson' possibly means something, though there is a great deal of prejudice against it. What I'm talking about is the *association of ideas* that comes with the name 'preacher', and when Wales loses this—the meaning of this name—and it becomes the same as 'clergyman', heaven help it. I can't help fearing that things are moving that way even today, you can see it in little things like the way announcements are made. When I was a lad, the elder would announce, 'We are expecting Mr Elias to preach here next Sabbath'; but nowadays you often hear, 'The Reverend Peter Smart will be ministering to us next Sabbath'. Again, don't misunderstand me: what I'm afraid of is that the reverence goes to the Reverend part of this, and not to Peter Smart. Thank God! There isn't a title on earth that can convey the reverence and love that is in a Welshman's heart for a true preacher. It borders nearly on worship, and long may it continue thus, so long as it does not become sinful, say I. But this reverence must be won in the pulpit. You know that nobody is keener than I for giving preachers the best possible education. If everyone were of the same mind as me, no-one would be considered for preaching in these enlightened days without him first having a university-level education, unless there was something really exceptional about his natural gifts and spirit. But in spite of all education, if a man is not a preacher, then his MA is no more use to him than the education of a girl who went to boarding school just to learn to say 'Ma' instead of 'Mum'. The respect, the fondness, the near-worship that is in the heart of a Welshman for the preacher needs to be won fairly, by merit. The other day I was reading something in the paper by some self-important fellow, making fun of the Welsh for their respect for preachers, without realising that this was the greatest compliment he could have paid the old land. I sometimes worry that the churches will be allowed to let anyone who happens to put themselves forward have a go at preaching, and the respect for preachers will be diluted and eventually vanish from the land. As I said, it would not be possible for you to aspire to a higher or more honourable station than being a preacher. The name 'preacher' is, for its owner, an introduction to the best men on earth, and a guarantee of a pure and irreproachable character, or at least it should be. I've often tried to guess what the consciousness of a preacher is like. It must be something glorious. His work is something that should endow him with the greatest happiness that it is possible to experience on this earth, and it is the best possible preparation for the terrors of death and the spirituality of the world to come.

In this world he receives the best things that any other men do, and much more besides; and in the world to come he is welcomed by the King himself as a good and faithful servant.[7] In my mind, the most successful merchant is only a beggar in rags beside a true preacher. The preacher is man's closest friend and God's next-door neighbour, if I am not blaspheming to say so. Where are the names of our wealthy men who were feasting in their castles sixty years ago? They have withered like their bones, and those of their hunting dogs. But the names of their contemporaries who proclaimed the Good News are still alive even in the hearts of those who never heard them.

Well, that's one way of looking at the preacher; but there's another. I don't want to discourage or frighten you, but I want you to be sober. The thing that determines a man's character is his motives; and perhaps there's nothing that a man, especially a serious man, feels more unable to do than to understand his real motives. There is so much corruption and selfishness in the character of every one of us that we're frightened of analysing our motives. Every young man who is thinking about preaching should fear and tremble. If he's not being driven by the purest motives, it would be better for him to hang himself. I have deep sympathy with a few men I know who intended to, and trained to, and started to preach, but were terrified into silence by the terrible responsibility of the work. The man who has his eyes on the pulpit to feed his ambition, to achieve a position of honour, or to satisfy something in his heart that can't be named, that man will have nothing but God's frown and will find himself one day lower than the demons in hell, being mocked by thieves and murderers. One of the English poets gives a terrible description of him. It starts like this:

> 'Among the accursed who sought a hiding place
> In vain, from fierceness of Jehovah's rage,
> And from the hot displeasure of the Lamb—
> Most wretched, most contemptible—most vile—

> Stood the false priest, and in his conscience felt
> The fellest gnaw of the undying worm!'[8]

I often think that Paul must have felt an electric shock when he said, 'Lest after I have preached to others I myself may be disqualified'.[9] But, as I said, I don't want to frighten you into setting your intention to preach aside; rather I'd like to be of some help to you if your motivations are pure. Perhaps it will be advantageous for you to look a bit more into the history of the first preachers—the apostles. They weren't perfect in their ideas or their motives, any more than we are. But there was one characteristic of theirs that should be a characteristic of every preacher: their love for and commitment to their Master was genuine—there was no doubt about that. 'To whom else shall we go?' asked Peter—not, 'To whom else shall *I* go?' as he was speaking on behalf of all of them—'You have the words of eternal life';[10] without You we'd be without words—we'd have nothing to say. I don't know whether Peter was conscious at the time that *saying* would soon be the main business of each of them; but I believe that he felt then that there was no-one else worth saying anything about, except Christ. Make sure that you are right on this point. If it's a natural enthusiasm that is driving you to preach, that interest will burn itself out soon, and you'll find yourself a cold lump living under the toleration of the church—filling engagements in places where otherwise there'd be no preacher of any sort and they'd have to hold a prayer meeting instead, to pass the Sabbath somehow—a burden to yourself and to everyone else. But if you are being stirred by the fire of God, that fire will never go out; and you'll find that sinners will crowd around you to warm their cold souls and warm themselves around your hearth. I don't know of any more pitiful creature than a preacher who is tolerated by men, and scorned by God, because

---

[7] Matt. 25:21.

[8] From 'The Course of Time' by Robert Pollok (1798–1827).

[9] 1 Cor. 9:27. [10] John 6:68.

of his worldliness and earthiness. Talking about worldliness, decide at the beginning, if you want to be a preacher, to give yourself wholly to the work. Don't even think about being a shopkeeper and a preacher. As a preacher the stock you'll have to look after will be so great that you won't have time to look after other stock, which is totally different. Whatever I can do to help you, I shall. Although I'm not poor, you know that I'm not rich; but perhaps I can do something for you in the way of money, because money is what you'll need. I'm often surprised how little is done by our wealthy people towards helping our young preachers, who as a rule are poor. I often think about how difficult it is for a student, even though he has a big and warm heart—how hard it is for him to get on with empty pockets, and how valuable to him a ten pound note from one of our wealthy people would be. When a little is given to a poor student, it has to be announced publicly in the Monthly Meeting, and he is branded as a beggar amongst his friends. This is scandalous, and it's no wonder that many a truly worthy boy—and the most worthy are often like this—suffers hardship quietly, rather than allowing his name to be published in the papers as the recipient of five pounds. I hope and believe that you are not expecting the work of preaching to be lucrative in a worldly sense. If you are, then you will be disappointed. There are a thousand better ways to make money. You often hear that preachers are materialistic. The accusation is a shameful libel, to my mind: and it is almost always the most materialistic people who make it. Most of the preachers I know who make their living by preaching live from hand to mouth. It's true that a special providence has been prepared for some of the most worthy, namely that God grants them favour in the eyes of rich women. Watch and pray against idleness and self-regard. You know—though I don't—whether self-regard had anything to do with your failure in the prayer meeting tonight. Was it giving praise or gaining praise that had the most place in your heart?"

Amazing! Abel understood my inner thoughts as well as I did myself, nearly.

33

MORE ABOUT WIL BRYAN

Wil Bryan's worldly wise observations, and the serious but thrilling counsels of Abel Hughes, drove me, I believe, to somewhere that I ought to be more often every day. My determination at the time was to give up for ever the idea of preaching; and I prayed much that the desire would go away; and yet I feared in my heart that I would be heard. I felt that I was two different persons—one desperate to be able to preach, the other doing his best to frustrate and discourage him. I believed that the latter was right; but my sympathy was with the former, and I always hoped that he would win the day. Perhaps in time I could have overcome my desire if David Davies had left me alone; but he did not. I was fairly certain that I no longer had the slightest inclination towards my bad old ways, and I felt that my chief enemy was Self. Since Abel Hughes had warned me against him, I saw this enemy trying to poke his finger into everything I did; and I was on the verge of ceasing to do anything public to do with religion until I had, through giving my full attention to myself, destroyed Self from inside me, and then... When I told David Davies about this, he nearly laughed; but as though he suddenly remembered that he didn't usually laugh, he smiled broadly instead, and said:

"An excellent intent; but the most selfish method you could devise. You'd be no better in twenty years with that plan. How will you defeat Self by not doing anything? Only by doing your duty can you get a grip of it and put its head on the block. If you go and spend your precious time searching for him, he's sure to hide somewhere. Self, you see, is like a mischievous lad that loves to play hide-and-seek. You cannot kill Self by closing up inside yourself—it must be crucified outside the camp. And don't be surprised if you find that Self is still alive by the time you reach my age. I've heard of people over in England who can do something they call *sleight of hand*—they can hold their hair with their left hand, and with their right hand take a sword and cut their head clean off, or at least that's how it looks—and then the next minute put a new head back in its place. When I heard that story I thought that I had been performing sleight of hand with Self. Many is the time that I have thought I had its head fairly on the block, and had cut it '*snug off*' as Evan Harris, Merthyr,[1] would say; but the next day Self would be as alive as ever. You're talking about not doing anything until you have killed Self! You'll never do a stroke of work if you wait till then. Self cannot be killed by child's play; but I think it's possible to starve it, and the best way to do that is to forget about it—neglect it, and give yourself body and soul to the service of God by doing good. And you have to *learn* to do good, as Isaiah said,[2] It's not something you can do in a day even to your own satisfaction, let alone God's. The first thing that the Gospel does is to apprentice a man to learn how to do good. And I'll tell you something else—we'll always be apprentices as long as we're in this world—we won't have learnt perfectly, and become free of our apprenticeships until we come to the next world. And time is so short, you see, that we need to get going with learning lest we appear odd, like those who haven't finished their training when we get to be among the master craftsmen. I often doubt my own motives—who doesn't?—but when I fail to reach any higher ground, I try to do a bit of good to spite the devil, and to show him that whatever else I am, I don't want anything to do with him."

He counselled me with many similar words, and I believe that they did me good. As I took part in public meetings, the

---

[1] A Calvinistic Methodist minister in Merthyr Tydfil for 50 years until his death in 1861; his biography was written by Thomas Levi and published by a Welsh-language publisher in Ohio in 1870.

[2] He probably has in mind Isaiah 1:17, 'Learn to do good; seek justice; reprove the oppressor; defend the fatherless; plead for the widow'.

consideration that I was not doing this at my own initiative, or without being pushed forwards by brothers with judgement and godliness, calmed a lot of my fears and transferred some of the responsibility to them. I was also comforted by the fact that I didn't suffer another breakdown like the one in Thomas Bartley's house; although I often felt the strain. When I had a little freedom while speaking in a prayer meeting, I would feel very happy and would come home with my head held high and humming a tune. I felt that it wasn't sinful to rejoice quietly in my spirit whenever David Davies or anyone else gave me a word of encouragement or praise; because I remembered noticing that when preachers came to Abel Hughes' house after a good meeting, and if Abel spoke highly of the sermon, then without exception they would enjoy their suppers, and vice versa. Perhaps the reason for this was that they felt they deserved their suppers, and vice versa again. I slowly came to understand that I was being looked upon as a 'candidate'; and when I realised that, my first reaction was to bridle at it, and to feel that everyone now had the right to give my bridle a tug. If I happened to be out late, I felt that the first man I met had authority to ask me, 'What are you doing out this time of night?' Whenever I laughed, I asked myself in the same moment whether I had, perhaps, laughed too loudly. If I happened to speak to young women—something I must admit I did from time to time—I felt that someone was always watching me, and planting both their feet in my face. Without going into detail, I felt that I had lost my freedom. Now I no longer had the right that others had to shake my head and refuse to go forward when asked to do so in a prayer meeting; and I didn't dare reply, 'I'd rather not' to any task that the Sunday School superintendent asked me to do. In a word, I lost the feeling of being my own man, and felt that I had been transformed into a piece of public property. Everyone great and small felt it was their duty to give me their pieces of advice, which varied enormously and were no doubt given with the best intentions. So much interest appeared to be shown in me, and so many were my advisors, that in the end I just came to expect everyone I met to give me advice, and I was rarely disappointed. Some said that if I intended to make a start at the work of preaching, then I should take my time and move slowly; and others said I should press on and not lose time. Some advised me to concentrate on reading at all times of day, and not waste time wandering around, while others said I should read less, and enjoy more fresh air, if I wanted to live long and be useful. Some urged me to familiarise myself with literature, politics and general knowledge, and with every new book that I could get my hands on—because that's essential for a young preacher in this day and age; while others advised me to leave those things alone, and to give my whole time to studying the scriptures, adding that the main fault with young preachers was that they were unfamiliar with the Bible and spent too much of their time with other books. "Whatever you do," said one person to me, "don't go to college to be spoiled, and to be made the same as all the rest of them." "Of course," said another, "you'll *have* to go to college, or you won't be able to do anything. Even if you don't learn anything, people will think more of you." "Remember," said one brother, "to be free and merry with everyone; I hate stiff preachers." "I hope, if they allow you to preach, that you will remember to watch yourself, and live simply, and not give occasion for anyone to talk about you," said an elderly sister. When I mentioned these different pieces of good advice to W.B. one evening, he said, "Use your common sense, man, if you have any common sense; and if not, then forget all about preaching. I admit you'll have to mind your *hegs an' pegs* now, and watch for your *centre of gravity*; but don't be as though you live in a clock case. There's no point in being like a cock walking through snow; something like that isn't *true to nature*, and I'll never believe that grace is contrary to *nature*—sinless *nature*, that is. I think there's a Bible verse on the subject, but I can't think of one just now.[3] '*Trust in God and keep your powder dry*' said old Cromwell, and he was no *duffer*. If you try to follow everyone's advice, you will have to work every hour of the day, and it will be *hic jacet* [4] and *Alas poor Yorick* for you very soon. I would just tell the *duffers* to go to Jericho; but there's no point in you doing that. You must be *civil* to everyone, try to spot the *wide-awakes* and listen to them."

I believed that there was quite a lot of sense in Wil's observations, even though it was put in a way unique to him. I spent a long time with the status of 'candidate' before my case was brought formally before the church; and the main reason was that it was my own wish. I was only young, and I was keen to have a fair proof of myself, and to prove to others, lest I make a mistake or others make a mistake that they would regret later. I had another end in view, namely avoiding having to give the 'test sermon' in the *seiat*. I knew that that was the general rule with those who sought permission to preach, namely that they had to give a sermon to the *seiat* to show what they could do. I considered that this way of testing the ability and suitability of a young man was the most unnatural and unfair thing that could be devised, and I was sure in my mind that I could not go through it. I often fancied myself being able to preach to a panel of judges, and only judges; preaching not for edification, but to show what ability I had. I knew that I couldn't act; and I would have preferred to spend an extra year in the state I was in rather than go through that trial. And there were many opportunities—and still are many opportunities—for every young man to show to the church and the neighbourhood whether he has any suitability to be a public man, without placing him in the unfair and disadvantageous situation to which I've referred. Another reason that caused me to delay putting my case before the church was that I was genuinely keen to have more certainty about the correctness of my motives and my calling to the work. I remembered hearing Abel Hughes talking about some who had

---

[3] I'm fairly sure there isn't.

[4] Latin, 'here lies'—sometimes rendered *hic iacet*, a common inscription on ancient tombs.

suffered a 'fit of preaching' and afterwards had fully recovered from the affliction. I was afraid lest I also was having a 'fit' and I reasoned that, if I were, then it would pass quickly. There was also in me something that I'm not entirely free of today, namely a deep desire for obvious and definite proof of some particular truths that bothered me—proof that likely isn't possible for me to have and, if it were possible, then it would render faith unnecessary. How that can be I don't know, but I often have a longing for the impossible. Months passed, but the 'fit' did not leave me. At every opportunity I had to talk to a preacher with whom I could be bold, I tried to tease from them as much information as I could about their experience and consciousness when they were in the same situation as I was in; but they could tell me very little about their own thought processes that I had not already experienced myself. Yet I always believed that they had received something that I had not, but that they were unable to describe it. I sharpened my imagination to call forth the terrors that were in store for me if I was deceiving myself; and in my mind I tried to put myself into a situation so fiery that hell itself would not be ashamed to call it its handiwork. The most I could say—and I certainly could say this—is that I was not, as far as I could tell, being driven by false purposes. I thought it was entirely possible that I was making a mistake and showing a lack of judgement in thinking about preaching; but I was sure that I had no unworthy motives as far as I was aware. I can't deny that every day I tried to guess what other people were thinking about me; and I often asked myself the same question that the Greatest once asked to some others—'Who do men say that I am?'[5] As someone who was inclined towards preaching, and who was doing a little in the way of it even without a licence, I was conscious that to many people I didn't appear in as favourable a light as I could. I knew some considered that one who has declared a desire to preach should

---

[5] Matt. 16:13.

have a fiery spirit, a high degree of experience, and a zeal to add a degree of compulsion to the things he had to say. I was not capable of being like that. Remembering my childhood made me unable to give advice to people. I also remembered a remark by Abel Hughes, 'I never like hearing a young man giving a lot of advice, and speaking to a mixed congregation as though he were an experienced old man. It's entirely unnatural, to my mind; and I question whether those who do it are doing any good. I'd rather see a young preacher half drowning than lazing about on the river bank. Listening to a twenty-year-old boy imitating an old man sounds as awkward to my ear as hearing an eighty-year-old man begging for a game of marbles. You do see such awkward things sometimes: but in both cases it's a sign of weakness'. I knew full well that my orations in meetings held in houses and small chapels were dry and essay-like—more so than they should have been, as I was keeping myself in check. Sometimes I felt zealous, but I made an effort to cool down lest I appear dogmatic or older than my years. It made a deep impression on my mind when I saw a young preacher in the *seiat* going around and talking with the gathered friends. When he came to old Betty Cynrig, he asked, "Well, old sister, do you think you know Jesus Christ by now?" and old Betty replied, "Well, I hope I knew him before your father was born, my lad." I don't applaud Betty for giving such a put-down to a young man who was visiting us; but she made an impression on my mind, nonetheless, and I'm sure the young man didn't feel as full of himself at the end of that *seiat* as he had at the beginning. I felt a degree of pleasure in helping the friends in small chapels out in the countryside to hold meetings when they didn't have a preacher; but when David Davies told me that he was going to bring my case formally before the church as a candidate for the ministry, I was filled with fear and depression. In one way I would have been happier to pull back, but at the same time I couldn't bear the idea. It was obvious that I couldn't remain as I was. If I permitted my case to be brought forward, I felt that I was claiming great things for myself, putting myself into a different category from everyone else in the church, and taking upon myself something that terrified me. Often I fancied that I heard a voice ask me, 'What will you say about My laws?' I longed for a clear vision, but none came; and I thought about what reason I could give for trying to be a preacher, when I couldn't state clearly and definitively that it was my calling. On the other hand, as I said, I couldn't bear the thought of laying aside my compulsion for the work, and snuffing out my most precious aspirations. I didn't understand myself, and I thought that was strange. How could others understand me? Was it possible that other people could form a more correct idea about me than I could myself? I decided to let circumstances take their course; and in a few days my case was brought before the church. I don't intend to give a detailed account of the matter. I was asked many questions, which I answered exactly as I thought and felt, without trying to colour myself in any way or claim more than I could in all truthfulness. I was sent out while the brethren discussed their thoughts about me. While I was waiting for their conclusion, I was afraid that my answers had given occasion for some to believe that I wasn't clear in my mind. I didn't really expect my case to be looked at favourably, and I almost hoped that it wouldn't be. Soon I was called back in; and I was told that the church was willing to pass my application on to the Monthly Meeting to ask them to send brethren to examine my case and to collect the views of the church on the matter. It was good for me that there was no need for me to say anything, as had there been then I would have been unable. Many thoughts went through my mind that night, which I would try to describe but something else happened that same night which is more vivid in my memory—something I'll never forget—and which is easier to tell because it has to do with somebody else.

It's possible that I've said more about Wil Bryan than anyone else. I won't say much more about him. As I've said more than once, Wil had made a deep impression on me since I was a young lad. Although he was some sort of a church member, I knew, and others knew as well, that from the point of view of his spirit and his inclinations he wasn't all that he should have been. I feared that his heart was very much a stranger to religion; and at one time I had decided to break off all contact with him, but that proved more of a job than I'd thought. His generosity of spirit, his open heart, his shrewdness, and especially his sharp and witty tongue, renewed my admiration for him every time I spoke to him and made me forget for the time being all his deficiencies—although they were many. Although he would never say so in as many words, I couldn't help think that he was fond of me; and I was sure that no-one living felt a greater interest in my success than Wil did. I had noticed lately that Wil was even lamer than usual in attending the services; and this was true of his parents as well. Even so, my old companion was present in the *seiat* when my case was brought forward; and I was glad to see him there, mainly I must confess because I knew that I would get a detailed account from him of everything that was said after I'd been asked to leave the room. Naturally enough I was curious to know what was said by various people in my absence; and I knew that Wil could bring me up to speed with everything. I have previously tried to convey on paper as much as I think is worth chronicling of Wil's words, as closely as I can for style and content to the way that they passed his lips, and I will attempt that again now. When we came from the *seiat*, I think that I for once was looking for Wil, rather than him looking for me, and he said, "*Just* the thing—I was wanting to have a chat with you."

"I know, Wil," said I, "that I'll get the full story from you. How was it after they sent me out?"

"If I were to give you a *verbatim et literatim* report it would do you no good at all. The only thing that tickled my fancy was the old scratcher insisting that you should preach before the *seiat* so that they could see what you were made of, and old Abel answering that that would make sense if you'd just arrived from

America and no-one knew anything about you. I don't know that there was anything else worth telling you, except for when that old *thoroughbred* Thomas Bartley, when they were raising hands to vote for you, raised both his hands—just like that picture of Whitefield—and that, I think, was by way of an *apology for the unavoidable absence of Barbara Bartley, owing to a severe attack of rheumatism*. But let that be. Tonight you have reached the point that I've been looking forward to for ages; and now all you have to do is go ahead. My conscience is a bit quieter tonight. I know very well that it was I who threw you off the *metals*; and I dreamed, the night that we nearly hanged Jones, that your mother came from the other world to tell me off, and she looked so cross with me; I'll never forget her expression. I was never happy after that night, although I put a brave face on it, until I saw you back on the *metals* again. Tonight you and I have come to the *junction* that I knew all the time we were sure to reach. We've travelled a lot together, but I always knew that we weren't going to the same place—and here's the *junction*. I'm speaking a bit figuratively, but you understand me properly, I know. The *fact* of the *matter* is, we need to say farewell, as the song goes, to the

'*Dear happy hours that can return no more*'.[6]

I'm about to beat it, and perhaps you'll never see me again; and there's a lump in my throat as I say this, I swear. Have you heard about us at home?"

"Heard what, Wil? I don't understand you," I said.

"It's UP[7] over there," said Wil, "and everyone will know within a week from now, and I can't stand it. Didn't I tell you that my father was a *duffer*? I remember a time when I used to think he made money as easily as carrying it, and that he was *clever at*

---

[6] From 'With Sighs, Sweet Rose' by John Wall Callcott (1766–1821).

[7] That is, 'up', as in 'the game's up'.

a bargain; but when I came to know what was what, and how things stood, this was the *verdict*: *duffer*. I saw it some time ago, but there was no use talking about a *change of policy*; my father just wanted to stay in the same old *rut*. He was just like another creature that we know about—*more noted for the length of his ears than for the sweetness of his voice*—who would cross a field of *clover* and head straight for the hedge to graze on nettles, dock leaves, coltsfoot and other such rubbish. What's the result? Other people have gathered the clover, and there's nothing left in the hedge—not so much as an old robin's nest. What's the *prospect*? *Liquidation by arrangement*, and *starvation!* So I'm going to peg it. Where to? I don't know. What can I do? *There's the rub!* I come of age next week, D.V., and I'll be as *well off* as I was *twenty-one years back to the date*. You know that I didn't get much more schooling than you did, and yet I think sometimes that I'm not a *perfect greenhorn*. When I got wise enough to see my loss, I made a *point* of keeping a *close observation* of human nature, as the Wesleys would call it. That's the best thing that a man without much schooling can do, study *human nature*. But I've made one big mistake—I haven't studied for my bread and cheese. What can I say that I am? I'm not a gentleman or a tailor. I haven't spent enough time behind the *counter* to learn how to serve—I never had an appetite for that, and my delight, as you know, was driving a horse; and I didn't mind whether I was carrying a truckload of bread or a truckload of young women, so long as I had a horse to drive; and I can drive one as well as any man, no matter where he comes from. But next week, Hugh Bryan, *provision dealer*, won't have any horses to drive. And there's a difference between driving your own horse and driving someone else's. Do you think I'd become a gentleman's servant? Never, even if I had to pound rocks instead. That's the most *degrading* job I know about. I couldn't stomach taking a salary to doff my hat all the time, and lend my legs to showing off the master's *cashmere*. Well, what am I to do? It's a brand new question for me, and I don't know how to answer it. You know how I was brought up—I never wanted for anything except grace and good advice. I don't think I've ever been a day without a good dinner. But how will it be next week? You know what? I've never been *really down in the mouth* before."

"Wil," I said, "you've quite taken the wind out of my sails. How did things come to this?"

"It would take too long to go over everything?" he said. "I don't want to be too hard on the *gaffer*—I'm genuinely sorry for him, I swear. But it's all his own fault. If he had minded his own business, things would have been *all right*. You know that my father was always *grasping*; and after he had made a bit of money, somebody persuaded him to speculate. I pleaded with him a year ago to drop it; but it was no use. *Fifty pounds a month*, for goodness' sake! How could he possibly keep that up? If he had taught me how to make a living, I wouldn't mind so much. It's an odd idea; but I've often thought lately that if I had happened to be my own father, I would have brought myself up much better. Perhaps people will think I'm *selfish* for *skidaddling*, but I can't bear the *disgrace*. And then there's Suse—*poor girl*—I can't look her in the face. It's lucky that there isn't anything *definite* between us. I have to go—something is driving me."

"You've made me sad, Wil," I said. "I remember many times when your sympathy and help was very valuable to me; but I don't remember you ever, before tonight, being in circumstances where you needed my sympathy. Will you take one piece of advice?"

"What's that, *old fellow?*"

"Whenever and wherever you go, will you take care to get a membership ticket[8]—and when you are set up in your new home, take care to find the nearest chapel, and present your ticket to the elders? I may as well tell you the whole truth, Wil: I'm afraid of you going on the wrong track."

"I was hoping," said Wil, "that you wouldn't mention that, but seeing as you have, I need to say something that's been on my mind for a long time. It would take me a whole day to tell everything.

It would be nothing but humbug for me to ask for a ticket. I've been far too much of a hypocrite. I know you think that you know about me pretty well, but you don't know anything. I can't hide from myself the fact that I don't have a *spark* of religion. Do you remember your mother telling me that there was an 'old man' in my heart, and I made fun of her? The old woman was exactly right. What she meant, as you know, was corruption, although she had an odd word for it. I don't know how to tell you about what goes on inside me, and I'd rather not try. I feel somehow as if I'm *Gospel-proof*; and I haven't been able for a long time to remember any Bible verses except for those that go against me. A lot of them come to my mind sometimes. To tell you the truth, I haven't read the Bible since I don't know how long—because when I did read it, it was the verses that were against me that I spotted in it all the time. I'm only a *youngster*, and yet I feel as if I've gained a *march* on the Gospel—or perhaps I should say, as if I've been left behind. Have I killed anyone? *No danger*. Have I wronged anyone? I don't know. Have I been drunk? *Never*. There's no need for *a chap* to do those things to get left behind. What have I done? Lots of little things: learning *comic songs* instead of learning the Bible and the *Instructor*,[9] going to the *billiard table* far more often than to the Lord's table, making fun of everyone and everything, and making *parodies* of the hymns of Williams Pantycelyn. In chapel, whenever a preacher was just on the point of bowling me out, I would always take care to use my bat; and now every sermon is a '*wide*'. I would be afraid of anyone seeing a tear in my eye; and whenever one was just about to come, I would call myself to *account*, and order it back. No tear has wanted to come now for a long time. Perhaps the blame isn't all on me. I wasn't raised the way you were. My father would make me go to chapel on Sunday; but there was never any talk of chapel or of religion at home, but 'Hoy!' and 'Hurry up!'

---

[8] That is, a certificate of membership in the Calvinistic Methodist church.

[9] That is, the catechism published by Thomas Charles in 1807.

and a *row* every day. My father did the same with me as you've seen Ned the smith doing with his iron. On Sunday, by driving me to chapel, he'd set my conscience on fire, and on Monday he'd plunge it into a bucket of water, with the result that by now it's as hard as a horseshoe."

"Wil…" I said.

"You may as well not say anything, I know what you're going to say—repent, start again, and so on. I know all those things. I don't want to know, but I want to feel. A man can't repent as easily as signing the pledge.[10] He must have a change of mind, as the 'Mother's Gift'[11] says. And doesn't the Bible say about someone who had no way to repent[12]—that's one of the verses that goes against me—there are a lot them. The worst thing is that it's as if I don't want to repent. I feel some impulse behind me, driving me on, as if I were being carried by a crowd of people, and as if I can't help it, and at the same time I'm always feeling that I'm going to the wrong place. Your mother, fair play to the old woman, gave me a lot of advice; and I remember you being rather annoyed with me for calling her the 'old Ten Commandments', but I always felt that she was telling me what to do. And so she was. Don't do that, but do this, is what she was always saying. I knew at the time that the old woman was quite right, and I would decide to do what she said after I'd had my *fling*. But I took too much of a *fling*, and now I can't come back. I'm afraid that I'm past *feeling*— nothing has any effect on me. I'm only a *youngster*, but I feel old in defiance and hardness. Fancy that! So young! I almost feel the same as Wolsey[13]—'*Had I served my God*'—you know the rest of the words. I feel disheartened, and I'm tired of myself, and yet I'm not repentant. I feel *remorse*, but not a hair of repentance— if indeed I understand what repentance is."

"Dear Wil," I said, "you're forgetting that God…"

"There's no point in you saying anything, you can't say anything new to me. I know what you're going to say—that God is merciful, and I should pray to him, and so on. But I've been trying on the *sly*, and every time I feel as though I'm *sponging*. You know what I think? I've offended God forever by making *parodies* of old Pantycelyn's hymns—because I swear that the Good Lord and old Pant are *chums*, and he'll never forgive me for that. But I'd better stop. Good night."

After shaking my hand Wil rushed away before I could say anything to him; but I was determined to see him the next day to try to give him another way to think. However, early the following morning a boy who worked for Hugh Bryan brought me a note addressed 'Rev. Rhys Lewis', and on opening it I read:

'*Dear Old Fellow,*

     Exit W.B.   *As the old song*[14] *says—*
                            "It may be for years,
                            And it may be for ever."

Stay on the path that you have begun[15], *and profit by the example of*
     Yours Truly.

P.S. I have snatched the honour of first addressing you as Rev., trusting that you will always well sustain the title. W.B.'

---

[10] That is, promising to be a teetotaller.

[11] 'Rhodd Mam', the Calvinistic Methodist children's catechism published by John Parry of Chester in 1811.

[12] Matt. 12:31.

[13] The last words of Cardinal Wolsey just before his death in 1530; there are many versions. Shakespeare's (Henry VIII, Act III, scene II) is: 'Had I but served my God with half the zeal I served my king, he would not in mine age have left me naked to mine enemies'.

[14] 'Kathleen Mavourneen', an Irish ballad written by Marion Crawford in 1837.

[15] In Wil's note, this half sentence is the only part that is written in Welsh.

34

THOMAS BARTLEY
ON COLLEGE EDUCATION

What is the essence of friendship? 'Like and like are rivals still'.[1] 'Birds of a feather flock together'.[2] Does the fact that two people are friends mean that they are always of the same inclinations, if not of the same ideas? Not always, I believe. When the ideas and inclinations aren't shared by the friends, then what is friendship made up of? The admiration one has for the other can't account for it, because admiration can exist without friendship, and friendship without admiration. I've often seen someone laughing at their friend, when the friend wouldn't tolerate anyone else doing so. Is friendship some special privilege of the heart, I wonder, which it holds without having to answer any other element of the soul? I don't know. I do know this—Wil Bryan and I were neither of the same inclinations nor ideas, but when he made his '*exit*' as he put it, my heart stirred and I wept inside. I didn't know until then that I had such a strong attachment, and I felt the effects of the separation for months afterwards. Wil went away, as I said, and I felt a great emptiness in his wake; and I'm afraid I will feel his absence in this story too in the future, since Wil won't enter it again for quite some time. His prophecy about his father was fulfilled within the week, but I won't say any more about that. I heard no word from my old friend after he'd gone away, and I

---

[1] In Welsh, 'Pob cyffelyb ymgais', which more literally means, 'All things that are similar will strive for the same things'. The proverbial form in English comes from *British Reason in English Rhyme* by Henry Halford Vaughan, 1889.

[2] In Welsh, 'Adar o'r unlliw ehedant i'r unlle', which means exactly what the English proverb does while sounding (in the translator's opinion) much more succinct.

took that to be a bad sign because I remembered him say one day that if he ever went away then none of his friends would hear from him unless he had good news to share, or something to report on a level with catching a wild elephant or fighting with a tiger.

A man gets tired of saying too much about himself; and I don't think anyone would embark on the task of writing a memoir unless he thought that others whom he had encountered would figure strongly in the work. What I find most interesting is what I learned from observing the strengths and weaknesses of other people. In the life of an ordinary young preacher there is quite a lot of monotony; the story of a particular week is also the story of the following week, and there are rarely circumstances whose description would be of particular interest to anyone except himself. And yet, as I said in the opening chapter of this story, the daily life of an ordinary man is *so* ordinary that no-one thinks it is worth putting down in writing. There are thousands of verses and sayings in common use which convey the true feeling and experience of the common people. They are not poetic or 'amusing', and no-one knows who their author was. Yes, someone *composed* the sayings, 'Good morning to you' and 'Good night'. Who were the authors? There's nothing diverting in these sayings and their like, and their only distinctive feature is the sheer ordinariness of the ideas they convey—and yet they are immortal! We common people use the same words and sayings every day in thousands of different places and circumstances, and we never tire of them or imagine accusing one another of being stale. If the day happens to be pleasant, how many thousands of tongues say 'it's fine today' as if it's the most original idea that was ever put into words. The same man may say 'it's fine today' twenty times in a day, with as much emphasis the last time as the first. It can almost be believed that the most ordinary things possess true and lasting interest. The little man never tires of the loaf of bread that is on his table three or four times a day, whilst one may tire of a 'club dinner' even once a week.

Although nothing *particular* happened for a while after what

I recorded in the previous chapter, except for what would have happened in the life of almost every young preacher, and although I am now jumping over a year of my life, I can't see why a detailed description of that period shouldn't be interesting if I can gather the courage to describe ordinary things that happen every day, and it will mean that the description is *true to nature*, as W.B. would say. Speaking of courage, it takes courage to call a spade a spade. The trouble is that a man is conscious that everyone knows—or at least ought to know—what a spade is called, and therefore he doesn't feel able to talk about it. Doesn't every young preacher with the Calvinistic Methodists lose many an hour of sleep in fear and anxiety about the night when two agents from the Monthly Meeting come to question and examine him? And isn't he disappointed when they arrive? Aren't the examiners much less frightening than his imagination portrayed them to be, and aren't their questions very much easier to answer than he had feared? How did he feel after his first sermon? Didn't he feel that he had undone himself, and that he'd never be able to preach again? Didn't he find that the sermon he delivered was something very different from how it had looked on paper? Didn't he think that there were various gaps and false steps in it, that he hadn't noticed before he delivered it? As he preached, wasn't he seized by a painful feeling that the sermon weakened towards the end, and finished abruptly and inconclusively? Many a Sunday night, in his bedroom, didn't he feel small and corrupted as he noticed he'd thought much more about who had admired his sermon than about who had believed? Didn't he drop in his own estimation when his only congregation was the night, and God? Didn't he lose hope a hundred times of ever reaching that desirable state of being able to shut from his mind every selfish consideration, and lose himself in the overwhelming urge to serve God and do good to his fellow men? At the same time, wasn't he often too fastidious to permit some things—the tithe, for example—to have a place in his thoughts? And didn't he eventually find that he'd become inured to taking such things into account? Wasn't he often shocked to find how similar he was to other people who did not profess the things that he professed? What idea did he have about the Monthly Meeting before he became familiar with it? Did he find the old institution as spiritual and heavenly minded as he had expected? He knew, of course, that everyone there was either a preacher or an elder, and hadn't he formed some silly idea that they would be almost like angels of God? As he got to know them wasn't he amazed how similar they were to other people, and especially to himself? Didn't he see it as a discovery that they actually ate and drank like other people, to say the least? That some were able to laugh heartily? That some would whisper among themselves whilst another brother was praying at the beginning or end of a meeting? Indeed, didn't he see some losing their tempers? He had used to think of _____ ,[3] hadn't he, as someone especially spiritual and devotional? Did he think quite so highly of him when he found out that he used to wait in the chapel house to have a smoke until after the brother who was opening the meeting in prayer had finished? On coming back from the Meeting wasn't he on better terms with himself, thinking, 'Well, we're all made of the same clay; we all have our weaknesses'? What was his experience of the members of the Monthly Meeting? Didn't he find that the most able and godly of them were his best and most faithful friends, who did the most to help him? Wasn't it the least Christ-like who were unfaithful to him, and who discouraged him the most? When he preached before the ministers of the county, wasn't it the ones he had feared the most who were the tenderest and most encouraging? And the ones he had feared the least who were the most patronising and snooty? As he went here and there to preach Sunday after Sunday, wasn't he alarmed more than once to see how he had cooled down to the point of doing it all mechanically? Wasn't he disappointed to find that preaching did not slay his own sinfulness? And didn't

---

[3] Again, the Victorian habit of leaving a blank space instead of a real person's name.

he find that this consecrated work put new temptations before him and woke tendencies in his nature that before then had lain dormant? Didn't he often fear that his preaching produced better effects upon other people than upon himself? Didn't he often notice that he wasn't as holy and flawless as others believed him to be? When he found that some people thought too highly of him, did he disabuse them of their ideas? No he didn't. When he found that others held similar ideas about him to those that he held himself, wasn't he annoyed with them? Didn't he regard those whom he knew thought well of him as men of ability and perception, and those who thought otherwise as being deficient in their judgement? After a dull and flat Sunday, didn't he decide never to preach again? And when he had a good Sunday, didn't he rejoice that he hadn't put that decision into action? Despite the painful consciousness of Self and corruption, which caused him a lot of deep sadness, didn't the suggestions he sometimes had that he was doing some good afford him a pleasure that he couldn't describe or place a price upon? Couldn't he say at times, 'You have put gladness in my heart, more than in the season that their grain and wine increased'?[4]

These things are just the common things in the life of every young preacher, and a chapter could have been written about every one of them; but who ever did that? They are things so common to a preacher's experience, as I said, that no-one ever thought it worth putting them into writing. I had intended to describe them in detail but I see, considering the size of this autobiography, that like my predecessors I shall have to leave the task to someone else.

I had been preaching almost every Sunday for about eighteen months—having been accepted as a member of the Monthly Meeting, and gone through the examination for acceptance into the college. I knew very well that I hadn't 'shone', as the saying goes, but my conscience was clear that I had done my best.

---

[4] Psalm 4:7.

Although my poor mother, when she was alive, felt she had done well by putting me in school for 'almost a whole year', I felt that I had to fight every step of the way with more energy, diligence and commitment because, in my early days, I'd had little more education than Robin the Soldier's cane had been able to impart to me. And yet I was sustained in going on by the encouragement and kindness of friends, and especially my master, Abel Hughes. I felt myself so far behind that I feared to be in the presence of young men who'd had a good education, and I'm sure I wouldn't have imagined going to college unless Abel had kept it as a target in my mind the whole time, and pushed me on towards it. I came through the exam for acceptance into the college somewhere near the middle of the ranking, and by that time it wasn't appropriate for me to hold back. I only had very little money to hand, because I had spent almost all my salary on books and clothes; and I depended on the promise Abel Hughes gave me for all that I would need while in college. I trusted completely that my master would help me, and do so quietly. He was a close friend to me, and he had renewed his promise many times when we spoke in secret. I knew that he hadn't said a word about his good intentions towards me even to his own sister. Whenever he performed a kindness, his delicacy and his respect for the feelings of the recipient were such that I sometimes felt he'd like to keep it a secret even from himself. I noticed many times that as he gave a gift to a poor man he would talk about some other thing, as if he were trying to call his attention and that of the recipient away from the action of his hands. I remember well one evening in August—about a fortnight before the time I intended to go to college. I was already beginning to prepare for the journey and feeling a bit fidgety, as I hadn't been away from home for more than two nights in my life. I had just closed the shop, and my master Abel Hughes sat on the sofa by the window in the parlour. He looked fatigued, sad, and listless. He immediately began talking about the time that I would be going to college. As he saw me put my hat on, he asked where I was going, and I answered that I had promised to call on Thomas Bartley. "Will you be long?" he asked, and I said, "I think it should only take a little time." I added, "What's the matter? Would you rather I stayed in?" "No, I don't want that on any account; but somehow I don't feel quite myself this evening," he said. "I'll stay in, and go to the Twmpath tomorrow night," I said. But Abel didn't want me to do that, and said, "There's not much wrong with me—I'll be better soon, and Marged will be in before long. Thomas Bartley no doubt is waiting for you." As I was going through the door he called me and said, "Wait a minute. Who knows what can happen?" Then he opened a cupboard, which was close by him, and pulled out the cash box, and after opening that he took out one or two bank notes; but he suddenly put them back in and smiled, and said, "What's wrong with me? Am I getting senile? Isn't there a fortnight to go? Off you go, don't mind me, but hurry back."

On the way to Thomas Bartley's house I couldn't help thinking that there was something strange about Abel's behaviour that evening, and I decided to return early. However, once under the roof of the Twmpath it wasn't easy to get away from there quickly. Doing so before having supper was out of the question, because I had barely sat down before Thomas cast a threatening eye upon the ham that hung from the ceiling. The best welcome Thomas could give was ham, eggs and tea, and not even a prince could need more. Amongst very many other things I remember Thomas saying the following things during my visit:

"Terribly strong food, ham and eggs, you see, if you have the quality. I wouldn't give a fig for a cartload of those American hams. How would you know what the poor pigs had been feedin' on? And I don't know how these town people dare to eat eggs. You know what I heard Ned my cousin say that he'd seen once with his own eyes in a proper respectable house in Liverpool? This was his story—at breakfast time the maid would bring about a dozen boiled eggs on a plate and set 'em down on the table; and then the family would break one after the other and smell 'em, and the maid would carry 'em away as fast as she could, and in the end perhaps they'd find two or three out of the dozen that were fit to eat! And the odd thing was, they didn't think anythin' of it—they did that every day. Well, they can keep their clean hearts, I say. Barbara, let's have those eggs that are on the middle shelf between the plates there—right opposite you—yes, they're the ones. These were laid today; game hen eggs. And you've decided to go to Bala? You know what, we'll feel very awkward for you, won't we Barbara? (Barbara nodded.) We shall, to be sure. I've never been to Bala nor anywhere up in the mountains, and I don't know anyone there except the two men who come here when there's a fair on to sell socks in the street—and they're fine enough fellows. I'd like terribly to go to Bala once in my life, if only to see the lake that that man walked across when it'd frozen. That was a cruel turn—when he understood what he'd done, he dropped dead on the spot. I heard James Pulford once saying an *englyn*[5] about Bala that he'd heard by Robin Ddu—'*Bala aeth* a'r *Bala eiff*'—somethin' like that—you'll hear it, I expect, when you go there. I remember that whenever my father was talkin' about somethin' that was really safe, he'd say 'as sound as Bala's clock'. Just take a look at it when you're there. You know what, when I hear of a cheap trip, Barbara

---

[2] A short Welsh poem with a very strictly defined meter; quite similar to a haiku. My personal favourite is this example by Gwilym Deudraeth:

'*Mae mewn byd i*
    hyd ei hwy,
	'In this world, for everything long
	    there is something longer,

i fawr ei fwy yn
    tramwy;
	for everything big, something
	    bigger looms;

Caffaeliad amhrisiadwy	It's a priceless thing

Yw dyn mawr yn
    gweld un mwy'.
	To find a great man who acknowledges
	    one greater than he'.

What Thomas goes on to quote is not an englyn at all, but a short two-line 'prophecy' attributed to 'Black Robin the Magician' (a poet from Anglesey who lived around 1450). 'Bala went, and Bala will go, and Llanfor [a nearby village] will become a lake'. It refers to a legend that Bala lake formed when a holy well in the old town of Bala was left uncovered overnight, against the dire warnings of the local folklore; the following morning, the old town was submerged by the lake, which at 4 miles long and a mile wide is the largest natural body of water in Wales. The present town of Bala was rebuilt at its northern end.

and I wouldn't mind comin' over to look in on you. You'd like that? I know for sure you'd like to see us. Get on and eat, boy, I don't see you eat much; you know you're welcome. Are there lots of 'em in Bala learnin' how to preach? What did you say? They're not learnin' how to preach there? Oh well indeed, you can say that again, because I've heard some of 'em who've happened to come here to preach and I haven't seen anything special about 'em—to my taste. I'd rather hear William Hughes, Abercwmnant, than the best of 'em—though I'm not much of a judge. Well, what on earth are they learnin' there if they're not learnin' how to preach?"

"Languages, Thomas Bartley," I said.

"What? What languages, say?"

"Latin and Greek," I said.

"Aha! I see now! In case they need to become missionaries, so that they can preach to the blacks, isn't it? A good thing, indeed. You're not thinkin' of going to the blacks, are you? I didn't think so. Can you say why so few of 'em go off to India to preach to the blacks, after they've learned their languages in the college? They tell me that there are scores of blacks who've never heard a word about Jesus Christ, and that's a terrible pity. They may as well not bother learnin' the languages if they're not going to preach in 'em. There'd have been no point in me becomin' a cobbler's apprentice if I wasn't thinkin' of mendin' shoes after that. You're not givin' up already? Have another cup of tea, my boy. Well, you've only got yourself to blame. But I was talkin' about the languages—what did you call 'em? To be sure, Latin and Greek—what the blacks speak, isn't it?"

"No, Thomas, Greek and Latin aren't what the blacks speak," I said.

"Whose languages are they, then?" asked Thomas.

"Oh, the languages of old people who died centuries ago," I said.

"Dead people's languages? Well, what on earth is the point of learnin' dead people's languages? Are you makin' fun of me, tell me, like your brother Bob used to?"

"I'm telling you the truth, Thomas. They teach the languages for their own sake, and for the treasures that are in them," I said.

"Well, I've never heard of such a thing! I always thought that a language was somethin' to speak. Well tell me, what language do blacks speak? They must teach that, or none of 'em could be missionaries."

"The blacks' language isn't taught in the college, Thomas Bartley; the missionaries need to go to the blacks themselves to learn that," I said.

"Well, my ears never heard such a thing," said Thomas— "Learnin' the languages of people who are dead, and not learnin' the languages of people who are alive! But now we've started talking about it, what else do they teach, tell me?"

"They teach mathematics," I said.

"Matthew Mattis? What's that, say?"

"How to measure and weigh and make all sorts of accounts, and that sort of thing," I said.

"That's somethin' handy enough," said Thomas, "and that's the reason, I suppose, why so many preachers become farmers and shopkeepers. Do they teach anythin' else there?"

"English and history," I answered.

"Quite a thing," said Thomas, "because I can see that if a man doesn't know a bit of English these days then he's bound to fall behind. And history is interestin' enough. One of the best men I ever heard for tellin' a story is James Pulford. When I was in the habit of goin' to the pub I used to love 'em; and there's nothin' I like to hear in a sermon more than a bit of a story. When Barbara and I have forgotten all the rest of the sermon, we'll still have a pretty good grasp of the story that the preacher told. But I don't think these boys in the college take the trouble to tell a story. I think William Hughes, Abercwmnant, tops any of 'em. You know what, William told a story the last time he was here about a little girl dyin', that I won't forget as long as I live. I couldn't for the life of me stop cryin' when he told it. I'm very glad to hear that they teach history in the college. But some of them are very slow to learn. There was a boy preachin' recently, and they said he'd been in the college for three years—but I couldn't for the life of me make head nor tail of him. He was talkin' about 'unity' or 'utility' or somethin' like that—I couldn't for the life of me tell which end of it was which. But tell me—I almost forgot—I knew there was something I wanted to ask you—what sort of food do they provide for you there? I'd expect it to be pretty good fare?"

"They don't provide for anyone, Thomas; everyone has to look after themselves," I answered.

"Well, how on earth do these boys get provisions? Do they get so much a week for livin' off?" asked Thomas.

"No, they don't," I said. "Every boy has to look after himself for food and drink, lodging and washing. They can go here and there to preach, they earn something from that and live off it."

"Well, I'll never go to Caerwys fair again if this college isn't the strangest place I've ever heard of!" said Thomas. "The boys, so you say, don't learn to preach there—they don't learn the language of the blacks, but they learn the languages of people who've been dead for centuries—they're not paid, but they have to pay their own way—whether they starve or not—and the only thing worth mentionin' that they *do* learn is history and that other thing—what did you call it? Matthew? To be sure, Matthew Mattis; what on earth are you going there for, tell me? Do they teach you anythin' about Jesus Christ there? I didn't hear you mention that."

"No doubt they do, Thomas," I said, "but the place is almost as strange to me as it is to you."

"Most the pity. If I were in your place, I'd want a month to try it out, and take my own food with me. You know what? It's struck me just now that everyone I see comin' here from the college has a look of hunger about 'em; and it's no wonder now you've told me how they manage there. The more a man lives, the more he sees and hears. I used to think that this college was a splendid place; and yet I used to wonder how the poor boys all looked so grey and discouraged; and I thought perhaps that they were a bit afraid, like a witness in the witness box, and that if I happened to see them on the Monday then they'd look normal, perhaps. They must've lived better in the college years ago, because I remember when I was a lad that I happened to go to chapel; and who was preachin' but John Jones, Llanllyfni[6]—he was in the college that time, I think—and his two cheeks were rosy as anythin'. Tell me: what if you don't happen to get called to preach for a month or two after you go to college, what will become of you?"

"Well," I said, "I'll have to trust to Providence."

"I never saw any good come from that story," said Thomas. "Providence looks after those who look after themselves. There was a man livin' in this neighbourhood many years ago—before your time—and he was a religious man as well—he was the most feckless fellow I ever saw, and he was always talkin' about trustin' to Providence. Do you know where he died? Holywell workhouse! Poor fellow! In a way, I'd rather you hadn't said to me what sort of place this college is, because once you go Barbara and I will be wonderin' all the time if you have enough food. I see you leavin' a good place and goin' to the mountains, where life is hard—or so the sock sellers told me; and for my part, I don't see that the game is worth the candle. I'd think better of it if they taught preachin' there. But you know best, and it's not my business to interfere; if your mother were still alive, I doubt that she'd let you go. What does Abel say? Is he in favour of you goin'?"

"Oh yes," I said, "Abel is encouraging me to go."

"Well, I'll give in to him; Abel's a shrewd old gentleman; I never saw him make a mistake," said Thomas.

"Talking of Abel," said I, "that reminds me that it's time for me to go home. Abel's not altogether well this evening, and I promised to go home early."

---

[6] Possibly the same man we met in Chapter 23, where he was called John Jones Talsarn—Llanllyfni is just the next village along in Dyffryn Nantlle, just outside Caernarfon.

"Worst of all," said Thomas; "I hope it's nothin' serious. I don't know what would become of us in that chapel if anythin' happened to the old sergeant major; it'd all be higgledly piggledy. You know what? When your mother was alive it was as good as a sermon just to hear the two of 'em talkin'. They never talked about 'utility', you know, and that sort of thing, but about Jesus Christ and heaven, and I would listen to 'em as happy as a pig in a field of barley; I never tired of it all night, and I hated to see Abel get up to leave—I felt that I hadn't had half enough. You know what I used to do?—I hope it wasn't a sin—when I saw Abel comin', I'd turn the clock back by half an hour; but I couldn't let your mother see me doin' it, because she was so strict, you know, about things like that. Well, I won't stop you, if Abel is waitin'. Remember the two of us to him, and good night to you. Wait! Here you are, as you've decided to go to college, if it won't be too much trouble for you to carry, you're welcome to a piece of this side of bacon, we'll still have enough. Well, well, you've only got yourself to blame, you know that you're very welcome to it. Good night."

I was glad to be able to leave so that I could laugh out loud; and I thought what if poor Wil Bryan had been there with me in the Twmpath that night, what sort of a report he would have been able to make of the conversation with 'that old *thoroughbred* Thomas Bartley', as he used to call him. A hundred memories came to my mind as I hurried home, about the way that my brother Bob used to smooth the creases on my mother's serious and wizened face after he had been at Thomas Bartley's house 'leading him on'. Bob could imitate him to a T; and I saw him make my mother cross because she had to laugh in spite of herself. I suppose there are times in every man's life when he looks like a lunatic; and if someone had taken a photograph of me that night, as I walked quickly past the Manor woods, the look on my face would have been very strange, as I was laughing and crying at the same time. Now I come to think of it, it's strange for me to think that Thomas Bartley was involved in so many of the biggest events of my life;

but I little thought during the minutes as I was walking back from the Twmpath, that I would always remember that evening but not only as material with which to entertain my companions.

I had been away from the Corner Shop for no more than an hour and a half; and when I was just a few yards away from it on my way home, I met Jones, who had been looking for me everywhere except in the Twmpath. He said that Abel was very sick. I didn't hear any other word he said; and the next minute I was in my dear old master's room. I'll never forgive myself for leaving him that evening. I found him lying on the sofa, where I left him when I started for the Twmpath. Sitting on a chair beside him was Dr Bennett, or, as we called him, the Works Doctor. Behind him, at the end of the sofa, was Miss Hughes, making an immense effort to hide the beating of her heart. The scene is alive in my memory; how could I forget it! With her left arm, which appeared as a piece of pure tenderness, Miss Hughes held the patriarchal head of the only man she loved with her whole heart throughout her life; and with her right hand she held a glass of some cordial, which her brother refused or rather was unable to take. I think there were two other women in the room, but I can't remember who they were. Beforehand, I wouldn't have believed it possible for a man to undergo such a transformation in so little time without somebody having attacked him from outside. The 'fine old fellow', as Wil Bryan used to call him, was a powerless wreck, like a ruined building struck by lightning, his glory laid low. The face, which had shone with wisdom, understanding and kindness just two hours before, was now like the face of a drunken fool. The tongue that never said anything except that which was sensible and edifying had now forgotten its function; and nothing came from its owner's mouth except an inarticulate noise, similar to the awful voice of the deaf and dumb. Apart from his right arm, it looked as though my dear master's whole body was paralysed. I had been in the room for some minutes before he took any notice of me. However, when he did, he became excited; and started to cry like a child. The next minute he pointed at me and then at the cupboard, trying hard to speak. I knew very well what he wanted, but I pretended not to understand. Again and again he tried to make his wishes understood; and the doctor asked me if I knew what he wanted, and I said... well, I said what wasn't true, namely that I didn't know. It was obvious to everybody in the room that Abel wished to say something to me. I knew exactly what that was. But if I had said to the doctor and to Miss Hughes that my kind master's wish was that I should have been given some of the bank notes from out of the cash box, wouldn't they have had cause to doubt me? But I was sure—as sure as I'm writing these words right now—that that was his only desire at the time. I thought that his mental powers were undimmed, but that the channels that had served them for seventy-five years were now refusing to be obedient to them. Again and again he tried to talk to me, and failing he burst into tears. The doctor urged me to leave the room, as I was obviously disturbing the patient; but respectfully I refused. I had left him when I should not have done, and I didn't want to do that again. I was in a very difficult situation. My heart bled with sympathy for the best, kindest and most godly man I had ever known. It was in my power to quieten his mind by making his wishes known; and it was very important to me personally, with my future depending on it to a large extent; but I didn't dare to do so for fear it would cause some to doubt my character. I prayed quietly and earnestly for my master to have the power to speak; but every minute seemed to drive him further from us, and lessen our hope that he would ever again talk to any of us. With a great deal of trouble we carried him to his bed, and used every means possible to try to restore him; but nothing had any effect. As I said, he hadn't wholly lost the use of his right arm. I sat by his bedside, and my hand was in his. He appeared to be in a happy sleep for many hours, but when I tried to pull my hand from his, he woke uncomfortably. The doctor said that he could continue like this for days, and went away promising to return in the morning. He had already persuaded Miss Hughes to go and take some rest, as there was nothing she could do for her brother; and he had secured an experienced nurse to wait with me and watch the patient. The weather was warm, and the room was quiet, and soon the 'experienced nurse' fell into a deep sleep. Dr Bennett held no hope for my dear master's restoration, and by now neither did I; but I continued to pray earnestly to God— not from any selfish motive—for his tongue to be freed if only for a minute. Was I heard? If I said yes, who would believe me? I had been watching for an hour, maybe two, and the 'experienced nurse' had been sleeping for just as long. The breaths of my kind old patron were so light and quiet, that I thought he had gone. I gently let go of his hand, and he awoke like a small child in its cot. He looked at me and said—well, I have never repeated his few words to anyone; because I thought Dr Bennett might say that the thing was impossible, and that I had been dreaming, and others might say that I told the story for selfish reasons, and others would say that the whole thing had been animal magnetism.[7] It doesn't matter now. I know this—that I made no use of his words to attain my own ends; but I keep them in my heart as a memento of how pure his intentions were towards me in his last minutes. The next moment his soul had crossed the great divide; and in the annals of death I don't believe that anyone better, more faithful, or more godly has passed through its dark doors, except One.

---

[7] The phrase had a completely different meaning in the 19th century from how it is popularly used today. Then, it denoted a sort of supernatural communication with somebody in a higher state of consciousness, closely linked to spiritualism but usually with a living subject.

35

TROUBLESOME

When an old oak tree falls in a storm, its roots having reached far and deep, the earth is rent about it and the other oaks for some distance around are less secure. Those which were closest to it feel the most from its fall: and some of them are wounded so deeply that neither the breezes of summer, nor rain, dew or warmth, can ever heal the scars. In the death of Abel Hughes, even the drunks hanging around on street corners and the worst characters in the town had the conviction that a good man had been lost. The tradesmen lost from their midst an example of a man who could deal with the world without telling a lie, while earning an honest living without wanting for anything. Let us hope he is not the last of such old-fashioned people! But it was the chapel that sustained the greatest loss. The inhabitants of the town could not conceive of Methodism without thinking of Abel; and Seth—the foolish boy—was right when he called the chapel 'Abel's chapel'; when he fell, everyone felt that the chapel had lost its heart. There weren't a dozen people in the church who could remember the Great Seat without Abel in it: and the majority of them had recited their verses to him when they were children, and been received into full membership by him. He knew the spiritual and temporal trials of almost every family in the church; and there was scarcely a Methodist house in the town where he had not at some time sat by someone's bedside praying with them and counselling them. The old men and women who were dependent on the parish, as well as others of higher status, were able to tell their stories to Abel without fear of their secrets being revealed. For many years he had acted as the pastor of the church, with this advantage: he could tell the truth, in public or in private, without fear that he'd be told to leave or that he'd see the church collection plate diminished. The truth stands; but how many of us are content to stand with it, without embellishing it in our own trimmings? 'They knew that they were naked'.[1] When we are possessed by truths we know we ought to tell, don't we tend to dress them up in clothes of our own making? On the other hand you meet people sometimes who boast that they are honest and that they love to tell the truth and 'speak plainly', but they show so much harshness and insensitivity that the wise look upon their 'plain speaking' as the result of bad manners and ignorance. In these people's thinking the truth is a knife, and 'the truth that slays' is their only truth. To this day many churches have within them religious butchers and executioners. The former like nothing better than slicing their brethren up into four quarters and a head, to display on their stalls; while the latter like to hang them and have done with it. To speak figuratively, Abel could use a knife, but not a butcher's knife. He would use it not to end life, but to save it. Once Abel believed there was a danger, he would not dilly-dally but would convince the victim that his life was indescribably precious, and that the severity of the procedure was necessary to save it. And as a rule, those who had spent the longest under his hand were his most zealous and faithful friends. I think it was the experience of everyone raised in the church that as a child they regarded Abel as too strict, sharp and bitter, but as they grew into age and sense, so their ideas about him mellowed. During their childhood they saw him as an unripe crab apple that set their teeth on edge; but as they grew they came to see him as a big, golden apple, round, ripe and sweet. Rarely, as Thomas Bartley said, would Abel make a mistake; and many times I saw church members who were zealous and enthusiastic about this or that, but when they learned Abel thought differently they began to doubt—not him—but themselves. Many times in the *seiat*, I saw John Lloyd rising to his feet to hold forth upon some gripe or other that he had;

[1] Gen. 3:7.

371

and one could think sometimes, to listen to him, that religion had disappeared from the land and that some particular people in the church, whom he wouldn't name, were guilty of every imaginable evil. Then Abel would get up, and with a dozen or so wise words would clear the air and calm everybody down, and then go straight to old Betty Cynrig or Thomas Bartley to ask them for a word about their experiences; and within two minutes everyone would have forgotten about John Lloyd and his lecture. Wil Bryan hated John Lloyd; and nothing amused him more than to see Abel 'sitting on him', as he'd say. Many times after coming home from the *seiat*, Wil would ask me, 'Did you spot Abel putting the old Scratcher's bonfire out by spitting on it? I swear that was the smartest move I've seen since I don't know how long'. Abel had a knack of deflating anyone who was boastful and full of themselves. Having done so, he would never talk about it, but I often thought that the task gave him pleasure; because after coming home, he would sit in his corner by the fire and a smile would spread across his face as if he were enjoying a private joke. He was a strict man and couldn't tolerate a harum-scarum believer; but whatever a man's flaws, if Abel believed he was honest, he could sympathise with him deeply. I said in a previous chapter that I've never seen anyone like Abel for knowing a man's heart. He had studied his own for a lifetime, and I often heard him say that it was more deceptive than any. Because of that he could understand and advise a young man fighting with temptations and doubts; he could sympathise with those in trouble, put up with the ignorant if he could see some good in them, and share the spiritual joy and sorrow of the experienced old people. But idleness, apathy, hypocrisy and false spirituality—these he couldn't stand at all. I had a better opportunity than anyone to get to know him well. To me he never once appeared to be proud of his own virtues; but when he saw those virtues shining even to a lesser extent in other people, his face glowed with pleasure. He had set himself such a high standard that he was always conscious of his failures; but he looked at others, who in my opinion weren't worthy to be compared with him, with envy. His sincerity and mental capacity gave him an authority in the church that no-one dared or wanted to challenge or spoil.

I must acknowledge that these weren't the considerations that filled my mind when Abel Hughes died. They were much more selfish. I felt that I had lost my most valuable friend, and that at a time when my future, humanly speaking, depended almost wholly upon him. I'm ashamed to think how selfish I was. At the time I feared that my prospects were diminished. I remember that I felt surprised and aggrieved that no-one appeared to show any sympathy towards me. Everyone said what a loss it was to the cause, and all the sympathy flowed to Miss Hughes. 'Poor Miss Hughes!' 'What will Miss Hughes do now?' 'Well, poor Miss Hughes will be all on her own after losing her brother'. 'Who will Miss Hughes find to run the business? There's that boy going to college; but it would be much better for him to stay home and help Miss Hughes if he has any feeling'. 'You don't think Rhys Lewis will think of leaving Miss Hughes in the trouble she is in now, do you? Shame on him if he does'. That's how people spoke. Everyone thought of Miss Hughes, and as far as I know no-one thought of Rhys Lewis. Why? Because no-one knew that Abel's chief wish was that I should go to college, and because he hadn't told anyone except me that I shouldn't want for a penny while I was there and that I should always think of the Corner Shop as my home. I realised the bitterness of my loss in his death, and I felt myself all alone and without support. I knew that I was being selfish, but I couldn't help it. I saw that my plans had been confounded, and at the time I thought that no course of action was open to me besides giving up the idea of going to college and getting stuck into the business again. At the same time Abel's words came back to me, 'Don't even think of preaching *and* shopkeeping', and I thought I would have to give up preaching as well. My heart fell within me. I had no taste at all for commerce; indeed I was set against it, and I felt that I wasn't to blame for this—my master Abel had led me to this, and had bred in me a distaste for business and directed my inclinations towards other things. For a long time before his death he had allowed me the greatest freedom; he asked me to do next to nothing in the shop if he saw me busy with my books, and I was not idle. By this time, though, I feared that all the trouble he had taken with me was in vain, and that all my own efforts had gone with the wind. The more I thought about this, the more I pitied myself and the less prepared I was to accept my fate. As I have described in an earlier chapter, Miss Hughes had been very kind to me even when I was a mischievous boy, and my debt to her was great. She was a simple and innocent old girl, not at all similar to her brother Abel except in her faithfulness and kindness. She took no interest in the things that Abel and I talked about; and I was often amazed at how little she realised the things that her brother was famous for. To her there was no difference between one preacher and another; they were all good, and she showed as much respect to the least as to the greatest. She read a chapter of the Bible in her bedroom every night without fail, and slept soundly after that; but I don't know that she ever read anything else except on the Sabbath, when she would pick up a copy of *The Treasury*,[2] open it somewhere at random, and immediately start to doze. Miss Hughes knew next to nothing about the business, and I feared when Abel died that she knew only little about her financial circumstances; and yet Miss Hughes was a good woman and perfectly filled the role to which she had been called. She kept the house clean and charming, and her hospitality was sincere to everyone whom Abel brought under her roof. Her brother's sudden death was a heavy blow to her, and I sympathised deeply with her; and it appeared that many others did as well, because 'many had come to comfort her concerning her brother'.[3] Seeing the sheer number of visitors—each one kind and well-meaning, no doubt—I think that I acted wisely in asking

---

[2] '*Y Drysorfa*', the Calvinistic Methodist magazine in which this novel was originally serialised!

[3] John 11:19.

a sensible woman to take care of Miss Hughes and prevent her from being drowned in sympathy. And one of the things that gave me the most comfort at the time was that I managed by myself to carry out the arrangements for my old master's funeral to everyone's satisfaction, without consulting anyone except David Davies. Or perhaps not. It's remarkable to think about the dream-like state that I was in at the time. With all the arrangements, I always felt that my old master was beside me; and it was as though I did everything according to his instructions. On the sad day when we buried him, when I was 'conscious of' rather than actually seeing the hundreds of people who came together, I remember thinking in amazement how small was the hole that he was placed into, and how big was the hole that he had left behind and that no-one else could fill. When David Davies and I returned from the cemetery, I imagined I could hear my old master saying to us, 'Thank you, Rhys—thank you, David Davies; you did well', while David and I answered, 'we have done no more for you than we should'.

David came into the house with me, and we sat in the old kitchen, as there were some women with Miss Hughes in the parlour. (If anyone reads these lines, no doubt they will think me foolish for recording such silly details.) I was hoping that David would sit in Abel's old armchair; but he didn't do that, and took instead the chair that he had usually sat in when Abel was alive. The old chair was empty; and beside it, on the wide mantelpiece, was his pipe, exactly where he had put it after using it for the last time four days before that evening. David didn't say it to me, nor did I say it to him; but we both felt as if we were still expecting Abel to come back in. How hard it is to come to terms with the final departure of someone who has for years been part of our lives! After speaking about this and that, David eventually asked me what I was intending to do next; did I think it would be wise, under the circumstances, to go to college? I said that I wasn't ready to answer that question.

"No-one would blame you," said David, "for not going to Bala now—the way things are—Abel being taken so suddenly—Miss Hughes left on her own—and she knowing nothing about the business. In fact, I think people would think more of you if you weren't to go. What about waiting for another year to see how things will be?"

He spoke tenderly and persuasively; but his words stung me to the heart. What, I thought, David Davies telling me not to go to college! I felt wounded, and I told him, somewhat agitatedly, "David Davies, if I don't go to the college now, I won't ever go. If I see, after considering the matter, that it is my duty to stay here, then I'll give preaching the fling for good; but otherwise, nothing will stop me from going. But tonight I can't see clearly what my duty is, and I don't want to talk about it."

"Pray for light, then," said David, and he got up to go home. But before he left, I took him into the parlour to see Miss Hughes. Her friends had left her, all apart from the one 'sensible woman'. I had only been able to speak to her a little since her brother's death. In her trouble she left everything to me; and whenever I asked her for advice, 'you know best' was all I could get from her. Naturally enough, when we appeared she burst into tears, and couldn't say anything for some time. I did the same, since to tell the truth, although I was selfish I wasn't hard-hearted. In due course, she said:

"David Davies, isn't Rhys doing well? I always liked him—he knows that himself. When he first came here he was very wicked, and Abel was so strict, and I always took his side, he knows. You won't leave me to go to that old college, will you, Rhys?"

David answered for me, and I was grateful to him. "You can talk about that another time, Miss Hughes," and after adding some comforting words, David went away.

I felt very sorry for myself that evening. I sat by the fire in the kitchen for some hours, thinking things over. The old clock had stopped, and everyone had been too distracted to wind it up again. I feared that Providence was telling me clearly that I wasn't to go to college, and if so then it was saying something else as well—that I wasn't to preach; because Abel had told me more than once that no young man in this enlightened age should consider the ministry unless he was prepared to spend years in university first; and at that time I thought it was impossible for Abel's judgement to be wrong. I thought that if I stayed with Miss Hughes then the whole burden of the business would fall upon me, since Jones was no more than a useful fixture. Responsibility for the business would take up almost all my time, and reading and preparing sermons would be out of the question for me. Yet, if I went to college, where would I find the means to pay? I had no hope of winning a scholarship. I saw that they would be won by rich and respectable boys, who'd had a good education while they were still young. But I remembered hearing some of the boys saying that they could live on very little in Bala; and I thought I would be glad to show them that I could live on less than any of them. Apart from a couple of shillings that were loose in my pocket, all the money I had in the world was in my purse. How much did I have? I took the purse from my pocket, emptied it into my hand and put the purse on the table. I counted my assets carefully: six pounds in gold, and ten shillings and sixpence in change—I remember well. While I was looking at my assets in the palm of my right hand, I heard Miss Hughes and her friend coming down the passage to say goodnight to me before going to bed; and I quickly put my wealth in my trouser pocket and pushed my purse to one side, lest they conclude that my meditations were about earthly things. Within a few minutes the house was perfectly quiet; and again my mind started to spin with the situation I was in, and the fact that my circumstances and plans had completely changed in less than a week. I don't know how long I spent in my reverie, but I knew that it was late because every sound in the street outside had ceased, and I could hear nothing except someone walking slowly past the corner of the house. I assumed it was the policeman, and I heard him go past three or four times. I knew that I wouldn't be able to sleep if I went to bed; and by now I felt uncomfortable and sick at heart. I thought a quick walk in the open air would do me good, and out I quietly went, closing the door carefully behind me. It was a lovely and pleasant moonlit night, the air thin and healthy without being cold, and the small happenings of the night are very clear in my memory. A deep silence reigned over the streets as if all their inhabitants had died. I turned down one street, and up another, as if I were going somewhere in particular, although I wasn't. In the second street I saw a light on in the upstairs window of a small house, and I remembered that there was a young girl there who was very sick. Yes, I thought, she is worse off than I am; and there were others around who could not sleep because of worry and 'the multitude of their thoughts within them'.[4] As I went on, I heard a sound in the distance and listened—it was the sound of a wheelbarrow being pushed along the pavement—and I realised that it was 'Ready Ned' at work. Ned always worked at night, and his was work which needed to be done at night. For more than one reason I took another route, and I remember a white cat crossing my path like a ghost. I hurried on, and before I had reached the top of the main road I met with a slightly built man wearing a soft hat, with the front of the brim turned low over his eyes. He looked like a tramp, who was tired and down on his luck. I greeted him with a 'good evening', but he did not answer, and I thought no worse of him for that; for it's possible, I thought, that he was tired and had an empty stomach, and was angry with the hardness of the world, and was too apathetic to answer, and was saying to himself, 'What is your "good evening" worth if you're not going to give anything to me?' We were just outside the town, and I could see no other creature besides William the Coal's mule grazing on the hedgerow. I knew before I reached him, from the sound of the chain, that it was William's mule. I remembered that 'Duke' had a tendency to wander, and William had had to put a chain on him to keep him within the bounds of his own parish. Duke was busy grazing, and

---

[4] Psalm 94:19.

was shaking his head emphatically, as if he were reasoning through something in his head and wanted to make a point; because that time of night it wasn't possible that he was being troubled by flies. As Duke heard me approach, he stopped grazing and the clicking of his jaw stopped in mid-mouthful; he looked as if he were astonished that William was coming to collect him so early, and his two ears stood up like two exclamation marks!! In any case, when he saw his mistake, Duke went back to grazing, and to his argument with himself. And so I went on. I thought about this and that, but eventually I came to myself. I was aware of a deep and honest craving for knowledge, and for being of some service to God and man, and yet it seemed that everything was forcing me back behind the counter to sell cloths, woollens and calico for the rest of my life. I tried to comfort myself and see things another way. What difference did it make? There was no shortage of young men more able than me to go into the ministry, who were in advantageous situations to be able to prepare themselves for the work. I looked up at the enormous sky above me, speckled throughout with stars. What difference would it make, I thought, if that small star over there in the distance were darkened forever? Nobody would notice it had gone missing. Yet it looked pretty as it sparkled, and no doubt it was serving somebody or something. Yes, there are a few clouds in the sky. How beautifully the bright moon shines! But there's a cloud that comes along and completely covers it. How similar it is to me! But I see that the cloud is going past—part of its face is already visible—yes, now the cloud has left it altogether, and the gentle moon is as bright as before. Will the cloud pass me, I wonder? All things are possible for Him! These are the thoughts that were going through my mind when I imagined that I heard somebody walking behind me. I looked back, but saw no-one. I suddenly turned on my heel, and started for home. I hadn't gone many yards when I saw a man get up from the side of the hedge and walk to meet me. I recognised that it was the tramp who I had seen earlier; but now he didn't appear to be at all tired.

The brim of his hat no longer covered his eyes. I thought that he had evil intentions towards me, and I thought of escaping—but how could I know whether he was armed? I though the wisest thing would be to confront him and make the best of it. When we came face to face, I recognised him straight away, and he said:

"You mustn't think that I was too proud to speak to you earlier on when I didn't answer you. No, no, I'll never be too proud to own my own family; but I take care not to lower myself by talking to every sort. Well, how…"

"Uncle," I said, cutting across his silly story—"do you remember what I said to you last time I saw you?"

"Good evening," he said.

"You know that's not what I mean," I said. "Do you remember what I said to you in Niclas' garden at Garth Ddu?"

"Well, wait a moment, my memory's not bad. What was it now? Oh! I remember—you'd give me a sovereign the next time you saw me. It's funny how a man can forget things!"

"You know different," I said, "and that this is what I told you—that if you ever showed your face again in this neighbourhood I'd give you straight to the police, and I shall too."

"Bosh!" he said carelessly. "Look—when you want to make a good aim, never use a double-barrelled shotgun. And that's the disadvantage of a revolver—it's good for nothing except at short range. Aren't I your uncle, your father's brother? Whose disgrace would it be if you handed me to the police? James Lewis', or Rhys Lewis'? What does James Lewis care about disgrace? But I know a young chap who wouldn't like it at all. Eh? But I don't want to argue with you. It's not a respectable thing for relatives to quarrel with one another. Let bygones be bygones. So Abel has gone to answer for himself, has he? The old miser, he'll have a lot to answer for, as will I."

"There you go, Uncle," I said, "I'd rather you killed me than made me listen to you talk disrespectfully about my kind old master."

"Well, well," he said, "I don't want to hurt your feelings. It was a good job for you that Abel legged it; you'll be the boss now, because what does the old woman and that born idiot Jones know about the business? If you don't make your fortune now, it will be your fault, and I hope you won't be shabby with me. I'm the only relative you have now; and I've been right unlucky lately. I haven't had a haul since I don't know when, and I was almost nabbed last week. I had to fight like a …"

"I can't abide your ungodly talk, Uncle, and I have to leave you," I said.

"I don't want to take up lodging with you, because that would be a loss to you and to me; but I need money, and I must get money or starve. Perhaps you don't have much with you tonight, but I can come round now and again when you're the boss, as I see you're a late bird just like me."

"While I'm there you won't be allowed to set foot in the house," I said. "And apart from that, I'm as poor as you are."

"That's your fault," he said. "If you hadn't swallowed that nonsense your mother taught you, you wouldn't be poor. I wouldn't be poor if I'd had your chance."

I must tell the truth, that when he mentioned 'that nonsense your mother taught you' I felt at the time that I could have strangled him with pleasure; and I had to hold myself back from rushing at his throat. I had such a struggle to control my sinful nature that I couldn't talk for a minute. When I managed to get a grip on myself—God forgive me for my foolish words—I said to him,

"You scoundrel! If you say one more disrespectful word about my mother then I'll tear you to shreds. My mother taught me to live honestly."

As I said these words, my uncle stepped back two or three yards and looked surprised at me, and I saw him fumbling for something in his pocket. I wasn't frightened; and I was quite happy to fall as a sacrifice to his anger while defending the character of the best mother in the world, as I saw it. After a minute's silence, he said with perfect self-possession:

"I'm glad to see that you have some of the family's pluck in you. I always thought you were a bit of a chicken. I think a hundred times more highly of you now. If I said anything disrespectful about your mother then I apologise. Your mother was a good sort in her way, and she did me many kindnesses. Why do you always want to fight with me? Let's be chums. When your father used to hit you, he was as cool as a turnip. I'm sorry if I've annoyed you; but you know why I'm here. I need money, I have none to buy food, and I know you'd like to keep me out of trouble."

"I don't want anything to do with you," I said. "Tell me which way you're going, and I'll go a different way. I'm not going to walk a step with you."

"Agreed," he said, "but give me what you have—perhaps you don't have much on you."

I was my mother's son, as I said before. I thought that I only had a few shillings and some small change loose in my pocket, and I emptied it for him. He thanked me, and went on, and I went home.

His meeting with me had driven me to a decision. Now I didn't dare stay home to be pestered by this accursed creature. I felt that he'd had the upper hand over me, that he understood my weakness, and that I wouldn't dare hand him over to the authorities without bringing myself to shame. It was obvious that he didn't know I was preaching; and when I went to college he would lose my scent, and he wouldn't dare to ask after me. I believed that Providence had brought me face to face with the scoundrel that night, and that it was urging me to throw myself into its arms. And I decided to do that, and go to college come what may. And I felt grateful to think that when I would be with the boys in college, none of them would know my background, although I wouldn't be able to take advantage of my family connections. And perhaps, I thought, some of them would have backgrounds that they wanted no-one to know about. Having made my decision, I felt happy and in my element. Indeed, I felt so cheerful that I could enjoy the different view I had of Duke when I went back past him. The old brother had had his fill and was dozing on his feet, with one leg hanging loosely, his head low and still as if he had won his argument some time ago. I thought that Duke would have his story to tell, like me, if he were able to tell it, and others besides—more interesting, perhaps. I walked past quickly and went into the house as quietly as I could. When I lit the gas, one of the first things I saw was my purse on the side of the table. I picked it up, and it was empty! For shame! I had given my last farthing to the 'Irishman', as I had called him since I was a small boy. I realised my situation with horror. I had decided to go to college, but I didn't have so much as a penny to pay my fare there! I stood, sad and astonished, in the middle of the kitchen floor where Abel had encouraged me many times to trust in God. I thought that he was testing me harshly. I sat, put my head in my hands on the table, and nearly cried my eyes out.

36

A FAMILIAR CHARACTER

I look on the night I tried to describe in the previous chapter as one of the big nights of my short life. I felt lonely and without support, as if everything had conspired together to deprive me of the thing I had set my heart on. I feared that I wasn't in God's favour, and that my convictions and all I'd had to do with religion were just falseness and hypocrisy. Without flattering myself, I knew that men found me a reasonably acceptable preacher; but why, I asked myself, did God in His Providence seem to throw every obstacle into my way? I can say clearly and honestly that I wasn't covetous for money, and that the desire of my heart was to preach and to train myself and to be trained for that work; and yet I had to think that I couldn't do anything without money, and because of my own folly I was now as poor as a church mouse. I thought so little about money that I hadn't learned to take care of it. As I said before, I believe there was a burning desire in me to be useful in my day and age; and yet by now I didn't have a penny to put towards preparing myself for that. I thought, I'm afraid to say with a resentful spirit, about the scores of men I knew who were swimming in money, without ever imagining serving anyone but themselves, and Wil Bryan's expression came powerfully back to my mind—'The old pockets! They're nothing but *intelligent pigs*. You can see that the Good Lord doesn't place much value on money or he wouldn't give so much of it to those rascals,' and added—'but Sir, said Mr Fox, aren't they sour?'[1]

A question came to my mind suddenly: had I perhaps trusted too much in Abel Hughes, and was Providence encouraging me to

---

[1] A reference to Aesop's fable of the fox and the grapes.

throw myself into its arms as I was, by stripping me of any other source of help? It seemed presumptuous for me to think of going to the college without anything around me save for plenty of clothes and a few books. I remembered the man whom Thomas Bartley mentioned, who, after trusting in Providence, died in the Holywell workhouse. Even so, I decided to do my best with the work that I had begun; and I sought to believe that God would soon give me some light upon my circumstances. Very early the next morning, I informed Miss Hughes of my decision to go to college. She was shocked! She couldn't believe, she said, that I could be so cruel towards her. I tried to reason with her, but there was no point. Miss Hughes looked at everything through her heart, not through her reason. She offered me a good salary if I stayed with her; but I refused. After much talking, she very generously offered me a share in the business; but I refused that too. Finally, she fell back on the most effective argument that any woman has—she burst into tears. She went through all the kindness she had shown to me— how poor I had been when I came to the Corner Shop—what a comfortable home I'd had there—what a kindness it was for me to be able to be trained by Abel—and what state I'd be in apart from that. She said I was without feeling, unkind, hard-hearted, ungrateful, and selfish. She used many other adjectives besides. She protested that I didn't care about anyone except myself, and that I wouldn't care in the least if I saw her forced to 'go on the parish'. She said that the fact that she knew nothing about the business, nor about her brother's affairs, kindled no sympathy in me. As far as she knew, she added, she could be homeless within three months. I listened to her quietly, and felt that I was guilty of all her accusations. My fears that Miss Hughes knew nothing about her brother's circumstances were confirmed. I asked her to calm down and wait until the next day, when, I believed, I would be able to give her some good advice. She replied pointedly that if she could do without my help, then she could do without my advice as well. I didn't say a word in reply, and today I regret that.

I went to the shop, and with the help of Jones I worked hard all day and all night. Miss Hughes didn't know, and I expect didn't care, what we were up to, and didn't say a word to either of us. I should have said that as soon as Abel died, Miss Hughes had passed all the keys into my hand; as in those hours she was perfectly indifferent to everything and ready to give up the ghost. After beginning my task, I didn't rest until I had taken a basic count of all the stock. Since Abel didn't usually give credit to customers apart from a few exceptions, it didn't take long to search through the shop's books. Within twenty-four hours, I had a pretty accurate idea of the estate that my master had left behind. As I wrote the last item down, Jones sat down on the stool; he placed his head, which had been swimming around for some time, on the counter, and slept like a top. Under different circumstances I would have thought this an unforgivable liberty; but considering how incapable Miss Hughes was, and also the consciousness I had that my old master would not disapprove, I didn't hesitate to open every cupboard, chest and drawer, and to search their contents. And I remember very well that when I opened one of the drawers, the one that was inside the oak cabinet where Abel kept all his private papers—I remember that as I opened that drawer the devil came out, and I had a fierce battle with him. In the drawer there was a wad of bank notes, and the devil said to me, "Do you hear Jones snoring? Do you remember that Abel intended to give a number of these to you? You know that there is no memorandum of these; and if there were, it would be easy to destroy it. If you took two or three, or four, of them, that wouldn't be anything that you wouldn't have had from Abel if he'd lived. It's just the same thing for you to take them as it would have been for Abel to give them to you. It wouldn't be theft at all because, in a sense, some of them are yours. It's likely you won't get so much as a thank you from Miss Hughes for all your trouble. Well, if you're not willing to take two or three of them then take one—just one; I'm sure Abel would have given more than that to you. Don't forget that you don't have a shilling to your name, and you can't go on without any money; and whatever sum you take, you of all people are sure to make good use of it."

With many other arguments my enemy tried to overcome me; but thank God! I remembered the armour that my mother had left me; and it was never so useful to me as it was that time, and with it I drove the devil away. When I had completed the task I had set myself, I went to speak to Miss Hughes with a clear conscience, and spotless hands; and this was worth more to me than a million pounds. I had a cold and indifferent reception from her; but I didn't care about that, and I greeted her with words as close as I can remember to these:

"Miss Hughes, you didn't need to remind me about all your kindness to me, because I've never forgotten it for so much as one day. I know that you think I am hard-hearted for leaving you and going to college. But I think that you believe that I am honest, or you would not have trusted so much into my hands; and I would not have done what I just have. I have cause to believe that you know nothing about the position you have been left in through the death of my master; and I find it strange that a man as wise as he would have kept this knowledge from you, and stranger still that he did not make a will. Without asking for your permission, I have made a pretty detailed investigation into all his affairs; and I have found, after paying all his creditors, that my master has left—between the stock, the cash that's on the books, in the bank, and in the house—assets of fifteen hundred pounds.[2] This will be enough to keep you fairly comfortably, and to live to a good old age; and my advice is—you can refuse it if you want to—to sell the stock and the business. I think I know of a friend of mine who would be happy to take everything off your hands. But as for me staying here to look after the business, that is out of the question. I am determined to go to college; and I'm sure that if you

---

[2] Somewhere in excess of £1 million in 2015 values. For comparison, a typical miner's wage at the time was £30 per annum and a miner's cottage would cost between £50 and £100 to purchase. Abel Hughes was a man of substance!

were able to ask my old master he would say that I am doing the right thing."

My words had an effect on her like magic: her sourness melted like ice on slate in the sunshine, but much more quickly. She looked at me incredulously for a moment—and then happily and kindly as had always been usual, for she and I were always great friends—and she said:

"I've spoken very hatefully to you, Rhys; I didn't know what I was saying. I know that you'll forgive me. I always liked you, you know yourself, and I know that you have more sense than me. Poor Abel always said that when you were a lad you could wrap me round your little finger. You know best, and I'll do as you say. If I had someone here instead of you, perhaps he'd rob me, wouldn't he? I've known for a long time that you have a going-to-Bala nature about you, and I won't try to stop you. You'll find everything that you want in Bala, and you'll be in your element. Must you go next week? Can't you wait a fortnight? What will you have for your lunch? Can I make you some stewed kidneys?" And so on and so on.

"*Simple woman!*' something told me; 'ask her for what you need—money'. 'No I won't', I said, 'no, independence is worth something; and I won't ask her for a penny, even though I know she wouldn't refuse me if I asked'. It was pretty obvious to me that Miss Hughes knew no more about the college than Thomas Bartley did, and that she looked on Bala as the next best thing to heaven, and that the students there were like the angels of God neither marrying nor eating nor drinking.[3] Poor thing! If she were to search the thing out, she would find that the students were guilty of each of these things to greater or lesser degrees. Thomas Bartley and Miss Hughes were not the only ones, it seemed, who thought that Bala was a town flowing with milk and honey and that once a boy got to go there he'd be all right. As far as I knew, no-one in church where I was a member was opposed to my going to the college; and the Monthly Meeting had unanimously urged me to go there. But not a living soul had asked me, apart from Thomas Bartley, what view I had of how I would support myself, even though by that time I hadn't lost so much as one of my teeth.[4] I don't say this with the intention of grumbling. The only man, as far as I could see, who realised how much of a challenge it was for a poor boy to go to college was Abel Hughes, and he was now in his grave. Yet I was determined to give a challenge to Providence. Did she accept the challenge? We shall see. I considered that it was my duty to do what I could for Miss Hughes before I left her. To cut a long story short, I succeeded, with the help of a man who was experienced with such things, to transfer the business to the friend who was keen to have it; and I calculated that Miss Hughes, when everything had been settled, would be worth fourteen hundred pounds, or just a hundred pounds less than I had estimated in the first place. In addition to this, I had arranged with the buyer for poor Jones to be regarded as one of the fixtures; and with this, I felt the burden that had been on my conscience since Wil Bryan and I had nearly hanged the poor creature was lightened by no small amount.

As I was gathering my things together, and packing my books into an old tea chest, I stood still and quietly several times; and something said to me, "What a fool you were to let go of a good job, with an excellent salary, and lose the opportunity to one day be a successful businessman! You must be out of your mind!" But something else said *in* me, "So what? The 'old pockets' can have the business and all the money as far as I'm concerned, so long as I can somehow go to college and make some sort of a living there." I believed that my aim was simple and honest, and I tried to believe also that Providence would not let me starve. I knew that if I told my best friends about my poverty, they would help me

---

[3] Matt. 22:30.

[4] The meaning of this idiom, not used anywhere else in Welsh literature as far as I know, is not particularly clear; it may refer to his youth, or perhaps to his poverty (too poor to afford many sweets).

heartily; but I was too proud to do that. It was Friday night, and the following Monday I was due to go to the college. I didn't have an appointment to preach on the Sunday, because I had refused one, thinking that I might need to get to the college sooner, but by now I regretted it. I remember Wil Bryan's comment about me, that I was '*poor and proud*'. But there was nothing I could do about that: I had inherited the foolish independence from my mother, and I prayed earnestly for help in keeping it, as in my view it was very precious. But that Friday night it seemed to me that Providence had decided to humble me, and to force me to do something I had never done before, namely, ask to borrow a sovereign, without knowing how I might pay it back. From whom could I borrow? There was only one man in the world I could ask, and that man was Thomas Bartley. As far as Thomas was concerned, I felt that the sovereign would be in my hand before I asked for it; and he was so innocent, I thought, that with a bit of skill I could maintain my dignity as I borrowed it. Thomas was the man. But I was determined not to ask even Thomas until the last minute, lest I run ahead of Providence; because I was trying to believe that she would take care of me. These things were going through my mind when Miss Hughes knocked on my door, and came in; and she said, "Rhys, William Williams, the elder of Blaenycwm, wants to see you." I was down in the kitchen before anyone could count to ten, although I had counted a hundred things in that time. Of course, William was a noble old creature, and his message was that he wanted me to preach in the Cwm on Sunday, since the Rev. _____ "had broken the engagement without giving any reason." My back straightened at that moment; and I don't remember that I have ever except for on that occasion rejoiced because somebody had broken their engagement. But what a knave I was! I gave various reasons for not going to the Cwm, the main one of which was that I would be going to college on the following Monday. William said that that was the best reason for me to obey, and if I did then he would make sure that I'd be home by Sunday night. After a lot of persuasion I agreed to go. I had, you see, learned to play hard-to-get at an early stage when negotiating preaching engagements, but, thank goodness, I learned also to give that up soon. I felt that Providence was beginning to smile on me; and I was in an excellent mood that Sunday, especially in the evening when I was being taken home with ten shillings in my pocket. Even so, I believed that it would be wise to borrow a sovereign from Thomas Bartley so that I would have something 'put by'. Thomas and Barbara had promised to come to the station on Monday morning to say farewell to me. As I was having breakfast, it struck me: what if Thomas didn't have a sovereign in his pocket? As I thought about it, it didn't seem likely that Thomas would carry gold about with him, even though he was reasonably wealthy. I saw that I would have to go to the Twmpath if I were to secure the sovereign; and I hurried through breakfast because there were only two hours to go before I was due to set off for college. "Why are you eating so quickly," Miss Hughes asked me. "Because time is short." I answered. "Remember, Rhys," said Miss Hughes, "I'll be expecting you to come home to spend Christmas with me, if you're not too proud. I'll keep your bed for you, and by that time I'll have moved to live in the cottage." I thanked her, and thought that Providence was seriously at work. "Did Abel owe you any wages?" she asked. "None," I said; "I received my salary up to last Saturday, a month ago." "Here you go," she said, "I know you'll have everything you need in the college, but you probably won't get much pocket money; here's five pounds if you will accept it." I almost cried out Hallelujah! Tears came to my eyes in spite of myself; but to try to hide them I coughed hard as if I had swallowed a piece of bread the wrong way, and I thanked her heartily; and I knew that Miss Hughes was happy that I had not refused it. There was no need, now, to go to the Twmpath, or to ask to borrow a sovereign. I was now as happy as could be. I departed from Miss Hughes on excellent terms. To tell the truth, I did something I hadn't done for many years, since I was a naughty child wanting to borrow a shilling from her—I gave her a kiss on her wrinkled old cheek; and while the simple, kind old girl was sobbing because I was sure to 'break her heart', I 'made my *exit*' as Wil Bryan would have said.

I felt very happy that morning as I left home for the first time, for two reasons: firstly, because Providence seemed to be showing me clearly that she approved of my action in going to the college; and also because I had good reason to believe that I had a place in the hearts of the many friends who came to bid me farewell. Not least among these were David Davies, and Thomas and Barbara Bartley. Whenever Thomas and Barbara went anywhere on the train, they were at the station at least an hour before the time. Although I was at the station that Monday morning a quarter of an hour before departure, Thomas protested that I had almost missed the train. Barbara sat on a hamper on the platform and nodded her head at the end of each paragraph Thomas spoke, and Thomas spoke continuously; and I tried to take in every word he said, thinking it would be useful to entertain whoever I'd be sharing a room with once I got to Bala. When the train came in, I shook hands with each of my friends, and with Barbara, whom I assumed was too tired to get up off the hamper. But as soon as I had taken my seat in the carriage, Barbara leapt to her feet, and Thomas grabbed the hamper and put it on the bench by my side, and said quietly in my ear, "This is for you; take care of it; and remember as soon as we hear of a cheap trip to Bala, Barbara and I are bound to come over to look for you;" and before I could say a word, Thomas was rushing from the station with Barbara leaning on his arm. I was amazed, and yet it was Thomas Bartley all over. I knew that the hamper would have in it valuable treasures for a young man with a healthy stomach; but I showed no curiosity to know its contents, such as weighing it or putting my nose by the lid to smell it, because there was another young man in the same compartment as me—my only fellow traveller—and I didn't want him to know that I wasn't perfectly aware what was inside it. The train sped towards Corwen; and soon I started to take stock of my travelling companion. I don't know whether there is anyone else who feels the same way as me—maybe there is, although it's a very silly thing—but when I travel by train, no matter how many people are in the same compartment as me, once I've been in their company for a little while I get the impression that I've seen them before somewhere, and ought to know them. Of course this is only an illusion, and I don't know how to account for it. Do we, perhaps, unconsciously place faces into classes—or categories—and when we come into the presence of strangers and look at them for a little while, we unconsciously place them into this category or that, and eventually come to think that we ought to know the individual because of our familiarity with the category that he belongs to? I don't know. I thought that I ought to know my companion, even though common sense told me that I'd never seen him before. I guessed that he was three or four years older than me. His skin was pale and his hair and eyebrows were very black, and his clothes a little threadbare, and I had him down as being from Caernarfonshire. He had a book in his hand, but he wasn't reading it, and he looked sadly out through the window—not at the countryside, I was fairly sure of that, but at something else that I didn't know about, perhaps his home, or his family, or his uncertain future. He seemed to be in a deep meditation for a long time. I was eager to be able to talk to him, and I was sure in my mind what sort of voice he would have, and there was no doubt that he was a Welshman. Eventually, I said to him in English that it was a fine day, and he answered in the same language with a Welsh accent. He didn't appear keen to talk, and I was sorry about that because I liked his face very much, and no matter how foolish it seemed I felt that the spirits of my fellow traveller and myself had been in each other's company before we'd ever met each other in the flesh. Soon I was lost in my meditations, as he was. We both disembarked in Corwen, since at that time the train went no further. After I had secured my valuable hamper, and while

I was looking for my clothes trunk and tea chest—which were in the van[5], with my name on—a man tapped me lightly on the shoulder, and said to me, "Mr Lewis, is that your hamper, Sir?"

"Yes," I said, "what about it?"

"Oh, nothing," he said, "except that I want to take care of it for you. What's the matter? Have you all gone on strike? Only two of you have come today, and I was hoping that I'd get a decent load. That's how you always are—coming in dribs and drabs, rather than all coming together and making a decent job of it. Have you got anything else apart from these two boxes and that hamper?"

At first I couldn't make him out. He was a large, cheerful and bold man, and yet his boldness seemed to fit him. It was hard to guess whether he was a farmer, a butcher or a horse dealer. In any case, I soon worked out that he wanted to take me and my things to Bala. When I asked him how he knew that it was to Bala that I was going, he replied,

"Good grief, even if I hadn't read the destination off your box, I'd know in a minute. I can pick a student or a Methodist preacher out of a crowd of a thousand. I've had so much to do with them, Sir. You know, I picked out the other one, and put him in the carriage before you'd even looked around."

"This is a strange man," I said to myself. "I didn't know until now that I looked like a student; and how could I, because I've never been to Bala before?" At the same time I wasn't sorry that this man, whoever he was, took me for a student, and I followed him like a dog following its master. I saw at once that this angel was very well known, and from the greetings he received I learned that his name was Mr Edwards.[6] I noticed that some people were quite bold with him, greeting him with the name of an ingredient that pudding is often made from. I couldn't tell at the time whether this was his real name or a nickname. When he led me to his carriage I was surprised to see that the 'other one' that Mr Edwards mentioned was my sad fellow traveller from the train. And this 'other one' was going to college just like me!

What a pity I hadn't known that before. How had Mr Edwards understood that the moment he saw him, while I had been in his company for quite some time without the idea crossing my mind? I took comfort in the fact that the 'other one' was just as dull as I was. While Mr Edwards was putting my things in his carriage, I looked at his horses; and the first impression they made on me was that there wasn't any danger of them running off and leaving us behind. I didn't know quite what to make of them; whether they were young horses who hadn't yet grown to full strength and put on some flesh, or whether they were old horses about to expire. Although I wasn't an expert on horseflesh, I thought after close inspection that these poor creatures' points were obvious, and so decided that they were in the 'about to expire' category. It took detailed observation to come to this judgement. 'New horses', I thought, 'would not be wise enough to take advantage of the pause in order to take a nap'. I noticed too that one had a smile on its face as it slept, as if it were dreaming about the time when it got to eat oats, and the other one gave a frightened start now and again as if it were conscious of the tanner aiming his gun at him. I suddenly thought that perhaps they, just like the students, 'lived on very little'. My fellow traveller from the train had already taken his place in the carriage, and seemed lost in thought once again. Mr Edwards wasn't prepared to start off with such a small load, and after going round a few times, asking, searching, and bargaining, he eventually succeeded in adding two women to his manifest; and as if to apologise for the delay, he said to me as I was taking my place beside him on the dicky, "We need to get a bit of ballast, you know, Mr Lewis, or we wouldn't be safe." It was one of the strangest things I have ever seen. The crack of Mr

---

[5] That is, the guard's carriage.

[6] In the author's usual fashion—and for reasons lost to posterity—the author refers to 'E_____' throughout this chapter. It becomes clear as the tale progresses that the character is based on some real-life person who would be familiar to visitors to Bala at the time. In the following chapter his identity is revealed as Mr Rice Edwards.

Edwards's whip, and some strange guttural sound that sounded a bit like swearing, had an effect on the horses like the voice in the valley of dry bones.[7] In a second, the poor creatures were all life; and such was their terror of their driver, that it was obvious they'd rather fall dead by the side of the road than to refuse to obey their master.

"You have excellent horses for travelling, Mr Edwards," I said.

"That just depends on who's driving them, Sir," he said. "The students complain terribly that they can't be made to go. Just look here," and Mr Edwards made that guttural noise I mentioned before, and used the whip without sparing, and the horses redoubled their efforts, panting in terror like I have seen animals do when a thunderbolt breaks suddenly above their heads. Mr Edwards added, "You know, Sir, I am the one who rents horses to the students for them to go to their engagements; and if they only did what I told them, the horses would go just fine. They are too gentle by half. You know what? Every horse I have knows the students. They know that the students are preachers, and they take advantage of them. It's no use, Sir, being too particular; if you want the horses to go, you have to _____[8] them. *Getmovingyoudamnedrascals!* Do you see now how they go? Where are you preaching next Sunday? I expect you'll need a horse. Come to me on Friday night. You don't have an engagement? You're bound to have one for next Sunday, because half the students won't have come back yet and there will be a lot of letters asking for preachers, you'll see. I know so much about them, you know, Sir. Have you been to Bala before? Where are you going to lodge?"

It would be impossible for me to describe clearly and in detail the information and advice I received from Mr Edwards during my journey from Corwen to Bala; and it was information that by its nature was of burning interest to me, and I took in every bit of it. Mr Edwards told me the history of the family I was going

---

[7] Ezek. 37:1–14.

[8] The implication being that an expletive was deleted here.

to stay with, in every detail. Without me asking any more than a couple of questions, he provided me with a full outline, in his own way, of the principal characters in Bala. Before I reached the end of my journey, I knew who was who in the Rhiwlas, in the big Bull, in the little Bull, the White Lion, the Plas Coch, and the Post Office; I knew the names of the chapel elders, the medical and theological doctors, and much besides. What I really wanted him to dwell on was the students. He knew the names of every one of them, which county they came from, and who they were staying with. He said of one, "He's very strict," and of another, "There isn't much to him" and of a third "He's a bit of a swell," and so on. He told me various stories about them, and I noticed that every story had something to do with his horses. I considered Mr Edwards a very interesting character, and I'm sure that I never learned so much in such a short period of time in all my life. I liked him because he showed so much interest in the students. I couldn't make out if he was a religious man or not, and it would have been too bold of me to ask him. His detailed knowledge of the chapel people and the cause, and his interest in the students, made me think that he was a believer; but when he shouted at his horses, as if in brackets, with his '*Getmovingyoudamnedrascals!*' I feared that he wasn't. I little thought at that time that I would have so much to do with Mr Edwards during my time in Bala. This minute, many entertaining stories about him come to mind, which were a rich pasture for amusement in the student refectory, and it would be a great pleasure for me to recount them. As it's not Mr Edwards' biography that I'm writing, though, I must leave them for another, more able hand. I wonder, in a world that is so full of pain, and with such innocent but effective material available for driving the clouds of depression away, whether someone else will take in hand the task of writing down the story of a character who was so different from everyone else, and yet in his own way such a good servant to Methodism?

Such was my interest in my driver that I completely forgot

my fellow traveller; but Mr Edwards hadn't, because as soon as we reached Tryweryn Bridge[9] he turned his head and said, "Mr Williams, where are you going to lodge?" and having received the answer, "How handy! The two of you are going to the same house. I'll put these petticoats (referring to the women) down by the bridge." The fact was even 'handier' in my view, as I felt a great interest in my taciturn colleague. Within a few minutes, he and I were sitting in a small, drab parlour, and the woman of the house—a small, merry woman, kind and very Welsh—was preparing tea for us, and telling us that we were the only students in Bala that day. "But," she said, "they'll all have arrived, I think, between now and the end of the week, or within a fortnight at the latest."

When two men of similar mind and aims meet together, and realise that they are likely to live together for some years—living in the same house, and sleeping in the same bed, some ceremony is appropriate to bring about mutual understanding and trust. The wedding takes place without the 'lesson'. Needless to say that Mr Williams and I knew a great deal about each other within half an hour, and we were old friends before the scattered students had gathered themselves together. Mr Williams *was* from Caernarfonshire, as I had guessed, and he was exactly as his face said he would be, an honest, serious and meticulous boy. It's not for me to say how he felt; but I felt happy and fortunate to come into contact for the first time with someone who understood me—someone who was walking the same path, possessed by the same goal, and fighting the same difficulties, someone with whom I could talk without reserve and without fearing that he would laugh at me. Although he was a few years older than me, I was certainly more of an Englishman than he, and I knew more about the way of the world; and I had Wil Bryan and the neighbourhood where I was raised to thank for that. But after a few conversations with Williams, I saw that he was a better theologian than I, and I knew before I ever heard him that he would be a better preacher than me. And so he was, and so he is today, an incomparably better preacher than I am. The boys of Caernarfonshire are fearfully good preachers. I believe the more anglicised the district in which a man is brought up, the worse a preacher he'll be, and vice versa. Williams lived up to be everything I could have dreamed about for a room-mate; and I can't help stating my great debt to him. One occurrence comes fresh to my mind this minute, and I can't help laughing as I think about it. I think I said before that Abel Hughes always took care to see I was well dressed. The day I went to Bala, I was wearing a good black suit. While Williams talked freely with me, I noticed that he was staring at my outfit, and it seemed that he was thinking about something else as he spoke with me. I guessed exactly what was going through the back of his mind. After I had taken a walk to see the town and the lake, and as we were starting once again to chat in front of the... I nearly said *fire*, but I remember that Bala people don't believe in lighting fires as early in the year as we do in Flintshire. Williams said:

"Mr Lewis (since at that time he hadn't started to address me as Rhys, nor I to address him as Jack), I fear that we have been yoked a little unequally.[10] I may as well tell you the truth at once: I am a poor boy; my mother is a widow and dependent on me, and the thing which is most on my mind tonight is whether I did the right thing to leave her. But it's obvious to me that you are from a rich and respectable family..."

Before he said another word I laughed loudly, and said, "Mr Williams, I am a bit of a poet, and do you know what my bardic name is? 'Job on the Ash-heap'![11] Of course you have seen the name many times, and I am he, Sir." Then I gave him a summary of my family history (without mentioning my father, or the Irishman, as such) and of my actual and probable resources. And it was remarkable! Williams was perfectly happy once he knew how poor I was! To convince him that I was telling the truth,

---

[9] The bridge over the river Tryweryn that marks the eastern boundary of Bala even today.
[10] 2 Cor. 6:14. [11] Job 2:8.

I told him the full story of the hamper that he had helped me to carry into the house. To demonstrate further, didn't he and I fetch the hamper into the parlour to search its contents? And didn't we sample it again the same evening to further explore their nature? And so on every day until we reached the bottom of it? Williams himself can testify that this is true. And lest I forget to say this again, the two boys, whose hearts had been satisfied by the contents of the hamper, never went a day during their time in college without a meal to come home to; because the two of them were trusting in the Master's care, and they were not disappointed.

37

THOMAS BARTLEY'S VISIT TO BALA

Before leaving home I had, foolishly I know, formed a strange idea of college life; and I don't know quite how to describe that idea. I knew that almost without exception the students were going to be preachers, and I portrayed them in my mind as a group of sad, serious and sombre young people; collected together from various parts of Wales, their coming together acting to deepen one another's sombreness. I fancied that what was called a 'term' would in fact be like a four-month-long funeral service, in which forty or so young guests all in mourning would hear the headmaster, or one of his assistants, reading the funeral rites over the dead languages, and some blessing would come out of it all somehow or other. My idea was something like that; but vaguer. But oh! how disappointed I was! I soon found out that the students could laugh and be merry like any other boys—they could enjoy harmless fun and let their hair down without any damage to their consciences. Indeed, I believe that if Wil Bryan had been there he'd have said that there was no '*humbug*' about them, and that they were '*true to nature*'. And I soon learned that seriousness and godliness were not the same thing, and that there was a world of difference between piousness and purity, and that the boys who were most natural and carefree—as opposed to care*less*—were the most well behaved and sincere. I know two birds that wear the same colours as a preacher, namely the crow and the blackbird. One croaks and the other sings, and I've yet to be convinced that the crow gives more glory to its Creator than the blackbird, even though they are more numerous and one encounters them more often. But many times I couldn't help asking myself, What if David Davies could hear and see us students? Wouldn't he see that we were much too high-spirited, and that he had his doubts whether we were really called to preach the Gospel? But if David were there, he wouldn't be able to see anything that didn't come up to his ideal of seriousness. But would he really be seeing the boys? No, he'd only see the particular show that they put on for him. What was the conclusion I came to? This: no-one can know a student properly except for another student. Isn't it a generally known fact that one can only be free, natural and uninhibited when one is in the company of those who are of the same class and temperament? The presence of a David Davies causes him to pull a veil over some part of himself or, worse, to pretend to be something that he isn't. To speak figuratively, doesn't every man and every class of society have their David Davieses that force them to behave in a particular way? And don't all creatures have their David Davieses? I see the sheep and the lamb playing on the hillside, enjoying themselves in their own element; but there comes David Davies in the shape of a small innocent dog, and the playing stops straight away. On a fine spring morning the birds warble in the hedge by the highway, and as he passes the traveller stops to listen to them; but the warblers have seen him, and they stop their singing. David Davies again. In June the Sunday School members in the big smoky town have their trip to the countryside. Young and old come together. After enjoying their picnic on the grass, you see twenty or more of the young people quietly disappearing to amuse themselves. In due course, as he takes a walk, a godly and respectable old man will come across them. They know him well, and think highly of him, and hope that they will one day be as he is now; and yet his appearing puts a dampener on their fun. David Davies! Isn't there some freemasonry, or whatever you would call it, running through all levels of society all the way down to a man himself? No man is entirely himself except for when he is alone. Everywhere else, he is adapting himself in some way to meet the expectations of some David Davies. Does it follow that no-one has ever really seen a man except the man himself, and that only when he was by himself? And does it follow that the more time he spends by himself, the better? I believe that the answer to the last question, at least, is 'no'.

* *

However different Bala and its students were from how I had imagined them before seeing them, I'm sure they were even more so for my old friend Thomas Bartley when he paid me a visit, which he did when I was barely, if I remember rightly, a student of two months' standing. To give a lift to my own sombre spirit, and before I forget, perhaps this would be the best place for me to give a brief account of that visit.

It was Monday. I was coming back from Trawsfynydd, where I had been preaching on the Sunday, and I had stayed a long time in Rhyd-y-fen, drinking tea and eating oat biscuits while waiting for my two friends with the carriage, one of whom had been preaching in Llan Ffestiniog and the other in Llanbedr and Gwynfryn. It was between one and two o'clock in the afternoon when I arrived in Bala, and when I went to my lodging I could hardly believe my eyes to see Thomas Bartley sitting in my chair having already filled the room with tobacco smoke, with Williams sitting beside him and smiling from ear to ear. Thomas' appearance was comical even to me who was long familiar with him, and more so than usual because I hadn't seen him in his blue dress coat for a long time. I knew that the thing that tickled Williams' fancy most was the enormous shirt collar that my friend from the Twmpath was wearing. If Thomas had blacked up his face he would have looked exactly like a Christy Minstrel.[1] He wore the collar only on special occasions, and I remember that at such times my brother Bob

---

[1] The Christy Minstrels were a song-and-dance troupe formed in Buffalo, New York, in the 1840s who blacked up their faces and performed in the style of American negroes. They spawned many imitations, and 'Christy Minstrels' became a generic term for this sort of act. It was revived between the 1950s and 70s in the form of the 'Black and White Minstrel Show' before the whole concept became too politically incorrect for public consumption.

would say, 'Thomas Bartley is going to fetch the cokes', referring to the false sides that waggoners would put on their wagons when they were carrying that particular cargo.[2] I'm sure that the collar had its own story to tell, if only it could be teased out. It was famous! Whenever Thomas wore it, for example to a club dinner, one felt somehow that it was the collar that was going to dinner and Thomas was just going to keep it company. And even though it seemed that the collar was the main thing and Thomas himself played second fiddle to it, yet it acted as a sort of herald for him; since you would see the collar some time before noticing Thomas. I think I've noted before that Thomas' forehead was very high, his nose was long and pointy, and his chin disappeared into his neck, so the shape of his head and face forced students to think of a problem in Euclidean geometry. But, as I said, I'm almost certain that the thing that was most striking to Williams in the appearance of my friend was the outrageous collar, as I could see him eyeing it in detail. Indeed I, though I had seen it many times before, couldn't help admiring it, and admiring Thomas as he nestled within it like a man of comfortable circumstances sinking into a cushioned armchair. But I digress. I was amazed, as I said, to see Thomas Bartley in my room; and he said, as if he hadn't seen me for years, "Well boy, how are you, it's been a long time?"

"Right healthy, Thomas," I answered. "Who in the world would have expected to see you in Bala?"

"To be sure; but six o'clock this mornin', as I was in the middle of feedin' the pig, it came into my head to come over to look you up. But I didn't think that Bala was so far away. You know what, it's a big step from home to here; I always thought there was a train the whole way, but I came to understand that Corwen was the last station. But you'll never guess how lucky I was! In Corwen Mr Williams here recognised me—I didn't know that he'd ever seen me, but it seems that he saw me in the station at home when you were goin' away—and I got a ride with a lot of students, and we had a right interestin' chat, didn't we, Mr Williams? They were all wonderfully nice boys, but *aren't* you all like one another? Incredibly so. Where were you all this time? Mr Williams was sayin' that you should have been here a while ago. Where were you at it yesterday?"

"Trawsfynydd, Thomas," I said.

"Trawsfynydd? Well hang on, isn't M_____ Ll_____ [3] from there? I thought so. He's a right one is M_____. I always say that if I happened to be in trouble then I'd go to M_____ Ll_____ for advice. Did you hear about that time in Ruthin, Mr Williams? No? Well I'll tell you about it—this is the gospel truth. You see, there was a man—this was at the time of the Assizes—being tried for stealin' bacon—bacon, mind you—and everyone was afraid he'd be transported. The shopkeeper who he'd stolen the bacon from—bacon, mind you—had chosen MacIntyre to prosecute, and the man, poor thing, had chosen M_____ Ll_____ to defend him. Well you see, MacIntyre was playing a blinder, and the man's cause was lookin' very black. But then it was M_____'s turn; and see him go! He called a butcher as a witness, and asked him, 'What did he think of as bacon?' And the butcher answered, 'the side of a pig, salted and dried'. 'To be sure', said M_____, and he called the shopkeeper forward and asked him, 'this piece of meat that you said the defendant had stolen— was it salted and dried?' 'No it wasn't,' said the shopkeeper. 'False indictment' said M_____, and he won the case straight away! He's a right one, is M_____. Tell me: are any of his family still livin' in Trawsfynydd now? There are? If I had the time I'd go over there to see 'em, if I can ever get away from here! You know what boys, it's very close in here—open that window a bit, Rhys. It's no wonder that the two of you look so grey—there's no air. You may as well live in a box as in a little room like this with the door

---

[3] The author using some Victorian literary convention just says 'M_____ Ll_____' throughout. He obviously had a real person in mind whose identity would be obvious to his original readers from this hint, but whose actual identity can no longer be accurately confirmed.

closed and nothin' in it except a table and chairs and books—you're bound to lose your health! If I were in a place like this for two days then I'd die on the spot. Hey! That's better; we'll get a bit of air now. Well, Rhys, how are you getting' on? D'you like the place? Are you getting' enough provisions here, tell me?"

"It's coming along fairly well here so far, Thomas," I said. "How is everyone at home? How is Barbara? And how come she's not here with you?"

"Well, Barbara's not too well, to be honest with you; she's havin' terrible trouble with rheumatic and pain in her arms and legs, and I had a terrible struggle to be able to come here today, and she'll be achin' to see me comin' home. She wishes to be remembered to you. You know what? I haven't been away from home for twenty-five years."

"What do you think of Bala, Thomas?" I asked.

"I haven't seen much of it yet," he said, "but from what I've seen so far, it looks very much, to my mind, like a town built in the middle of a field. Why on earth don't they cut down those trees? Don't the crows cause 'em trouble sometimes? I've never seen a row of big trees, like the ones near the Manor, in the middle of a street. Don't you have a Local Board here?"

"The people of Bala think a lot of their trees, Thomas Bartley, and put a high price on them," said Williams.

"Now I come to think of it, indeed, Mr Williams," said Thomas, "I wouldn't be surprised if they're quite handy on a fair day to tie cattle to 'em, but they did strike me as odd when I saw them. But there you are, Rhys, are you going to take me around a bit to see the town? I don't have much time, and Barbara will be on tenterhooks until I get back. Do you have time?"

"Yes, I expect so," I said. "I'll show you as much as I can. I take it for granted, Thomas, that you've eaten?"

"Yes indeed, I had lunch with Mr Williams here, sufficient for anyone, and I ate heartily."

"Jolly good," I said, "I'll take you out once I've washed."

"Washed? What do you want to wash for? You're like a pin in paper[4]—there's not a speck on you. You're not gettin' fussy here, are you?"

Williams laughed, and I rushed to get washed. In a minute, Williams followed me into the room and rolled onto the bed, his sides splitting with laughter. He said, "Rhys, this is the best Original I've ever seen. The boys have had a pound's worth of fun with him from Corwen to Bala; and they've told me to tell you to keep him here as long as possible. Do you think you can smuggle him into the class? That would be a perfect treat."

"That wouldn't quite be the thing," I said. "It's a bit of a trial for me, because I'm the one who has to go around with him. I'd have been glad if the creature had left the big collar at home; everyone will be staring at us."

"Don't be silly," said Williams, "he wouldn't be a quarter as good without the collar. The collar alone is worth a hundred pounds! Can I come with you? If I can, then the mathematics, at least for the afternoon, can go to Jericho!"

"Of course you can!" I said, "I was about to offer you five shillings to come and share the embarrassment."

When we went down to the parlour, Thomas was on his feet and reloading his pipe; and when he saw that we were ready to start off, he said, "Is Mr Williams comin'? Well, clean shoes! Wait Rhys, I haven't seen you puttin' anything in your head since I arrived. Haven't you eaten?"

"Yes, Thomas, I had some food in Rhyd-y-fen."

"Rhyd-y-fen? Where's that, say? Is it a long way from here?"

"No, the Rhyd-y-fen is a pub, about halfway between Bala and Ffestiniog," I said.

"What? What?" said Thomas, "Up here in the mountains do they let preachers go into pubs? Although there's no harm in it, as far as I can see, and I always said that Abel Hughes was too strict

---

[4] A common and quite expressive Welsh idiom.

about that. Anyway, let's go, people!" and Thomas lit his pipe.

"Perhaps it would be better if you didn't smoke in town, Thomas," I said.

"Is there any harm in that? Or are people here in Bala a bit fussy?" asked the old brother.

"There's no harm in it, as far as I know, Thomas; but no-one respectable does that here," I said.

"Huh! And I'd heard that you were fine smokers here. But be that as it may, as that odd fellow from the South[5] puts it, let's go and see what we can see. There are three things I want to see—the green, that your mother was always goin' on about; the lake; and the clock. My father always used to say about anything that was really safe—that it was 'as sound as Bala's clock'."

"We'll go to see the lake first, Thomas," I said, because I was keen to go through the town towards Llanycil as quickly as possible so we didn't draw attention to ourselves. But that was more of a task than I'd expected. Thomas wanted to stop and look at everything. He stood in the middle of the road with his hands in the lapels of his jacket, and his hat on the back of his head, and when I went a little bit ahead he would shout loudly at me "Rhys, stop for breath, my boy! Well, these trees in the middle of the road are funny things, if I were ever from here. This is a champion pub, what's its name?" "The White Lion," I said quietly, hoping that he would take the hint and speak the same way. "Oh, the White Lion!" he repeated at the top of his voice. People stopped to look at us—shopkeepers came to their doors—children piled in all around us; and I was sure that Thomas' big collar and his generally strange appearance were making everyone expect he was about to gather everyone around in a ring and start performing in front of the White Lion, and I didn't know where to put myself with embarrassment. I was also feeling a bit annoyed with Williams, who I'm sure was enjoying himself as much as Thomas, to whose side he kept close. I moved on and heard Thomas shouting loudly, "What's wrong with you children? What are you staring at? Haven't you ever seen a man before? These are the strangest children I've ever set eyes upon. I've often heard about 'the children of little Bala'.[6] You know what? If you don't go away I'll use this stick on your backs, so I will! Rhys, why are you in such a hurry? Is this town just one street, Mr Williams? I don't see anything particular about it, there are no special shops here, and the place looks quiet enough. I always thought that Bala was a town full of chapels, and churches, and bells, and schools. You know what Mr Williams, here's another terribly impressive pub, what's its name?" "Bull *mawr*,"[7] said Williams. "Bull *mawr*?" said Thomas, "a bit of a funny name, isn't it Mr Williams? Do you Bala people talk like they do in Buckley,[8] a bit of Welsh and a bit of English? Hello Squire! I've found you, I see; is it possible to have a light?"

This 'Squire' was Mr Rice Edwards, who was standing on the pavement outside his house with a white pipe in his mouth. Thomas crossed the street towards him, Williams followed, and I went on slowly. Having gone on a few steps, I looked behind me and saw a remarkable scene. Mr Edwards and Mr Bartley looked like two doves cooing together. The points of Thomas' collar were dangerously close to Mr Edwards' eyes, while Thomas had put

---

[5] South of Great Britain? South Wales? South Flintshire? Whether politician or entertainer, this mysterious person's slogan '*let's go and see what we can see...*' was presumed by the author to be well known to the Welsh reader of his times.

[6] 'Plant y Bala bach', a phrase attributed to Bala native Ioan Tegid who was a popular Welsh poet and author in the early 19th century. Later in life he was a canon of St. David's Cathedral in Pembrokeshire.

[7] The Welsh adjective 'mawr' meaning 'big' comes after the English noun 'Bull' in the original text. Thomas' subsequent comment is on the strange mixture of a noun in one language with an adjective in another. This is by now, quite a common feature of modern spoken Welsh, much to the dismay of some.

[8] A small town just outside Mold. Buckley became synonymous with the production of various fire-clay and pottery products, as well as for coal mining. By the early 19th century, there were fourteen potteries in the town manned, for the larger part, by immigrant pottery-workers from the Staffordshire Potteries. Buckley subsequently developed its own distinctive 'Potteries' culture, and English dialect. People also moved into the area from Ireland and Liverpool to find work in the mining and brick industries, further contributing to the town's distinctive accent, and the anglicisation of Welsh language and culture.

the end of his pipe right on the end of Edwards'. The latter was blowing his cheeks out as if he were playing the bugle, while the former was pulling his cheeks in and panting, making it clear in the process that he had lost his molars. I could see that the grand objective they had in view was to get Thomas Bartley's pipe lit, and I could also see that Williams was holding his sides with laughter at the scene. My advice to Thomas not to smoke in the street was in vain, and I heard him whistling and then shouting at me—"Slow down man, the end of the world isn't due yet!" I was in a hurry to get out of town, because everyone was looking at us like we were a comedy act, and I felt very cross with Williams as he encouraged the conversation between Mr Edwards and Thomas Bartley, the latter of whom, once he had got his pipe lit, looked like he had all the time in the world. I walked on slowly like a man in a sulk, and very soon I heard Thomas behind me speaking at the top of his voice:

"The Baptist chapel did you say it was, Mr Williams? Ho! It's not much of a one. I suppose they're not doing very well here? To be sure. I don't like their way of doing things at all. If you think now about someone like Barbara at home who has the rheumatic and pain in her arms and legs, well, it would be more than her life's worth. So it would. I heard—I don't know if it's true—but I heard that in cases like that they warm the water up, but to me that's too much like what they'd do if they were going to slaughter a pig. I much prefer the Methodist way, though it was in the Church that I was baptised in the year—oh let's see now—I don't remember, but it was written in my father's Bible, all our names were. Rhys, are you trying to disown us or what?"

Although my old friend's appearance was strange, and drew no small amount of attention, I wouldn't have minded so much if he had stopped shouting whenever he spoke; and I was glad of heart when we finally made it out of town. No sooner had I escaped one trial, though, than I found myself in another. When we were a hundred yards outside town, Williams gave me a jab in the ribs with his elbow and signalled to me to look ahead, and I saw one of our lecturers coming towards us after having taken his usual afternoon walk. 'Out of the frying pan into the fire', I said to myself, and I started to think about how I could get past him without doing anything more than raising my hat, when Thomas said, "Wait there, boys, who's that man there comin' to meet us? Is that the Master?"

"Yes, sure," said Williams, readily enough.

"I thought so," said Thomas, "and he looks like a terribly noble man. They say that he's very wise, and understands a devil of a lot of languages; and I think he does—you can tell that from lookin' at him. I heard that he's the best man of the lot when it comes to the push. I only heard him preach twice, and I liked him an awful lot. I understood every word of his sermon, because he gave you time to think, not like John Hughes from Llangollen who grabs you and lets you go again until you don't know where you are. I've never been so lucky! I must talk to him, so I can tell Barbara all about it when I get home!"

"He's a busy man, Thomas," I said, "and perhaps it would be better for us to walk past and just say 'good afternoon'."

"No danger," said Williams, "you can be sure, Thomas Bartley, that he'd be pleased to have a talk with you, as you're a visitor to Bala. And if you ask him if you can come to the college I'm sure he'll give you his permission, and then you'll have even more to talk about at home."

"To be sure," said Thomas.

I could almost have strangled Williams, and he knew that very well. I could see that there was no point in me trying to persuade Thomas to give up on this plan, as Williams was determined to encourage it. I was dripping with sweat, whilst Williams was dripping with laughter. Even if Thomas Bartley had not been in the company of two students, I knew that his appearance would have caught the attention of our respectable teacher; and long before he reached us, I could see on his face an indication of the sense of humour that genuinely great men possess almost without exception. Before I had time to introduce my friend from the Twmpath, he strode out in front of me and, holding his hat in his hand, said, "Well how are you, Sir? It's been a long time. I haven't seen you since the time of that Session at home, and that was years ago, and you still look just the same, Sir."

"Mr Thomas Bartley, Sir, one of our members at home—he's come up to visit Bala," I said.

"Very good," said our teacher. "I'm pleased to see you, Mr Bartley, and I hope that Bala has satisfied you."

"You wouldn't believe how little I've seen of it so far, Sir, only one street, but I think, from what I've seen, that that is sufficient," said Thomas.

"How is the cause coming along over there these days, Mr Bartley? You had a great loss with the death of Mr Abel Hughes."

"Splendid, Sir, splendid! It was all higgledy-piggledy for a while after Abel died, but now we've come on quite well, considerin'. When are you comin' over to preach again, Sir? I'd like it an awful lot if you would, because I understand every word of your sermons; and I'd like it terribly much if you'd teach these young preachers to speak more plainly—they're much too deep for me and my sort. You know what, Sir? There was one of them over there lately, and I couldn't make head nor tail of him. He was talking about 'unity' or 'utility' or somethin' like that—I can't quite remember the word, to be sure, but Barbara and I couldn't tell which end of it was which; and I told David Davies that I'd tell you the next time I saw you, Sir."

"Well, indeed, Mr Bartley, I tell them a lot; but it needs someone like you, and other people with influence, to give them a word of advice, and that would do them the world of good."

"To be sure, Sir," said Thomas. "I was thinkin' of asking you, Sir, if you would mind lettin' me see the school while you're all at it there?"

"Well, perhaps Mr Lewis could bring you to the class at five o'clock, Mr Bartley."

"Thank you very much to you, Sir, and good afternoon to you now," said Thomas.

We had only just parted when Thomas turned on his heel, and shouted, "Mr _____,[9] beggin' your pardon Sir, would you happen to have such a thing as a match in your pocket? To be sure. I don't know how I left the house without one…"

I heard no more, and I was afraid to turn my head. I was burning with shame, and ready to be swallowed up by the earth, while Williams was almost bursting when Thomas said, as he came back to us, "No, he didn't have one—he doesn't carry 'em, else I'd have been welcome to one, so he said. But I must get a light from somewhere soon—is there a house nearby? You know what? That there master of yours is a fine, kind gentleman. I'm as happy that he's let me come to the class with you as if I'd been crowned—I'll have so much more to tell Barbara when I get home."

My debt to Thomas Bartley was great, but I'd have been quite happy to give all my worldly wealth to see him turn for home at that precise moment. After the permission for him to attend the class, I didn't know what new embarrassments were in store for me. It didn't seem appropriate to point out that if he came to the class then it wouldn't be possible for him to make it home that night; that would have seemed inhospitable. In my home I could enjoy Thomas' humour perfectly well; but in Bala it made me feel miserable, and I felt like he was an embarrassing dad. Although I tried my best to appear carefree, Thomas protested that I had taken a turn for the worse, and that he was sure that something was on my mind. On the other hand Williams could not have been happier, and he and Thomas were like a spinning top and a cord. With great delight Williams took to himself the task of 'showing Thomas around', and I knew that he took great pleasure

---

[9] The author follows his usual pattern of 'Mr_____'. It is probable that he intends the character to represent Lewis Edwards, who was Principal of the college at the time.

in Thomas' matter-of-fact way of looking at things. When we came to a place where we could see a full view of the lake, the most poetic utterances that descended from Thomas' lips were: "You know what, Mr Williams? This lake would make a half-decent sea at a pinch. I'd expect there are plenty of fish in it? What sort of feather do you use to catch 'em with? A coch-y-bonddu?[10] I never saw a better place in my life for breeding ducks." Thomas declined the opportunity to visit Llanycil cemetery[11] because, he said, all cemeteries looked the same to him and reminded him of Seth, and also because he wanted to go back to Bala and see the famous clock. Williams took some trouble to explain to Thomas that this clock was just a figment of people's imagination, or at least he and I had failed ever to see it. "Ho!" said Thomas, "I think it must be a bit of a scam then, like those people who say that the best thing to heal wounds is snail-foot oil."

Despite my best efforts to delay our return as long as possible, with the intention of keeping my old neighbour and sponsor from going to the class at all, Williams was too cunning for me and made sure that we arrived back at our lodgings by half past four, by which time I came to understand that he'd already arranged for tea to be ready. When I saw the spread that he had ordered—although we could hardly afford it—I could see that he'd done what I ought to have done, namely give a proper welcome to Thomas Bartley; and I felt guilty, and glad that Thomas didn't know that. I also saw the danger that Thomas would think that our 'provisions', as he called them, were better than they were in reality, and that he would tell everyone that because I knew that he had no sense of discretion. The idea had hardly gone through my head when

---

[10] A type of fishing fly, known by this same name even in English textbooks today. It resembles a black beetle, the name meaning roughly, 'red with a black base'.

[11] Final resting place of various prominent people from this period in Welsh history, including Thomas Charles (founder of the Bible Society), Dafydd Cadwaladr (father of Betsi, the Crimean-War-era nurse nowadays best known for having the North Wales hospital trust named after her), and, later, Lewis Edwards himself.

Thomas said, "You know what, boys? You live like fighting cocks! But you can do no better, since if a man can't have decent food he may as well give up and go home." Thomas little realised that this was a 'club dinner' for us.

The meal was over in a few minutes; Williams wanted us to leave for class straight away, and I knew that his intention was to give the boys a bit of insight into Thomas Bartley before the teacher arrived. But I beat him this time, I said, "Thomas wants to have a smoke first." "To be sure, if there's time," said Thomas. Even so, Williams took care that we were in the class by five o'clock to the minute. It was to be a class in the Greek Testament. Although we 'new students' knew no Greek as yet, we nevertheless benefitted from the explanations in a language that we did understand, and almost all the students were present. There was a particularly large gathering there this evening, and as we entered there were some deafening cheers, and I saw at once that some of Thomas' fellow travellers from Corwen to Bala were joking around. I was uncomfortably conscious that it wasn't Thomas himself that they were cheering, but rather his enormous collar. Thomas made a courtly bow, which raised more cheers; and then he sat down between Williams and myself. In a moment, Williams rose to his feet and announced: "Mr Thomas Bartley, gentlemen—a friend of Mr Rhys Lewis," but before he could say any more the Professor came in, and everything fell silent. Thomas whispered in my ear—"You know what? There are a lot of you here, and you are all so alike—apart from that chap over there with the crooked nose. Is he a pupil teacher?" Thomas nodded at the Professor as if he were an old chum, and he acknowledged the nod respectfully and turned his face away; as he did so I noticed that his neck was unusually red, as though it had been sunburned. Then the work of the class went on normally for about twenty minutes. For the first five minutes, Thomas looked careful and discerning, like an adjudicator judging poetry; for the second five minutes, he looked a little patronising; during the third five minutes, he looked uncomfortable, and asked me quietly, "Is this goin' to take much longer?" and for the last five minutes, he sank into his huge collar and I was afraid that he was going to start snoring. All through this the boys were looking sideways at Thomas, and Williams, and myself, and making faces that spoke volumes. I was very afraid, as I said, that Thomas would start to snore, and perhaps it was similar fear that caused the Professor, at the end of the twenty minutes, to speak along the following lines…

"(*Speaking first in English*) Perhaps we had better leave off there. You see that Mr Lewis, with my permission, has brought a friend with him to the class this evening. This is an unusual thing, and must not be looked upon as establishing a precedent. But I thought that Mr Lewis' friend might give you as preachers a word of advice. Words of wisdom are not to be despised from whatever quarter they come. (*Switching back to Welsh*) I was saying, Mr Bartley (and Thomas woke up, and came up out of his collar as if to say, 'Yep, that's my name'), to the young men that you may perhaps have a word of advice to give them. Say something, Mr Bartley, there's a lot that needs to be said to our young men nowadays."

"You never saw anyone worse than me for sayin' anythin', Sir," said Thomas, "but I never like to be odd or disobedient. I've heard a lot said about Bala, Sir; and when Rhys came here to you—his mother and I were great friends—it was she who turned me to religion, and I didn't know anythin' until she explained it to me, and she was an amazin' woman—I often told her that if she happened to belong to the Ranters she'd make a champion preacher (*cheers*)—

"Wait a minute, what was I goin' to say? Oh yes! When Rhys came to you I decided I'd come to see him in Bala sometime, and this mornin', as I was in the middle of feedin' the pig (*cheers*) I said, today's the day. From Corwen to Bala I had a ride with a lot of you young preachers, and I *was* very surprised by 'em, Sir. I'd always thought that students were timid things with their heads under their wings—their hearts half-broken, starvin' themselves. But I never seen smarter boys—nothin' at all like preachers, because they were so funny. You know what, Sir? Mr Williams here (*putting his hand on his shoulder*) can impersonate you to a T; if I closed my eyes I wouldn't know that it wasn't you."

When Thomas said this, there was thunderous applause from all the boys except for Williams, who blushed all the way up to his fringe. And I wasn't sorry to see him put on the spot, since all afternoon he'd been amusing himself at my expense. For a second or two, Thomas looked as though he couldn't make out the reason for the applause—whether he'd made a 'good hit' or a mistake. After hesitating a little, he added—"and that's the gospel truth, Sir"—which brought out more applause and reassured Thomas that he had said something excellent, so he carried on:

"But I must tell the truth to their faces, Sir; I don't see 'em so clever when they're preachin'. I admit that I'm dull —because I came to religion in my old age; and I confess that I've only heard a few of 'em preach, and perhaps they weren't the best of 'em. When *you're* preachin', Sir, I understand you just champion; but to tell the truth, I can't make head nor tail of the students who've been over in our chapel, and Barbara can't make anythin' of 'em. They don't say enough, Sir, about Jesus Christ and about heaven. Someone like me can understand about them fairly well. There was one of 'em over there talking about unicycles or somethin', and I couldn't even figure out what he meant by that. Rhys told me that you didn't actually teach 'em to preach, and that's a terrible pity. I know that you're wiser than me, but if I were you, Sir, I'd make them all preach in front of me—one every week—and after he'd finished I'd tell him where he'd gone wrong, and if he didn't do what I said I'd kick him out. These boys are expectin' to make their livin's by preachin' in Welsh, so there's no point 'em learning the languages of people who died hundreds of years ago if they can't preach in a language that everyone can understand 'em in. That's what I think, Sir, but perhaps I'm wrong, because after all

I can barely read. I'm surprised that you're runnin' this college in an old empty house, and I'm glad now I've seen you that I gave half a sovereign to that sick little man who was collecting money for you to get a new building.[12] He was one of the noblest men, Sir, that I've ever seen—I'd never tire of listening to him. He was saying that Bala is where the singing cocks come from, and I'll never hear our young cock at home singing in the yard without remembering what he said. If you've ever noticed, Sir, young cocks make a pretty strange screechin' sound for the first four months, especially if there isn't an old cock around to show 'em how it's done. But whichever one you take they eventually come to sound noble. I take quite an interest, Sir, in fowls—Rhys knows all about it—and the thing I hate most is those chicks where you can't tell whether they're cocks or hens. If they don't show soon which one they are, I cut their heads off. Well, I'm heartily glad to see you are all so comfortable here, and I hope you'll forgive me for taking up so much of your time."

Thomas sat down to long and loud applause, and I heard him ask Williams, "What do all these cheers mean, Mr Williams? Did I talk tidy?" "Champion!" said Williams.

"Well, Mr Bartley," said the Professor, "I very much hope that the young men will remember your valuable advice, and your purposeful observations. The next time you have students in your chapel, pay close attention to them—see if they've got any better. If they don't show clearly whether they're a cock or a hen, let us know, Mr Bartley, and we shall cut their heads off!"

In the midst of more deafening applause the Professor shook hands with Thomas Bartley and went away. As soon as he had left the room, one of the students got up and closed the door. "What's happening now?" asked Thomas. "I don't know," I replied, and I didn't know, but I understood that something was

---

[12] The current college building in Bala, an imposing building on the road to Porthmadog, with a statue of Lewis Edwards outside it, was built in 1863.

afoot. Immediately, D. H. Aberdaron (he about whom Thomas had asked if he was a 'pupil teacher') said, "Friends, it appears that talking about unicycles, as our friend Mr Bartley has mentioned, is not the only crime that we students are guilty of, though there is a close connection between them and the thing that I must now bring before you. It appears that our brother from Flintshire—a harsh county—as he came back from his posting this morning, through unforgiveable negligence and incompetence, was the occasion of causing Mr Rice Edwards' valuable horse to fall, and break its legs, and thereby cause great financial loss to the said Mr Rice Edwards and terrible pain to the poor horse. We should not look upon such a thing lightly—we must handle the case. According to our rules, we must put the brother on trial. I shall act as Judge; Mr V.P. can act as Prosecutor, and to ensure fair play for the accused, Mr Rhys Lewis, since he comes from the same county, can defend him. I appoint Mr Thomas Bartley to be Foreman of the Jury, and Mr John Jones to be the interpreter."

"Is this serious, or a joke, tell me?" Thomas asked me. "It's a joke," I said. "Ho! A bit of a skit, then," said Thomas with relish.

In less time than it takes me to write the words, the 'trial' was in full swing. I will not attempt a detailed account of it, although I could do so. The proceedings were conducted in English. The accused looked like an accused—his head hung low. D.H. the Judge sat in the Professor's chair, which had been placed on top of the table. A white cloth had been wrapped round his head, in place of a wig. Thomas gave every appearance of appreciating the importance of his role as foreman, and paid close attention to every word. V.P. was a talkative and amusing boy, and performed his role as Prosecutor without missing a beat. He called forth numerous witnesses to the character of the horse as one who was trustworthy and entirely disinclined to go down on its knees other than through the shameful negligence of its rider. No matter how much I tried to shake their testimony about the health and integrity of the horse's knees, nothing succeeded. Amongst the students, and only them,

I had lost the sense of imprisonment I'd had all afternoon, I felt entirely uninhibited, and I was able to throw myself with all my heart into defending my friend from my own county. But it was no use—it was a bad case, and every witness gave a good word for the horse. The trial went on for an hour and a half, and the witnesses who were the best English speakers had great fun refusing to speak in that language, forcing Mr John Jones to translate when he was the worst English speaker of all. I made the best speech I could in defence of my compatriot, but I was conscious that I did not have a leg to stand on; so my only hope was the sympathy of Thomas Bartley as Foreman of the Jury. My reasoning was torn apart by the Judge when he gave his summing-up, and I think it was probably the weakness of my defence that made him go out of his way to give the accused a chance to add anything in his own defence to that which I had said on his behalf—before he (that is, the Judge) handed the matter over to the consideration of the Jury. While the room was as silent as the grave, the accused said— "False indictment, my lord—it was a mare that I had, not a horse."

I remember the scene that followed as if I were there now. Some of the boys, overcome by laughter, lay prostrate on the benches; others, with no regard for their clothes, were rolling on the floor. Thomas Bartley stood on a bench waving his hat above his head, shouting at the top of his voice as if it were an election. In the midst of these raptures, the meeting was dispersed. On the way home, I had the greatest of difficulty stopping Thomas from shouting loudly and drawing the attention of the neighbours. He said over and over, "Every bit as good as M_____ Ll_____ in Ruthin! Every bit as good. You know what? That's the best meetin' I've ever been to, but as for that first part, that was the dullest thing I've ever seen, and I didn't know what on earth was going on. Where has Mr Williams snuck off to, tell me? He's a good lad, is Mr Williams. Don't you think he's awfully like your brother Bob? What will you have on tomorrow night? I'd like very much to stay with you for the week, but I'd better get home or Barbara will have a fit." When I explained to Thomas that it wouldn't be possible for him to get home that night, he was terrified at the thought of Barbara having to spend the night by herself. But he had to give in to the inevitable. Even so, he said many times how sorry he was that he didn't bring Barbara with him "even as she was." When Williams appeared, and with him three other students, Thomas cheered up considerably. I could see that my house-mate was determined to make the most of Thomas Bartley. There were six of us packed into our small room for supper that night. For Thomas Bartley, the supper was the highlight; Thomas Bartley was the highlight for the other five. If I had not already gone on for too long, I would give a summary of the conversation. The boys enjoyed the evening greatly, but the sighs that Thomas gave now and again made it clear to me that his thoughts were with Barbara in the Twmpath. His sojourn with us brought about a thorough change of billet; the lady of the house had to sleep with the maid—I went to sleep with the master—and Thomas and Williams chose to share our room. At cock-crow the following morning I heard Thomas walking back and forth shouting, "Wake up, people! It's a splendid day," and no-one had a minute's peace until they obeyed the call. Thomas insisted on making the first train from Corwen; and as the clock struck six, Thomas, Williams and I were crossing Tryweryn bridge in Mr Rice Edwards' carriage. Before I said farewell to him in Corwen, Thomas took me aside and said, "How's the pocket, my boy?" "I haven't suffered any hardship so far, Thomas," I replied. "Well, here you are, you can borrow this for ever," said Thomas, as he pushed a sovereign into my hand despite my protests. Credit to him, that wasn't the only sovereign I had from him while I was in Bala. Having charged Williams strictly that he must come and spend a week at the Twmpath, Thomas went home to tell the tale of Bala and the college. And what a tale it was! After the visit, of course, Thomas knew everything there was to know about the students. I knew from his question, "What do you have on tomorrow night?" that

Thomas thought that the scene he had seen with his own eyes that Monday evening in the college was representative of what went on every day. He little knew that a 'trial' like the one he saw took place perhaps once every two or three years, and that what he called 'the dullest thing on the face of the earth' was our daily work. Poor Thomas! He went home with the impression, that no-one could ever eradicate, that being a student was one of the most fun things 'on the face of the earth'; and as for the long hours, the hard work, the fear and worry that every student knows something of, these never crossed his innocent mind.

Thomas Bartley is not the only one, alas, who has the wrong idea about college life. I gather from various comments that I've heard around the country that some, who ought to know better, have ideas that are just as strange though not of the same kind.

38

A FORTUNATE ENCOUNTER

As far as learning goes, I think that I was as 'honest' as virtually anyone who has been to college. During the four years that I was there, I let other boys take all the prizes. Because I wasn't particularly talented, and because the 'start' that I got in Robin the Soldier's school was not the best, I soon found that it wasn't an easy task to compete with boys who'd had a good education before they came to Bala. Besides that, I needed to preach, and my ability to stay in the college depended on that. If I stopped preaching, I'd need to stop eating; and at the time I couldn't see my way clear to doing either. My Sabbath journeys were usually long, to places such as Trawsfynydd, Ffestiniog, Tanygrisiau, Maentwrog, Rhydymain, Corris, Aberllyfeni, Machynlleth and so on. I only ever once preached in Llanfor, something which Edward Rowlands told me off about many times (I have fond memories of the old Christian), and the main reason was that I couldn't afford it; that and the fact that I disliked seeing a dozen students coming to the service at Llanfor instead of attending the Sunday School in Bala. Everyone had their measure. What fun we had once when a friend of mine, preaching in Llanfor, referred to 'Adam in his state of *uncircumcision*'![1] He didn't hear the last of that for as long as he was in Bala. How could I know that I wouldn't say something stupid in Llanfor, which by the following morning would be written on every wall in the college. But I must stop talking about the walls of 'the old college'—*Mirabile visu*![2]

---

[1] Funny, partly because circumcision was only introduced at the time of Abraham, many generations after Adam; but mainly because it was usually administered to the recipient while an eight-day-old baby—something Adam never was.

[2] Wonderful to behold!

But as I was saying, the journeys were long. The planning took up Saturday morning, the journey itself took up the afternoon; returning home took up Monday morning, and recovering from the shaking that I got from riding Mr Rice Edwards' old 'sixteen' took up the whole of Monday afternoon. That's two days over and above the Sabbath itself, while the other boys who didn't *have* to preach could be working at their books. These things, combined with a lack of talent, prevented me from distinguishing myself in the exams. Yet, the trouble that Bob my brother took to teach me, my own motivation, and my decision to follow the classes as rigorously as I could, kept me from being at the bottom of the list; and I had the comfort of not being an extreme man, never being at the top or the bottom but somewhere in the middle! And I flatter myself that I have continued thus, trying to walk the middle path. But this is what I've been trying to get to for a while: although I didn't 'make my mark' in college, I am sure that a mark was made on me that will never be scratched away. I received a great deal of good, I learned hundreds if not thousands of things that I didn't know before, and I couldn't now put a price on them. A new world was opened up to my mind, and although I couldn't, as others could, dig deep into the depths of it nevertheless it was a discovery for me to know that it existed. It was something for me to be able to see the leaf upon the water with my own eyes. It's worth it for a boy to go to college, if he can find any way in the world to do so, to know how much there is to know, to cast his net wide and to shake away the dust that will have accumulated in his home. It's not saying much to say that in the church I was brought up in there was no other boy, besides Wil Bryan, who was stronger than me in terms of natural gifts; and it would be hypocritical to deny that this caused me to form a certain idea about myself. But when I went to college, it didn't take me long to realise that I was a nothing and a nobody, and some of my fellow students could have put me in the pockets of their waistcoats. I'd have needed the skin of a hippopotamus to fail to get some benefit from rubbing up against these boys who were my superiors in every meaning of the word. If a young man can spend three or four years in college, and come home without having benefitted from them, then the blame is on him, and he doesn't deserve to eat. My own experience was that this was the happiest and most blessed time of my life, and I look back on it with bittersweet longing. I formed many knots of friendship that will never be unravelled by either time or distance. With only a little effort, my memory can this minute call forth the faces of each of my companions as clear as if they were here. Where are they now? Two or three of them were called home[3] before they finished their schooling, and one or two others followed them before they had been able to 'do' much. But most of them are still alive and spread all over the world. Some were called to pastor churches, and are already useful ministers—some of them famous; others went back to their occupations; some are doing the best they can, making a living preaching here and there on Sundays without doing anything in particular during the week. Talking of that, I remember, when the time was approaching for us to leave college, that this was the question we'd ask each other: what are you going to do? It was an important question, especially for some of us. We had left our old occupations, and to a large extent rendered ourselves unsuitable for resuming them. We didn't all have comfortable homes to go back to, or rich families to depend upon; and some of them, as they saw the day approaching, felt themselves to be in a real fix. I felt especially that way. During the four years that I had been in the college, Miss Hughes had been very kind to me by welcoming me into her home to spend the holidays. But I could see that circumstances would be different once I had completed my education, or at least left the college. Even if Miss Hughes were willing to receive me back home, I felt it would be a shameless imposition to take advantage of that. I couldn't stand the thought of living all week like an idle gentleman, and going

---

[3] Here, 'called home' being the Christian euphemism for having died.

around preaching on Sundays. Williams, my house-mate, was in exactly the same predicament, and we had many serious confabs about what we should do. At times Williams would joke about the question. He said to me one evening, "It's no wonder that Methodist preachers go on the lookout for old widows with plenty of money! Here we are: we'll be leaving Bala within a month, and what are we going to do to earn a crust? I swear no-one will be able to say about me that I do nothing all week except wear a frock coat. I see you've got a much better chance than me. Four years in college have softened my hands too much for me to think of going back to the quarry; but as for you, you can just put an advertisement in the *Liverpool Mercury*:

'WANTED—By a young man who has spent four years at college, knows a little Latin and Greek and a lot of Divinity, a situation as a draper's assistant. Can preach well. Salary no object, provided he gets his Saturdays to go and his Mondays to return from his journeys'.

"But as for me I don't see anything open for me to do except try for a job on the railway as a ticket collector, or to go to the blacks like your old friend Thomas Bartley suggested. What if you tried to work on the Bishop of St. Asaph, and I did the same with the Bishop of Bangor? If we succeeded, I wonder if we'd have to start this business all over again in Lampeter? Whether we're scholars or not, I'd defy anyone to say that we can't preach better than half of them. What do you say? Have you got a better plan?"

Williams had plenty of sly humour; and I couldn't help laughing at his portrayal of our future, although the subject was serious and my own heart was heavy. As the time for us to leave drew closer, the question came back with more urgency every day—*if we have to just go back to what we were doing before, what on earth was the point of being here for four years?* We were both keen to find somewhere to work where we would feel in our element, and we believed—rightly or wrongly—that we had some suitability for it. But at the time, although we were—to tell the truth—listening carefully, there was no suggestion coming from anywhere that either of us might be called to take responsibility for a church. We had given ourselves over, and humbly believed that we had been consecrated for the work, and our hearts and minds were set on it; and the thought of going back to our day-jobs was devastating. Yet as far as I could see, that was all that awaited us; since we were determined that neither of us would dawdle about after leaving college. Williams was more optimistic than I was; and he could afford to be, as I knew he was conscious of being an excellent preacher. Indeed, he was the best preacher in the college at the time, in my opinion. It seems that the 'friends' were of the same opinion, since Williams preached *twice* in Bala itself during the four years he was there, which was definitely a good sign and a sure omen of a bright future.

Despite all of this it is true that 'the last shall be first'.[4] A few weeks before I left Bala, I received two important letters—that is, important to me. Williams was an early riser, and I rather a late one. By the way, isn't it a talent to be able to rise early in the morning? I'm sure it is. Bob my brother *had* to go to work early every morning, but he'd never get out of bed without my mother calling him a dozen times. But Bob could stay up at night as late as he needed to. I'm exactly like him, but Williams had the talent for getting up early. One morning, a few weeks before leaving college, as I said, I came downstairs about eight o'clock and found that Williams had already gone out for a walk. On the table there were two letters waiting for me. I recognised the handwriting on both of them—one looked like Miss Hughes', and the other Eos Prydain's. I always gave the priority to Miss Hughes' letters. I opened it, and found that she had enclosed another letter, the writing on which was unfamiliar to me. It was written in English:

---

[4] Matt. 19:30.

Old Bailey, Birmingham[5]
May 1st, 18__

Sir,

This morning a man called John Freeman died in this prison. Six weeks ago, having been found guilty of poaching, he was sentenced to three months in prison with hard labour. He wasn't strong to begin with, and soon after arriving here he caught a cold, and then quickly deteriorated. A little while before dying, he expressed a wish to speak to me in confidence. I had thought from the beginning that he was an 'old bird'; and he confessed to me in the end that his real name was James Lewis. He pleaded with me—and I promised—to inform you of his death when it came. The thing he emphasised that I ought to tell you was this: not everything that he told you was true. He did not know your address, but I believe you will eventually receive this letter through addressing it as I have done. I have now fulfilled my promise to the deceased. He will be buried tomorrow. We would have buried him today had we not been short of coffins, as we didn't expect him to die so soon.

Yours faithfully,
J.F. Breece, Governor.

I read and re-read the letter in amazement. My uncle James, as I have said many times in this story, was the author of most of my misfortunes and I really hated him. Yet, when I read of his shameful end, and of what he had said, I felt a pang of something that I won't try to describe. I held the letter in my hand, and looked out through the window at Tegid Street—I don't know exactly how long for—and my mind raced back to my earliest memory of my uncle, when I called him 'the Irishman'. De Quincy[6] speaks of someone who fell into the sea from the deck of a ship; he was only under the water for a few seconds, but when he was pulled back on board and had come to himself he testified that all the events of his life, and all of his sins, had come alive in his mind during those few seconds. I don't believe I was looking through the window for more than half an hour, but in that time all the main events of my life went through my mind in the order in which they had occurred. I knew that our landlady had been in the kitchen preparing breakfast, and was saying something to me, but I didn't know what, and I remember Williams breaking into my reverie by shouting behind me, "Well, the seven sleepers, have you got up? What bad news is it today? You look like you're by your grandmother's graveside!" I made an effort to come to, and to look comfortable, and as I began breakfast I remembered about Eos's letter. It read like this:

May 1st, 18__

Dear Brother,

We understand that your term at Bala is nearly at an end. We don't need to tell you, who knows the history and circumstances of Bethel church as well as we do, that the cause is suffering because of the lack of anyone to take care of it, especially since the death of our old master Abel Hughes. We've been feeling for some time that our children and young people have not been having the care and attention that they should. There has been talk among us for some time about having a pastor; and last week the two of us put the question before the church, and took the liberty of suggesting your name as one who was nearing the end of his term at Bala, one who was raised in the church, and who therefore knows us very well. Our suggestion received widespread support. Of course, we did

---

[5] There doesn't seem to be any record of a prison in Birmingham called the Old Bailey at this time; in 1849 the main Birmingham prison had relocated from Moor Street to Winson Green.

[6] Probably Thomas Penson De Quincey (1785–1859), despite the variation in spelling.

not take a vote, and we have not yet received the permission of the Monthly Meeting; but we thought it would be wise to tell you that this is our intention—indeed, you can look on it as a fact—lest you promise too quickly to go somewhere else. We don't believe that you need worry about anyone here despising your youth.[7] We expect you over here within a few weeks, and then we can talk further about the matter. Until then, wishing you every success and with kind regards, we are on behalf of the church,

Yours,
David Davies
Alexander Phillips (Eos Prydain), Deacons

I threw the letter across the table to Williams, and I will never forget his joy. I'm sure he couldn't have shown more joy if he'd heard that someone had left him an estate all of his own. A call for me to pastor the church I had been brought up in was the most unexpected thing that could have happened to me, and I considered it a huge compliment; and were it not for the other letter that I've just mentioned, it would be a cause of rejoicing for me also. But in the wake of that letter, which was very sad news for me, I had immediately been possessed by my old disease—depression. I sent word straight away to my old friends, David Davies and Eos Prydain, to thank them for their kind letter, adding that I would be returning home within a few weeks. Having done that, I said to my companion, "Williams, don't tell the boys or anyone else about this, since I cannot accept the call on any account."

"Don't be absurd," he said, "I'll tell everyone I see. What's the matter with you? Are you mad? Not wanting to accept the thing that you've most wanted? I used to think that you weren't capable of being snobbish."

"You know the story about the skeleton in the cupboard," I said

---

[7] 1 Tim. 4:12.

to him. "I have my own story that I can't even tell you. Perhaps I shall be able to tell it one day, but not today. My spirit is low and sad, and I know that you'd be willing to share some of my burden, but you cannot do so today. The fact is, I must go away for two or three days, and that without delay."

"My dear fellow," said Williams sympathetically, since he had a very tender heart; "you're not telling me anything new. I've known all along that there's some hidden bitterness in your history that I have no right to demand an explanation for. Can I help in any way?"

"Yes you can; don't say anything about this call, because I can't accept it; and, if you would, go to Rice Edwards and ask him to send a cab after me to Corwen. I must leave straight away. Perhaps I can explain this to you some other time."

Without taking anything with me besides my outer coat, and the little money that I had, I started at once; and Williams went without asking any further questions to get Rice Edwards to send a cab. The journey was long, and it took nearly the whole day to arrive; but I was determined to go, as I was fed up with wearing a mask and living in fear. Rice Edwards overtook me and whisked me to Corwen, just in time to miss the train. After a long wait, I was happy to be in the seclusion of the carriage, where I could think without having to talk to anyone. A thousand and one things went through my mind. I read Mr Breece's letter many times over. Sometimes I thought that perhaps it was a forgery—my uncle was enough of a rascal to do that—but if so then I couldn't see what purpose it served.

If the letter was accurate, then I thought I understood the meaning of the sentence 'not everything that he told you was true'. This opened before my mind a possibility that caused my heart to freeze, and made me decide right away that I couldn't accept the invitation to pastor Bethel church. It amazed me that a church in which half the members where familiar with my family history could yet have called me to be their pastor. But in twenty-two years people forget all sorts of things. During that time, many things were revealed to me that caused me sadness, but they knew nothing about them, and I couldn't do anything about my own family connections. Were 'the sins of the fathers being visited upon the children'[8] in my case? I feared that they were. Was Providence going to set me up in my own home to have my teeth set on edge by the sour grapes that my fathers had eaten?[9] How could I even think of accepting the call? And yet what reason could I give for refusing it? I had nowhere else to go, and I longed for an excuse to go as far as I could—to Australia or somewhere. Yet I'd had no part in the making of my misfortunes. I thought sometimes that I was blowing things out of proportion, and fearing things that would never come to pass. Even so, that day I had vowed to shed as much light as possible on my living nightmare, and I hoped to have that before I slept that night. My plan was to visit Mr J. F. Breece, whoever he was. If the letter was not a forgery, my uncle might have said a great deal more to Mr Breece than he had passed on to me. I could see that the journey would not be wholly in vain however it turned out; and my anxiety had worked its way up to a point that I couldn't hold on any longer. If things turned out as I feared, then my future was clouded over, and I would not be able to accept the call to pastor Bethel church. Not only that; I feared that, before I could be happy, I'd have to leave the land of my birth. But, on the other hand, why did I have to do this? I had tried to keep a clear conscience before God, and if the worst came to the worst, no reasonable person could blame me. But, I thought, everyone would sympathise with me and pity me, which would be every bit as bad. What! Was it the pride of my heart that caused me to fear what was possible, indeed likely? Didn't I have enough religion and moral strength to bear any shame of which I myself was not the cause? And yet something told me that blood was thicker than water.

---

[8] Ex. 20:5. [9] Ezek. 18:2.

I had never been to Birmingham, and I didn't know anything about it except through stories—a fact which did nothing to raise my spirits. It was a dull and heavy day, with the rain drizzling down persistently. Besides that it seemed that fate was against me; since I missed the train again in Chester, and I had to wait two hours for the next one. I saw by now that I would be very late arriving in Birmingham, and I was afraid I would not be able to see Mr Breece. I was sick of heart when I arrived in the big, busy town. It was nearly ten o'clock when I jumped out onto the platform. I woke up from my reverie when I saw all the lamps lit up, and the hundreds of people weaving past one another in the station. Was it too late for me to be able to see Mr Breece? Well, I'd be no worse off for having a go. I headed quickly for the cab stand, and before I arrived a young man hurried towards me and said "Cab, Sir?" and I nodded in confirmation. "Old Bailey," I said as I took my seat; and he replied, "Old Bailey? Know the place well, Sir. Better to be outside than inside that place, as the worm said to the blackbird when he was about to be swallowed by him," and he shut the door and off we went. The din of the carriages on the streets was deafening to me who was used to the tranquillity of Bala. I looked out of the cab and gazed in wonderment at the endless flow of people who were coming and going from every direction. Looking just to one side for a few minutes, I saw hundreds of faces that I'd never seen before and never would again; and each one of them had, I realised, their own story and troubles as strange to me as mine was to them. Although there were many lamps, all they did was to show up the dirty fog that filled the streets. I figured that the smoke that had risen from the chimneys throughout the day had descended back to ground level and was keeping company with the drizzle that continued to fall. I saw that the main shops were all closed, and so the small shops stood out: the ones selling tobacco, the pubs, and the gin shops, all of which were busier than they could possibly be in broad daylight. I don't think I passed one vault or gin shop without seeing someone going in or out of it. Coming out from one I saw a soldier in his red coat, and by his side a young woman with no bonnet, but her shawl over her head and pinned under her chin. As I went past another, I saw a man—about whom it was hard to say whether he was old or young—lame, ragged, who seemed not to have an intact pocket to his name and so had to carry his money in his fist until he could lay it down on the counter. Outside one pub a man leaned with his back to the doorpost, his chin on his waistcoat and eyes looking as though they were counting the buttons; and outside another I saw a dandy in a frock coat buttoned up to his neck to cover a multitude of sins, sniffing the air by the door for want of anything better to do. What ugly faces I saw by the lights of the pubs that night! Had their owners, fifty years ago, been locked up in a dark room and half starved, and only just been able to escape, some out of the chimney and some by squeezing through the locks? How proud I felt of the Welshmen with their rosy cheeks, looking healthy and honest. This was what was going through my mind when I noticed that the lights were thinning out. I looked out, and saw that there was nothing to see except large warehouses, dark and still. By now there was almost nobody to be seen walking along the street. I couldn't hear anything except the noise of the cab and somebody whistling. It was as if the whistler was following us. I stuck my head out to listen, and realised that it was the driver who was whistling. I recognised the tune: it was the hymn tune 'Caersalem'. I didn't know at that time that the English used it as well. I kept my head out, and felt as if I were in a Welsh chapel, and imagined I could hear the words '*Diolch iddo, byth am gofio llwch y llawr*'.[10] I concluded that the cabby must be a chapel-goer. I was soon in the grimmest part of the town. I began to think how foolish I had been to imagine I could meet with Mr Breece at such a time. I soon saw a huge, high, strong wall, that seemed in

---

[10] 'Thank Him forever, for remembering the dust of the earth', from the hymn 'Dyma Geidwad i'r colledig' ('Here is a Saviour for the lost') by Morgan Rhys (1716–1776).

the lamplight to have been blackened with age. The next minute the cab came to a halt opposite a wide door, which was almost completely covered with the heads of nails. Beside it there was a bigger-than-normal lamp fixed to the strong wall. "Here we are, safe and sound," said my driver, and he opened the door. The cabby stood with his back to the light, which shone onto my face and he was just about to hold his hand out to receive his fare, when he pulled it back suddenly while looking at me in amazement, and he said in Welsh, "Well, the old Hundredth! Is it you?" My heart jumped, and I almost embraced him, because he was none other than the old companion of my youth—Wil Bryan! But before we could exchange a dozen words, a small door opened in the middle of the big door to the Old Bailey, and a tall hunchbacked man came out and slammed the door behind him. He needed to walk past us. He didn't look at us, but kept his eyes down. Even so, he couldn't stop the lamp shining, and when he was out of earshot Wil said, "I'm blowed if that chap wasn't old Niclas!"

"You're right Wil, I said; "it was definitely Niclas, and for my sake, follow him, and find out where he's going, if it takes you two hours; and then come back here. I'll tell you why later. I'll try to complete my errand, and whether I succeed or not I'll wait here until you come back."

"At your service as detective in chief," said Wil, in his old manner of speaking, and he jumped into his cab and off he went. I watched him for a moment, but soon lost sight of him, then turned on my heel and rang the bell of the Old Bailey with gusto. But I see I'll need to take another chapter to tell of the adventures of that strange night in my story.

WIL BRYAN IN HIS CASTLE

I rang the bell of the Old Bailey with gusto, as I said, and felt excited
and apprehensive. The unexpected appearance of Wil Bryan and
old Niclas had done nothing to calm my thoughts. Immediately I
heard someone coming quickly to the door to answer the call, the
clanking of his keys demonstrating his important but onerous job.
The next moment, the door was opened, and the opener shone the
light of his lamp onto my face so that I was nearly blinded. "Who
was I, and what did I want?" "Was the Governor in?" "Yes." "Can
I see him?" "Yes, if your message is important." It was. "Very well,
come in." I was led to a small, square room in which there was
nothing but a table and two chairs, where I was left by my host
who closed the door which then locked by itself. I wasn't without
fear at being taken into the presence of the prison gatekeeper, even
though that was my whole reason for having come this far. Mr
Prichard, the warden of Flint prison, was the only jailer I had ever
seen before, and the very sight of him was enough to make even
an innocent man quake in his boots. What fearful authority he
had in his face! It was as if his wild, piercing eyes could stare into
you and see your backbone. I never heard of anyone who was sent
to Flint prison and who wasn't terrified of Mr Prichard, except
for old Ned James. When Ned was sent to Flint for the second
time, Mr Prichard shouted at him, 'Well, Ned! Ned! Ned! Are
you here again?' Ned answered calmly, 'I've never been anywhere,
Mr Prichard, where they wouldn't invite me back.' I thought that
if Mr Prichard, the warden of Flint jail, was so frightening, how
much more the keeper of the Old Bailey? The door opened, and I
was led into the presence of Mr Breece with my knees shaking. But
there was no need—Mr Breece wasn't at all like Mr Prichard. He

was a small man, weak and harmless-looking. Mrs Breece was also in the room, darning a sock. She was a big, fleshy woman, very self-satisfied in her appearance, and her husband looked like a sort of appendage to her. As I entered the room the jailer rose to his feet, gave me a welcoming look over his yellow spectacle-frames, and asked me to take a seat. He said:

"Mr Lewis, I understand?"

"Yes, sir," I said, "and I must ask your forgiveness for disturbing you at such a time."

"Don't mention it! Don't mention it!" he said, "when business is in the question, I don't pay any attention to what time it is."

After some polite general conversation, in which I noticed that Mr Breece had a habit of repeating the same words, he added, "Excuse me Mr Lewis; are you in the ministry?"

"Yes I am, Sir," I said.

"I guessed that," he said, "and therefore would you accept a glass of wine? Mother, if you would, pass the..."

"Don't trouble yourself," I said, "I won't have any wine. My business is short and simple, and I won't detain you for more than two minutes. This morning I received a letter from you informing me of the death of someone named James Lewis, a prisoner in this place, and my visit may be attributed to curiosity more than anything else."

"Oh!" said Mr Breece, and his expression altered in a moment; he looked at me with narrow, penetrating eyes and added, "Yes, I wrote to you, and I didn't think anything more of it—anything—more—of—it. He was your father, it appears, eh?"

"No," I said, and I felt glad that I could say that, "but he was some sort of relative of mine, not something, I can assure you, that I was proud of. My business is to find out, if I may, if he said anything else to you that wasn't mentioned in your letter? I have my reasons for asking this that would be of no interest to you, and which you wouldn't benefit from knowing."

"I understand you, I understand you," said Mr Breece, and

resumed his previous geniality. "No, no, not that I remember, he said no more than I wrote to you about. Do you have many relatives, Mr Lewis?"

"As far as I know, he was my last one," I replied.

"Ah!" said Mr Breece in surprise.

"Of course, you buried him today, as you said in your letter?" I said.

"No," he said. "No. Wait, did you say, Mr Lewis, that he was the only relative you had?"

"I swear it," I said, as I could see that he had his doubts, "as far as I know, he was the last of my family."

"That is strange," said Mr Breece, "if indeed such a thing is strange, since we are all deceived from time to time—all of us; but I must take your word as a clergyman, yet this morning, when I had just issued the order to place the body into a coffin, a visitor came here who claimed to be the brother of the deceased—(I felt uncomfortable as Mr Breece said this)—although I must confess that he bore no resemblance to the prisoner. Indeed he was a strange character, and obviously a wealthy man. He pleaded to be allowed to give a fitting coffin to his unfortunate brother, as he called him, and he put a five pound note down on the table to pay for it—on the table, Sir. Tell me, could I have refused him? Sir, I always say that when death comes to do its work, the law must draw back—draw back, Sir. Will I punish a dead man? Never! Never! That would be as if I were fighting against Almighty God. I ordered at once that a good coffin be made for the dead man; and it is a good coffin. Indeed, in a manner of speaking, it's a pity to bury such a valuable coffin in the ground. The man who paid for it liked it very much; and if you had been here ten minutes earlier, you would have seen that strange man—a character—a real character, Sir."

I rose to leave, and said, "I am very grateful to you, Mr Breece, for your kindness, and I again beg your forgiveness for disturbing you at such a late hour."

"Don't mention it, don't mention it," he said. "These things happen sometimes. Tell you what—would you like to see the coffin? I'm sure you'll like it."

"Please, Sir," I said. Mr Breece rang a bell which was by his elbow, and in a minute the man I'd seen before made his appearance, and Mr Breece said, "Gloom, is coffin number seventy-two screwed down?"

"That's what I was doing just now, Sir," said Gloom.

"Take this gentleman to see it. Good night. Don't mention it, don't mention it, you're welcome."

I was led across a wide yard, then through a door that opened into a long corridor, through another door, and another, all of which closed themselves; then down some stone steps, and along another corridor; and there was something in the air, in the heavy doors, and the damp walls, that made me think that everyone here had been dead for ages, besides my guide, and Mr Breece and his wife, since everything looked so sad and hopeless. At last we came to the mortuary where, or so I thought at the time, there had never been a breath of fresh air, and where the living were bound to behave like the dead—not breathing. The ceiling of the room was low and the walls dripping with damp, as if snails had been slithering across them for centuries, and the stench of death lay heavily on it. When I first entered the room I thought it was the subterranean nature of the place that caused me to imagine rats running over my feet and between my legs, until my guide swore and tried to kick one of them; which showed me that I wasn't imagining them and that he too was being annoyed by the creatures. I hadn't had much to eat that day, and I felt weak and faint, but I tried to be brave because I hadn't gone all the way there for nothing. In the far end of the room, which was long and narrow, there was a table, which had upon it the 'good coffin'; and beside it there was a man in shirtsleeves with a paper cap who, when he heard us come in, turned his face towards us, holding a screwdriver in his hand, with an expression exactly as if he had been caught graverobbing. They took a lot of trouble to show me how excellent the coffin was. But what did I care about the coffin? My aim was to see who was inside it, and I had to give a shilling to the joiner to unscrew it. No matter how silly it sounds, I was afraid that my uncle James was only pretending to be dead, and that it was part of a cunning plan to escape from prison; and I must admit that I was half expecting, as the joiner took out the last screw and opened the lid, to see my uncle sitting up and laughing at us. But that's not how it was, and however bad it sounds, I felt a huge sense of relief. There he was in his old clothes, in his coffin, as dead as a doornail. He who had turned my father away—who caused my mother and me the greater part of our troubles—who spent every penny that I had saved up to go to college—for whom nothing was too wicked to perpetrate—there he was lying still and powerless, conquered by the great conqueror! To be really sure, I felt his hands and his forehead, and they were as cold as the wet walls all around us. Before that night I had only seen two dead faces, that of Seth and that of my mother. How different this was! The devil had left his mark, and I could see that the pains of death had been something terrible for him. I thought that there was as much difference between the cheerful face that Seth had when in his coffin, and that which was before me now, as between heaven and hell! He was my uncle, my father's brother; but I'm afraid that few worse men than he were ever laid between four boards. While I looked at him, I felt a sense of horror; and yet, I felt that everything around me contributed to making a fitting end for such a defiled and sinful life. Although my clothes were sticking to me in cold sweat, I felt a chuckle rise within me as I realised he could no longer hurt me. Whatever other trials awaited me, half of my nightmare had passed, and I hurried out. When I found myself outside the walls of the Old Bailey, I took a deep breath and said unconsciously to myself, "Oh, blessed freedom!"

The streets in that part of town were quiet and peaceful, and I didn't see a living soul as I walked back and forth waiting for Wil Bryan. As I walked my thoughts went to back to Bala, and I longed to be back there. Williams, back in his bed, knew little of where I was or of what thoughts were going through my mind. If he had known, he wouldn't have slept a wink. It had stopped raining some time ago, and the moon was up, and I was glad to see it—I knew it, and felt that it had known me since I was a boy, and I believed then that we Welsh owned it. Wil took a long time to come, and I began to fear that something had happened to him and that he wouldn't come at all. At times I felt so hungry that I could have fainted; but then I'd forget my hunger as my mind went back through many of the events of my life. As I looked back, I saw that God had brought me safely through many dangers. What purpose did he have in bringing me here? My thoughts were like a thicket, but was dawn breaking? Wil was long in coming, and I remember a saying of my mother's that waiting always takes a long time. I imagined that I could hear in the distance the sound of a cab approaching, and I listened carefully. Was it Wil's cab? No, it was going the other way. A church clock nearby struck twelve o'clock. After a while I thought I heard someone walking along the pavement, and I strained my ears to listen. Yes, someone was coming towards me. I walked quickly and whistled. To avoid suspicion, I walked to meet him, intending to turn around after he had gone past. When I was some forty yards away from him he broke into singing part of a duet called, if I remember rightly, 'The Larboard Watch',[1] which contains the questions and answers: *'Who's there?' 'A friend'. 'The word?' 'Good night'. 'All's well'*. Wil was the singer; and his familiar voice healed my spirit. He said:

"Well, my old radish soup, are you tired of waiting? You must excuse me for not bringing the cab; the nag was tired out, and it's not far to get home. Now let's have a bit of your stranger-than-fiction. I can tell from the look on your face that you've been in a pickle. Where in the world have you come from? You know what, I've

---

[1] The author nearly remembered rightly; but not quite; the lyrics quoted come from 'All's Well', a duet written by Thomas Dibdin and John Braham as part of the comic opera *The English Fleet in 1342*, first performed in 1803. 'Larboard Watch' was written by Thomas E. Williams in 1869, and described by its author as a sequel to 'All's Well'.

thought about you thousands of times, and have often wondered whether Providence would tumble us across one another's paths some time. But now, *thou weary pilgrim, tell thy tale.*"

"First of all, Wil," I said, "did you find out where old Niclas went?"

"Yes, and I got sixpence for it," said Wil. "After I left you I thought how hard it was to follow a chap while I was in a cab, so I went straight to him and said, 'step in, Sir' as if I wanted nothing in return, and he took the bait. "sixty-five Gregg Street," he said, and when I set him down, he gave me sixpence. We'll be going past the house in two minutes—I'll show it to you. But what's the row? What is the *meaning of all this*? Go on, spout!"

It wasn't hard to explain to Wil why I had come to Birmingham, since he knew more of my family history than anyone else. I gave him a short summary of what had happened to me since he made his '*exit*', as he'd put it, and Wil listened with deep interest. I knew that I could rely on his trust, and his help. Indeed, if I hadn't met him so providentially the other half of my mission in Birmingham would not have been achieved. We walked arm in arm, and I didn't look where we were going although I was conscious that Wil had led me through many streets and had turned to the left and to the right many times. I had just finished telling him about what I had seen in the Old Bailey, when Wil stopped and said quietly, "Here it is." I looked around, and saw that we were in a long, narrow street. The buildings were tall and, to judge from the number of windows, contained many dwellings. There were shutters over the lower windows. Wil whispered again—"This is the house— sixty-five Gregg Street—where old Nic went—shall we ask whether supper is ready?" A strange feeling, which I can't describe, came over me. It was made up of fear, strange thoughts, and curiosity. It appeared that the occupants had gone to bed—but Wil pointed out to me that there was a glimmer of light around the shutters of number sixty-five —and he walked as quietly as a cat towards the window, and I followed him. We could hear talking inside, but I

442

couldn't make out any of the words. The sill of the window was low. Wil placed his right hand on my shoulder, and his left foot on the sill, and lifted himself up to his full height to try to peep in through the top edge of the shutter. But he couldn't—and he climbed down quietly and gestured to me to have a go, as I was about an inch taller than him. I did so, and I could see into the room, but my heart was pounding so hard that I felt I was about to lose my eyesight. Even so, I could see a bed in the far end of the room, and someone sitting up in it, but I couldn't see his face because Niclas, whose form I knew well, was standing between me and him and was at the time pouring something from a bottle held in his right hand into a glass held in his left. I was keen to see the face of the man in the bed, but my attention was diverted by a clicking sound close to me, like the sound of a key in a lock. As I looked, a tall and strong policeman lifted me cleanly off the windowsill and before my feet reached the ground my wrist was tightly held in one half of a pair of handcuffs, the other half of which was already round Wil's wrist. It took about six seconds for the officer to carry out this manoeuver, without saying a word. He held the collar of my coat firmly while he looked carefully at the house number. I was nearly fainting with fear; but Wil came to himself in an instant, and was the first to speak. He said, "Officer, I must give you credit; you are a smart fellow." Looking thoughtfully at me first and then the handcuffs, he added, "just as it should be—we've always been attached, even from childhood." Then Wil tried to reason with the officer, but he did not listen to anything Wil said—the only word we had from him was "March!" And so we did. The officer walked close at our heels saying nothing except "right" or "left" whenever we came to a street corner.

"This is the tightest spot I've ever been in, I swear it," said Wil. "We've blown it, and there's no point trying to reason with these bluecoats." Wil was uncharacteristically speaking fully in Welsh, with no English words thrown in, and added, "We'd better keep it grammatical, or he'll understand us. The thing is now, how do we get out of it? Put your mind to work for a decent plan, now. What are you shaking like that for? There's no need for a man to shake if he's not guilty. You know that we're as innocent as William the Coal's mule. *Bye the bye*, is old William still alive? And is he still putting the blame on Satan? I'm afraid I must blame him for this job. How are we going to manage it, tell me? The bluecoat will swear on a lot of things first thing tomorrow morning, you know. Speak, there's no point in being downhearted."

"There's nothing to do except to tell the truth and take the consequences," I said. "But whenever we get out of the grip of this man, I must go back to that house."

"They'll never believe the truth," said Wil. "If we tell them the truth, namely that all we wanted to do was to see who was in the house with old Nick, do you think they'll believe us? No danger! And there are many ways of telling the truth; you need to speak figuratively sometimes, you know. If the bluecoat doesn't tell too many lies, I don't think they'll be able to do anything with us. Perhaps we'll get fourteen days; and that will be a terrible shame for two innocent boys. I never saw such a pity—and there was I thinking we'd have a happy evening going over old times! If I knew whether or not this bluecoat was an exception, I'd try bribing him; but there's no telling, he's so quiet. If we pretend to be drunk, that will just be five shillings plus costs. Do you have any ideas? Say something, there's no point giving up the ghost. I'm trying not to use a word of English so this bluecoat doesn't understand me; and I don't think I've ever spoken such pure Welsh—I'm surprised at myself. Let's agree what we're going to say, so we don't get our story mixed up. What if we say that we wanted to see the maids? There are bound to be maids in a house like that? But what if they ask us their names? And we answer—Ann and Margaret. And what if they ask us what colour hair they have? And we say—black. But then what if their names turn out to be Maud and Cecilia, and they both have red hair? How will we look then? No, that won't work. What's your idea? You know what? I never knew you had so little pluck. You may as well not hide in your shoes—you'll be no better off. At the same time, I really feel for you. I don't give a fig about myself, because some chum will look after the nag for me. But the idea of it! A Methodist preacher in the clink! I hope to goodness that they don't hear about this in the college. It would be a thing and a half for them to hear about this in Bala. You'd lose all the bookings in your diary straight away! But it wouldn't help if you tell them in the morning that you're Rhys Lewis. You must be a good Welshman, and take on a pseudonym. If you say that your name is—say, Melltathranorosllanerchrugog[2]—they won't know any different here. I'm bound to think of a pseudonym, because I dabble in poetry; but haven't you anything to say?"

Wil was quiet for a few minutes, and I said no more than a few words. Indeed my mind was too troubled to be able to hold a conversation with him; and I wondered how he was able to treat the whole thing so lightly. I was about to tell him how upset I was, and my fears that news of the event would reach Bala and my home, when Wil started up again…

"I really can't see how we're going to get out of this fix, because appearances are against us. It all depends on what the bluecoat will say. It just struck me, has Providence decided that every member of your family should go to prison for a spell? Some of them, you know, were quite at home there. Then there was your brother, one of the best of men—he had a spell; and now here are you. Are you Ffynnon Elian,[3] tell me? But the point is, how can we prove our innocence? Wait a minute, weren't Paul and Silas held in *durance vile* once?[4] I'm slipping into English. Well, we're just as innocent

---

[2] 'Thunder and lightning from Rhosllanerchrugog', referring to the village on the outskirts of Wrexham.

[3] Elian's Well, a rather controversial 'holy' or more appropriately, 'cursing' well near Colwyn Bay, the colourful and dubious history of which can be read in the appendix at the back of this book.

[4] Acts 16:16–40; the term *durance vile* doesn't occur in the Bible account, but is an archaic English idiom for being in prison.

as they were. And how did they get out of the fix. Wasn't it by praying and singing? Well, if you'll pray, I'll sing until the place falls down, I swear!"

As Wil said these last words we were both surprised as the police officer roared with laughter, and said in Welsh, "Boys, what were you doing by that house?" "Hello! John Jones from the land of my fathers! Where's your latch key to open these cuffs? Long live the Welsh language! Yes, there you are! Welshmen will always be free!" said Wil merrily as the officer released us. As he pulled the handcuffs from our wrists, Wil heaped words of praise upon him, among the most honourable of which were '*trump*', '*old brick*', and '*A1*', mixing up humour, gratitude, and a full and satisfactory explanation of what we had been doing, all in one torrent, without pausing for breath, and finishing with an offer to reward the officer with the price of a good dinner. "No," said the officer, "this 'bluecoat' is an 'exception', and won't be bribed. Go home like good children." "You are *true to nature* and an honour to your country, and you ought to be made an Inspector straight away," said Wil. After some further conversation with the officer, we parted on good terms and in good spirits.

"You know what?" said Wil, I'll never again say that all *bobbies* are *humbugs without exception*. There are *good sorts* even among them. I sometimes think that it's worth getting into a scrape for the joy of getting out of it. Those chaps have only ever had their hooks into me once before—about a year ago. I knew a girl in this town—there was nothing *definite* between us, you understand, but we were *extra* good friends—and one evening I walked her home, and went into the house with her, and stayed there for a while—longer than I thought—I promise you it must have been eleven o'clock. All of a sudden we heard the mistress coming down from the sitting room, and the girl—instead of being straightforward and saying who I was—pushed me into the pantry or something, and it was terribly close in there. Well, I heard the mistress ordering the girl to bed, and then I heard her close the front and back doors, but I didn't imagine that she'd take the keys with her. Then I heard the two of them go upstairs, but I expected that the girl would be back to let me out. I was just about to suffocate, and I opened the door of the pantry, or whatever it was, and the house was as black as the inside of a black cow's stomach, and I didn't know what to do. Well, I waited for a bit, and soon I heard the girl coming down in her stockinged feet, very quietly. I was never gladder to see the light of a candle, and I was in a hurry to get out because I know it's not right to be in anyone's house on the sly. I really felt for the girl as well when she said that her mistress still had the keys, and that I wouldn't be able to get out. But I had to get out, even if I had to cut a hole through the wall, because it wasn't *true to nature*, or *honourable*, to stay in the house all night. I said to the girl, what could be easier than going out through the window of the front room? 'Well yes' she said, in Welsh, since she was a Welsh girl; and she put the candle on the table and off we went to the parlour. I remember well that the moonlight was shining in through the window. There was a flower pot stand by the window, and in my haste I knocked one of the pots over and smashed it to smithereens. Fair play to the girl—she said, 'the cat will get the blame for that'. The bottom part of the window hadn't been opened since I don't know when, and once I'd got it open about ten inches it wouldn't go any further. There was nothing to do except to squeeze through. As I was halfway out I got stuck as sound as Bala's clock, and thought I'd be stuck there for good. But help came. In two minutes I felt someone pulling me out, and I felt all the buttons on my waistcoat being scraped off one by one. It was the bobby—and this is what I was coming to, though I've been a while telling the story. When the girl saw that I was in the hands of the bobby, she burst into tears, and that's when I knew she was fond of me. I said to her, 'Don't cry, Gwen dear—Gwen, her name was—I'll come to see you once I'm out of jail' and she cried all the more. I didn't see her again after that. But here's the point—the bobby knew very well that I hadn't done anything wrong, but he still wanted five shillings to let me go.

After a lot of argument I got him down to half a crown. But their wages are so low, you know, they have to do that from time to time. Are you tired? Or aren't you as fit on your feet as you used to be? You're dragging your feet like anything. Have you got rheumatism, tell me? We don't have far to go now."

"The less the better," I said, "because I'm tired out. But you know what, Wil? sixty-five Gregg Street is still in my mind. How can I get into that house?" Then I told him what I had seen before the policeman put us in handcuffs, and added, "I must, before I leave this town, shed some more light on what I saw. It's obvious that Niclas isn't staying there. His hat was on his head, as if he were about to leave. Do you understand what I'm worried about?" After quite a bit of discussion between Wil and myself, he said:

"*I have it!* Do you remember that I told you not to wear a dog collar too soon? *But circumstances alter cases*—you need to start tomorrow. There are men in this town called *town missionaries*— men who go around looking, not for their friends, but for people who are sick or ungodly, trying to do some good for them. Somehow they find everyone who is sick, as if they can smell them. I've only been sick for four days since I came here, and one of them came to see me three times during it, and said a lot of things to me that would be good, if I did them. There are two things I don't like about them: for one, they expect a man to believe on the spot, and don't give him time to consider; and they push the Gospel too hard, in my opinion. They're not like the Calvinistic Methodists, you know, who think the Gospel is too good to push, and that those who need it will come to chapel to look for it. No, these *town missionaries* are like those people who sell *patent medicine* and *advertise* every day, posting letters into every house that tell of all the people who've been cured by it. What bothers me most about them is that they never seem to be down in the dumps, like your mother was sometimes and old Abel, and some of the other people I knew in the old chapel who were *extra* godly. No danger! The *town missionaries* are always jolly, as if they'd never sinned!

I swear they're good people, because they don't want anything from you except to do good for you. Yet I can't stomach how they're always so cheerful. And they expect everyone else to be the same. I sometimes think that if the angel Gabriel had sinned as much as I have—even if he'd been forgiven—then he'd get a fit of the *glums* occasionally, even in heaven. But the *town missionaries* never get the *glums*; and the ordinary people and the poor respect them, and let them visit their houses and give them advice. Do you see the plan? You speak English well, and there's nothing to stop you going to sixty-five Gregg Street and killing two birds with one stone. Anyway, here's my house. Don't expect anything smart— I haven't taken on a butler yet."

Wil took a key from his pocket and opened the door of his lodging, and after I had followed him in and he had closed the door, we were in total darkness. Wil lit a match, and I saw a small candlestick on the table behind the door, and once Wil had lit the candle he said, "I'm the last one to come in tonight, or you'd see a lot of candles on the table here. This house is the nearest thing you've ever seen—follow me upstairs and don't make any more noise than you have to, because everyone's snoring—the nearest thing you've ever seen to a pigeon shed. There are eight of us lodging here; and we each have a room of our own, and none of us know which room the lady of the house, her daughter, or the maid sleep in, but they're here somewhere. This is my room; and the best you can say about it is that it's clean. Make yourself at home while I get some *grub* ready. You can wash just here, and you can't eat in my house without washing after you've been handling the remains of that *son of a gun*."

I was amazed to see that the room was barely four yards in each direction, but contained a bed, a cupboard, two chairs, a round table, and various other necessary things. On the table there was a clean white tablecloth, one cup and saucer, two plates, and two knives and forks. By the fireside there was a kettle and a coffee pot. "I see," said Wil as he took off his coat and washed, "that you are taking stock. What's it to be then? Tea or coffee?"

"Well, dear Wil, have you come to this?" I said, and couldn't help laughing.

"Come to what?" asked Wil, "to one room? I maintain that it's *true to nature*; every one of God's creatures except man lives in one room once it's left the open air; it's just *humbug* to have a lot of rooms. How can a man live in more than one room at once? That's a *physical impossibility*. You mustn't think I'm *hard up*, as I'll show you in a minute. Say the word. Tea? Or coffee?" "Tea," I said, and "*same here*" replied Wil, opening the cupboard and pulling out the necessaries, and preparing a meal with great aplomb.

"You wouldn't want a better woman than the landlady here," said Wil. "Sometimes I don't see her for a whole week; and whenever I want something, I put the order on that slate there, and put the money on the mantelpiece, and the next time I come home there it will be on the table. When I first came here I didn't always lock the cupboard, and I must admit that my landlady would borrow some of my things from time to time. I'll tell you how I caught her. I was finding that I got through tea remarkably quickly, and what did I do but get a live fly and put it in the canister? The next time I went to open it, the fly was gone. That was certain proof. But it was my fault—the lady was honest enough so long as I kept my cupboard locked."

Wil said all this as he was on his knees before the fire grilling some ham on a fork. In a few minutes the meal was ready, and after a little thought Wil said—"I can see that there's one drawback— there's only one cup and saucer here; but for now, you have the cup, and I'll have the saucer." And so we did; and from that day to this I don't remember ever enjoying a meal more than that one. Next, at my request, Wil told me his own story. Although I believe I could recite it word for word, I will only attempt to chronicle the main points; and that in more or less his own words, which were as follows…

40

THE AUTOBIOGRAPHY OF WIL BRYAN

"You know," Wil said "what made me leave home; I can say it with one word—pride. I had been used to holding my head so high—driving through the streets like *wild fury*, acting the *gallant* with the girls there—that no, I couldn't bear the *disgrace* of my father's *liquidation*. I had a bit of money put aside, but not enough to emigrate; and I came to this big town thinking I'd hit on a job within three or four hours. But when I got here and saw how many people there were, I felt lonely and discouraged, and I was afraid to ask for a job because I hadn't really learned to do anything properly except drive. I knocked around a bit until I ran out of money; and you'd be amazed how hard it is to be proud on an empty stomach. For a few days before the money ran out I'd been loitering around the stables to pick up what information I could, as I could see that it would come to that. You know that I wasn't in rags, and perhaps I had a bit of a swagger, and at first the cabbies would make a bow to me as if I were someone; and to tell the truth, I was ashamed to see them do that. I was cut to the heart when I had to sell the *guard* that my mother had bought me when I was eighteen, but what could I do? I kept going to the stables, and I think the cabbies thought that I was some gentleman's son who had fallen out with his father, as they were very respectful towards me. They'd spotted that I was *hard up*, and they quarrelled with each other to see who would get to buy me a beer thinking that, one day when I made things up with my father, I'd think nothing of dropping them a five pound note in return. This made it even harder to tell them my real story. I pawned my overcoat. By this time, I'd become *chums* with the man who owned the stables, and the horses, and everything. He'd shake hands with me, and quietly try to pump my story out of me, but Wil was too deep for him and remained a *great mystery*. One day—I think the day that I took my watch to the pawn shop—I asked the gaffer for a job as a cabby, and he laughed until he was almost sick, thinking it was just a hobby of mine. But I kept at it. Within two days, one of the men was taken sick with *inflammation of the lungs* after being out at night. I applied for his place until he was mended, and as a bit of fun they gave it to me. When I went out on the *dicky* there were *roars of laughter* in the yard, and the master was laughing the most. But Wil was laughing to himself, and hoping, I'm afraid, that the poor man would be sick for a long time, as I was in dire straits. They soon saw that the *young swell*, as they called me, could handle a horse as well as any one of them, and I was remarkably lucky that day, and the next day, and all week, and I agreed a salary, and the master laughed at the thought of feeding my hobby, or so he thought.

Hanging out with the cabbies, I'm afraid to tell you I came to live the same way as them, and to call for the *everlasting twopenn'orth*.[1] But I wasn't seasoned like they were, you know, and one day I had too much and fell head-first off the *dicky*. They carried me to this bed, and here I stayed for four days, during which the *town missionary* came to look in on me, and give me some advice. He could tell from my accent that I hadn't come from China, and he took a great deal of interest in me. He reasoned with me, and counted up on the slate how much a cabby paid every year to paint his nose black and blue, besides damning his soul, and the amount was staggering. I decided, before leaving the bed, that not one more *twopenn'orth* would be going down Wil's throat ever again, and none has. Remembering how I was a long time ago, this will amaze you. After I became a teetotaller, I became a regular miser. After starting to save money, and getting a taste for it, I was afraid to spend a penny of it, and the last thing I'd do every night before going to bed was to count it

---

[1] A tuppenny glass of beer.

all. Within a few weeks I had pounds, and I'd put them under my pillow every night, and carry them in my waistcoat pocket during the day, for fear that someone would take them. I was afraid to put them in the bank for a reason that I'll tell you soon enough. I lived on bread and butter and tea, and would rather put sixpence in my purse than put *relish* on my supper. One morning in the stables, I was a bit slow with the horse. There were two other cabbies standing near me, waiting for me to finish. I had undone my waistcoat and I was folding it up by the horse's feet, and my purse fell out and about fifteen pounds spilled onto the floor. The two of them nearly fainted to see so much money, and it confirmed in their minds that I was a gentleman's son, and worth thousands, so that they were amazed that I had such a *queer hobby*. They didn't talk about anything else with their chums all day, and next day the gaffer challenged me about my *antecedents*. He knew that I hadn't robbed him—because I was turning more profit for him than anyone in the stables. I kept them all in the dark, and went out and bought a *swell suit* which had pockets everywhere, and then beat myself up over the amount of money I'd spent on it, although I didn't need to because the customers started picking me out for being *respectably dressed*, and I'd get *extra fees*. I had more money than it was safe to carry around in my pocket, so I bought a *lever lock* to put on that box there, and I put it on myself so that no-one spotted it. It cost four-and-six, and I spent eightpence for a gimlet, screwdriver and screws. After coming home in the evening I would entertain myself by counting my money many times over, and then I'd grieve over how much more I'd have if I hadn't spent so much on *twopenn'orths*. Sometimes I'd be amazed at myself and wonder if I was myself, and my conscience said that I was a *humbug*, and that I wasn't *true to nature*, but the way that I made it *shut up* was to recall all the old godly Methodists I knew who were just like me, and how they would groan to part with a shilling. By now I was able to sympathise with them, remembering how when they were in my father's shop they would turn their backs to the counter as they got their money out of their purses, and I remembered how I'd see their shoulders rise as they groaned. And yet my conscience insisted that I was no better than I'd been when I was on the sauce. Yet I taught it to say better things. I had an idea of striking out on my own, because I'd never been reconciled with the thought that I was someone's servant. You know that horses have always been my delight, and that if I know about anything, then it's horses. That's why Mr Edwards of Caerwys and I have always been such *chums*. Anyway—let me know when you're tired of hearing this—anyway, I knew almost every horse in this town, and knew about their *points—good and bad*. One *chap* here had a horse who was a *real good sort*—a horse with a backbone, if you know what I mean. But he was starving him. This *chap* was permanently *three sheets*, and thought he was putting *feed* in the *nosebag* whenever he called for a *twopenn'orth*. You know what, my heart would ache for the creature, and sometimes I'd give it my own horse's nosebag out of pity for it. And Bob—Bob was the name of this horse, the same as your brother—Bob came to know me as well as you do, and perhaps you won't believe this, but I saw him, when I drove towards him, standing to attention out of respect towards me, as if he were expecting something from me—I don't know what. Whatever, Bob was getting worse every day, and in the end just failing to come up to scratch. He was so quiet and sad that even if someone had shot a gun an inch from his ear he wouldn't have winked. One day, in the cabstand, he started shaking terribly, and lots of people gathered round expecting him to fall over any minute. They pulled him from the cab, but it made no difference. Everyone said that the best thing to do would be to finish him off. But before they did that I offered a sovereign for him, as he was, and I got him. I remembered a recipe from Mr Edwards of Caerwys, so I threw my rug over him, and aimed straight for the druggist shop across the street, and I was afraid he'd be dead before I got back. But I knew that he was hungry—because he was panting terribly, just like a hungry man would. By the time I got back, Bob was paying no attention to anybody, and I thought it was all over, and the chaps were asking me how much I'd take for the carcass. But as he was panting I managed to get him to take the medicine, and I asked the chaps to help me rub his legs, to get the circulation back—and they did so, to humour me. Well, I tell you, within ten minutes Bob was reviving and starting to look at what we were doing. There were hundreds of people watching and laughing, and one of the chaps working on his front legs—an Irishman, a wonderfully *witty chap*, jumped five yards and said that Bob had bitten him—and there were *roars of laughter*. You'll find it hard to believe, but within half an hour Bob was eating warm *mash* as well as I'd ever seen him, and the crowd were shouting 'Hooray!' The man who'd sold Bob to me for a sovereign always looked a bit sheepish; but this time he looked like a complete fool. He tried to go back on the bargain, but the crowd protested. I got a reputation for being a *sharp fellow*, but what did they know about Mr Edwards of Caerwys? Well, I rented a stall for Bob, and I tended him, fed him, and did what I could for him, and he got better every day—he wasn't old, you see, and eventually he was kicking and biting everyone around him except me; with me he behaved like a Christian. Between everything, I reckoned he had cost me five pounds by the time I gave a week's notice to my master. I bought a second-hand cab cheaply, and as I started out by myself Bob was brimming with health and shining so much that the other chaps swore I'd been putting *Day and Martin's blacking* on him. *To a certain extent* I became famous, and I had as much work as I needed. The man who sold Bob to me for a sovereign had a go at me every time he saw me, but I paid no attention to that. The more money I got the more I wanted, and I didn't think about anything else—I never looked at a book or a newspaper. I made a lot of money as well by pretending to be a bit of a vet. Are you bored with my story?"

"Since ages ago, Wil," I said, "if you haven't got anything better to talk about, then put a sock in it. You're not yourself."

"Be patient for a minute," said Wil. "When you're preaching do you say your best bits at the beginning or at the end? If you say them at the beginning then you're not *worthy of the craft*. Well, one night, I'd had a good day, and had a quarter of a sausage for my supper; and I counted up my money and found I was worth *forty-eight pounds exclusive of the concern,* and I was feeling happy and *independent.* I think it was the sausage that did it. Without thinking, I started to hum a tune. And what do you think the tune was? The old 'Black Spot',[2] and I don't think anyone has ever had a blessing from singing it except me. Well, I started on it to see if I could remember it, and when I came to the words:

> 'How fare my father and mother,
> How stands their estate?'

"...I broke down, a terrible homesickness came over me, and I couldn't stop crying. I started thinking about the old things, especially my mother, and what a *selfish old devil* I was to collect money for I don't know what, and I felt, I think, something very much like religion. I hadn't written home since I had left, and I didn't know whether they had enough to eat or even if they were still alive. *This is not true to nature,* I said to myself, and I cried for a while more after that, and then I wrote to the gaffer to ask whether he was still alive, and how he was getting on, and what was the total *amount* of his *failure*, and I put the letter in the post that very night in case I changed my mind by the morning. After posting that letter I felt I was no longer a cabby, but that I was Wil Bryan, and I can't tell you the pleasure I had when I felt I was becoming myself again. I didn't change my mind by the morning, and I was burning with desire to have a reply to the letter, and I had one *by return*. The old woman had written it, because my father, so she said, was too *cut up*. But I knew that this was a *dodge* on the old woman's part, in case my

---

[2] 'Y Flotyn Du', obviously not the well-known First World War poem of the same name by Hedd Wyn, but an earlier 18th century traditional ballad about a boy sent into the navy and shipwrecked in India, where he made his fortune, returned home, and in a case of mistaken identity was murdered by his own father for the sake of his gold.

father said something nasty that would send me *fifty miles further*; because I know that old Hugh was never as tender-hearted as that. The old woman was pleading like a cripple for me to come home, and saying how good it was to hear from her prodigal son. She was making a *mistake* in that case, since there's no *analogy* between the prodigal son and me. That *chap's* father was a gentleman, who gave him half his estate, and he spent thousands of pounds, then went to tend pigs and then went home in rags. My father was broke, and I never had a chance to spend so much as five pounds of his money, I never lowered myself to tending pigs, and I swear I'll never go home in rags. There's no *analogy at all*. The old boy's failure was four hundred pounds, and the creditors agreed to accept one shilling in the pound; he'd paid them, and he was getting on all right, and had given up *speculating*, said my mother. But I expect you know all about it. And just fancy the old woman's cunning: 'Suse is still a young girl', she said. The gaffer would never think of *tactics* like that, you know. And although I knew that it was my mother's cunning that made her mention Suse, it had a terrible effect on me, and that moment I'd have given all I had to have a sight of her. But although I was feeling terribly homesick, and I felt that I was coming back to myself—I got a grip, and said that I'd never go home until every farthing of my father's debt was paid back, because I couldn't think of going there unless I could hold my head up high. I wrote to them that I was in good place (though they don't know I'm a *cabby*, and don't you *split* on me), and I made a bargain with them that I'd come home when they had paid the debt, and that I would help them. And that's been going on for a while now. We've paid back about two hundred between us. Here's a receipt I got from the gaffer this morning for ten pounds—read it."

Wil held the letter out to me, and after looking at it I said, "Walter Bateson is the name on this, Wil."

"*Certainly*," said Wil, "that's the reason why I'm afraid to put my money in the bank. I didn't want anyone to know my name here, in case they thought I was Irish, and for other reasons as well."

"That's not worthy of you, Wil," I said.

"What harm is there in it?" said Wil. "Look at them in Wales: no-one of any note goes by their own name there. I have more reason to call myself Walter Bateson than any John Jones has to call himself Llew Twllylwl.[3] '*What's in a name? A rose...*' you know the rest. And *yours truly's* initials, W.B., still stand. But the old folk don't like it at all; and to tell the truth, when I started to come to myself again, I'd have liked to get rid of it if I only knew how." "I heard when I was home," I said, "that your father was paying his debt and regaining his old status, but I had no idea you were helping him. That's a great credit to you. You're doing well, but you'd do better still if you went home to help them. I'm very glad to have met you, Wil, but permit me to say that you have changed a lot. Hearing you talk about nothing but money and..."

"Hold on!" said Wil. "I know that myself. I know I've lost my talent, and can't say anything worth listening to. But you must remember that I'm still in the process of coming to myself; I haven't reached myself yet, but I *am* coming. I don't want to come too fast, but when the *real* W.B. arrives I'll go home."

"Wil," I said, "you haven't said anything about religion, or chapel; do you go to any church or chapel?"

"Not much—I may as well own up. You know that I've never liked the Church. I went once to one of those *dissenting* chapels—*Congregationalists* they called themselves—and I sat near the door. The minister is a Welshman, by the name of Price, and they're *advertising* him all the time. Well, out of *curiosity*, I went there. And what do you think his *text* was? Old Morgan Dyffryn's text, about the little foxes—I don't remember the verse, but it's somewhere in the Old Testament,[4] but I remember a lot of the sermon because it tickled me more than a little. Well wait a minute, I said to myself,

---

[3] 'The Lion of Twllylwl', the latter meaning roughly 'sleepy hollow'.

[4] The author probably has in mind a book in the Bible called The Song of Solomon and chapter 2:25, '*Catch the foxes for us, the little foxes that are ruining the vineyards, while our vineyards are in blossom*'.

can you do as well as Old Morgan on that verse? And I settled down to listen. But I spotted inside ten minutes that all *my nabs* was doing was translating Old Morgan's sermon, and I bolted for it, since someone who steals sermons is no better than a man who steals sovereigns, nor even as good, since he gets paid for the sermon and the other guy gets *three months*. I didn't go anywhere for a while after that. But by *accident* I went one Sunday night to one of these Wesley chapels, and I'd have thought the minister's praying was *first class*—if he'd had peace and quiet to pray, but you've never seen the like of it! A lot of the congregation were passing remarks loudly about his prayer as he prayed, and I don't know how he wasn't distracted. He preached about Peter after he'd slipped up and made a mess of things, and I was quite *well up* on the story so I took an *interest*. But if Peter had heard him he wouldn't have thanked him, because he was running him down terribly. I didn't like the man's theology either. He said that a man could find religion and then lose it again, and that many times, and that everything depended on the man himself. If it's like that, I said to myself, then it's *good bye to Wil Bryan*. I reasoned that if the man was bungling it with things I was *well up* on, how could I know whether he'd be *right* about things I didn't know about? I never went there again. I didn't spot a Welsh Calvinistic Methodist church in this town until a fortnight ago. I went there. It was nothing like the old chapel at home. A lot of *swells* sitting in the Great Seat. As I looked around, I could see the occasional Abel Hughes here and there, but the *swells* were in the Great Seat. A young chap was preaching, and I could tell from the cut of his jib that he was one of these *postage stamps* from Bala—*no offence*, mind. Don't you think it would be good if a new sect came up combining the *good points* of all the denominations? Like this: the *style* of the Church of England, the *smartness* of the dissenters, the *go-aheadness* of the Wesleyans—and the theology of the Calvinistic Methodists. I don't know much about the Quakers, but I suppose they must have their good points too. Every sect beats the others in some category or other. I like the style of the

Church of England—so devotional; they don't look around or talk to each other when they're in church; but they're terribly ignorant. Then there are the dissenters; look how *smart* and *witty* they are. They're terribly clever, but there's too much politics about them and they're too much into their eisteddfods. Almost every one of them can write an englyn, and almost every one of them has a bardic name, though I'd better not criticise them for that. Then there are the Wesleyans; look how zealous, warm and *jolly* they are. But I think they're terribly *clannish*. They all pray the same as well, and too boldly—as if they're talking to the bloke next door. Then you have us Calvinistic Methodists—I say 'us' because I still count myself an *honorary member*. I think the Calvinistic Methodists are the *John Bull* of Wales. The dissenters won't admit it, of course, but they may as well. The Calvinistic Methodists make me think of a fat, lazy man who's hard to move; there's no use trying to tickle him, his skin is too thick, he'll move when he's good and ready; but when he does he's like an elephant, and it doesn't matter what you hook on to him, he'll drag it with him. You understand that I'm talking figuratively here? You know Duke, William the Coal's mule? I don't know how he is nowadays, but a long time ago there was no stronger mule in the land; yet he wouldn't move a step until he was ready, and nothing had any effect on him besides old William's crop. In the summertime other mules would have a hazel branch tied to their heads to help them brush the flies away; but what did Duke care about flies? Nothing had any effect on him except William's crop, and I swear that if they do a *post-mortem examination* on him they'll find that his skin is like a pepper box. But I've seen Duke, when it suited him, pull twelve hundredweight of coal up the terrace like a fly. I look at the Calvinistic Methodists the same way. Perhaps you'll say I'm showing a *want of taste*, and am guilty of an *anticlimax*, but you must remember that I've never been to college. That's what I think; that the Calvinistic Methodists are too *slow*; they have plenty of *power*, but no go. They're too solemn as well, too much like a funeral. Well, don't you think it would be possible to start a new denomination to combine the good points of all the others? What do you think?"

"I think, Wil, that you're 'coming back to yourself' but you've lost none of your old sharpness. But as for starting a new denomination, don't you think it would be better to combine the virtues that you were talking about in our own selves? What do you think about starting a new *life*? Don't you sometimes long for something that you don't have, and when you do have it you won't have to give it up like the twopenn'orth and the miserliness? You're doing well to pay back your father's debt; but what about your own debt? *That* will have to be paid by someone, you know. In other words, what do you think about the terrible future that awaits you and me? What do you think now about religion?"

"I was expecting you to talk about things like that," said Wil seriously, "and if you hadn't then I'd have said you weren't fit to be a preacher. I don't think that your words are just *cant*, and I know that you want what's best for me; but I don't know how to answer your question. I'd be lying if I said that religion wasn't on my programme; but so far it's still on the *second part* of it. There was a time when it was very low down on the second part, only just above *God Save the Queen*. I made that same *remark* to the *town missionary*, and I'll always remember his reply: 'What if you had to leave in the *interval*? When you fell head-first off the *dicky* you came very close to leaving before the end of the *first part*'. He did well, didn't he? Well, to tell you the truth, for some time I've thought that religion has moved higher up the programme, and sometimes I long for its turn to come. Although I'm still a young chap I've had just about enough of the *comic songs* of my life—if you get my meaning. I'm almost always *jolly*, but I've never been happy. No matter how jolly I am, I always know that there's something that smells off in my heart's buttery. That's the difference between the happiness of a godly man and the happiness of a natural man—nothing stinks in the godly man's buttery. What I want to know is, how can I give the buttery a *clean sweep*? Because ever since I came to this town—no matter how jolly I've been when in the pub, or with my *chums*, or after counting my money—as soon as I go to bed I can smell the bad odours coming up from the buttery. Do you get my meaning?"

"Perfectly, Wil," I said, "and I'm glad in my heart that you're tired of the smell, and that your mind longs for cleansing and true happiness. I hardly need say…"

"There you go again," said Wil, "I don't need a sermon—I've heard thousands of those, but I want some *sound common sense* advice. Because I never go to chapel I don't have a proper *chum*, and that's not *true to nature*. As for the *chaps* I work with every day, there's nothing in their heads and they never think of anything besides drink. Although I never got religion properly—because I don't think it's possible for a man to get *the real thing* and then lose it again—I sometimes think that I've had some sort of inoculation in the old chapel at home, so that I'll never get the smallpox heavily. I had a *slight attack* of it when I came here first, but it didn't leave a deep impression. Do you get my meaning?"

"Of course," I said. "The two of us were brought with religion from childhood, and even so we've lost the way and wandered around a lot; but I've always hoped, Wil, that you hadn't lost the good impressions, or the 'inoculation' as you call it."

"But your inoculation has taken more than mine; I'll need to have a fresh one before I'm safe," said Wil.

"Go to the doctor, then," I said, "and ask for the surgery. By now you've 'spotted' the Welsh chapel. I don't want to suggest that other denominations aren't as good as ours; but our upbringing, and perhaps our prejudices, prevent us from receiving as much blessing from them as we can expect from the Calvinistic Methodists. What's stopping you from going to chapel regularly? You'll find friends there quickly, since you're so good at introducing yourself. And who knows whether you'll find the Friend who sticks closer than a brother.⁵"

"That's where I'd like to be solidly, every Sunday," said Wil. "But if I were to go, the minister and the elders would spot me, and ask me

462

my name, and where I live, and I'd have to say William Bryan, and my house number, or I'd be a *humbug*. So, the minister will come here to visit, and he'll ask, 'Is Mr William Bryan at home', and the landlady will say, 'There's no-one here with that name'; and how will I look? If I give my false name in the chapel then it will look like I'm trying to trick the Good Lord, and I'll never do that. I'd be able to overcome the difficulty by changing my lodging if it weren't Walter Bateson who'd registered the cab, and I don't think they allow just the initials. But I see every day, as I come to myself, that sooner or later I'll have to drop the 'alter' and 'ateson' and substitute 'illiam' and 'ryan' before I arrive. If I can't find any neat way to get out of it I'll just throw my *inverness* away—I'll show a *bold front*, and take my seat in the chapel—*take my word*. But there you are, if you want to be in trim tomorrow to visit the sick, then we'd better go to the kennel, because it's now quarter to three.

There was only a single step between us and the bed, and I was glad that the journey was so short. I slept hard: and I remember that for some minutes in the morning when I was half awake, I couldn't make out whether I was feeling bacon or smelling someone shaking me. When I woke up properly I could see that the two things were vice versa. Wil was by my head, having had great trouble waking me, and the smells of bacon and coffee filled the room. While I rubbed my eyes, I felt like I had been in a dream, although the room and everything in it corresponded exactly with what I'd been dreaming about, except that there were now two cups and saucers on the table instead of one. Wil and I spent a few more hours talking about old times, before starting on the day's work.

---

[5] Prov. 18:24, in this context a reference to Christ.

41

THE FIRST AND LAST TIME

"Now for the dog-collar,"[1] said Wil, "if you want to get into that house; and if I were you I'd give the *idea* a *fling*, because what else can you do? I'll go and look for the choker in two minutes, and while you're decking yourself out I'll go and fetch Bob, because I'm donating today to the Queen."

When I was a boy Wil had a habit of ordering me about, and I felt myself once again in his hands and under an obligation to wear a dog-collar and follow his instructions. I was willing to subject myself to almost any scheme to achieve my end that morning, since I felt the duty towards the one that I'd loved most, and if I lost the opportunity then it would trouble me for ever afterwards. I understood that Wil had borrowed a trap, so that he wouldn't be hailed. Although I had heard so much about Bob the previous night, my mind was too troubled with thoughts about how my venture would turn out to take much notice of him when I got to see him in daylight. But I do remember that he looked quite healthy, and Wil said that the other 'chaps' called him 'Lazarus'. Our programme for the day was that Wil would take me by carriage to Gregg Street and leave me there to carry out my errand; then, after half an hour, he would come and collect me to spend the rest of the day in whatever way we thought best. But 'a man's life is not his own'.[2] When we were within a hundred yards of the place where we'd been taken prisoner the night before, Wil pulled up the reins and said agitatedly, "My word! That's the bobby who nabbed us last night, and he's coming straight for us!" That was the

---

[1] In the original, Wil uses the English word '*choker*'.

[2] 1 Cor. 6:19, Jer. 10:23.

case; and within a minute he was alongside us ordering us to stop. Wil and I were thoroughly shaken. "Rhys Lewis," said the officer, "come down!" I obeyed; and although I was trying to appear brave I felt myself shaking, and I knew that I'd gone pale. Wil jumped down at the same moment, saying, "I'll follow you wherever you're going, even if the whole concern ends up in Bryn Eglwys," and he threw the reins onto Bob's back. The officer smiled, and said, "Don't be frightened. Do you know me, Rhys Lewis?" "*To be sure*," said Wil, "it was you who lent us a pair of cuffs last night." "Wil," said the policeman, "don't you remember being lent the end of my cane more than once?" After staring at him hard for a few seconds, Wil said, "Well, I'll be a bedpost! If you're not *Sergeant* Williams. No wonder you turned up trumps last night! How are you, old A1? Can't you get a *leave of absence* for today?" "Perhaps I can, Mr Bateson," said the officer. Wil looked flummoxed, and said, "*True to nature, Sergeant*, but a Welshman must have a pseudonym—just a bardic name, you know." "I didn't know that cabbies were famous for their poetry," said the *Sergeant*. "Hush!" said Wil, "*least said, soonest mended*. I feel just as if I were home; I'm here, and Rhys Lewis, and *Sergeant* Williams—all we need is William the Coal, and Duke, and that old *thoroughbred* Thomas Bartley, and we'd be a *compact*."

At first the appearance of *Sergeant* Williams caused me a great deal of discomfort, as my memories of him were not sweet; but my fears were soon laid aside. After some conversation, Wil leapt into his carriage and off he went. The *Sergeant* came with me to 65 Gregg Street and knocked on the door. It was opened by a large woman, rather masculine in appearance, and I saw at once that she and the *Sergeant* knew one another. He informed her of my errand, and left. The woman led me to the room that I had been trying to peer into the previous night, and after she had said "the minister," she left me and closed the door behind her. Since I had got up that morning my heart had been beating heavily, as I felt I had a task to accomplish that would not be pleasant for me; yet I couldn't avoid it even if the heavens fell down. Before me I saw the one whom I'd partly seen the night before, and in the same state—sitting in his bed. I pulled myself together as best I could, and greeted him in English as soon as I entered the room, though many thoughts went through my heart before I spoke, and before he answered. This was the first time I had ever seen his face; but my breast carried the burden of his story, and the story was anything but comforting. When I asked him how he felt, he answered in one word—"*Bad*." When I asked him whether he held any hope of recovery, he shook his head sadly. When I asked him again for his thoughts about his prospects, he would only shake his head. I tried to lead him to think about God and His mercy even to the chief of sinners, and about as many of the Bible's promises as I could remember, but the only answer I could get from him was a shaking of the head that displayed the greatest misery and deepest despair. After I had run out of things to say I fell silent, and felt myself being carried back in time to a bedroom in Thomas Bartley's house, where I heard my mother, at death's door, charging me again and again—"If you ever meet him, and who knows whether you will, try to remember that he's your father—try to forget his sins, and if you can do some good for him, do so." Then my mind went back to the night that Seth died, when I met my uncle in the Manor woods, when he said the words that opened my eyes to my family's history, and when Bob my brother told me that same night, after I had gone to bed, talking quietly in the darkness, my father's story—his decline, his prodigality, and his cruelty towards my mother. I remembered how I had to bite on my bedclothes to stop myself crying out when Bob told me how my mother would have to stay home from chapel to hide her two black eyes when my father had beaten her. I remember being amazed at how she could pray for him when he had just hit her, before the blood on her apron was even dry. Oh! How I hated him at that time! How glad I was that I had never seen his face! But now here I was by his side, and I heard the words—not as a recollection from the past—but as if they were being spoken for the first time in the same voice, "If you ever meet him, and who knows whether you will, try to remember that he's your father—try to forget his sins, and if you can do some good for him, do so." Here I was looking at him, and I could hardly take it in. He, who had once been a strong man, appeared before me as a worthless wretch; and I didn't need the help of the smell of whisky that permeated the place, to understand what brought him to this state. My uncle and he had pretty much followed the same path. Should I reveal myself to him? Would that be wise? Would it do any good? It was obvious that his life was about to end, and I had done my best to draw his attention to the seriousness of his situation, and to put before him the graciousness of the Gospel, and how it held out hope to the chief of sinners even in their last hour. I had reminded him of those who had been called at the eleventh hour, and about the thief on the cross, but nothing I said seemed to touch him or excite any interest in him. I had tried to pray with him, but he flatly refused to do so. What else could I do for him? I'd never seen anyone looking so pitiful, and I hope that I never shall again. He looked like one who had bidden farewell to any hope or comfort, and who was sinking into a deep and fearful darkness; and any mention I made of the Bible seemed to make him plunge yet deeper. The verses I reminded him of, instead of comforting him, seemed to frighten him, like old acquaintances that he was terrified of meeting again, and I noticed that he was using what strength he had left to recoil from me and press harder against the wall behind him. Sometimes he appeared agitated as though his heart was pounding, and he would grip his bedclothes tightly; and other times he would relax as if he were taking a long journey deep inside himself and forgetting that I was in the room. But he'd soon return, and after looking wildly around the room and seeing that I was still there, he would turn again uncomfortably towards the wall. I knew that I was a burden to him, and that he was longing for me to leave, because he reached his hand more than once towards the bottle of whisky that was on the bedside table, yet pulled it back when he remembered that I was watching him. By now he was not taking much notice of anything I said, and I was afraid that I could not do him any good, so I rose to leave. But the words came to me again—"If you ever meet him…" as if they came from the other world. Would I have done my best for him if I had failed to speak to him in Welsh, or to tell him who I was? Wouldn't it mean something for him to know that my mother had forgiven him for his inhuman treatment of her, even if that was the only forgiveness he ever experienced? I decided to reveal myself to him, and I tried to pray that it would have a good effect on him. I said to him in Welsh:

"Robert Lewis, do you know who it is that's speaking to you?" He was startled by my question, and looked harshly at me, something he hadn't done before. He kept his eyes on me without closing them, and they were remarkably clear—like two lanterns lighting his way into the depths of his hopelessness, which would, I thought, be put out once he had passed away. I guessed that his mind was going back to find any recollection about me, but unsuccessfully of course, so I spoke to him again:

"I am your son, Rhys Lewis. My father, be pleased to hear that my mother forgave you everything before she died."

I repented a thousand times for letting these words descend from my lips. It was only a short sentence, but it caused me more pain than anything I've ever said. If I had poured a bucket of fire over his head the effect could not have been more terrifying. He flailed and writhed as if in the most indescribable tortures. He screamed madly, with strength beyond what I thought he had, for me to get out of his sight, "Go away! Go away!" and recoiled from me as though I were a snake. He pressed himself close against the wall and would, if he could, have gone through it. Frightened by his groans the lady of the house rushed into the room and stared at me like a lioness. She asked angrily what I had done to the patient, and I was afraid that she was going to plant her fingernails in my face. I was too frightened to try to give her an explanation, and I fled for my life. Remembering the scene, my memory has often returned to the words of the unclean spirits, 'Have you come here to torment us before the time?'[3] and the words of Ellis Wynn from Lasynys,[4]

> 'I wouldn't want to see it again,
> For ten thousand worlds;
> Even though it was not my own suffering'.

My visit lasted no more than twenty minutes, but it forms the darkest part of my story. I must confess that I didn't feel the pang that would be natural for a son seeing his father in such a state, as there had never been any love for him in my heart. 'Horror' is the best word to describe what I felt. The sight had made me myself pitiful, and my only comfort was that I had discharged, to the best of my ability, my mother's last wish.

The Sergeant and Wil were waiting for me in the appointed place. I reported the outcome of my visit to them, and was told off by Wil for failing to take his advice and forget the whole idea of it. By now I was anxious to return to Bala, since my final exam was due to take place the following week. I could tell that the Sergeant had something to tell me, and I was right because he pulled me aside and asked, "Lewis, do you have anything to hide from Bryan?" "Nothing," I replied. "Jolly good," he said, and then added more loudly, "Well boys, where can we go?" "I would like to start for Bala at once," I said. "You're not leaving here today if we have to put shackles on your feet, like William the Coal used to do with Duke to stop him rambling," said Wil, but neither Wil nor the Sergeant were able to persuade me to stay. Wil told me that there was no train for an hour and a half, and I took his word. The Sergeant and I were led by Wil to a hotel where we could get something to eat, or as he put it, "*a last blow-out on yours truly's account.*" I ate only a

---

[3] Matt. 8:29.

[4] A clergyman and poet who lived from 1671 to 1734.

little, as I was hanging on Sergeant Williams' every word. Here is a summary of what he said:

"It's many years, Lewis, since I last saw you. In fact I haven't seen you since the night I came to your house to arrest your brother. I won't forget that night as long as I live. I knew that Bob wasn't guilty, and yet I had to take him. Your mother's pale face has haunted me ever since then. Bob and I were great friends, and I knew your mother well. I think you remember, because I saw you leaving the house, about the two men who attacked us just as we left the yard? You know who they were. I made the other policeman swear not to mention it to anyone. Their intention, as you know, was to give Bob a chance to escape, if he wanted to take it. The next day, which was the Sunday, I met the Squire as he was going to church and I told him that I was sure that Bob, John Powell and Morris Hughes were not guilty and that it was a mistake to arrest them. He flew into a temper and swore at me, calling me a fool many times over. I told him that he should hurry to church and pray. I knew right then that my own fate was sealed, and that the knave wouldn't rest until he had got rid of me. Do you remember the destruction which was wrought upon his pheasants the night that Bob was taken to the county jail? The colliers were blamed for it. Was it them? No chance! I knew very well that there were two men in the land who had more daring than all the colliers put together. Bob knew that, and so did your mother, poor lady. I wasn't going to tell the Squire, though; in fact, if everything he owned was on fire and I could have put it out by spitting on it, I wouldn't have done so because he always treated me like a dog. After all this had happened, I felt very unhappy because I knew I was hated by all sides and there was nothing I could do about it. Indeed, I don't think I'm really cut out to be a policeman. Before that trouble I had many friends back home, but afterwards everyone showed me the cold shoulder, and not just me but every policeman in the place. I wasn't sorry to have to leave. I've lived here ever since then, and have been quite comfortable. About three years ago, quite accidentally, I came across your father. He took fright when he saw me, as he remembered that I knew he was guilty of something much worse that poaching. But he didn't need to be afraid, and I told him so. I'm a good policeman, aren't I? But I felt that I owed a kindness to your mother, and to Bob, and I didn't want to air things that were best left hidden. After that I met him many times; and before he became totally enslaved to the drink, I visited him at home from time to time, to chat and to get news from home, since he often went over to visit with your uncle and they helped themselves to the old Squire's game. They didn't hide that from me, and I wouldn't have cared if they had every pheasant in the place, such was my grudge against the old bastard. I never liked your uncle, but I could get on all right with your father. Perhaps it was because we both had the same deadly enmity towards the old Squire. Your uncle didn't care whose game it was, so long as he could get his hands on it, but your father took particular pleasure from being able to say of his prey, 'This is the *Squire's* game—it costs him ten shillings a head!' Your father and uncle were systematically plucking the estate over the years, and if I were put on oath I couldn't swear that none of the pheasants had found their way onto my table over the last three years, as I was friends with your father. I'm a good policeman, aren't I? As I ate the pheasants, the sense of revenge was better than sauce on them. I always wondered how they managed not to get caught after so many years, until it was explained to me. You remember Niclas from Garth Ddu? He managed the whole thing, and provided a bolthole for them. Your father told me that Niclas was a game dealer, who knew half the poachers in the kingdom and did business with most of them. He'd made a great deal of money that way, and your father and uncle had dealt with him a lot before he retired. Your father persuaded him to buy Garth Ddu, which became a *city of refuge*[5] for him and your uncle. The two maintained a continuous correspondence with Niclas. As you know, no-one at home thought that Niclas was quite the full package; but your father

---

[5] Referring to cities set aside in Old-Testament Israel for manslaughter suspects to flee to.

said, if anyone was ever thirty-seven inches to the yard, it was Niclas! He was their scout, and he took pleasure in his work. He walked along all the roads, and through the Manor woods, and Berth Goch, all hours of the day and night without anyone suspecting him, but rather they feared him as an idiot. He knew where the keepers were watching every night of the year. Everything that happened in the town was relayed to him by Modlen. How your father would laugh when he told me about the merry evenings they had in Garth Ddu after making a great haul! But it's all over now. I expect you know that Niclas has sold Garth Ddu? Oh yes, he sold it three months ago, and he lives here now, and looks just the same as the first time I saw him. He looks after your father. When your father dies, no-one knows where Niclas will be the next day. Well, you must remember that everything I'm telling you is strictly confidential.

By now I had completed my mission in Birmingham; I'd had more light shed on what had previously been dark to me than I'd expected, so I was in a hurry to return. The Sergeant and Wil came with me to the station, and the latter said to me, entirely sincerely, I know, "If I'd known you were going to go away again so abruptly, you'd have had no *drag through the sheets* last night; because I haven't said to you a thousandth of the things I want to. It's like a preacher ending his sermon just as he's catching the *hwyl*. It's not *true to nature*, and by the time I've come to myself and gone home, you won't be there; because by then you'll be the minister of Llanygogor[6] or somewhere, and I won't have a single *chum* there."

"You don't know the half of it, Wil," I said. "What do you think?" (The train was by now just about to start.) "I've been called to pastor Bethel church, and now there's nothing in my way to stop me from accepting it." Wil looked joyfully at me and said "*Fact?*" (The train was starting.) "Well, *bye bye*, and remember to be *true to ...*"

I didn't hear the last word but I could guess what it was, as I'd heard

---

[6] A wholly fictitious place.

it from him hundreds of times. If I'd known at that moment that that would be the last time I'd see him, my heart would have been heavier than it was; since despite all his deficiencies Wil's affability, honesty and naturalness, together with his great faithfulness to me when I was a young lad, had made for him a place in my heart that I couldn't despise even if I wanted to, and I long to see him now. While I was rushing back, I made an energetic attempt to forget about the past and set my sights upon the future. My nature had received such a shaking, and my mind was so badly unsettled, that I dreaded the day of the exam. I knew that my score would be much lower than would have been the case were it not for the events that I've just described. This caused me a great deal of pain. I knew that some would be all too ready to say that I'd been lazy, and I couldn't imagine a more hateful accusation, nor one from which I was more innocent, whatever else my faults were. Then my mind returned to my father in his pitiful state. So terrible! And yet I felt a quietness of conscience because I had done my best for him, and I imagined, if indeed I was imagining it, a familiar voice saying to me, 'Don't worry, my boy, you have done your duty, as I did for him also. It's between him and God now'. A ray of light shone into my mind. My journey to Birmingham had not been in vain. I believed that my meeting with Wil had been a blessing. I had reason to believe that he was not untroubled by the seriousness of his situation. He had given his word that he would go to chapel, and I knew that Wil didn't consider anyone who broke his word to be *true to nature*. Besides that, I felt that I had been delivered from the nightmare that had haunted me for years. Now I could throw myself into the work of preaching without fearing that my name would be dragged into shame. The thing that worried me most by now was the exam. I knew that I cut a sorry figure. But I was saved. When I arrived in Bala, I felt very strange. I thought that the whole town had been transformed in two days, and I wondered if I'd made a mistake and that I wasn't in Bala after all. I was glad that it late at night, because my legs were shaking and I was afraid that people might

473

think I was drunk. I had a great deal of trouble finding my way to my lodgings, and then opening the door. But I was right after all, because Williams met me and shook my hand welcomingly. I don't remember anything else.

Nine or ten days after this, I found myself in bed. It was daylight, and I tried to sit up, but couldn't. Then I saw Williams by my side, and he said, "Well, boy, how do you feel?" And I said, "What's the matter? Who hit me? Where have I been?" I saw his face relax as he saw that I was coming to myself. He urged me to relax as well, and told me that I'd been very ill. "What day is it?" I asked, "when does the exam start?" "It was all over yesterday, lad, so you can't be at the bottom or at the top this time round. You need to keep quiet, as you've been in a heavy fever, and have been shouting night and day for Wil Bryan and some Sergeant, but you've taken a turn for the better and I'm heartily glad to see it. Oh! Here's Dr Hughes. Well, Doctor, you'll get some sense from him today." "Has he tired of talking about Wil Bryan? It's about time he changed his story," said the doctor. Dr Hughes was a popular, genial and merry man (who had one failing: he never sent a bill to a student), and he joked with me a lot that day. I asked him when I could go home, and he answered, "You need to go to Jericho first to wait for your hair to grow back."[7] I felt my head and, oh! My hair had all been shaved. I was sad to find out how much vainer I was than I had thought. I asked how long it would take for my hair to grow back enough for me not to frighten myself and anyone who saw me. Weeks passed before I was strong enough to return home. Williams stayed with me for a fortnight, and his kindness was beyond description. A few days before we parted, I told him the essentials of the long story that I've now nearly completed; and I believe that no-one alive knows it besides Williams and Wil Bryan, and if it ever sees the light of day after I myself have gone the way of no return, the facts will not be unfamiliar to either of them.

---

[7] 2 Samuel. 10:4–5.

THE MINISTER OF BETHEL

I now need to bring my autobiography to a conclusion, for the same reason, partly, that I was compelled to start it. What was that? I'll state it in a few words. I have now spent some years in Bethel in the role of its pastor. When I started to write my memoirs, I imagined that the history of these years would form the greater part of it. I now see that that is out of the question, and I regret having taken so much time to talk of things far less important. It wasn't without a great deal of trepidation that I started, aged less than thirty years, to pastor the church that I had been brought up in. I feared myself rather than the church, because I knew every one of the members and they were genial and kind people. I didn't need to take any time to make myself at home. In going to lodge with Miss Hughes I was going to my old home, and the only thing new to me was the work. It's not my place to say how qualified I was to do the work, but I can say that my heart was full of it, and my longing to fulfil it in the best possible way was overpowering. I felt that taking up such a job presumed a high level of ambition, and I was often ashamed of myself. But I think that the responsibility that was upon me caused me to pray more. If I were to fail, I was determined that it would not be because of idleness, negligence or a sense of self-sufficiency. I worked hard—perhaps too hard—though I don't take any credit for that, I couldn't help it. My salary was small, but it was enough; my needs were not great. Indeed, I often took comfort in how small my salary was. It was not big enough to cause me discomfort of mind, and it was too small for anyone to go to the trouble of grudging it to me. If anyone had, I'm afraid I might have declined it altogether, as quite a lot of the foolish sense of independence that my mother had was in me also. However, no-one did. I strived to do my duty; and I had an ambition, or a principle or something, to satisfy those whom I served. The harder I worked, the quieter was my mind, and the sounder I slept at night. The minute I stepped back from the plate, my old enemy—depression—would come upon me. I haven't had many causes to complain since I have been here; and when I have, the many causes for gratitude that I've also had have caused me to keep quiet. I was not neglected by the Monthly Meeting, and I was chosen for ordination much sooner than I deserved. I had every help and encouragement from David Davies and the *Eos*, and every kindness from the church in general, especially the young people.

About two years ago, I felt that everyone's kindness to me was increasing. If I had a journey of six or eight miles to make, David Davies would lend me his horse. Miss Hughes would take more care than usual to make sure that I was well bundled up. Thomas Bartley charged me every day to eat plenty of meat and eggs, and everyone else urged me to take good care of myself. The interest that was taken in me caused me to think hard about the cause of it. I knew that I didn't deserve it. What could the reason be? It didn't take me long to find out, and once I did, I found I could see it in the look and the behaviour towards me of every one of my friends. I was getting weaker. I had always been a bit of a weakling, and for some time I'd noticed that I wasn't as strong as usual, but I didn't imagine I was in danger. Others had noticed it before I did. When I did, my spirit fell further. The doctor tried to encourage me, and said that there was nothing wrong with me but a bit of weakness, and I needed a change of air and some rest. Where would I go? I liked the seaside. No, I couldn't go to the sea; it would be better for me to go to Trefriw.[1] I understood the suggestion. Ah, Sea! You were the first part of the Earth that I had to pull myself away from!

---

[1] A village in the Conwy valley, with a spa that had been known since Roman times and in the late 19th century was known by some as the 'healthiest place in Wales'. Mary Owen, born in Trefriw in 1803, lived to be the oldest person in Britain when she died in 1911 aged 108. The translator's grandmother had family there.

And what a painful parting it was. Although you always made me sombre, I liked to be beside you. I felt that your sound corresponded to something in my breast that I was not able to describe. I felt that you carried something of the unknown to me from a great distance away. But, I was forbidden to go to you. I went to Trefriw, and there I met with a few of my old friends, some of whom were foolish enough to say that they were surprised to see me looking so much better. Even so, they tried to comfort me and be merry with me, and help me to forget myself; but underneath their cheerfulness I could see the sadness of their pity towards me. How I envied their health and vitality! But Trefriw did me a lot of good, and before I left I enjoyed a bit of harmless fun around the springs there; I felt better, and I can hardly describe my joy, the deep feeling of happiness that I felt in my breast. When I came back to Bethel the friends there were astonished at the improvement to be seen in me, and they were glad. I preached the following Sunday without feeling tired, and my joy was great.

Weeks passed, and I found myself in decline again, and thought that I needed nothing more than to go back to Trefriw. I went. It was the first day of October. As far as I could tell, I was the only visitor in the village. The weather was cold and wet. I stayed in my room for four days and returned home in a worse state than when I had left. I feared that my doctor didn't understand my condition, and by now the first things I read in any newspaper would be the advertisements placed by the quack doctors. Secretly I spent a lot of money before realising that the advertisements were lies, and that most of the 'letters of testimonial' were figments of the quack doctors' imaginations. I couldn't hide the fact that I was weakening, as I felt that the work of preaching was getting harder every Sunday, and the offers of various kind elders to lead the service for me were an index of my true state of health, which saddened me further. To begin with, I refused their kindness, but afterwards I accepted it gratefully. It's now a year since I last preached; but I think I would have stuck at it for longer if I hadn't been advised by a new doctor who told me the truth and commanded me to cease work at once. Shouldn't one always tell the truth? There is one truth I must tell—that I often regretted the fact that that doctor didn't withhold the truth from me. The truth was terrible for me, and my spirits sank into a terrible depression. For a while I didn't want to speak to anyone. From somewhere within me stirred a manic desire to grip onto life, that I hadn't been conscious of before. I felt that I had been deceived by what I had previously trusted in the most. For days and nights I argued in my head with doctors, with fate, with Providence, and even (I'm afraid to say) with God. Every day I would see going past my window men who were much older than me, who were broad-shouldered, strong, barrel-chested; yes, and some of them swore, cursed and got drunk; and here was I, poor man, my chest like an old basket! Who ordered things this way? Was everything just down to chance after all? All my plans had come to nothing, and I felt keenly the power of the saying, 'And then all his plans come to naught'[2] coming home to me. I had various sermons on death, and on the world to come, and similar subjects—but how empty they seemed to me now! How cold and soulless! If I had opportunity, how much better I could have preached! It took me weeks before I could submit to the inevitable, and I tendered my resignation. How hard the effort was! By now, everything was appearing in a new light. Things that I had used to take a great interest in, like politics and literature, lost all their charm, and I was amazed to think that they'd ever held any charm for me. The number of things that I thought about decreased every day, until my mind was given wholly to the question of what my spiritual fate would be. By now the Truths that I had rejoiced in so much as I preached them only saddened me and sunk me into depths of sadness that I can't describe.

Yet it was by heaven's grace that I eventually gained victory over my depression. I became more willing to humble myself under

---

[2] Psalm 146:4.

the hand of God, and to cast myself into His arms. At times, I experienced glimpses of profound joy, and flashes of light at the grand design of the Gospel, that I had never experienced before I was so troubled. From time to time I would quietly rejoice in my state, and feel a powerful longing for the perfection and glory of the spiritual world. Sometimes I would look upon my body and its weakness as something separate from myself, and would laugh at it. Then I would relax into a joyful quietness, guessing what unpleasant things I had been spared through being waylaid along the road in this way. If I had lived, perhaps I would have met some temptation that was too strong for me and would have brought me and my testimony to shame. I thought of some that I knew; what a mercy it would have been for them to die young! Again there came some periods of sadness, and I lost myself in morbid and unedifying thoughts. In the midst of one of these times, I was struck by a remarkable idea: if Providence was going to take me away in the midst of my days, couldn't I play a trick on it and re-live my life, in my mind, and so in effect double it? Couldn't I, so long as my strength allowed me, spend a few hours each day going through the chief events of my life? This kept me from thinking over useless things, and from eating away at myself before my time. While on my own I felt reasonably well, and perhaps writing my autobiography would do me some good. This great volume is the result of that idea. It has been written by a sad man. This may appear remarkable considering how many amusing things are described in it; but that's not at all strange. Even if there's too much here about Wil Bryan, I flatter myself that there are also some things here that every serious-minded man—every man who has been awakened to the big questions of life—needs to think carefully about. If not, then the fire would be the best place for this manuscript.

I'd have liked to be able to record something more definite and comforting about Wil Bryan; but I've heard nothing from him in ages. In his last letter to me, he said that he had finished paying his father's debt, and that he was still going to the Welsh chapel, but that he still 'hadn't come to himself'. My last letter to him was returned, with '*left without address*' written across it. That was months ago, and I haven't heard anything more from him. Has Wil gone with the tide? No, I have a presentiment that Wil shall return.

I received a charge, as I said, from my mother when she was on her deathbed, that I should pay back Thomas and Barbara Bartley for their kindness to her; but I was never able to. The boot is on the other foot. The kindness of the pair of them towards me knows no bounds, and their sympathy towards me in my weakness is immeasurable, and very valuable to me. They understand little, and I've often asked what the purpose of their lives is. Yet I envy them. They are healthy and happy and, by all appearances, likely to live on for many years. If they put their heads together they wouldn't be able to read so much as a verse; yet they enjoy religion, and without question experience its power. There's such unity and similarity between them, that I almost believe they'll die on the same day. I can't see how Thomas and Barbara could ever live apart.

If anyone goes to the trouble of reading this story, perhaps they'll be surprised that I've said so much about some aspects of my family that weren't very honourable, and they might ask, in Wil Bryan's words, is this *true to nature*? But how could this story be any different and still be true? And when I have gone away, who will be harmed? Nobody will need to hide their heads, since I am the last of the family.

Looking back over what I've written I see that I have, through oversight, left out some things that I'd have liked to have said something about; and there are other things that I've left out on purpose. In all likelihood, I'll never be able to revise this memoir, since writing the final parts of it have been burdensome to me and I fear that the reading of it will also be. If that is the case, then the reader can do the same as me—put it to one side when he is tired of it.

THE END

IV

APPENDIX

In the summer of 1869 a riot occurred in the town that had considerable effect on the subsequent policing of public disturbances in Great Britain. On 17 May, 1869, John Young, the English manager of the nearby colliery, angered his workers by announcing a pay cut. He had previously strained relationships with them by banning the use of the Welsh language underground. Two days later, following a meeting at the pithead, miners attacked Young before frogmarching him to the police station. Seven men were arrested and ordered to stand trial on 2 June. All were found guilty and the convicted ringleaders, Ismael Jones and John Jones, were sentenced to a month's hard labour. A large crowd had assembled to hear the verdict, and the Chief Constable of Flintshire had arranged for police from all over the county and soldiers from The 4th King's Own Regiment (Lancaster), based temporarily at Chester, to be present. As the convicts were being transported to the railway station, the crowd of 1,500 to 2,000 grew restive and threw missiles at the officers, injuring many of them. On the command of their commanding officer, Captain Blake, the soldiers opened fire on the crowd, killing four, including one completely innocent bystander, Margaret Younghusband. She was a nineteen-year-old girl, a domestic servant from Liverpool, who had been innocently observing events from the nearby high ground. The musket ball entered her thigh severing her femoral artery and she bled to death. The others killed included Robert Hannaby a collier from Moss, near Wrexham. He was shot in the head in the act of throwing a stone and died instantly. Edward Bellis, another collier, was shot in the abdomen. A local doctor, Dr Platt, performed surgery to remove the ball but Bellis died shortly afterwards. Elizabeth Jones, living at Coed Talon, wife of Isaac Jones, was shot in the back and died two days later from the injury. The Coroner's inquest regarding the first three deaths was held by the end of the same week of the riot, on Saturday 5 June. The Coroner, Mr Peter Parry, was described as being "exceedingly old and infirm and being so deaf as to be compelled to use a 'speaking' trumpet, to which affliction must be added that greater one of partial blindness". He was assisted by the Deputy Coroner, his brother Robert Parry, surgeon, of Mold. The verdict of the Jury, following clear direction of the Coroner, and after retiring for five minutes to consider the matter, was that of justifiable homicide. Later that afternoon the Coroner held a further inquest on the death of Elizabeth Jones who had died at 11pm the previous night. The same verdict was reached. The following week Isaac Jones, a collier at Black Diamond, was one of a number of men tried for their involvement in the riot. He was allowed bail to attend the funeral of his wife. The other men tried were William Griffiths (medical herbalist, former collier, Mold), Rowland Jones (age 25, collier, Pontyblyddyn), Gomer Jones (age 17, collier) and William Hughes (collier) At the conclusion of their trial they were found guilty of "felonious wounding" and Lord Chief Justice Bovill sentenced them all to ten years penal servitude.

Although he strenuously denied the connection, Daniel Owen (who lived in the town) features some very similar events in his first novel Rhys Lewis, which was published in instalments in 1882–1884.'

https://en.wikipedia.org/wiki/Mold,_Flintshire#The_Mold_Riot

Chapter 25, Footnote 9

'Caethforwyn fy nghydwybod,
Sydd imi o'i rhadau hynod, yn rhoi dy hanes,
Mai ti yw'r Proffwyd pena',
Sy a'i ymwared yn Samaria, i'w dda orddiwes ;
'Mhob llun darostwng di fy ngwŷn,
Nad imi drydar am Abana a Pharphar,
Afonydd siomgar fy hagar wlad fy hun ;
Tro fi i'r Iorddonen gyhoedd, sef dyfroedd Mab y Dyn;
Nid oes all olchi bryntni f'oes,
Ond gwaed yr Iesu, yr hwn a ddarfu
Drwy angeu drengu, gan grynu ar bren y groes,
Ow! gad, er imi bechu, Dduw, lechu yn dy loes.
Ni roddaist, Iesu tyner,
Mo'th werthfawr waed yn ofer, dros fyd anafus, &c.'

Chapter 39, Footnote 3

Ffynnon Elian is sited on the Denbighshire/Caernarfonshire border, in the parish of Llandrillo-yn-Rhos and was part of a farm called Cefnyffynnon. Up to about 1775 the well was known only for its healing properties, and the parishioners even tried to promote it as a bathing place, no doubt influenced by the popularity of Holywell. In the later 18th century however, the well acquired an ambiguous reputation as a place where wrongs could be righted, and by the early 19th century it was well-known as a cursing well, with numerous stories circulated of the tragedies connected with it.

The keeper of the well lived at Cefnyffynnon Farm, apparently rebuilt from the profits of the well as the keeper was paid a substantial fee to impose or retract a curse. The intended victim's name or initials were written on a piece of slate, which was then placed in the well to an accompaniment of curses and imprecations directed against the person, their property or cattle. The well worked by power of suggestion—people were understandably anxious, if not terrified, if they heard they had been cursed there and could apply to the keeper to be taken out of the well. Those who enquired if they had been cursed were usually replied to in the affirmative, and it seems that slates with every possible permutation of initials were kept at the farmhouse. Curses were invariably found and cancelled—at considerably more than the initial cost of imposing a curse.

The well resulted in a law and order problem as hundreds, if not thousands, cursed their neighbours. The magistrates seemed powerless as the well was on private property and no obvious crime had been committed. In 1828 however, the congregation of the adjacent Rehoboth Methodist Chapel took matters into their own hands and destroyed the well, planting potatoes on the spot. An enterprising villager, John Evans (alias Jac Ffynnon Elian), diverted the spring water to his own garden, opened a well and continued in business for another thirty years. Tried for fraud in 1831, he was imprisoned for six months, but continued after his release. Towards the end of his life, in the 1850s, he confessed to a minister that the well had been a hoax, and became a Baptist'.

http://www.rcahmw.gov.uk/HI/ENG/Heritage+of+Wales/Hidden+Histories+III/Episode+3/

V

EPILOGUE

On page 61, Mary Lewis, in the heat of her argument with Bob, quotes a line from the hymn *"Mae'r gwaed a redodd ar y groes"* (literally, '*The blood that flowed upon the cross*') by Robert Williams of Eifionydd (Robert ap Gwilym Ddu), 1767–1850. Although this was in some ways a theme song of the Welsh revivals in the 19th and early 20th centuries, and is still well-known among Welsh-speaking Christians, it has not previously had a significant hearing in English-speaking circles. A rather halting translation by Howell Elvet Lewis (Elfed—after whom Elfed High School in Buckley is named), '*From age to age the memory of Jesus' blood grows fonder*' appeared in around 1887 but does not seem to have caught on. We (that is, the publisher and the translator) decided that the hymn deserved to be more widely known and sung, and circulated a request at the Hymn Society conference in Cambridge in August 2015 for someone to come up with something both more modern and closer to the spirit of the original. Martin E. Leckebusch, author of '*More Than Words*' and '*Songs of God's People*' rose to the challenge, and the verse quoted on page 61 comes from his brand new rendering of the hymn based upon the literal version supplied by the translator.

Gill Berry, a trustee of the Praise Trust and a member of the translator's church in Shropshire, also wrote a tune "in the Welsh style" (and, at the translator's insistence, in a minor key).

The following pages present the new hymn and tune in full, followed by the words of the original Welsh version. This is offered in the hope that both will become more widely known and sung in years to come.

Ah, The Bloodstained Cross of Jesus!

Calvin Lansdowne (87 87)

Ah, the blood - stained cross of Je - sus!
While e - ter - nal years un - fold,
ne - ver shall it be for - got - ten,
nor its ri - ches ful - ly told.

1. Ah, the blood-stained cross of Jesus!
   While eternal years unfold,
   never shall it be forgotten
   nor its riches fully told.

2. Where the heavenly harps are sounding,
   one theme rings through every song:
   highest praise, eternal glory
   to the Lamb of God belong.

3. What can match his blood, its virtue
   saving souls by mortal pain?
   Not the finest strings of heaven,
   nor the sweetest angel strain.

4. Wonders from that costly suffering,
   fresh delights to understand,
   shall we find revealed through ages
   numberless as grains of sand.

5. Ah, the sacrifice of Jesus!
   Priceless to infinity—
   to the end of endless ages
   ever new the song shall be.

WORDS: © 2015 MARTIN E. LECKEBUSCH
Based on the hymn *Mae'r gwaed a redodd ar y groes*,
by Robert Williams of Eifionydd
(Robert ap Gwilym Ddu) 1767–1850
MUSIC: © 2015 GILL BERRY/PRAISE TRUST

Mae'r Gwaed a Redodd ar y Groes

1. Mae'r gwaed a redodd ar y groes
   o oes i oes i'w gofio;
   rhy fyr yw tragwyddoldeb llawn
   i ddweud yn iawn amdano.

2. Prif destun holl ganiadau'r nef
   eyw 'iddo Ef,' a'i haeddiant;
   a dyna sain telynau glân,
   ar uchaf gân gogoniant.

3. Mae hynod rinwedd gwaed yr Oen,
   a'i boen wrth achub enaid,
   yn seinio'n uwch ar dannau'r nef
   na hyfryd lef seraffiaid.

4. 'Mhen oesoedd rif y tywod mân
   ni bydd y gân ond dechrau;
   rhyw newydd wyrth o'i angau drud
   a ddaw o hyd i'r golau.

5. Ni thraethir maint anfeidrol werth
   ei aberth yn dragywydd:
   er treulio myrdd o oesoedd glân,
   ni bydd y gân ond newydd.

gan Robert Williams o Eifionydd
(Robert ap Gwilym Ddu) 1767–1850

Other titles in the

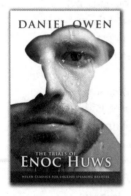

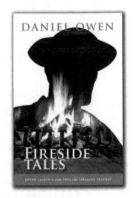

The Trials of Enoc Huws
ISBN: 978-0-9567031-0-1

Fireside Tales
ISBN: 978-0-9567031-1-8

To purchase a copy, visit your local bookshop or

www.browncowpublishing.com